The GLASS ARROW

BOOKS BY KRISTEN SIMMONS

The GLASS ARROW

KRISTEN SIMMONS

TOR®
TEEN

A TOM DOHERTY ASSOCIATES BOOK
NEW YORK

THE GLASS ARROW

Copyright © 2015 by Kristen Simmons

Designed by Greg Collins

A Tor Teen Book
Published by Tom Doherty Associates, LLC
175 Fifth Avenue
New York, NY 10010

www.tor-forge.com

Tor® is a registered trademark of Tom Doherty Associates, LLC.

The Library of Congress Cataloging-in-Publication Data is available upon request.

ISBN 978-0-7653-3661-3 (hardcover)
ISBN 978-1-4668-2878-0 (e-book)

Tor Teen books may be purchased for educational, business, or promotional use. For information on bulk purchases, please contact the Macmillan Corporate and Premium Sales Department at 1-800-221-7945, extension 5442, or write to specialmarkets@macmillan.com.

First Edition: February 2015

Printed in the United States of America

0 9 8 7 6 5 4 3 2 1

*To Melissa Frain, for many reasons,
but mostly for making me better*

PART ONE

THE GARDEN

CHAPTER 1

Run.

My breath is sharp as a dagger, stabbing through my throat. It's all I hear. *Whoosh. Whoosh.* In and out.

They're here. The Trackers. They've followed Bian from the lowland village where he lives. The fool led them right to us.

The forest I know as well as the lines on my palms is dense and shrouded from the midmorning light. I keep to the shadows, skirting around the bright open patches where the sunlight streams to the forest floor. My calloused feet fly over the damp leaves and gray pebbles, keeping me stealthy as a fox.

I run a practiced pattern, just like my ma taught me as a child. A zigzag through the brush and trees. I never run in a line; their horses will catch up too quickly on the straightaway, and they're not all I have to worry about. I know the Tracker hounds have picked up my scent too, but they're scroungers, weakened by hunger, and not as nimble as me in these woods. I'm banking on their starving stomachs leading them directly to the bait meat in my hunting snares.

My thoughts jolt to the traps. There are six placed strategically around our camp. I know they're good because I set them myself, and checked them only this morning.

In my mind I see a Tracker's heavy black boots clamber over the loose branches, see him fall ten feet down into a muddy hole.

Another might trip the spring of the rabbit cage so its razor-sharp teeth bite down through his leather shoe.

Trackers are cunning. But not as cunning as me.

I swing around a stout pine, locking my body in place behind it so that I'm absolutely still. The coarse bark imprints onto the naked skin of my shoulders but I hold my position. That's when I hear it. The thunder of hoofbeats.

A shot pierces the air. Gunfire. Someone yells—a man's voice, strained, hurting. It's either one of them or Bian. He's the only man old enough to make a noise so deep. Tam's not yet seven, and if he were caught, his cry would be shrill. Childlike.

Tam. I must find Tam and Nina, the twins. They count on me when they're scared. Though when I conjure them in my mind—Tam's black hair and button nose, Nina's ever-watchful eyes—I am the one who's scared.

I've prepared them, I tell myself. I've prepared them like my ma prepared me. They know the hiding place—the abandoned wolf's den in the south woods. An image of it breaks through from my memory: the narrow, shale entrance and damp inner chamber, smelling of mold. The rocky floor lined with the brittle bones of squirrels whose souls have long since passed to Mother Hawk. At first it looks to be a trap in itself, but if you squeeze past the tapering stone walls, the rock gives way to soil, and the twisting roots of an old pine create a ladder to climb upward into sunlit freedom.

This has been our hiding place for my entire life. The twins know this. I've drilled them on this plan since my ma died four years ago, when I was eleven. Since they were toddling, crying in that cave for fear of the dark, and I had to carry them the entire way, singing their favorite lullabies, saying, *you're so brave, you're so brave.* Lifting them out myself, because they weren't yet strong enough to climb.

I made them practice hiding even when Salma told me not to—that I shouldn't "frighten them." Stupid—readiness was how we'd survived two raids from the Trackers in our youth. But

10

though Salma is two years older, she acts like a baby. She hates the mountains, and hates my ma, even in death, for stealing her away here, for giving her freedom. And why she hates *that*, I'll never know.

Salma. I've lost sight of my cousin, and Metea, Bian, Tam and Nina's mother. They're my only family, the only ones who live with me in hiding.

Another shot. My hearing sharpens, hones in on the sound, and I alter my course. I have to see if it's Bian that's in trouble. In his panic I'm sure he's run for the wolf's den. If the twins are there, if Salma and Metea are there, he'll give them all away.

I'm running westward now, aware of the heat and the moisture coating my skin. The trees spread, and I enter the clearing where the moss beneath my feet grows plush and soft as fur. Most days I love it here, but today this area is treacherous. There are few places to hide, and at any given moment I am exposed on all sides.

The hoofbeats have faded behind me, and the stillness makes me leery. Only a fool would think I'd lost them. No, they're stalling, waiting to box me in.

I am less than a mile from our camp. For a flash, I debate running back to get a weapon. Any weapon—a bow, a knife, a steel pan. Anything that can be useful to defend myself, but I don't have time. My usual obsidian blade is now in Tam's tiny hands. I pray he won't have to use it.

The sound of labored breathing, of something wounded, cuts through the trees. I skid to a halt, swinging myself onto a low branch so that I can get a better view of the surrounding area. Just north, thirty paces or so, I make out a figure crumpled over the ground.

Bian.

His long, dark hair is matted with mud and leaves. His tunic— the one he trades his T-shirt for when he comes to visit us in the mountains—is twisted around his body and stained with an ink darker than berry juice. From the corner of his chest a spear nearly as tall as me juts out at an angle like a sapling after a windstorm. Weakly, he reaches for it with his opposite hand. Then his arm drops and he grows still. Too still.

I will not approach him. I *cannot*. My heart twists for the boy I have called brother all my life.

Silence. Even the birds are voiceless. Even the stream has stopped.

I must get closer. If he's alive, I can help him.

I climb down, one painstaking step at a time, crouching low to sneak towards him. As I close in, I feel my blood grow slow and thick.

Bian is dead.

The spear is planted straight through to the earth. There is a wound in his leg where a bullet has pierced his jeans, and another in his chest. Dark blossoms of red are still seeping out across the sweat-dampened fabric. His mouth and his eyes are wide open in shock.

Still ten paces away and sheltered on one side by the thick, tri-split leaves of a wormwood bush, I fall to my knees. I don't understand why they've done this—why he's been shot *and* speared. Trackers carry guns, and for their grand prize, use nets. They don't use the antique weapons of the upper class.

The answer pops into my mind as soon as I ask the question. These Trackers are not bounty hunters out on a slave-catching mission. These Trackers are hired thugs, paid for their services by some rich Magnate businessman looking for hunting fun. A bit of adventure.

It sickens me but I can picture it: The first shot, to Bian's leg, was meant to slow him down, to fix the game. He'd stumbled, made an easy target for the men pursuing him. The Magnate managed to spear him in the chest, but the wound had not been fatal. So the Tracker had shot him again.

Poor Bian. Poor stupid Bian. Who never heeded his mother's

desperate pleas that he cover his tracks when paying us a visit. I hate him for bringing this upon us. I hate him more for dying.

Enough time has been wasted. There is nothing I can do here.

Find the twins. Find Salma and Metea, I order myself. But though the grief has dried, my feet are clumsier than before.

The woods are unnaturally silent. I doubt the Trackers have taken the Magnate home. They would have returned to collect his spear, and besides that, they haven't gotten what they've come for. The real trophy.

Me.

They'll want Salma, and Nina too, though she's still too young for auction. Metea is in real danger. She's too old to bear children—she was already forty when she had the twins. If she's caught, they'll kill her, just like they killed her son, Bian.

But they'll bring the girls—Salma, Nina, and me—to the city. My ma's stories flash through my mind, blending with Bian's, brought back from the civilized world. The Trackers will sell us to a farm, where we'll be groomed and fattened, and sold at auction to any Magnate who can pay the price.

To be free means to be hunted, and there aren't many of us left.

I begin to follow one of my hidden hunting trails up a steep embankment towards the cave. I don't know how long we've been under attack; the sun is high now, it must be almost midday. Surely the Magnate will be tiring, slowing atop the show pony that has replaced his electric car as a sign of status. I'm tiring too. My muscles have grown tight, my tongue thick, and there's less sweat pouring down my face and between my breasts than before.

"Aya!" Metea's faint cry steals my focus.

I cut sharply left, scaling a large boulder that leaves me momentarily exposed to the sunlight and any roaming eyes. Without delay, I hop down into a small clearing where I see Metea lying on her stomach.

Now I don't think about consequences. I don't care if they see me. Metea has been a mother to me since my ma died. It scares me to the core that she is down; she's fit and able to run. She should be heading for the cave.

"Go, Aya!" she cries, twisting her face up to meet my gaze. "Salma has taken the twins!"

I look at Metea and see Tam's small nose and Nina's dark eyes. Bian's broad shoulders. Her hair has become more salt than pepper these days, and her eyes and mouth bear the marks of too much smiling. But now her face is all twisted up with a pain that makes my whole body hurt.

"Come on, get up!" I say, scanning the trees for movement.

"I can't. Go, child! The Trackers, they . . ." She cries out, and the sound is like a pestle grinding my heart into the mortar. I lock my jaw.

Metea had gone into hiding when she learned she was pregnant with the twins. My ma helped her through the birthing. She didn't cry out once.

"I'm not leaving you!" I say.

I try to force her over onto her back. A groan comes from deep in her throat, and draws a whimper to my lips. Now I'm certain the Trackers have heard us.

I succeed in turning her but can't hide the gasp, or stop the sick that fills my mouth. There are deep lines scratched into her shins and thighs, and a serpentine gash across her belly, sliced straight through the yellow dress Bian brought her for her birthday. The red blood seems darker next to that bright fabric. When I look closer, I can see the white and purple flesh within the wounds that I recognize from cleaning a kill.

My throat is knotting up. I can heal most cuts, but nothing so deep. Metea will need a hospital. She will need to go into Bian's village for treatment. I press down on her stomach to stanch the bleeding and to my revulsion, my hands slide away from the slippery surface of her skin.

Metea grasps both of my arms.

"The Trackers have wires!" she sputters, and her eyes are now so wide I can see the perfect white rings around her brown irises.

"Wires," I repeat. Long, metal, snakelike whips that stun and slice their prey. This can't be right. Only Watchers, the city police, carry wires. Trackers belong to the Virulent caste, the bottom-feeders of the city. They are thieves and murderers. Thugs. They have guns, not the complex weaponry of the Watchers.

Then I remember the spear protruding from Bian's chest, and I remember my conclusion that the rich Magnate has hired these thugs for sport and entertainment. Maybe he's outfitted them with wires. If that's true, who knows what else they got.

"Is Bian with Salma?" Metea asks me. There is a slur in her words, as though she's drunk on shine, and my fear catapults to a new level. I don't have to answer her. She sees the truth flicker across my face. Her eyes slip shut momentarily, and I shake her.

"You know what to do," she tells me.

I must sing his soul to Mother Hawk, who will carry him to the afterlife.

"Yes," I promise. Though now my voice sounds very far away. Then, as if struck by a bolt of lightning, she rouses, and sits straight up.

"Run, Aya! I feel them! They're coming!"

I know a moment later what she means. The horses' hooves are striking the ground, vibrating the gravel beneath my knees. I look to the brush beside us and quickly consider dragging Metea into it, but the horses are too close. If I'm going to save myself I don't have time.

"Get up!" I am crying now. The salty tears blend with my sweat and burn my eyes.

"Leave me."

"No!" Even as I say it I'm rising, hooking my arms beneath hers, pulling her back against my chest. But she's dead weight and I collapse. She rolls limply to one side. I kiss her cheek, and hope she knows that I love her. I will sing Bian's soul to the next life. I will sing her soul there too, because she surely is doomed to his same fate.

"Run," she says one last time, and I release her.

I sprint due north, the opposite direction from the cave where I hope Salma has hidden the twins. I run as hard and as fast as I can, fueled by fear and hatred. My feet barely graze the ground for long enough to propel me forward, but still I can feel the earth tremble beneath them. The Trackers are coming closer. The Magnate is right on my heels.

I dodge in my zigzag pattern. I spin around the pine trees and barely feel the gray bark as it nicks my arms and legs. My hide pants rip near the knee when I cut too close to a sharp rock, and I know that it's taken a hunk of my skin, too. No time to check the damage, no time for pain. I hurdle over a streambed and continue to run.

A break in the noise behind me, and I make the mistake that will cost me my freedom.

I look back.

They are close. So much closer than I thought. Two horses have jumped the creek. They are back on the bank now, twenty paces behind me. I catch a glimpse of the tattered clothes of the Trackers, and their lanky, rented geldings, frothing at the bit. The faces of the Virulent are ashy, scarred, and starved. Not just for food, but for income. They see me as a paycheck. I've got a credit sign tattooed across my back.

I run again, forcing my cramping muscles to push harder. Suddenly, a crack pierces the air, and something metal—first cold, then shockingly hot—winds around my right calf. I cannot hold back the scream this time as I crash to the ground.

The wire contracts, cutting through the skin and into the flesh and muscle of my leg. The heat turns electric, and soon it is shocking me, sending volts of lightning up through my hips, vibrating my insides. My whole body begins to thrash wildly, and I'm powerless to hold still. The pressure squeezes my lungs and I can't swallow. I start to pant; it is all I can do to get enough air.

A net shoots out over me. I can see it even through my quaking vision. My seizing arms become instantly tangled.

"Release the wire! Release it!" orders a strident male voice.

A second later, the wire retracts its hold, and I gasp. The blood from my leg pools over the skin and soaks the dirt below. But I know I have no time to rest. I must push forward. To avoid the meat market, to keep my family safe, I must get away.

I begin to crawl, one elbow digging into the dirt, then the next. Fingers clawing into the mossy ground, dragging my useless leg. But my body is a corpse, and I cannot revive it.

Mother Hawk, I pray, *please give me wings.*

But my prayers are too late.

My voice is only a trembling whisper, but I sing. For Bian and for Metea. I sing as I push onward, the tears streaming from my eyes. I must try to set their souls free while I can.

Out of the corner of my eye I see the boney fetlocks of a chestnut horse. The smooth cartilage of his hooves is cracked. This must be a rental—the animal hasn't even been shod. An instant later, black boots land on the ground beside my face. Tracker boots. I can hear the bay of the hounds now. The stupid mutts have found me last, even after the horses and the humans.

I keep trying to crawl away. My shirt is soaked by sweat and blood, some mine, some Metea's. It drips on the ground. I bare my teeth, and swallow back the harsh copper liquid that is oozing into my mouth from a bite on the inside of my cheek. I am yelling, struggling against my failing body, summoning the strength to escape.

"Exciting, isn't it boys?" I hear a man say. The same one who ordered the release of the wire.

He kneels on the ground and I notice he's wearing fine linen pants and a collared shirt with a tie. If only I had the power to choke him with it. At least that would be vengeance for one death today. His face is smooth and creaseless, but there's no fancy surgery to de-age his eyes. He's at least fifty.

He's wearing a symbol on his breast pocket. A red bird in flight. A cardinal. Bian has told me this is the symbol for the city of Glasscaster, the capitol. This must be where he plans on taking me.

He's ripping the net away, and for a moment I think he's freeing me, he's letting me go. But this is ridiculous. I'm who he wants.

Then, as though I'm an animal, he weaves his uncalloused, unblistered fingers into my black, spiraled hair, and jerks my head back so hard that I arch halfway off the ground. I hiss at the burn jolting across my scalp. He points to one of the Trackers, who's holding a small black box. Thinking this is a gun, I close my eyes and brace for the shot that will end my life. But no shot comes.

"Open your eyes, and smile," the Magnate says. With his other hand he is fixing his wave of stylishly silver hair, which has become ruffled in the chase.

I do open my eyes, and I focus through my quaking vision on the black box. I've heard Bian talk about these things. Picture boxes. They freeze your image, so that it can be preserved forever. Like a trophy.

I'm going to remember this moment forever, too. And I don't even need his stupid picture box.

CHAPTER 2

I'VE BEEN LOCKED UP one hundred and seven days.

That's one hundred and seven days of meal supplement pills crammed down my throat, skin scrubbings, and whippings.

That's eighteen fights I've won, six escape attempts I've failed, and nine runs in solitary.

That's four auctions, three I've managed to avoid.

Tomorrow is number five, and I'm not going, even if it means taking down the Governess herself. I'm not getting sold. Not now. Not ever.

I walk to the far corner of the recreation yard, the side nearest to the rising sun. Not that I can see it—you can't see anything through the gray-green haze that blankets this poisoned city—but I still remember what it looks like, and how it feels on my face. For now, that's all I have.

I glance behind me at the facility they call the Garden. The black glass walls reflect the light from the electric lamps that hang from the red sloping roof. Most of the girls are huddling under a wooden gazebo near the doors. We get let out each morning before breakfast, and they're all waiting, tired and hungry, for the first chance to get back inside where it's warm. The iron benches and neat bricked walkways all stand empty until our afternoon break, leaving the lower part of the yard clear.

But I'm not alone. I look up at the black camera box staring down from the high chain-link fence that surrounds the property.

It adjusts its position as I approach, tracking me as I move closer to the boundary. I give my nastiest look and gesture rudely, but the lens continues to stare, unblinking.

The buzzing of the fence grows louder as I near. It's electric; every once in a while a stray cat or bird will get fried when they venture too close. Most of the girls keep their distance, and most of the men who come to gawk from the street outside do too.

The grass is a little longer here; the workers that cut it short never venture this far away from the main viewing areas. No sense in making it nice if no one that matters has a chance to see it. I pull off my pointy, knee-high boots, flexing my feet, and kneel on the ground, feeling the dew soak through the skintight uniform dress.

As my eyes drift closed, I wind my fingers in the grass and pretend I'm back in the mountains. The birds are chirping and the branches are clicking together as the breeze rustles the pine needles. I'm bringing home fish from the stream, and Salma's there waiting to cook it, while Tam and Nina chase each other around the fire. Bian and Metea are there too, but the vision fades when I see them, and my stomach feels sour and hollow.

I'm not in the mountains. I'm stuck inside this electric fence, listening to the distant beat of the music from the all-night clubs in the Black Lanes and smelling garbage in the air.

And Tam and Nina are with Salma, and that scares me straight through. Salma can take care of them, but she's never had to before. She never wanted to. I can only hope that they're all taking care of each other, and hiding from Trackers like I taught them.

My hands have turned so that my palms face the sky, and I sing, softly so the others don't hear me. I sing to *Her*—Mother Hawk, guardian of the afterlife—and try to find comfort knowing she will keep the souls of my family safe. Without any way to receive word from home, prayer is all I have.

"Told you she's cracked."

I jolt to my feet, turning sharply at the same time. Four girls are standing before me, all in the same black, low-cut dress. None of them are wearing shoes—probably how they managed to sneak up on me. One of them has bright red hair, cut at an angle to her chin—Daphne, my half-friend, who can only barely stand to be near me when I'm not embarrassing her, and refuses to acknowledge me at all when I am.

I don't blame her. We have nothing in common besides the fact that we're both stuck here. She's the daughter of a computer-programming Merchant, and has prepared her whole life for auction. She's looking away now, arms crossed in a tight shield over her chest.

My shoulders rise and I steel myself for a confrontation. I learned early on not to look for help within these walls. Everyone here is out for themselves.

It's a curvy girl with a turned-up nose who's called me cracked. Her white hair is braided in two ropes that reach down to her waist, and she's painting circles on her cheek with the end of one. I think her name is Lotus—she's only been here since the last auction. I bare my teeth at her and she takes a quick step back.

"Did you hear that screeching? How dreadful," says another. She's a singer; I've heard her practicing all week for tomorrow. Her hands are planted on her bony hips. They call her Lily.

"She probably doesn't even know what she's doing," says Lotus. "I've seen people like her before. Not right in the head. She's probably a witch." She whispers the last part.

They talk about me like I'm not right in front of them. Like I'm deaf or something. Daphne's examining her nails now, as if they're the most interesting things she's ever seen.

"Well she is from the *outside*," says Lily.

I wonder how well she'd sing if I punched her in her skinny little throat.

Lily's delicate fingers lift to one of her long beaded earrings, the sign of the Unpromised. They don't let me wear mine anymore.

The last time I ripped one out right before they tried to put me on stage.

"Yes," says Daphne in a small voice. "And it's because of that she's going to fetch twice your bidding price." She peels a hangnail off her thumb; a nervous habit I knew from our time here together. She always gets nervous on auction days. I don't suppose this situation is making her feel any calmer; even I can feel the tension in this murky air.

Lotus scoffs. "I don't see why. It's not as if she's prettier than me . . . than any of us, I mean."

"I don't know about that," I tell her. She sneers.

"It's her insides that are different." Daphne says this as though she's bored, but her words have a bite to them. "She's fertile, like the girls brought in from the outliers. She doesn't have to have the treatments to activate her babymaker."

Daphne was the first to tell me why the hunters were so eager to sell me to the Garden. The city scientists think it's the fresh air or the real food—as opposed to the meal supplement pills pumped down their throats in the early, *formative* years— that make wild girls like me, and those born in the outlying towns, like my mother, different. Whatever the reason, I'm worth quite a lot. I'm twice as likely to produce a living, healthy boy child than any other woman born in the city.

Daphne cringes slightly, and I wonder if she's thinking about the fertility injections. A lot of the girls here complain about them. The medicine gives them the shakes, and makes them throw up, and cry for no reason. The whole process seems a huge waste if they don't even conceive a boy, but the docs do it because treating the girls they have is more reliable than pulling stock from the outliers. The census works for women, just as it works against us. There must be a steady pool of childbearing females to populate the city.

"Rumor," says Lily. "It can't be true. If it was, they'd move all of us outside the gates."

Now it's my turn to laugh.

"Right," I say. "You wouldn't last a day." I try to imagine her setting a trap or cleaning a kill, but I can't. "Besides, if the men set us all free, it'd be just a matter of time before they'd have an uprising on their hands."

"Stop it." Daphne glances up as the camera above focuses with a buzzing noise. She's warned me before that talking this way could get me in trouble. I'd do it a lot more if I thought it might actually get me out of here.

"Deny it if you want," I say with a shrug, "but it's the truth."

These girls don't know freedom. Men own women in the city, right down to the Virulent—those whose crimes have been recorded with a permanent X on their cheek—pimps and their whores. Not even the women in the surrounding towns are safe. Maybe they can still choose a husband, but the moment the female census gets too high, they'll be collected, along with their girl children, to be sold in the city. Sometimes their families even offer them up early for credits.

"It's an honor to be chosen," snaps Daphne. "I'd rather be pampered than end up a poor housewife in the outliers, or a prostitute in the Black Lanes, or living in a *tent*."

Her voice hitches on that last part. I shouldn't have told her how we lived. She never understood how much warmer it was there than within these cold glass walls.

"The wild girl might think she's better than everyone else, but she never gets bids." The fourth girl finally speaks. She's tall, with a round face, and has been shoved in the Garden's weight shifter so many times her waist is half the size of her hips and breasts. She looks like her back might break if she bends over too far. "She's not worth the credits."

It shouldn't bother me—a buyer is the last thing I want—but my cheeks get hot all the same. I size her up.

She's big, but not too smart. She likes to pick on the smaller ones around here and no one tries to stop her. Sweetpea is her name, sent over from one of the packed dorms on the south side of Glasscaster, where Keepers collect girl children and raise them for auction. She's been on a registry since birth, groomed to be obedient and mild mannered. I don't think any of their training stuck. She's a brute.

"Exactly," says Lotus. "Look at her hair—it's like sheep's wool. I bet her mother laid down with a sheep and that's how she came to be."

Daphne snorts. I glare at her for only a moment. My blood's turning hot, and my fists clench at my sides.

"I bet *she* laid down with a sheep," says Sweetpea. "I bet the wild girl broke the purity rule with a sheep." She laughs, and even her laugh sounds stupid. *Huh huh huh.* They all join her. They're all laughing at me.

I crack my knuckles.

Before any sale is final, every girl is forced to have a medical test to determine if she's pure or not. Magnates—the wealthiest men in the city—pay a lot of money for First Rounders; they want to be the first to own their brand-new toy. Then, when they tire of her, or when she gives them what they really want—a boy child—she's returned to the Garden and resold as a Second or Third Rounder for childbearing, or pleasure, or anything else, to a man with less money. Her baby, if she has one, is handed over to the Keepers to be raised.

The First Rounders will call her a Sloppy Second. Sloppy Seconds don't call the Third Rounders anything. Sloppy Seconds don't talk much.

My ma used to tell Salma these stories to convince her to stay clear of the city. When she got to the bit about the medical exam, she always reached for my hand, as if to assure me she'd never let something like that happen to me.

I take a step towards Sweetpea and her full lips tilt up in a smirk.

"Clover," warns Daphne.

I cringe at the name. Larkspur, Thistle, Lily, Daphne . . . There are fifty or so of us here at any given time, all named after flowers, myself included. *Clover*. Most of these plants are at least somewhat poisonous, which I'm sure the Governess doesn't know because she's never been outside the city walls.

And of course, Clover is a weed. Which she probably does know.

Lotus and Lily stand on either side of Sweetpea, glancing to her for their next move. Behind me, I hear the camera swivel, and know that I don't have much time.

"You think you're so much better than me, don't you fat face?" I say to the biggest of the four. It's a low cut, but I need to get her riled up, even if calling her names makes my insides feel ugly.

Sweetpea tilts her head to the side, her dull eyes narrowing. I take another step up. In order for this to work, she's got to come at me. I was planning on doing this closer to breakfast, but now works too.

"I don't have to think it," she says. "I know it."

There are more girls gathering now. Ten or so more have made the trip down and have formed a half circle behind Sweetpea.

"With a face like that it's no wonder no one wants to take you home," I say, trying to sound as cold as she does. "Sour-faced Sweetpea. Has a nice ring to it."

She twitches. "At least I get bids," she says.

The girls around her agree.

I scoff. "You've been here a lot longer than me, that's all I know."

"*Clover*," says Daphne again. She's not crossing over to my side. I don't expect her to anyway. She is only a half friend, after all.

A girl with straight black hair and slanted eyes comes up beside her. She's been named Buttercup, of all things. Daphne immediately blushes.

"The Keepers are coming," says Buttercup.

I glance over Sweetpea's broad shoulder and see she's right. Three Keepers—or Pips as I call them—are rushing out of the building, black caftans floating behind them. The Pips are assigned to take care of the youth in this city, whether at the Garden, in one of the children's dormitories, or even in some wealthy Magnate's house. They're male—but you couldn't tell by looking at them. Their faces are smooth and hairless. Too smooth, like their skulls are made of clay, and their features have all been softened. The rumor is that when they were children, their parents signed them over to the city in payment of their taxes or debts. In a Keeper facility in the medical district, their boy parts were removed, and they were given strange medical treatments to alter their hormones and stunt their growth. I guess they're still sore about it, because they have nasty tempers and are snide even on their best days. I can't blame them, but that doesn't mean I like them.

I don't have much time.

"Ooh," I say. "Keepers. Scared, fat face?"

Sweetpea twitches.

"The Governess says I'll be chosen by the end of the week," she says.

"That's what she tells you," I say. "I heard her talking to a buyer the last time I was sent to her office. She tried to throw you in two for one with Rose, but he wouldn't even take you for free."

"Shut up," she says, lunging forward, but stopping just before we collide.

Not good enough.

"I promise I'm out of here before you," I say, closing the distance between us so that I have to look up at her. Quick as I can, I grab a fistful of her hair. I yank and a chunk rips away in my hand. Her upper half wobbles on her skinny waist. Her eyes go glassy with tears.

"Oops," I say, looking at the long strands hanging limply from my grasp, and then back to her face. "That won't look good on stage."

Crack.

I cough and choke on the fountain of blood that gurgles down my throat. It's thick and vile, and if I wasn't so busy concentrating on standing upright, I would puke it up.

I've got to hand it to her. Sweetpea's knuckles are like iron. My nose is definitely broken.

I blink and the girl before me wavers in my vision. Her hands stretch out to her sides as though she might want to embrace me. The Pips are closing in now—I can hear that strange noise they all make when they're flustered. It must be a side effect of the treatments that make them into Keepers, because every Pip I've ever met does it.

"Pip, pip, pip!"

I blink again and wait for the world to stop swaying. When it does, I smile.

A whip smacks down on my arm and I jerk back. Another comes down on my shoulder.

Stupid Pips and their stupid little beaters.

They use their whips to herd me away from the crowd. As I pass, the round, shocked mouths of the girls melt into snide little gossip holes.

As for Sweetpea, she's now looking just as surprised as they are. Poor thing. She's about as sharp as a brick.

I've really put the Pips in a buzz. Two of them stand on either side, slapping at the backs of my arms with their beaters to usher me forward. Sour looks scrunch both of their pretty faces, and even their flowing dress shirts seem to have deflated. I can tell from their greenish tint that the blood has made them sickly.

"Pip, pip, pip, pip, pip!" one sputters before he can even speak. He's picked up my boots and is holding them away from his body as if they're a dead animal.

I'm impressed. Five Pips is a new personal best.

"The Governess won't be pleased, no she won't! *Pip!*" he finishes. I wipe some of the blood on my dress sleeve and he can't hide his "eww."

The Governess runs the Garden, the facility where I've been held since my capture. She has the final word on our *conditioning,* how we're readied for the suitors.

She's a wretched peacock of a woman.

She calls herself an artist, claiming that her decorations up our auction price on market day. But she's no artist. An artist creates because she has to, because if she doesn't, she'll explode. Bian was an artist. He was handy with sculptures, which is why he left our camp in the mountains to make a living in town. I can still see his skilled hands forming figures of horses and wolves and birds from shapeless blocks of wood. The Governess is his opposite. A false artist; she creates so others will pat her on the back, and that makes her more a slave than me.

I hear the cheering now. The small early crowd has come to gawk at us from the street and I've put on quite a show. I don't worry about their attention; they're mostly work staff, too poor to place a bid on the auction block. They just come to drool.

The Pips direct me down the stone walkway out of the recreation yard and its flat, mosquito-infested lily pond, and towards the automatic doors of the East Wing. I hesitate, as I always do before these sliding doors, and only proceed when they're fully open and I'm sure they won't change their minds and crush me.

A year ago I'd never seen such stuff. I'd heard about it secondhand from my ma's and Bian's stories, but that's all they were: stories. I'd stayed my distance from the city because of the danger. Though I've since learned they're not magic, things like automatic doors and messageboxes and weight shifters still make me nervous. I don't trust machines. I trust what I know. That thunderheads bring rain. That cool stream water will quench my thirst. That a punch to the face will sting like a dog's bite, but ultimately accomplish a greater purpose.

The hallway we pass through is painted bruise purple, and the windows are draped with pink velvet and white lace. No matter how much they dress them up, the windows still reveal the electrical fence surrounding the building. They can't hide the fact that the Garden is nothing but a prison.

My nose continues to bleed, though now I make no attempt to stop it and instead lean forward, so that my blood rains down on the Governess's perfectly clean floor.

"*Pip, pip!*" coughs one of the Pips disgustedly. If my face wasn't frozen by swelling, I'd smirk.

One of the Pips knocks on a broad oak door, and it pleases me to see his soft hand trembling.

"Enter," calls a singsong voice from within. I hope my swollen face isn't hiding my disgust. I want the Governess to see how much she revolts me.

The Pip opens the door and reveals the bright room with the white, lavish couches that I know so well. I've been in to see the Governess at least once a week since I arrived here.

Her office is one of the nicest rooms in the facility. She does a lot of business here with buyers, and she can't have them thinking that she leaves their potential purchases living in any less-than-desirable conditions. If they knew we slept on moldy mattresses in a packed hall that reeks of nail paint and girl stink, they might not be so quick to pay. They only see what she lets them see, which is what they want to see anyway. A girl who's been groomed, shaved, slicked-up by the Pips for auction.

In my least delicate manner, I stomp across the bone white carpet, and take my usual place on the couch. I still can't get used to the feel of sitting on something so plush. I sink into the cushions, and it feels as if I'm being swallowed whole.

"Oh!" cries the Governess, launching out from behind her large, glass-topped desk. Today her hair is done up in a long golden braid that twists around her forehead like a crown, and she's wearing a dark blue suit with a neckline low enough that you can practically see her belly button. On her right breast pocket is the cardinal, the symbol of Glasscaster. Her face is covered with makeup that's so dark over her cheekbones and so black around her eyes, it looks like she's the one that's taken a beating.

"She's bleeding everywhere!" shrieks the Governess. "Do something, Keeper!"

One of the Pips scurries from the room, his black linen uniform wafting behind him. He's only too happy to have been dismissed. The other one is gnawing on his lower lip now, and refusing to look me squarely in the face.

On the coffee table in front of me is the leather-bound bodybook. I glare at it, knowing what will be within, but can't help myself. I snatch it off the table as the Governess listens to the Pip recount what he knows of my fight.

I turn through the first few pages. There are color photos of each of the girls here, beginning with the First Rounders. Most of them have sparkling smiles, their faces glowing with glittery makeup and white powder. Beside some of their pictures are full body shots from market day, showcasing every inch of their costumed forms.

The Governess always themes our monthly appearances at market. Once the theme was "A Day in the Sun," and we all had to wear skimpy swimsuits and bronze paint to make ourselves look like we'd spent the last week baking in an oven. Then we were waxed and plucked in the most disgusting places; just thinking about it is enough to make me shudder. They'd taken my body—my strong, healthy body—and turned me into a monster.

I turn to another page and see a girl I know as Violet dressed like a gardener to go along with the Garden theme. She's wearing tight-fitting, see-through overalls, a floppy hat, and is holding a plastic spade. I'm feeling the urge to gag again, though not because of the blood.

I turn to the page I'm looking for. My page. There is only one picture here since I refuse to pose for the camera, and the sight of it burns me up. Still, I can't help but stare, because it is the only photograph I know that exists of me.

It's the picture of my capture, with the spear-wielding Magnate jerking my head back. Though my face is screwed up in pain in the picture, I look over my long-muscled form, my curly, long, raven-black hair, my deep brown eyes and thin lips drawn back in fury. I look menacing, even in that position, and this pleases me.

My finger traces absently over the penned scratches beneath my photograph that must say something about me. My previous scores on past market days. My stupid weed name. I wish I could read what has been written about me.

"CLOSE THAT!" wails the Governess, who seems to have only now noticed what I'm doing. "You're bleeding all over it! I need that for the customers!" She makes a move to grab the book from me, but doesn't want to get too close for fear that I'll bleed on her. I snap the book shut, and toss it on the table, as though I was done anyway.

There is a scuffle outside, and I see that they've brought Sweetpea to the office too. My jaw tightens as I prepare for the next stage of my plan.

If the Governess knows I don't want to go to market, she'll do everything she can to get me there. I need to show her how upset I'd be to be left behind.

Only one Pip has ushered Sweetpea from the corner of the red yard. This doesn't surprise me. At over a head above me and three times as thick, Sweetpea is easily the biggest girl here. But no one worries about her like they do about me.

"Is it true that you called Sweetpea *hefty*, Clover?" the Governess asks in her squeaky voice. My other Pip has returned, and he hastily shoves me a wad of tissue and a damp rag.

It also doesn't surprise me that the Governess has immediately blamed me for the fight, even though I'm the one bleeding. She blames me for most of the trouble around here. She's probably right to.

"I tink I called der *thour-fathed Thweetpea*." I can barely get the words out because the blood is now jelly in my nostrils.

"Sweetpea is not sour-faced, she is . . . beautiful. In her own way. She will fetch a lofty price to any of our customers who are looking for a . . . a . . ." the Governess stammers, hands on her hips.

"A thour fathe?" I offer.

The Governess narrows her eyes at me. "We can fix Sweetpea's hair with a wig, but there's nothing we can do for your *fat* nose before market. You've done this on purpose, haven't you?" She's wagging her finger at me. "You're just trying to avoid the auction tomorrow, and the theme is Body Paint, and it was going to be my best show ever!" She is on the brink of tears.

Body Paint? The Governess has reached a new all-time low.

I try to look hurt. "I can still do id!" I whine.

"No, you can't!" she snaps. "Don't play your games with me, Clover! This is just like that time when you mutilated your ear so I couldn't put you on the stage!"

I touch the thin scar left from where I ripped my dangling beaded earring straight out of my flesh two auctions ago. I'd told her it got caught on my collar. It was painful, but I was able to avoid the meat market.

I feel my face flush against my will. *It's okay,* I tell myself, *let her see that I'm upset.* I know it's time to push a little harder.

"I didn'd do dat on burbose!" I object. "And dis eeder! Sweedpea starded id!"

"I did not!" counters Sweetpea.

"She did! She dold me thad I was neber going to ged chosen, and thad I'd be Unpromised foreber!" I open my eyes wide, trying to make them water.

I know that the Governess's desire to punish me will prevent her from giving me what I want. So I pretend that what I want, more than anything, is to still go to market. Which we both know is impossible now that I look like I've just been kicked in the face by a horse.

"She's the one that said that!" Sweetpea has begun to cry.

"Please!" I beg. "I hade it here! You know thad, Governess! Getting chosen is my only way oud!"

"Oh, shut up, you!" The Governess paces back and forth, twisting her high heel into the rug before she changes direction. "I'm never going to transfer your papers unless you go to auction!" She sighs, exasperated, because she's tired of me and wants me gone just as much as *I* want me gone. I hide the cringe at her self-righteousness. As though she's really the one who signs my paperwork. She's illiterate, just like the rest of us. Her Pip assistant has to sign for her.

"Then led me go!" I beg.

"No. That's it. Tomorrow is a big day for me, and I can't have you ruin it like you try to ruin everything else. Sweetpea will go to auction. I almost had her sold last market day anyhow. And I don't want to see your skinny, bruised face for a month! Do you hear that, Keepers? Put her in solitary! I'm calling a Watcher to come supervise. Someone smarter than the last one," she rambles on.

My heart swells in my chest. In solitary, I'll get to see Brax, and it's been weeks since the last time we were together. I wonder if he's changed at all. If he'll still let me sleep on his shoulder. It's not as good as getting out of the city, but at least I won't be sold.

I fix my face to hide my relief.

"No!" I bellow. "Please led me go! Nod solidary!"

"You've left me no choice. You're going just as soon as I get a Watcher. Which will have to wait a few minutes. We've got a new shipment today and I've got to make a presentation."

I roll my eyes. Another stupid presentation. I wonder what

it'll be this time, ten ways to please a Magnate? The thought brings a flush to my cheeks.

"Should Clover wait here?" asks one of the Pips in a clear, pristine voice. His color is returning now that my nose is cleaned up.

"No, bring her. Clover needs a reminder of what deceit can cost her." The Governess smiles, and her painted face looks as deadly as a rattler.

Whatever joy I have felt at my success crashes. Someone's about to be punished. And her punishment is far, far worse than a month in solitary.

CHAPTER 3

I FOLLOW SWEETPEA BACK down the hallway of the East Wing, a Pip flanking me on either side. We're heading towards the amphitheater, where the girls are gathered for announcements.

Passing the sliding doors that lead out to the rec yard, we continue through an open doorway and into the entertainment parlor. This room is even more dressed up than the Governess's office. The walls are peach and draped with lace, and there are big leather couches and loungers atop the bearskin rugs. In the back is a huge stone fireplace—the kind that burns real wood, not the fake press-a-button flames I've seen in the city on market days. There's no fire now, but soft, velvety light glows from lamps which are placed on each of the fancy wooden tables sprinkled around the room.

It still feels strange being here; once, places like this—and people like Pips—only lived in my ma and Bian's stories. Finding them real makes me wonder what other nightmares exist.

"Come *on*," says one of the Pips in a high voice. "Don't dally." He smacks my lower back with one of the beaters.

I growl at him and he holds the little stick out before him like a knife.

"The only time she ever comes through here is when she's in trouble." The other Pip has stopped, and motions to a couch with a twisty little smile. "Would you like to sit down, dear?"

I swallow. He's got me pegged and he knows it.

It's here that the girls will meet their prospective buyers for the first time; a very wealthy Magnate may even send an assistant to finish the sale. He might interview her on the couch, drink a cup of tea brought in by the Governess. We're prepped on all the right things to say should this happen. City men like to hear they look young and powerful. They want to tell you about all the nice things they have, and you're supposed to listen and smile down at your shoes and hope that you might be one of those nice things, too.

"Sure," I say, forcing myself to relax. "I wouldn't mind putting my feet up on one of those fancy chairs." I wipe some of the blood drying on the back of my hand on the side of my dress.

"*Pip*," says the first, making a gagging noise. "Get on already." He smacks me again. I reach to snag the beater, but he pulls it away too fast.

We exit into a hallway where four smaller sitting rooms, two on each side, are left open to air. I clip Sweetpea's heels, trying to make her hurry. This place makes my skin crawl. Should a buyer want a closer look at the property, the pair will be escorted into one of these private rooms. Here, he can request almost anything. *Almost.* A First Rounder must pass a medical exam verifying she's not done it with anybody before any sale is complete. Nobody paying that much wants damaged goods.

I've never been brought into one of these rooms. Never the parlor either.

"Don't worry, Clover," says Sweetpea. "You'll never make it this far." She still thinks she's better than me.

"Good," I say with a snort, and she shoots a glare my way.

The curved outer walls of the amphitheater are broken by more sliding doors, and the last of the girls are going in. I'm held back until the end, and again I hesitate before I pass through. Just in case.

The first three descending rows of seats are filled, though the room can fit twice that. A Pip motions for me to sit in the fourth row, alone, and I find a seat behind the girl with red hair.

"Hi Daphne," I whisper. The Pip doesn't hear me. Before us is a stage the shape of a half-moon. The heavy maroon curtains are drawn.

She turns, her narrow nose scrunched as though she's smelling something foul, and glares at me with her green eyes. I can see that she's had her eyebrows waxed in preparation for tomorrow, and the skin treatments to remove her freckles are almost complete.

"Don't speak to me," she says. Buttercup, the skinny girl beside her with the slanted eyes, tries to hide the fact that she's looking at me by pulling her long, smooth, black hair over her shoulder.

I lean back, only mildly stung. I didn't expect Daphne to talk to me anyway.

"Your face looks terrible," she whispers after a moment. "I'm glad Sweetpea hit you. You deserved it." She smirks when Buttercup giggles.

I shrug. I'm glad Sweetpea hit me too. Now I don't have to go to the meat market tomorrow. I, of course, don't say this to Daphne. She's only a half friend after all. Really, she's not even that. More like a nonenemy.

"I got a month in solitary," I say.

"A month!" she nearly shouts. Several girls nearby have heard her, and are now staring at me and whispering feverishly to one another. "A month alone out there? With that Driver stink? I can't imagine it." Buttercup isn't hiding her stare now. Her mouth is open in shock, but pulls quickly into a smile.

The *Driver stink* Daphne refers to is the horse rental station the solitary yard butts up against. It's the last facility in the business district before the city walls. But when she says stink, she's not just referring to the animal smell, she's referring to the people that own the horses.

The Drivers are horsemen who breed and tame their animals in the wild, then bring them into town for sale and rental. They're a wild people, considered only a step above dirt—even lower than the Virulent who have broken city laws and are marked so that everyone knows it—because they are strange and unclean, skittish as rabbits, and too stupid to speak even the common language.

I'm not biased. Anyone within the walls of this city is an equal threat.

Buttercup's distracted in conversation with another girl when Daphne turns back again.

"Why do you do that, anyway? Sing like that? If that's even what it is."

I lean back in my seat. The girls from the city don't believe the same stuff I do. They don't believe anything, really, unless the Magnates tell them they can, and the Magnates only worship themselves.

"It's praying," I say.

"Praying is for heathens," she says. "The Magnate council outlawed it before any of us were born."

Of course they did. Believing in anything other than the Magnate would mean that there's something more powerful than them out there.

"You can't outlaw praying," I say.

"You can," she argues. "Praying promotes false courage and a lack of personal responsibility. Besides that, it's childish to believe in things that aren't real. They did tests after the Red Years. Scientific tests. And they proved that gods don't exist."

I guess someone pays attention in the Governess's lectures after all.

"You can't prove that," I say.

"Of course you can," she says. "Have you ever seen your bird . . . woman—whatever you call her?"

"Mother Hawk." I fidget. "No." There are others too, but I don't bring them up.

"Exactly."

I pull the stretchy sleeves of my dress over my hands. I know Mother Hawk exists because she does. Because my ma told me she did. Because a long time ago, before scientific tests and Magnates, Mother Hawk gave the first people their reincarnated souls, and the only reason any of us walk and talk and live today is because of that gift.

I know she exists, because without her, I'm all alone.

I shake off the cold feeling that I *am* alone.

"Lots of people pray," I tell Daphne. "My ma's people were from a village on the other side of the mountains. They all prayed. My ma taught me how."

"A lot of good it did her," Daphne says. "She died, didn't she?"

I wish I'd never told Daphne that. "Her soul lives, even if her body dies."

Daphne doesn't turn around, just whispers over her shoulder. "Grow up. There's no such thing as a soul. There's just us, Clover. Just bones and blood and body."

Daphne doesn't know. If the scientists here are so great, how come they can't do what we can do? How come they can't make a boy? The Governess once told us they've tried, but the results were deformed, or sickly, or not right in the head. That's why we're so important.

That's what they get for messing with nature.

The curtains pull aside then and reveal three new girls standing on the stage beside the Governess, who is preening behind her lectern. She likes to welcome the new acquisitions this way, showing them off to the rest of us like livestock. I've heard her say it's the first hint at what the auction stage will be like. A screen has already been lowered behind them, and as the pictures of wildflowers begin to rotate through, I feel my throat go tight. I miss home. The mountains. My family.

Daphne's wrong. There is a soul. Something inside of me is pulling me away from here. Aching for my old life.

The Governess begins the way she always does, by asking us to observe a short period of silence in reverence for the Magnates and the Merchants, and all the men we serve. I keep quiet because I cannot risk her taking back my punishment, but I offer no such thanks.

It seems not all prayer has been outlawed.

The Governess has launched into her speech about how our great country Isor was nearly destroyed by the vicious workings of our ancestors. How simple things used to be, when free women could be trusted to know the value of their place in the shadows. Before greed infected their minds and their hearts and they used their bodies to seduce the very men who cared for them. She talks about how our grandmothers' grandmothers tore down the barriers between men and women with their trickery, and destroyed cities with their petulance. How they began to poison their wombs so that they could not bear children, and murdered men with their wicked powers.

"These were not women," the Governess preaches. "They were witches. And so we thank the Magistrate for their abolishment and give ourselves openly to the service of their sons, so that we never again lose our path."

It was during the Red Years—so called for the evil that poisoned the nation—that the Magistrate Brotherhood was charged with returning the rightful balance. They were the original witch hunters, killing women by the thousands. Cutting down anyone who stood in their way. I imagine them with swords and spears, like the Magnate that caught me, chasing down demon women who have three heads and layers of triangular, pointed teeth.

My ma used to tell this story differently. In her version, women walked free and proud. No one owned them. No one hunted them. Their bodies and minds were their own. That was until two Magistrates fell in love with the same woman. Competing for her affection, they turned against each other, forcing other men of power to take sides with them. The Brotherhood began to crumble. A council was called to rectify the issue, and when they learned that she had willingly given herself to both, had her killed. The rules changed then. My ma said it was because the men were scared by their own weakness and how easy it was to succumb to temptation. Women in power—merchants and healers—were accused of using dark magic to gain their status. Girls became the property of their fathers and husbands. And the Magistrate became monsters, making slaves of innocent girls and slaughtering those who stood against them.

One woman had infected two men. Two men, the Brotherhood. And the Brotherhood, the whole of Isor. The Red Years were called that because they were stained with the blood of our sisters who fought and died in the struggle.

The Governess finishes with the raise of her hands. "And so the Magistrate purged the country of witchcraft, *honoring* and *celebrating* those who were loyal by bringing them into their home."

"And their bed," whispers Buttercup. Daphne hides a laugh in her shoulder.

She's all giggles when she's talking to anyone but me.

Ten generations later, the world isn't much changed. The Magistrate has become the Magnate, and our numbers are still monitored by the Watchers—the genetically enhanced soldiers that police the city. We're hunted and sold for breeding. And if there gets to be too many of us, they control the population and destroy our girl babies so that the same problems don't resurface.

My eyes switch to the new girls on the stage. Two have braided hair and eager smiles. Judging by their makeup, they've been prepped by house Pips for today. The third has a clump of yellow straw hair on her head and pale skin. She is crying softly, her hands knotted in the sides of the same uniform dress I wear. It is short and slinky, and stretches over her flat chest and stomach. All three of the girls wear the beaded earrings of the Unpromised and are about my age. Fifteen years. Sixteen, maybe.

"It's my sincere hope you make something of yourselves," the Governess says. "Some of our girls have gone on to be forever wives. Some movie stars, even."

"Like Solace," whispers Buttercup. "I'd just *die* if a big-shot movie man picked me."

The other girls all fawn over mention of the skinny actress who's always half naked in all her posters and billboards. Rumor is her name was Marigold when she lived here, but that her owner changed it when he bought her. Somehow they've convinced themselves that the rich men she ends up with in her movies are real, and that we'll all be so spoiled.

The reality is that most will be returned to a facility like this one, but for those who've already been through the system. Daphne's told me only one in a hundred girls gets made a forever wife. Even that big-time actress will probably get dumped back into rotation at some point.

The Governess is patting down a stray hair. "I once sat where you did and look at me now. Governess of the Garden. My own apartment in the city."

"And sterile as a steel glove," whispers one of the girls. The Governess stiffens.

She can't make babies. Everyone knows it. Few women live to be her age. Most, after they've been all used up by their buyers, are freed to work for Merchants, but they're so bone tired and burned up from all the birthing treatments, they don't make it long. Most of them end up scrounging around the Black Lanes until they succumb to the plague.

"Have your fun," she says quietly. "But remember: I control who takes you home." She takes a deep breath and beams, as if she remembers she's in charge here. There's a gleam in her eye as she rests a hand on her waist. "Take care of your men, and they will take care of you."

I don't know who she belonged to, but she must have done

a thorough job keeping him satisfied to land this position. Especially after being such a disappointment in the childbearing arena.

The Governess clicks off the main projector and her mouth forms a grim line.

"The rules of the Garden are outlined by the original Magistrate," she says. "The Unpromised must not be compromised prior to their first sale. It has always been this way. It must always remain this way. This is how we assure the quality of our *product*."

My stomach is hurting now. I know what will come next. Someone's broken the Purity Rule. Someone hasn't passed their medical inspection during a pending sale.

It's a girl with dark skin named Jasmine. She's brought out onto the stage by a Watcher, wearing the pressed black jacket of his station. He's enormous, nearly twice her height and thickly muscled. He's got a messagebox on a belt cutting across his chest, right beside the metallic handle of his wire. I shiver, and immediately the old scars on my right leg begin to ache.

In one of his hands is a sickle-shaped, silver knife.

Even the new girl that was crying on stage is quiet now, watching him with wide eyes. I try to look away, but I can't. Jasmine is the only one making a sound. She can barely support her weight and bobbles about as though her head is too heavy for her neck.

"As you all know, Jasmine was Promised to a Magnate last month after auction. She fetched a high price, and was in the midst of her ownership transfer when she was discovered impure."

"I had to," Jasmine whimpers, so quietly we all strain to hear her.

"Silence," says the Governess softly.

Jasmine doesn't have to say any more. We all know what

happened. During the interview process she was brought into one of the private rooms for an inspection, and within, the Magnate made her lay down with him. Now he's discarding her, saying that she's impure. It happens more often than anyone would like to admit.

The Watcher's face is blank and uncaring. He has a dimple in his chin, and all of his hair has been removed by treatments. He looks as if he hasn't even registered what the Governess has said.

I shiver. If anyone's truly soulless, it's a Watcher. After they're plucked from the pool of criminals at the jail they're biologically altered, not unlike the Pips. But instead of becoming obedient, the Watchers are made more aggressive. Their emotions are turned off somehow and their bones are fused with supports, making them bigger, stronger, and more powerful.

They're the walking dead. They don't feel. They don't speak. They're lethal.

The Watcher is stiff as a board, waiting for the Governess's go-ahead to proceed.

My hands begin to tremble. This is one of the worst parts of being here. It hits far too close to home.

I close my eyes and see my ma. She has curly hair, just like mine, though hers is much longer, down almost to her waist. Her skin is sun kissed from years of living in the mountains, and her mouth is fuller, more shapely, than my thin lips. She smiles easily, but when she's serious, when she drills me on our escape plan, I stand at attention.

Her cheek bears the puckered scar of the Virulent, which she tells me she earned at a facility just like the Garden. Though she never shares the details, I know I was conceived in the same manner that has led to Jasmine's punishment. I am the spawn of some nameless, impatient buyer who took what he wanted before he signed her papers.

When I open my eyes again, the Watcher is holding Jasmine tightly against his chest with one arm, almost like they are lovers, but for the knife he holds over her face. She pinches her eyes shut and grips his muscled forearm to steady herself. Her arms are so thin and fragile. Like little Nina's arms.

In a quick, practiced motion, he slices a large X across her right cheek. A short scream bursts from her throat, and then she sags against him, passed out.

AN HOUR LATER I am sitting on the floor outside the Governess's office, still thinking about Jasmine. She'll be out on the streets now. I wonder if her wound will become infected and kill her, or if she'll be forced to live in the Black Lanes, selling herself as a Skinmonger. She's pretty; she'll find that kind of work easily.

If I was her, I'd break out of the walls; the gatekeepers won't hold one of the Virulent back. *Better she die in the wilderness than die in here,* they'd say. That's what they told my ma when she left anyway.

The Governess's raised voice begins to leak through the doorway as she relays her instructions to the Watcher who cut Jasmine.

"Clover is a sneaky girl. She has tried almost everything to escape. You must be on guard at *all times.*"

A moment later, the Watcher, the Pip, and the Governess all emerge through the heavy door of her office. She is smiling smugly. Pleased, I'm sure, with the prospect of a month away from me.

The Watcher types a message on the small black screen that is his messagebox and tucks it back into the pouch in his utility belt. He's holding a wide silver bracelet in his right hand. The sight of it makes my fists tighten.

The Governess instructs me to hold out my right hand, and I do as she says. She smiles, showcasing her gleaming white teeth. I try to relax, knowing what's coming.

The Watcher clicks the bracelet around my wrist in one smooth movement. It reaches from my wrist to my elbow and is so heavy my arm automatically falls before I jerk it back up. The Watcher then pulls a narrow silver cylinder from a pocket on his chest strap and presses it into the middle seam of the metal, where it makes a sharp hiss. The sheath becomes so hot I have to bite my tongue to keep from wincing, but soon it is cool again. The bracelet has now been welded to my arm, and only the Watcher's device can remove it.

"*Finally*. Get her out of here. I've got *so* much to do before tomorrow," says the Governess, and she turns and slams the door behind her. The Pip scurries away like a field mouse.

The Watcher grabs my arm stiffly and leads me again down the bruised hallway, past the parlor and the dangerous private screening rooms, and through the main foyer. We pass the amphitheater and make a sharp right. He pauses while a Pip presses the button that releases the magnetic hold on the door.

We travel down a long hall, this one rimmed with dust and cobwebs, and overhead lights flicker, on the verge of death. There are no windows here, but I know if there were, they would show the metal-and-glass high-rises of the city on one side, and the rec yard on the other. But the passage extends past the edge of the pond and its high containment fence, and finally we reach an office.

The Watcher types a code into the lockbox outside the door and it pops open. I memorize the pattern his finger makes, but know the code is useless without his thick leather gloves. If I touch the keys they will melt my skin to the metal with a clear acid, pinning me there until someone else can release me.

I know this, of course, because I've tried. The attempt cost me three skin-grafting surgeries and two weeks in the infirmary.

The Watcher's office for the solitary paddock sticks out like a leg from the Garden. The walls are glass on all sides except for one, which is plaster. He seals us inside with another lockbox code, and then crosses the small room to a glass door. It slips open just as soon as he approaches it.

One more step and we're outside. Here the weed-infested yard wraps like a horseshoe around the office. On one side, fifty or so paces away, I can see the outer edge of the rec yard; its buzzing fence sounds like a honeybee is somewhere close. On another side is the crumbling gray stone wall of the facility's trash incinerator. And on the third side, completely hidden from the rec yard, behind the office wall, is the yellow Driver rental barn. Only a runoff stream separates this back lot from the back fence of the horses' paddocks. The Pips don't maintain this area of the Garden; no potential buyer will ever come back this far into the facility.

There are a dozen places I could sneak out. Over the stone wall, cut through the barn, follow the stream down to where it disappears into the sewer. But the Watcher's hand is heavy on my shoulder, and as I twist, his tightening grasp becomes painful.

A stake sticks out of the ground, and attached to it is a long tarnished chain that curls like a snake. The Watcher lifts the end of it, and holding my arm steady, attaches it to my bracelet with his key. It makes a hiss, welding into place so there's nothing I can do to remove it.

When he's released me, I round the corner to the plaster wall, the chain dragging after me through the dirt. Here, I'm hidden from view from the office, but the Watcher follows me, seeing if I'll try to cross the stream. Once, there was a metal roof shelter out here, but that has since rusted away. All that's left is the orange line where the plate attached to the wall.

Before I reach the water the chain stops me. I've gone as far as it will let me.

I look up and the sun is only a pinprick of white through the grayish-green haze. I breathe in the soot-filled city air.

At least I'm not going to auction.

I HAVE BEEN IN solitary nine times in my one hundred and seven days at the Garden. The first few times for three days. The next few for a week. Then two weeks. This is the longest I will have been here.

Sometimes I wonder why the Governess puts up with me at all. My body may be healthier from growing up outside the city walls, but I wonder if that makes me worth her trouble. As hard as I push to stay away from the auction, I sometimes worry that she'll try to dump me early—give me to some pimp from the Black Lanes, like the others who don't make the cut.

At least while I'm here I'll get to see Brax. If he's stuck around, that is.

The Watcher goes inside and sits in his rigid metal chair before the window. If I'm going to get out of here I have to get that key on the belt across his chest. I can't be too quick about it though; I need to sit back, bide my time. Wait until he stops expecting me to bolt. That's when I'll strike.

I just need to get close enough to slip it off without him noticing. Not an easy feat, but there's no way around it. The bracelet can't be cut off—I've tried with every sharp piece of metal and rock I've managed to smuggle back here. I have to get the key, and for that I've got a plan.

Once this bracelet's off, I'll wait until dark and then follow the runoff stream through the weeds into the sewer. It's big enough for Brax to fit through, so it's big enough for me.

Then, freedom. I'm getting my family, and going so deep in the mountains the Trackers will never find us.

I unlace my slender black boots and set them aside. My toes curl around the grass and weeds, and I cringe at a bite of pain from the gravel beneath. My feet have been spoiled by these city-wearer's shoes. They've lost their calluses from my life in the mountains. I add this to my checklist of things I must remedy before my escape. If I'm going to run, my body's got to be ready to move.

The Watcher stares at me blankly as I pass in front of his station. The way a dead person stares at some fixed point in the distance. The way my ma saw through sightless eyes after her soul left her body.

Daphne's words return to me—about men proving that Mother Hawk doesn't exist. The idea of it sours in my stomach. But the thought of my ma's soul going to the next life, of her bearing more children and loving them as she loved me, feels even worse.

I feel my brows draw together and ignore the guilt I feel for putting her out of my mind.

After I'm sure the Watcher's bored with watching me drag my chain through the dirt, I walk back around the other side of the office, beyond where he can see. When I pause to listen I can tell he hasn't got up to follow. Good.

Behind the back wall I see something that surprises me.

A man leading a tired bay mare in a red halter. He's tall for a Driver; his outstretched arm rests on the mare's withers without having to reach up. His lanky body fills the typical garb of his people: scuffed leather boots, rawhide pants, a dirt-streaked tunic, and a faded maroon handkerchief rolled around his neck. His hair is messy and ragged, but as golden as the sun in the mountains, and his face has been darkened by a lifetime of outdoor work.

My next thought is that he must be new, because he's about

to do something incredibly stupid—something I've never seen another Driver try in their time here.

Thirty paces away, he's leading the mare through a break in the fence towards the narrow runoff stream. He clearly doesn't realize that it flows from the pond in the rec yard, where it's been treated with chemicals to keep it looking clean. It's poisonous. If I hadn't heard the girls whispering about it the first time I'd been sent here, I would have tried to drink it.

Just like this boy's about to let his horse do.

I don't think about what I do next. I don't consider that he's a Driver and dangerous, maybe even lethal. I don't think about how the Watcher will react when he hears me. I'm thinking about that horse and how her stupid owner's about to get her killed.

"Stop!" I shout, waving my free arm and running towards the stream.

The Driver sees me a second later, and before I can take another breath, he whips a gleaming dagger from his belt and hurls it directly at my chest.

CHAPTER 4

I'M STRETCHED OUT ON the ground, where I threw myself after I saw the weapon. I roll over, and my hands fly over my chest, my stomach, making sure I'm still in one piece. There's no knife, and when I turn my head I see it planted in the plaster wall behind me. I'm breathing hard, and my body is already humming with the need to get up and run. But I can't go far. The chain has made sure of that.

I'm stuck here. A stone's throw away from a boy who just tried to kill me.

Scrambling up, I run for the knife. I have to work it back and forth to pull it free, but I never take my eyes off the Driver. When the grip is in my hand I start edging sideways, towards the Watcher office, whipping the chain after me so I don't trip.

I take a closer look at my attacker. He's got wide, shocked eyes, high cheekbones, and his mouth is hanging slack. He must be surprised I'm not dead. He's young—the youngest Driver I've ever seen. He can't be more than a few years older than me. But it's hard to say exactly, because his face is smeared with dirt.

His spooked horse is bucking behind him, and though he holds the lead tightly in both hands, be barely turns to calm her. Now that the shock has passed, I can see the horror in his face.

"That's right," I say, trying to puff myself up. "They'll hang you for that. I'm Unpromised." I've never used this as a shield before, but I do now. I wish I had my earrings to prove it.

His look remains unchanged, and I remember that Drivers don't speak the common tongue. They don't speak at all actually—they're mute.

"*Unpromised*!" I yell slowly. As if this will make him understand.

A few seconds later, the Watcher comes careening around the side of the building. The metal handle of the wire is ready in his hand and his black eyes are narrowed. I try to hide the knife up my sleeve, but he's seen it. His thumb presses down on the wire, and with a click, a glowing green rope inches out. The electric whirring sound makes my blood run cold.

He doesn't even look at the Driver. He's only looking at me. As always, everyone thinks that I'm the biggest threat around.

"Wait," I say. "Wait, it was him." I point across the poisoned stream.

The Watcher is suddenly before me—he moves so fast a short scream bursts from my throat. I drop the knife and hold up one hand. The other, weighed down by the chain, is out to my side. I'm shaking, and the links rattle together.

I might be scared, but I'm not stupid. Even with a blade I'm no match for a Watcher. He'd break my neck before I could take my next breath. But even though I know this, I hate that I'm not stronger.

He picks up the knife from the ground, then presses a button which retracts the wire, and replaces it in his chest strap. Then, right in front of my face, he breaks the knife in half with just his hands. His face shows nothing. No emotion at all.

Only now does he glance at the Driver.

The boy's done. There's no way the Watcher will let him live. Much as I hate being trapped here, I'm worth a lot, and for the first time I'm glad about that. But the Watcher only tosses the hilt of the broken knife across the stream, where it lands at the Driver's feet. The boy is shocked too; he doesn't even pick it up.

"Don't kill her," my guard says in a flat, bored voice.

That's *all* he says.

And the Driver probably doesn't even understand anyway.

Solitary was a bad idea. I've kept myself off the auction block, but at a huge price. None of the other Drivers have come back here before. No one at all comes back here. But now that this crazy boy has found out I'm here, unable to escape and without so much as a fence for protection, who knows what he'll try.

But for now, the Watcher is distracted.

My mind springs back into action, and I know it's reckless, and I know it's too soon and I should stick to the plan, but I can't let this chance pass me by.

Much as it revolts me, I fake a sob and bury my face into my guard's rock-hard arm. I don't even have to force a tremble; my body is still reeling. I feel his shoulders move as he looks down at me slowly.

"He tried to kill me!" I say, moving subtly so my face is against his chest.

And before the Watcher can figure out what to do next, I slide my hand into his utility strap and latch my fingers around the small metal cylinder beside his wire. The key to my bracelet.

He knows what I've done when I jerk ever so slightly as I pull away. In a flash, he's lifted me off the ground. One hand squeezes my shoulder in a vicelike grip. The other is clutching my throat.

I can't breathe. I struggle, kicking my legs out at him, and drop the key on the ground so that my fingers can peel away his grasp. But though my nails dig into his thick leather gloves, they cannot release his hold.

My spine pops as my weight pulls me down and stretches my back. I begin to panic. I can no longer see his cold stare; my eyes are beginning to slip out of focus. He's going to kill me. The Driver needed a knife to do it. The Watcher just needs his bare hands.

An instant later I am weightless. Light as a feather. And then

I collide with the plaster wall against the back of the office. A bright explosion of color bursts before my vision, and instantly everything is clear. The Watcher has thrown me, and now he is picking up the key I have dropped on the ground. Straight before me is the Driver. Staring. One of his hands reaches towards me, but it's empty.

And then I slump to the ground, and everything goes black.

It's the pounding in my head that wakes me up. At least it's dark; that helps a little. I groan, and slip a hand around my neck. The skin is sensitive, like it's been rope burned, and my throat is dry. The muscles ache as I rotate my head in a slow circle.

The memories come back in one sharp pang. The Driver barn is quiet, and the boy is nowhere to be seen. I think of hiding on the other side of the office, but I'd rather take my chances back here than face the Watcher again. Still too dizzy to stand, I crawl away from the wall, filling the stretchy fabric of my skirt with small rocks and then placing them in a wide half circle around me. It's not much of a trap, but anyone trying to sneak up will trip over them in the dark. I gather a hunk of chain in my hand—it's heavy, but if someone gets close enough I can use it to defend myself.

My eyes close again, and the trickle of the water in the stream reminds me of home, where the moon changes shape and only hides behind clouds, not this nasty haze from the city. I listen to these sounds until the hammering in my brain filters in the other noise as well: the metallic clang from the factories in the business district, the soft thump of club music from the bars and brothels in the Black Lanes where the Virulent live. And if I focus, the faraway scream of sirens from the housing sectors of Glasscaster. The more I focus on it, the more my head hurts.

Beside me are a water bottle and a metal bowl with three pills inside. The Watcher must have brought it when I was out. Guess he doesn't want me dead after all.

I grab the bottle and drink greedily. It took time to become accustomed to this tepid water. Even though it shows mountains on the label, it's hardly fresh; I can taste the bitter tang of the pipes it's flowed through. Then I grab a pink pill the size of my thumbnail and swallow it. It's a meal supplement. The very thing they suspect makes the city girls infertile. If it worked, I'd take a hundred a day just to poison my babymaker so nobody would want me anyway. But Daphne says it doesn't matter because my body's already developed.

As my stomach begins to swell with the overdue lunch pill, I rotate another pill between my fingers and think about the Driver boy. I can't figure out that look on his face in those last moments after the Watcher threw me. He was probably still confused over why his knife didn't hit the mark. I can't believe the Watcher didn't kill him. If we were in the rec yard, the boy would have been arrested, and at the very least fined.

Maybe the Governess really does want me gone.

There are two pills left. The Pips always give me one and a half pills per meal. Most of the other girls get only one, but I can't keep on weight. That's because I eat a whole ration only when I'm sure a Pip is watching. They say rotten pills, the outdated ones that turn yellow, make you sick—give you what the city people call plague. It makes your eyes bleed. The Pips screen our pills to make sure they're good, but I trust them about as much as I trust the Governess. I'd rather starve, thank you very much.

Why people don't just eat real food—something you can chew—is beyond me.

When I'm sure the Watcher hasn't moved, I crawl to my boots and drag them towards the backside of the building. It's been three weeks since I was last in solitary, and no one else has been brought in the meantime. Carefully, I count ten hand lengths from the corner of the plaster wall and dig.

Below the surface my fingers scratch something solid. Plastic. I clear away the surrounding dirt and find a water bottle like the one I'm drinking from. I remove it and give it a shake, then smile when the contents inside rattle.

I've stored some items within that I might need for my escape. Ten or so meal pills—I don't like them, but I'll keep them just in case. Strips of fabric from a dress I tore two visits ago. And some herbs I've picked from the Garden. It's not much, but I save what I can.

The lights from the factories reflect off the gray-green haze, and I can see just a little. I remove the items inside the bottle, even though I don't like to pull from this supply. Still, my head hurts too bad right now to worry about it.

Carefully, I remove two dried tear-shaped leafs from the bottle and crumble them between my fingers. If I had a fire at my disposal, I'd make a hot drink, but instead, I place the powder of the teaberry plant on my tongue and swallow it down with another swig of water. My throat burns again, though this time with the minty taste. The teaberry should kick my headache and lower the swelling in my face from Sweetpea's punch.

I empty my boots. A small piece of fabric wrapped around five more meal pills is inside, as well as a sewing needle, complete with a bobbin of thread that I stole from the costume room. Finally, I remove the slender metal tip of a beater a nasty little Pip broke over my shoulder one day when I refused to get my leg hair zapped off. I roll it across the palm of my hand, hoping I haven't ruined my chances of escape with my earlier stunt. These items have been hiding in my boot, crushing my toes for the last week. I place them in the bottle with the rest of the items, seal the lid, and bury it again.

A couple minutes pass and I begin to feel better. Metea's voice in my head reminds me to be thankful for that.

I pull myself to my knees, but when I open my lips to pray, the song is missing. It's dried up inside of me. I can't even think of how to start, and this scares me a little. Sweetpea and Lotus and Lily's voices are in my head, calling me cracked, saying I lay down with sheep. Laughing at me like I'm some kind of freak. Daphne's in there too, telling me the city scientists have proven there are no gods. Up until this morning I was convinced Mother Hawk would hear me, but now I wonder if the pollution in the city is too thick or, worse, that my call has fallen on deaf ears.

Because I am still here.

If my ma was still alive, she'd come for me. Bian would've tried something. But Salma—she's got enough to do just worrying about herself, and with the twins, she's surely stretched to the limit.

I chew my nails, fighting back that feeling I get sometimes. That something's happened to them—maybe that day I was caught, maybe one day since. It sticks to me like sap, that feeling. I try to focus on a new camp and what supplies we'll need in the colder elevations, but my worries are hard to shake.

Something crunches lightly over the grass, and I startle. These are not the heavy boots of a Watcher, but someone else. I roll to my feet and crouch low, gripping the chain. Ready to defend myself if needed.

The noise is coming from the sewer behind the Driver's barn. I hear a soft whimper, and my heart soars.

"Brax!" I whisper. "It's okay! The Watcher's inside! Come on, Brax!"

Brax knows to run if the Watcher's door slides open. It was the first thing he learned when he first came to visit me. I force myself to take a deep breath, and feel my chest expand. The swelling in my nose is down, thanks to the teaberry.

A large gray wolf, no less than hip height, comes stalking across the grass towards me. He avoids the brook after he leaves the sewer—I suspect Brax can smell the bad water—and sneaks straight up against the outer wall of the facility.

Then he springs through the air and tackles me.

I cannot swallow the giggles that bubble from my throat as Brax kisses my cheeks and my neck with his long, rough tongue. He licks and sniffs and snorts through my mess of hair, as though he believes I've hidden treats inside my curls. His paws are on my shoulders, pinning me down, and his breath smells a little fishy, but I am overjoyed. Brax is the only good thing I have in my life since I was taken.

"You've gotten so big!" I croon, feeling like a mother must as she watches her child grow up. His eyes are still ice blue and glassy with love and a bit of wildness. I grip his shaggy silver mane and play-shove him to the side. He knows this game well. He pounces, attacking me again with kisses, and then rolls onto his back so I can scratch his belly. His tongue lolls to the side.

"You're dirty," I say. He doesn't have Pips scrubbing him clean every time he refuses to bathe.

Brax was only a puppy when I found him, small enough to fit in the cradle of my arm. He came from the sewer, reeking of garbage, too thin. I suspect he wandered through the grating when he was small enough to fit, and then couldn't get back outside the city walls. He was wary of me, and I was just as suspicious, not trusting even the wild things in the city so soon after my capture. But eventually he crossed the stream, limping and whimpering because his stomach was twisted by hunger and worms.

He felt better after I convinced him to eat some mayflower leaves that I found growing wild by the office. I could tell he trusted me.

Later that night, he nipped at me, and made a playful growling noise that sounded almost like a bobcat. "Burrrrrax!" It seemed only right to assume he was telling me his name. And when I called him Brax he licked the back of my hand. I felt like I had finally done something right. I was so happy I'd hugged him until he'd bitten me to stop.

He disappeared that night, but returned the next. And on my

next turn in solitary, he came back out of the sewer like before. When I'm sent back to the other girls, I'm always scared that he will move on. But he hasn't yet.

After we play for a while, Brax quiets, and I lay my head across his shoulder and stare up into the haze. The Watcher has probably thrown a cot for me out into the yard on the other side of the office, but I don't need it and I don't want it. If he truly wants to treat me like a dog, leave me out here on the ground with Brax. I'd rather be a wolf than a girl any day.

I train my eyes on the barn, which is ghostly now in the darkness. I can hear the horses within moving over the straw. They're probably all padding down for the night, like Brax and I. But something else is awake. I can feel eyes upon me. Watching me. But with Brax as my guard, I am safe.

I drift off.

I AM WOKEN JUST before dawn by Brax's sudden shifting. In an instant he's on his feet. My head, which had been resting on his furry neck, cracks against the ground.

"Ouch!" I grumble, rubbing my tender skull.

Brax is hunkered down in a pounce position and the hair on the crest of his neck has begun to stand on end. His black lips have drawn back menacingly over sharp teeth, but he does not growl because he's smart and knows the value of silence.

I rise up onto my elbows and listen intently for what has spooked Brax. A moment later, the office's automatic glass door slides open.

"Home, Brax," I command. Brax tilts his head at me, and there is a sharp edge of resentment in his blue eyes, almost as though he's angry because I won't let him be a hero.

But he already is my hero. He is my only real friend.

"*Home,*" I say again, just as the Watcher's boots scuff against the dirt outside the office.

This time he listens. I barely catch the silver of Brax's tail as he scrams into the sewer. My heart relaxes when he completely disappears from view.

The Watcher rounds the corner of the office and stares at me for long enough to make me fidgety. Not as though he's interested, but as though this time he will fulfill what the Governess has asked of him. As far as Watcher positions go, guarding a girl in solitary probably rates up there with shining boots or scrubbing latrines.

I glance at the key on his chest strap and feel the frown pull at my lips. I'd have gone for it today if I hadn't blown it yesterday. Now he's more wary than before. His gaze flickers down to where I was looking, and immediately I turn away.

The morning is cool and has left a glossy layer of dew on my skin. Without the warmth of my Brax pillow, I'm beginning to feel the cold. When I rub my now shivering arm, a glimmering black streak remains. The tiny bits of coal floating in the morning smog will continue to paint me until a breeze clears it from the valley, which might be weeks.

I rise, and rotate my sore wrist as much as I can within the metal bracelet. With the moisture, the skin is already beginning to chafe, but I can't focus on that. There are things I have to do today.

I begin by jogging around my horseshoe-shaped pen, the chain tossed over my shoulder. At the end of my run I do sprints, hiking my slinky dress up around my thighs and racing around the office like a caged animal. I do push-ups, sit-ups. The things the Pips beat me for in the rec yard because the men who come from the street don't need to think the Garden is for loons.

If they think I'm a loon, so be it. When I break out of here, I'm going to run so fast they'll never catch me.

The Watcher tracks me every time I cross in front of his view, but he doesn't get up to stop me. There are plants here in the solitary yard he probably thinks are weeds. A fat purslane bush with its purple forking stems. Ivy and hotrod. Near the brook I find the flat lobed leaves of the bloodroot, and I pull it up from the roots and lay it on a large rock to dry. In small doses bloodroot can aid a cough. In heavier doses, the red, bleeding stems can be used as a sedative, so strong it will knock you flat. A little more and you won't wake up again.

I've made it that strong one time. I hope I never have to again.

Finally, when the sun is swallowed by the evening haze, I make a big show of gulping down my dinner pill in front of the glass office wall and stare across the open area to the rec yard, where the girls are milling about near the building, fifty paces away. I can see them strutting around like that actress—Solace. Repeating her words that are played on the media booths downtown like she's some icon, not the property of some man, like most everyone else.

Several of them are taunting the men who stand on the street gawking. It's a smaller crowd than usual, but rowdier. I can tell by their bold invitations that they've been drinking. I remind myself with a sigh of relief that it's market day and I've avoided the auction yet again.

I can't see Daphne and wonder if she's inside meeting with a potential buyer. Probably not. She's been here longer than me and nobody's wanted her yet.

Some of the girls see me, and though I can't hear what they're saying, I know it ends in laughter. I fight back the bitterness that bites into my stomach and remind myself that I'm better off alone than stuck with them.

A moment later, the new girl with the straw hair breaks away from a group standing by the pond and runs to the high fence. I strain my eyes, watching her curiously. What is she doing? She must know that it's electric.

She halts a few feet in front of the barrier, and even from the distance I can see her shoulders heave. She's bawling now, and a strange sadness cracks my hardened heart. She didn't want to come to the Garden, and if I understand nothing more about her, I get that.

I wonder if she's been to auction. The Governess usually holds back the new girls for at least a month of conditioning, but if she already had a prospective buyer she could have gone today. I'm too far away to see if she's still wearing her Unpromised earrings. One would have been removed if she's progressed to the paperwork stages.

And then I see a figure break from the crowd on the street and approach the fence.

One of his hands stretches towards her, and for a moment I think he'll touch the metal, but he backs away suddenly and kicks the ground. She's still crying, and has wrapped her arms around her midsection. In his other hand is a bottle, and I see it only moments before he heaves it at the ground near the fence. Pieces of glass clang against the metal, and sparks fly as the liquid spurts out.

Straw Hair is wailing now, chasing him down the fence line as he strides away, head down.

He's right to make a quick escape. He'll be fined for throwing that bottle. If he's a Merchant, he might even lose his business license. If he ever wanted to buy her, he won't be able to now.

She's lucky he didn't throw a knife at her chest.

I keep staring at her like she's putting on some kind of show.

It's dark now, and the Watcher is rising from his chair. I think he'll come out and watch me for a while, but instead the door slides open, and he throws a thin bedroll on the ground outside. It rolls through a patch of dust until it's coated on all sides by dirt. I sneer at him, but he simply turns around and lays down on his mattress inside the office.

Though the bedroll would make a nice mattress atop the rocks, I refuse to take it, and march back behind the office to the little privacy I have. I keep my eyes on the barn, just in case the Driver boy wants to break the Watcher's command and come at me, but only the horses are moving within.

Tam and Nina love horses. Tam especially. He'd probably have chewed through the chain by now, just to get to that barn. The thought makes me smile.

At last Brax arrives. He's happy again to see me, though probably not as happy as I am to see him. We play for a while, and soon I've forgotten all about the straw-haired girl and her visitor. About the Watcher and his stupid bedroll. About everything ugly in my life.

Brax has laid down, and I am just about to rest on his fluffy neck when he jumps back up and snarls, so quietly I can barely hear him. He's facing the barn, and I strain my eyes to see what he's looking at. Maybe a horse out in its paddock has startled him.

A moment later, the Driver boy appears, and this time I can see that he's wearing a plain white T-shirt and dirty, tie-on linen pants, and he's barefoot.

An ice-cold fist closes around my heart. He's walking straight towards me.

CHAPTER 5

I REMEMBER HOW FAST he flung the knife. How I would be dead if I hadn't reacted quick enough. He wants to finish the job. He's going to come in here and try to kill me, since he didn't succeed before. Or if not, at least try to hurt me—the Watcher didn't seem to have a problem with that.

If I scream, my guard will come out, but after the way things went before, I doubt he'll do anything. He'll probably think I baited the horseman and punish me for it. Strong as I am, I'm not ready for another choke out.

I should flee around the side of the office. The Driver won't follow; he has to be afraid of the Watcher. *Everyone* is afraid of the Watchers. My pulse is pounding in my ears. A freezing line of sweat rolls down my spine.

Just as I'm about to take off to where my guard can see me, the boy stops, three paces away from his side of the barrier. He lifts his hands to show they're empty, like this is supposed to mean he's safe or something. He's trying to tempt me to drop my guard. Well, I'm not going to do it. He must think I'm ten kinds of stupid if he thinks I'll fall for that.

My toes claw at the dirt, but my feet stay planted. I don't know why I'm not running. Some unseen hand is holding me in place. Fine. If my body won't run, it can still fight.

I wrap the chain around my right hand and drop down and

pick up a fist-sized rock with my other. I stand behind Brax, waiting for him to strike. We'll take this boy together.

The Driver climbs down to the edge of the stream and lowers himself to the water. For a moment I think he's about to drink it—this time I'm not objecting. His hands plant in the mud and he sniffs at it. There's a subtle sour scent to the water, the only clue that it's poisoned, and he must smell this because he jerks back and stands. His face is shadowed, and this makes me even more nervous. I can't tell what he's thinking.

Brax is lowering himself to the ground, a low growl rumbling in his chest, but the Driver seems oblivious to the wolf's killer instincts. Maybe he's insane. Or maybe the city people are right and Drivers really are thick.

But I remember that look on his face right before the Watcher knocked me out. He didn't look thick. He knew exactly what he'd done.

The Driver wipes his hands on his thighs. Shifts from side to side. Then, very slowly, he reaches his foot forward over the water.

Without another thought I wheel back and hurl the rock right at his head. I've got a strong arm; I've killed squirrels and rabbits at this range before.

The Driver reaches up and snags the rock out of the air with one hand.

He bounces it to the other, as though it's too hot to hold. He's wincing; I've hurt him with my throw. This should please me, but it doesn't. I don't know how he caught it. He wasn't paying enough attention to have seen my attack coming.

I bury my fingers in Brax's coat, gripping the chain even harder in my other fist.

The Driver looks down at the rock, and then, to my complete surprise, tosses it back to me. I catch it. His brows raise as if he's impressed, and I fight the urge to smirk. He thinks I'm like any other Pip-groomed, doe-eyed house slave in this place. Like I've never caught a ball before.

I've got news for him: I wasn't always locked up.

He's trying to distract me, play games so I won't be ready for whatever he's got coming, but I still can't figure out what that might be. While I'm trying to, he again stretches his bare foot forward, just over the waterline, and dips his toes in. Nothing happens—what did he expect? His toes to burn off? In the reflection of the city lights off the cloud cover, I see him smile.

His white teeth gleam. *Like the teeth of a bear,* I tell myself, *right before it eats you.* Still, he's not smiling at me. He's not looking me at all. He's smiling at himself, as though he's outwitted a runoff stream. It's the same dumb look I probably had on my face the first time I went through a sliding door.

A warning tears through me and without thinking, I throw the rock again.

He catches it again. And tosses it back to me.

This is infuriating. He doesn't make a sound—probably because he can't. His people are born mute, according to Daphne. Still, if he's smart enough to be here, he's got to be smart enough to know I'm trying to hurt him, to send him back to his barn and his horses. Doesn't he get that I don't want him here?

I feel like I can run now—the freeze is gone—and I will. Just as soon as I figure out what he's doing.

He paces awhile on the bank, glancing back at the barn and then around the edge of the solitary office. Each time he passes in front of me he takes a deep breath. Brax has fallen back on his haunches and is panting. Great. He no longer sees the Driver as a threat.

Finally, the Driver moves upstream towards the sewer, where the stream is at its thinnest. Then he climbs back up the bank. My shoulders relax because I think he's going home, but the next thing I know, I hear his sharp intake of breath and he's running down the slope. He catapults over the stream, which is almost twice as wide as I am tall, in a single bound.

Now I'm in trouble.

I stumble back, slamming my shoulders against the wall with a yelp. The rock is still in my hand. I can run. I can still run. It's only thirty steps around the side of the office. Or I can scream. And maybe the Watcher will come. Despite what he's done, he knows I'm more valuable alive than I am dead.

But I don't scream. And I don't run. My body is betraying me.

The boy takes a few steps towards me, and I grip the rock in my hand so hard my fingers go numb. The chain weighs me down. I feel more trapped out here than I did in the net when the Magnate and his hired Tracker thugs captured me.

Brax jumps back up. The Driver's gotten too close to us, and Brax is still my protector. He growls a low, menacing sound from his throat, and though I can't see his face, I know his ice-blue eyes are slits and his teeth are bared.

My mind flashes to the Watcher, only an arm's length away, but it could be miles thanks to the thick plaster wall that separates us.

The Driver stops short and frowns, eyes on Brax. He falls back a step, hands outstretched cautiously. I swing the slack of the chain in a circle, and hurriedly shove the sweat-dampened hair away from my brow so that I can see.

If he wants a fight, he's got one.

Brax holds his position. He seems to relax the longer the boy remains still. But I don't. It just makes me more nervous.

I stare at the Driver's face and watch for any sudden moves. Very slowly, he reaches into his pocket. Something silver flashes in his hand—it's another knife, I know it—and that's all I need to fling the rock and take off running.

I get all of ten steps before I realize he's not following. A quick glimpse over my shoulder reveals that he's on his knees.

For a moment, I think I've hit him, so I stop and turn, but he's still conscious. In his hands is the broken knife handle. He places it on the ground before me, and shoves it my way. Then he stands, and turns out his pockets.

They're empty.

My fist, still holding the chain, drops an inch. Brax repositions himself between us, the hair on the back of his neck still raised.

My mind runs through any other weapons he might have on him, and like he's reading my mind, the boy lifts his pant legs one at a time, showing off his bare ankles. He opens his sleeves and shows his wrists. Then he lifts his shirt, and I see the pale skin of his stomach and the lines of his hips that cut down beneath his waistband.

"That's enough," I say. But either he doesn't get the meaning of my words or he's ignoring me. He turns around slowly and shows me his back too.

"You don't have a weapon, I get it." I try to swallow, but my mouth is completely dry.

The incinerator is grinding, a consistent hum that makes me jump as it switches to a higher gear. I chance a quick glance towards the end of the wall for the Watcher, but there is no movement. I'll have to get all the way around the corner if he's going to hear me yelling over the noise, and I don't want to risk turning my back on this Driver boy again.

Keeping my eyes on him, I creep closer, sink down, and snatch the broken blade from the dirt. There's still a jagged piece of metal sticking out of the handle. Enough to cut him if I wanted. I don't know why he's giving it to me. It's either a trick or a peace offering.

His face is clean; I can see that up close. I've never seen a Driver with a clean face. Maybe they bathe at night. I think of the makeup we wear to auction and wonder if they wear dirt the same way. There are tons of ways I've tried to make myself appear horrible and disgusting to avoid being Promised.

In the gray shadows, the boy's golden hair looks silver and it waves around his face. His mouth is closed, but his eyes are glimmering like Tam's do when he's lying about something. I don't trust him.

"What do you want?" I hear myself whisper. My voice is trembling.

A look of pity slashes across his face, but quickly disappears. He continues to wait silently.

"Don't get any closer," I warn him. "I'll scream for the Watcher. Or I'll . . . I'll hit you." These are the only threats I can think of. I raise the chain looped in my hand, hoping he understands that at least.

Then he does something very odd. He sits down on the ground, long legs splayed out in front of him, and leans back on straight arms. Brax follows his cue, and lays out on the weedy grass at my feet.

"Brax!" I hiss. So much for being my hero.

The Driver and I stare at each other for a long time before I finally back into the plaster wall and sink down to a crouching position. I've made sure that he's not blocking my exit; I can still dart around the corner, and I'm ready to spring should he rise.

I keep my eyes trained on him. He's staring up now at the starless sky, and for some reason I wonder if he's ever seen the moon away from these city lights, from the mountains.

"I knew a Driver once," I say, surprising even myself that I have spoken. He turns towards me at the sound of my voice.

"You don't understand a word I'm saying, do you?"

He continues to stare at me. Brax has more language than he does. It seems odd. He must deal with city people. Maybe there's something wrong with him. Or maybe he's new here and hasn't learned much yet.

"*Driver,*" I say again.

He nods, but doesn't say anything.

"Horse."

He points to the barn. All right, he's got at least a couple words under his belt, but just in case . . .

"You're uglier than a rotting deer carcass. You probably grow another head at the full moon, don't you?" I test. He tilts his head to the side, brows lifted, as though I've just told him a very interesting story. He's bolder than most Drivers in the city. None are brave enough to look an Unpromised girl in the face.

"Anyone who touches the stream dies," I continue. "Poison. They only live for about three hours unless they get the antidote from a city doctor." This of course isn't true. If it were, I'd be dead from all the times I've stuck my foot in the pond just to feel a little bit of home.

Still nothing.

He's trying to do exactly what I do with the Watcher: get me used to him hanging around so that I never see the attack coming.

"How do you talk to your people?" I ask. The Drivers I saw in the city the last time I was there for the auction kept to themselves. I never saw them communicate with anyone. Daphne said that's because they've got brains the size of sparrow eggs. I know better, though. The Driver I knew in the mountains may not have spoken a word, but he seemed to understand us just fine.

He looks back up at the sky, and I'm reminded again of the moon and my home. I don't like him for bringing those things up, even if he hasn't said them out loud.

I groan, frustrated. "If you're going to try to kill me you should just get on with it, so that I don't have to wait to kill you back."

He's got me rattled. I never talk this much. But he's just sitting there acting plain-as-day normal, and I can't seem to stop.

"You should know that I'm not like any other girl you've ever met. I've killed animals twice your size in the mountains. And they've had teeth and claws, and . . . I'm not afraid of you," I finish.

He crosses one straightened leg over the other and lays back on the grass.

"Hey!" I say sharply. He rolls his head lazily to the side to look over at me. As intimidating as I possibly can, I stretch the chain across my neck and gag, showing him I could choke him dead if I wanted. "I am *not* afraid of you," I repeat slowly.

He only cocks his eyebrow and then looks back up at the sky.

My face begins to feel very hot, despite the cooling temperatures. This crazy Driver boy is making me feel like an idiot.

The time passes slowly. I've remained wide awake, and he hasn't moved. Brax, on the other hand, has sprawled out on the grass and fallen asleep with his tongue lolling out.

My legs are cramped, and out of exhaustion, I finally sit down. My toes slide under Brax's body for warmth, and I wrap the long slinky skirt around my ankles.

"There's a Driver I know named Lorcan," I say almost in a whisper, breaking our silence. "Well, *knew*. Before they brought me here."

The second the words leave my lips, the Driver turns his head, and I pop back up to my feet. Then I relax. He's recognized the word *Driver* again.

Warily, I sit back down.

I can picture Lorcan as clearly as if he is standing right in front of me. He's a wiry man with long silver hair and a pointy nose. Not a handsome face, but a peaceful one. Eyes that beckon trust like a moth to the flame. His skin is the color of oiled leather, but for the thin white scar running from his chin down to the notch in his collarbone. My ma told me once that a Watcher did that to him, and if Mother Hawk had not loved Lorcan, he surely would have died.

I clear my throat. "We called him Silent Lorcan because he never talked. I didn't realize until I got here that none of you can. He bartered with me when I lived in the mountains. Not with Salma or Metea or even Bian. Just me. He brought us clothes or wheat or yeast in exchange for the jewelry I made. He sold it at Trader's Day—the market they hold in the city every other week."

I glance at the Driver's calloused hands, thinking how my own used to look like that. "One time, when I was little, he brought me back a blueberry pie."

The Driver is still watching me curiously, with no sign to indicate that he's understood a bit of what I've said. For some strange reason, I continue.

"He had a yellow horse with white socks and a star between her eyes. She was crankier than Salma in the morning and liked to bite. I tried to ride her." I grin, the memory coming back to me in vivid colors. "Bian helped me up on her back while Lorcan was down by the river. I didn't last long—I ended up on the ground with a broken arm. Lorcan was furious when he found us."

Furious, and something else as well. I'd thought Lorcan was mad because I hadn't asked permission to ride his horse, but he seemed angrier that I'd been hurt doing it. The way my mother would get angry when I disappeared in the woods for too long.

My ma had died before his next visit. After Lorcan found out, he never came again. That's when I realized Drivers weren't to be trusted.

For a moment, I fiddle with the scar on my earlobe from the earring I pulled out, then realize I've become so consumed with the memory, I've completely forgotten the Driver boy is still sitting less than ten paces away. I jolt up, feeling a flood of heat rush through me.

"I know all about your tricks," I say. He doesn't move. Doesn't even lift his brows. "You can't fool me. I know . . ."

He rises quickly, and I brace myself to attack. But he's already turned around and is walking back towards the stream and the barn. He has a smooth, confident stride, so contrary to every other skittish Driver I've seen in the city. He leaps over the stream without hesitation and doesn't even glance back before disappearing into the darkened entrance of his quarters.

I remain standing, shocked. He didn't try to hurt me. He

didn't even come close enough to touch me. He just sat there, letting me ramble on about things he doesn't understand.

When I'm convinced he's not coming back, I slide back down to the ground and lay my head on Brax's shoulder. But it takes me a long time to go to sleep. I'm thinking about the Driver and his golden hair. About how much I miss home.

And about how long it has been since I've talked that much to anyone.

The Watcher doesn't even come outside for three days. He sits behind the glass, tossing meal pills out into the dirt from behind the slider door, infuriating me, because now it's me that's watching him, not him that's watching me, and I'm starting to think I really missed my chance.

During this time the Driver stays away. I see him sometimes, leaning against the paddock fence on the left side of the barn or leading a horse around to the other side, where a Magnate is probably waiting for his rental. I see him mucking stalls or tossing hay into the long wooden troughs. He's dirty again during the daytime. He seems to wake up dirty, as though he slept in a mud puddle. His clothes are soiled with white lines from sweat and horse slobber he doesn't bother to wipe away. On top of that, he walks differently during the day than he did that night when he visited me. His pace is short and clipped. His gaze stays aimed at the ground. He looks jumpy. So unlike the curious boy who stared and smiled.

Although I don't completely understand why he does this, it makes me think of all my attempts to sabotage a sale. My torn earlobe. Broken nose. Last auction I even lay down on the stage and pretended to be dead during my individual exhibition.

My days are spent exercising, eating my meal pills, bathing as modestly as I can with a sponge and a pail of water, and watching that girl with the straw-colored hair wait by the fence. The boy has not returned to visit her, and I can't help but think he's been paid a visit by the Watchers. Daphne's back outside during rec time. I can see her across the yard, lazing about with her friends. I guess she didn't get Promised at the auction after all.

Sometimes what's left of Sweetpea's pack—Lily and Lotus and a few new ones—head towards the back of the rec yard, towards where I sit. Not that I'm scared of them or anything—they're the ones behind a fence—but when I see them coming, I head behind the Watcher office, pulling my chain as far as I can. It's not far enough that I can't hear them singing prayers to make fun of me.

At night, I wait for the Driver, the broken knife and chain ready in my hands. But he doesn't come.

MY FIFTH DAY IN solitary, I wake alone, a damp meal supplement in the dirt beside my head. I wipe it off and swallow it down. Then I dig up my bottle and retrieve the broken end of the Pip's beater and hide it just under the cuff of the bracelet.

Today I'm getting that key.

Thoughts about the Driver boy keep bouncing around in my head. I peer over at the barn, wondering where he sleeps inside. If he is already awake.

I shake my head, irritated with myself. The boy tried to kill me. He's trying to fool me into relaxing so that he can do something to me. What, I don't know, but it can't be good. No man spends time with a woman just to lay ten paces away in the grass and listen to her babble.

Then I think about Lorcan. We didn't make enough jewelry

to truly make the trade worthwhile—Bian told me that once, after he'd been living in the city for a few years. But Lorcan still came up to the mountains. Sometimes, it seemed, just to walk with my ma.

If he just wanted to walk, maybe this Driver just wants to listen.

I kick the ground with my bare foot. That's the bad thing about solitary—you think too much. I've got more important things to do.

In my third month here, as part of our lessons, the Governess let us watch one of Solace's movies. In it, she plays a singer, the property of a big, fat man who owns a club. Somehow she loses her voice, and poisons herself. Daphne said it was because she was so sad to disappoint her owner, but I thought she was just stupid. Either way, he carried her to the doctor, who gave her medicine so she could sing again. Probably because she was bringing in a lot of credits. The Governess told us we should learn from Solace's dedication.

I guess the Governess isn't *always* wrong.

I lie on the grass behind the office and curl into a ball. Then I begin to whimper as loudly as I can, just like Solace did in the movie. If the Watcher thinks I'm sick enough, he'll have to take me to the medical wing.

It's not long after I've started that the Watcher's boots approach and halt beside me.

My eyes flutter open, and with a groan, I grasp my stomach. The white dot of sun is directly behind his hairless head, leaving his face shadowed.

"I'm sick," I groan quietly. "The pill . . ." I begin to writhe.

He doesn't move.

"Please!" I beg him. "I'm sick!"

The Watcher tries to haul me up, but I collapse again into the grass. There is a scuffle outside, and both of us turn to see the

Driver. He's just outside the back entrance of the barn, holding two large plastic buckets. He's pretending not to look at us, but I can tell he is.

I push him from my mind and pull the broken tip of the beater to the edge of the bracelet with my middle finger. I'm close now, almost close enough to grab the key and put the little metal piece in its place.

The Watcher lifts me again, trying to make me stand. I stumble forward, one hand on his chest, the beater pin in my palm. I lift my other hand to snatch the key.

More commotion from the barn makes the Watcher jerk, and his chest strap is too far now to grasp. I'm going to miss my opportunity because of all the noise made by a mute boy.

Once again the Watcher attempts to haul me up, but I refuse to use my legs, and this time he hauls back and slaps me. The metal pin in my hand, which I was going to use to replace the key, goes flying. We both watch it skid across the dirt.

My knees lock as I catch myself. My face feels like fire, and there are bright patches in the left side of my vision. My eyeball is about to explode. When I can, I suck in a breath.

The Watcher says nothing, but his eyes have narrowed. I glance down and see the messagebox on his strap and think of the Governess and the Pip who gave him his orders. They must have told the Watcher to be ready for this kind of thing. And now that I'm standing and glaring at him, I hardly look sick anymore.

Fury surges through me. I grab at the only thing I can: the messagebox. Without a thought of the consequences, my fingers snatch it off his chest. There is a word typed in block letters on the screen and I recognize it from the bodybook in the Governess's office. It's my name. Or the name they call me here anyway: *Clover*. The weed.

The Watcher reaches for the messagebox, but I scramble away and with all my might, hurl the box into the electric brook. There is a loud hiss and a crackle, and the messagebox is carried away into the sewer.

I turn back to the Watcher, who looks mildly bothered, but won't get angry on account of his treatments. He's lifted his hand again and reaching for my shoulder, to hold me in place while he beats me.

I kick him in the shins as hard as I can and try to wriggle away, but it's too late, he's got the back of my dress. All I can do now is curl into a ball, arms up to protect the delicate bones of my face.

Bang!

The Watcher pauses, one hand still gripping my shoulder, the other stretched up above my head.

Bang!

I turn to see the Driver slapping together the two large plastic buckets with great force. He's not looking directly at us. Several horses are startled by the noise, and race out to their paddocks, bucking and whinnying.

The Watcher, distracted, releases me, and I retreat towards the back wall to hide.

But the Watcher seems to have lost interest. He turns, picks up the piece of broken beater, and stalks around the office. I hear the automatic doors open, then shut, and through the wall comes the loud suctioned release of the internal office door that connects with the hallway. The Watcher is going to get another messagebox. He's gone.

I look across the brook towards the barn, but now the Driver is gone, too.

I could run inside. The automatic door may let me in, but I still can't get through the main exit because of the code box with its acid keys. I've failed. Yet again. Because of the *Driver*. And what's worse than the failure is knowing that every time I screw up, it makes my next attempt to escape that much harder.

I sink to the ground and press the heel of my hand into my

eye socket. The pressure has lessened, but my head is still aching, and my cheek stings. At least my nose was avoided.

Someone is back outside, and I lift my head, expecting to see Brax nosing out to check on me. But it's not Brax. It's the Driver. He's striding towards me, this time with purpose.

He hesitates only momentarily at the brook, then jumps over.

But my mind reverts back to the danger at hand. The tricks are over, now he's ready to get on with it. I'm still pinned in the corner. Why didn't I run when I first saw him coming? Why don't I *ever* run from him? Now even the Watcher can't help me.

My pulse begins to climb, and soon I'm breathing hard. I bend to retrieve a rock, but this time when I throw it, he simply ducks out of the way. He moves as fast as a Watcher, I swear.

I guard myself in the only way I know how. I crouch down, ready to spring like a cornered wildcat. The Watcher may be too big to beat, but I will not let this Driver better me.

He's five paces away when I pounce. My muscles quiver, as though I've just touched the electric fence and been given the shocks. He's expected this and ducks low, guarding his gut. I reach with the chain, but he slaps it aside. My nails catch him around the face and scratch at the skin of his neck. I bite, and get nothing but a dry mouthful of fabric.

He shoves me back and I charge him again, but he slips to the side, locking my head beneath his arm. I twist, but he won't let go. Then, somehow, he's pinned me against the wall. Both of my wrists are trapped in one of his large, impossibly strong hands. My legs are locked together, squeezed between his. His whole body has smashed mine against the plaster. I can feel his heart beat in my own chest. Feel it as though it is my own.

I've never been this close to a man before. Not Silent Lorcan. Not Bian. I'm petrified as to what he's about to do.

I struggle, but he's locked me in place so tightly I can barely move. I tilt my chin up to see his face. There's no hunger in his eyes like I've seen in the men at auction. No deadened stare like the Watcher. Instead his expression is angry.

Before I can make sense of it, he jerks back. The lump on his throat bobs. He bites his bottom lip so hard it turns white.

He points at my jaw and I flinch, but plant my feet. I touch my face, already feeling the heat and swelling from the Watcher's slap.

"Yeah," I say. "He got me. So what?"

He turns around, paces away, and then comes back. My muscles have all flexed, but I don't move. I don't know what's come over me.

I don't even move when his hand lifts and he touches my cheek with his fingertips, gently, like my skin is made of eggshells. He pushes aside my nest of hair and looks over my jaw. Over what the Watcher's done to me.

I gape into his Driver eyes, and for the first time I notice how there are flecks of copper in the deep brown.

The anger in his stare is dying, and in its place comes pity.

CHAPTER 6

"Stop that," I say.

My heart's pounding in my ears, harder than it did with the Watcher here.

His fingers brush over my eyebrow and a spark of pain lights me up. When he pulls away there's blood on the side of his hand.

It brings me back from wherever I went, and I punch him, hard as I can, in the gut.

All the air empties from his chest in one hard grunt; it's the first sound I've ever heard him make. As he staggers back, I scramble for the ground and pick up a sharp, fist-sized rock, and the jagged knife handle I've left just under the surface of the dirt against the plaster wall. He makes no attempt to stop me. His hands are resting on his thighs and he's bent over, still trying to catch his breath.

"You don't touch me," I say, my voice wobbly. "Nobody touches me without my say-so, got it?"

I've knocked the wind out of him. It's now that I've got my best advantage. But I don't attack. Just like I didn't run when he'd come striding across the yard.

"I said, you got it?" I nearly shout. I want him to nod, leave, *anything* to show he understands.

He glances up at the sound of my voice, a grimace pulling at his mouth.

"You ruined it," I say quietly. "I was *this close* to that key. I was almost out of here, and you ruined it."

His head tilts to the side.

"What do you want from me?" My fists are shaking now. My wrists are warm from where he grasped them and my cheek is still tingling from his touch.

It doesn't make sense. I didn't ask for his kindness, if that's what this is. And if he thinks he's going to try to make me break the purity rule he's got another thing coming.

My ma taught me one thing from the beginning: My body is mine. My own. No one else's. Just because someone thinks they have rights to it, doesn't make it true. I thought I understood that before, but here, in this place, it's become more clear than ever how right she was. My flesh and blood—it's the only thing I own, and I'll defend it until I can't fight anymore.

After a minute the boy stands upright and swallows a deep breath. He takes a step towards me, now just an arm's length away. I grip the knife. He points a finger at me, then he points at the Watcher's office. And then he shakes his head and slices both hands through the air as if to say *no*.

"What?" I say, trying to figure out what he's getting at. "You think I started it?"

He completes the same series of gestures, this time bigger and faster.

"Well what am I supposed to do?" I ask, throwing my hands up. I've forgotten about the weapons I'm holding. "I can't stay here forever. I've got to do *something*."

He leans closer, but I'm no longer afraid of what he'll do. Maybe that's unwise of me, but I don't care. I'm too frustrated.

He's closing in on me slowly, like I'm a fallen bird with a broken wing, and that irritates me even more because if there's one thing I'm not, it's fragile. When he's close enough he raises his hand as though he's going to touch my face again, but I jerk away. Instead, he points at my cheek, and then he mimics a choke hold on himself, and then he taps his nose, right where I know mine is still bruised from my run-in with Sweetpea. He slices another *no* through the air with his arms.

It's as if he's telling me not to fight anymore.

"It's the only way," I explain, not knowing why I feel the need to explain anything to him. "I need the key." I tap my bracelet, and point to the office, which has become our sign for *Watcher*. "So I can get out of here. Go home. *Home*." I point beyond the city walls to my mountains, and the worry sinks its claws into me again. Are Tam and Nina safe? Is Salma taking care of them?

He repeats the same series of gestures, now adding a point outside the city. I can almost hear a voice, *his* voice, in a clear, steady tone, telling me, "*Your freedom's not worth your life*." I'm probably making it up—I know he doesn't use my words— but I can't help feeling like we're getting through to each other.

"You know what they'll do. I'll be auctioned off, and some rich Magnate will lock me up in his fancy house and . . ." I can't say it. "I'll be his broodmare, you understand *that*? I'll be made to make him babies. And if they're girls, they'll just be sent to auction like me, and if they're boys, they'll be just like him, buying people like property! And *me*, I'll just keep coming back here again and again, till I'm all used up and no one wants me, and then I'll be shunned." I'm so worked up I'm almost shouting. I drop the rock and jab him hard in the chest with my finger, making the links of the heavy chain weighing down my arm clink together.

It can't happen. I've got Nina and Tam and Salma to look out for. I don't even know if they've gotten food or shelter for the winter. I don't know if they've been captured. I don't know what's happened to them.

My chest is so tight I drop the knife handle too and begin to rub a trembling fist across my collar. My skin is damp, and I'm surprised by the tears streaming down my face. Suddenly realizing what I've just said, I wipe my eyes on my sleeve and try my hardest to will the heat in my cheeks to cool off. At least the Watcher hasn't heard; the office door has yet to open.

I've never confessed so much to anyone, not even Metea. Thanks be to Mother Hawk that the Driver doesn't know what I'm saying, and even if he gets some of it, can't repeat it. Still, I wish I could shove all those words back inside my mouth.

He straightens so that I have to lift my chin to see his face. He pushes his hands down his hips, like he's trying to stick them in pockets, but his pants don't have pockets, so instead he weaves his fingers behind his neck. His jaw is twitching, as though he's chewing on anger.

And his eyes are gleaming. River silt and copper.

It strikes me that they look just like the stones my ma and I would gather to make jewelry. *Kiran,* we called them, for the copper streaks that reflect the light. We found them in the streambeds, worn smooth by water and sand. Silent Lorcan always traded more for any piece with a kiran stone because they were so rare.

This Driver's eyes are like kiran, and once again, I'm missing home so badly the pain feels like a living thing inside of me.

He raises his hands and mimes pushing down slowly on something very heavy. I again hear his made-up voice inside my head.

Calm down. Don't bait him.

"Don't tell me what to do," I snap. "You don't own me. Nobody owns me."

One of his eyebrows cocks up, and I can't tell if he's surprised by my tone or that I seem to be answering his gestures as though we're really speaking. Fine. Let him think I'm cracked, just like all the others here. I don't care what he thinks.

The sliding *whoosh* of the automatic door breaks my concentration, and a moment later I hear the Watcher's heavy boot crunch into the gravel right outside the office.

My breath catches. He's back.

At the sound, the Driver sinks an inch or two, bending his knees as though the ground's shaking. All the long, lean muscles in his arms and chest contract, and I notice for the first time that he's not just tall, but strong as well.

For some reason, the same shredding fear I feel when I think Brax might be caught rips through me.

"Go!" I hiss, jerking my arm towards the barn. I kick dirt over the knife handle I've dropped by my feet.

The Driver gives me one last warning look which I meet with a hard glare, and then darts back over the runoff stream. But he doesn't make it all the way back to the barn before the Watcher comes around the corner.

The Driver knows he's too late. He stops, spins, halfway up the bank. He's facing me. The Watcher's mouth pulls into a straight line—the most emotion I've seen him show yet. And then he reaches below his new messagebox to the silver handle of the wire, strapped on his chest.

The Driver drops to the ground, grabs a handful of pebbles, and throws them at me. I avoid getting hit just barely by jumping sideways. Then he crosses his arms over his chest and stares at me with a smug grin. His teeth shine in contrast to his dirty face.

My mouth drops open. Then snaps shut. I know what he's doing. He's trying to make it look like he's taking the Watcher's advice not to kill me and has decided just to torture me instead.

I play along. Whimpering, I cower against the office wall. I hide my face, fearing the Watcher will see the truth there.

The Watcher buys it. He releases the handle of the wire and stalks away, back to his chair in his nice cool office. I can hardly believe he's left until I hear the silence following the close of the automatic door.

I whip my head around towards the Driver and see that the smugness has turned to awe; he's just as surprised that this

84

worked as I am. And then one of his hands presses against his lips, and I can see in his kiranlike eyes and by his bouncing shoulders that he's laughing, though he doesn't make a single sound.

I feel a strange sensation brewing inside me. It tickles my throat and forces my lips into a grin. Before I can stifle it, I giggle. And then I laugh. We are both staring across the poisoned stream laughing at how we've managed to outwit the Watcher.

The feeling takes me over. My arms begin to tingle. My legs too, right down to my bare feet. I can't stop laughing. I have to bite my hand to quiet myself so that the Watcher doesn't come back to check on me. I haven't laughed like that since . . . since before they got Bian.

We both hear a noise coming from the opposite side of the barn. The low rumbling of a city car. Someone's here to rent a horse. Probably a Merchant. Most of the Magnates are too snooty to use that kind of old-fashioned transportation. They want something classier—a fine horse or a carriage.

Either way, the Driver's got to go.

He smiles at me once more before turning and jogging into the back door of the barn. He's got to change before the customer arrives.

When he disappears, I'm hit by a sudden sensation of loss. It's like all the happiness is sucked from my body.

I remember where I am and why I'm here. And that the only plan I had worth anything is ruined.

THE DRIVER IS GONE for most of the afternoon. His business must be keeping him busy, because he's not out throwing hay or cleaning stalls as usual. That or he's realized, like I have, that he shouldn't come back. It's too dangerous, for both of us.

I wander around in front of the glass wall for a while so that the Watcher can see me, or at least so he doesn't feel the need to come outside and check on me. From here I've got a clear view of the rec yard. It's past dinnertime and the girls who are left from Auction Day have been turned out to stretch their legs before bed. I can't see Sweetpea anywhere. Maybe that weight shifter worked after all.

Watching them gives me the shivers. Nina can never come to a place like this. The prospect of her being prodded and groomed then sold to a wealthy bidder makes me ill. I hope Tam protects her, like I taught him. She's worth more to these city people than he is. She'll always be in more danger.

Daphne's red hair stands out even across the space separating us. She and Buttercup are sitting on a bench facing the gathering crowd of workers on break. Buttercup's legs are up on Daphne's lap, and even from this distance, I can see Daphne lean over to kiss her. I never saw two girls kissing before this place, but Daphne says it helps raise their stock at auction. I don't know about that—it obviously hasn't worked for her yet—but from the hollers of the men in the crowd, I'd say she's definitely got their attention. Even the two new Pip-raised girls are watching.

Only one girl has stayed away from the fence. Straw Hair. She's meandering down by the pond, completely ignoring the others.

As I watch, she steps into the tepid water, kicking aside a lily pad. Daphne glances over, and soon she and Buttercup are laughing and pointing over the back of the bench. A frown pulls at my mouth. Daphne never laughed at me when I was praying. Maybe she's just bitter because she wasn't chosen. I'm disappointed in her. My half friend.

Straw Hair takes another step in. Then another. Her dress is soaked up to the knees. The pond isn't much deeper than that. Then she sits, the slinky fabric fanning around her like another lily pad. She lays back, dunking her head underwater. The other girls are laughing like loons now. But I'm not laughing. Poison aside, I'm pretty sure she's trying to drown herself.

I don't breathe again until Straw Hair stands up. She's soaked, and her dress is clinging to her flat little body as she sloshes out of the pond. Daphne's laugh, which is high pitched and rises over the others, stops suddenly. She and I both realize at the same moment what's about to happen.

"No," I say aloud, just as Straw Hair takes off at a sprint towards the fence. The electric fence. Where I saw her meet the boy on her first night. My gaze shoots to Daphne. She sees what's happening, but doesn't move to intercept.

"Daphne!" I cry. "Stop her!"

I run forward, but hit the end of my chain hard and am yanked to a stop. I strain against the chain, but have no way of getting inside the rec-yard fence. Daphne is standing now; she hasn't moved from Buttercup's side.

"*Daphne!*" I shout again. I know she can hear me—I'm less than fifty paces away—but she only watches, like I'm forced to do. I'm vaguely aware that my guard has come outside to see what I'm yelling about.

Straw Hair hits the fence at a dead run.

I'm unable to tear my eyes away. There's a flash of light, and a deafening metallic *zap*! Straw Hair is stuck to the fence, as though she's a piece of cotton stuck to tree sap. And she's shaking. Her whole body is shaking.

Her hair catches fire and her yellow head goes up in orange flames. It rolls back while the rest of her—her arms, her legs, her torso—are all still attached to the fence, dancing uncontrollably. I can smell her burning flesh in the pure white cloud of smoke that's rising around her. I can taste the sick in the back of my mouth.

There is a loud popping sound, and I know the fence's power

has been shut down. I can't help but think that if I were on that side, I would have taken this chance to climb over to freedom.

What's left of Straw Hair crumples to the ground, smoking. All that is left of her hair is a charred scalp. A moment later, the fence buzzes. The power has been turned back on.

And then three Pips are scurrying towards her. They don't run, but they walk speedily, and though I can't see their faces, I'm sure their expressions are that of disgust. My bloody nose was nothing compared to this sickening mess.

They don't pick up her body. They're calling on the radio to someone within the Garden. The Governess probably. She won't come outside, but she'll have her Pip assistant contact someone to pick up the body. Who knows how long that will take.

I stumble back a step, turn to the side, and puke.

I've never seen anyone do anything like that in all my time here. The most desperate attempts to escape have been mine. But Straw Hair has beaten me. She has escaped. *Truly* escaped.

Straw Hair. I didn't even know her name. Her Garden name. Or her given name. I feel another bout of sick coming on.

A short time later I register the Watcher's presence. When I turn he's holding a meal pill in one hand and a bottle of water in the other. Weakly, I take them from him. And then he promptly turns away to go inside. As though there isn't a dead body lying fifty paces away. As though a life has not just been lost in fire and smoke.

I throw the pill at him as hard as I can. I don't care if he does come back here to knock me around. I think, in all my fury, I might be able to take him right now.

But he's already inside, and the pill bounces harmlessly off the glass and lands in the dirt.

I'M BACK IN MY normal hiding place behind the wall when Brax comes. It's dark now—as dark as it gets here—and the night is unusually quiet but for the traces of bass booming from the clubs in the Black Lanes.

Brax can read my moods. He always has been able to, even when he was a puppy. He crawls towards me with his jaw closed, and sniffs my face and hair before lying beside me with his head in my lap. He wiggles there, until I lift my hand to pet him. The soft feel of his fur comforts me.

But only a little.

I'd never do what Straw Hair did. I can't, I've got the twins to think about. But it's out there. Even if it's an option I refuse to take, I know it's out there.

A tall figure emerges from the barn. It's the Driver, and I can see that he's clean again, even though his clothes are a mess. He doesn't descend the bank. He stands just outside the closest paddock fence. I can see his white teeth in the dim light.

I stand, leaving Brax lying on his side. This time, he doesn't bother getting up to defend me. I don't even grab my usual rock to defend myself. My hands feel empty, loose, and open like this.

The Driver's holding something, and for a split second, I kick myself for not grabbing a weapon. But soon I see what it is. Round. Palm sized.

A ball. He's tossing and catching it in one hand.

My jaw falls open. Surely he doesn't want to play *catch*.

The Driver tosses me the ball underhand, and I catch it easily. It's light and rubber, a little squishy in my grip. I toss it back, and he catches it. Then he throws a little harder. I grin, swiping it out of the air above me, muscles remembering the game Bian and I grew up playing. When I return the throw, he has to shake the sting out of his hand.

We go on this way for a while, and in that time I think of nothing but our game. Chains and auctions and girls with yellow hair all fade away.

My muscles get sore after a while, but I don't stop until he does. Winding his arm in a large circle, he comes to the stream, preparing again to hop over. As always, he sighs just after he clears it.

When he's walking towards me, my stomach tightens. Things weren't so bad when he was on the other side of the barrier, but now that he's close again I don't know what to think. I don't know what he wants or why he's here, but to show him I'm not afraid, I hold my ground. When he gets within ten paces, Brax jumps up and begins to growl.

I scoff. "Nice of you to wake up."

I pet Brax's back, soothing his raised fur back down. The Driver is regarding Brax warily.

He gives the wolf wide berth on his way to the wall, then slides back against it. I feel my eyes narrow—this is the place where I usually sit. He pats the ground beside him.

Tentatively, I approach, coaxing Brax to follow. Just because I'm pretty sure I won't be knifed doesn't mean I'm about to sit beside this boy unprotected. With my eyes ever on him, I sink to the ground. Brax insists on sitting between us. He faces the Driver, giving a warning snap each time the boy jostles.

The bass from the Black Lanes changes rhythms twice while I wonder what to make of my visitor. Absently, I trace patterns in the dirt with my fingers while he tosses the ball from hand to hand. After a while he seems to notice what I've done and taps the ground beside him, where I've scribbled a picture of a four-leafed weed. He looks at me expectantly.

"It's what they call me here," I say in a hushed voice so that I don't wake the Watcher up. "Clover. Eck. It's not my real name."

I look at him from under my lashes, waiting until he turns away so he doesn't see my face when I whisper, "My real name's Aiyana."

It's been so long since I've said it, I scarcely recognize its feel on my tongue. The word sounds strange, like I'm speaking a foreign language. I almost wonder what else has drifted away, but the Driver boy is watching me again, so I don't worry about that right now.

"*Aiyana*," I repeat, then point to him. "What's your name?"

He looks back blankly. Even if he did follow, he wouldn't be able to tell me.

"Your name should be Kiran," I tell him. "Because your eyes, they look like . . ." I pause. I don't know why but I feel like I've said something stupid again. The Driver, *Kiran*, looks over at me when I stop talking, and nods as though he wants me to continue.

"Well, what do you want me to say, Kiran?" I ask him. The name fits. I'm pleased with myself for thinking of it.

He leans back against the wall again, not understanding a word I'm saying. So I talk. Because no one has listened for a long, long time.

CHAPTER 7

"You're a long way from the Driver camps," I say, not expecting an answer. Though Silent Lorcan came to trade with us, we never went to his home. It's somewhere in the valleys where the rivers meet. At least, that's what my ma always told us.

Kiran's leaning against the plaster wall, looking towards the barn. There's a chestnut mare out in the back that's sleeping standing up. One of her rear hooves is cocked, and her head hangs low.

I go on.

"Ma was raised in Marhollow, one of the towns in the outskirts, where people still live the old ways." When he doesn't respond, I explain, "With families, I mean. All living together because they want to. Anyhow, the Magnates sent Trackers to raid the town when the census was low and took all the girls that were auction age. That's how she came to the city."

She was torn away from her family, her sister left behind. Not unlike I was.

"She got kicked out of the Garden when they found out about the baby—about me. They gave her a Virulent mark, and sent her to the Black Lanes. But she wasn't having any of that, so she left." I picture my ma's fierce smile. The way the puckered X scar would stretch when she was mad. "The gatekeepers figured she'd be better off dying *outside* their city." I shiver at the words, but that's how my ma told the story.

"She was alone in the mountains when I came. For years it was just her and me. Sometimes Lorcan too—the Driver I told you about. He came to trade with us. I wasn't more than hip high when he taught me how to set a trap."

By five I was cleaning my own game while Ma cooked. Fishing on days I couldn't hunt. Gathering the roots and plants that my ma had told me weren't poisonous.

I look at the Driver boy and for the first time I wonder if my ma named Lorcan the way I named Kiran. It's not like he could talk to tell us his real name. Strange that I never questioned it until now.

"When I was seven, Ma and I went down to the outskirts of Marhollow so she could visit her family. She made me stay above the tree line while she snuck in to see her parents and her sister at their farm."

The bitterness returns to me as I say this. I'd never been to a town or met my grandparents before. I didn't get to meet them then either.

"She came back at nightfall, carting the whiner. *Salma*. Her sister's daughter, my cousin. The census in the city was low, and so the Magnates hired Virulent thugs—Trackers, we called them—to raid the towns for young girls to bring to the meat market."

Lots of women fled into the mountains then. Some of us even became friends. But as the Tracker raids increased and more Magnates started hunting, our numbers dwindled. Soon it was only Lorcan that came to call.

"Salma was nine when we took her in. She hated my ma for what she did, for saving her life. She never really got over it. I used to tell her just to go back to town if she missed it so much, but she never did that either. She's all bark and no bite, Salma is."

I turn to Kiran who, when he hears me stop, motions for me to continue again. I wonder if he just likes the sound of my voice. This makes sense to me. I like the sound of the wind through the trees. I don't speak tree language, but the whisper is soothing all the same.

"We lived that way for a while, just the three of us. My ma trained us to hide from Trackers. And when Lorcan visited, he'd teach me to fight. Salma hated that he was mute and couldn't bring her news from the city.

"Then one day, I think I was eight or nine, I found a woman sleeping by a nearby brook." I smile a little at the memory. "She was all swollen up with babies. Two of them." I motion to show her belly. Her feet were thick too, and bleeding from all the walking they'd done to get away from town.

"Her son jumped out of the bushes while I was watching and he hit me with a stick, right between the eyes." I laugh at the memory now, but at the time, I was so mad I shoved him into the stream and held him under until Metea pulled me off.

"Bian," I say. "A year older than Salma."

It feels better to remember him at ten than the last time I saw him.

"It wasn't long before Metea's labor started. We worked all night, Ma and me, cleaning her, cooling her. We made her tea from baneberry roots to ease the pain. The twins were born just before dawn. Tam and Nina, she named them. Nina after her ma. Tam after the man she loved—Trackers had raided her town and killed him."

I take a deep breath, remembering the night of Tam and Nina's birth as though it has just happened. Blood and sweat. Metea's silent struggles. Bian's crying. And my ma's reliance on me. How proud she was of me. How proud I was of myself.

I'd never been so scared in my life. I think about telling Kiran this—but for some reason, I don't.

My stomach begins to hurt at the next part of my story. I want to stop, but the words just keep coming.

"I was eleven when she got sick. My ma. Fever."

My voice cracks. But this time, Kiran does not encourage me

on. He's watching me intently, mouth closed around a long piece of grass he'd been chewing.

I remember how she told me that this was the way of things. That to have life there must be death. To have joy there must be sadness. And that I must not be angry with Mother Hawk because of it.

But I was angry. I'm *still* angry.

"Metea and I gave her herbs for the fever, but the sickness took her eyes, made her see things that weren't there." It makes my heart pinch to remember my ma's crazed words during those last hours.

"I tried to remember the fever cures, but none of them worked. And when Metea said Ma couldn't take any more we made her a strong sleeping draught from bloodroot. So strong she didn't wake up again. I don't want to talk about this anymore," I finish suddenly.

I'm exhausted. The story has left me with a hollow feeling inside. I don't care that Kiran is still here. I don't care if he wants to kill me even. I just want to lie down and sleep. And for the first night in some time, I *don't* want to dream about the mountains.

I lay my head on Brax's neck. He's already passed out, and his steady heart calms me. I close my eyes. I must fall asleep quickly, because I don't hear Kiran leaving.

Maybe he stayed a while. I don't know.

THE NEXT MORNING I see that the Watcher is no longer wearing the key to my bracelet. I stop looking at his chest strap because it's such a disappointment. I don't know where he keeps it— somewhere inside, but unless he opens the door with his hand scan, there's no way to get in.

The days grow shorter, not just because winter is coming, but because Kiran begins visiting every night. With the motions of his arms and his pointing fingers, he tells me he's got some kind of plan in the works to get me out. I don't know what it is exactly, but he seems confident. At first I'm skeptical, but every day brings new hope, and every night he shows up empty-handed, more disappointment.

But it's not all disappointing. We talk a lot.

At least, *I* talk a lot.

A Pip comes by on my eighth day and gives me a few changes of clothes and two wool blankets—my only shelter against the rain that pelts me half that afternoon. I find myself reluctant to change out in the open, because on one side of my yard the Watcher can surely see, and on the other, Kiran might.

Not that he'd be looking.

During the daytime I can't help but glance over towards the barn. Sometimes I see Kiran outside doing his normal working routine. He wears his riding pants, his boots, sometimes a button-down shirt. His clothes are always filthy, but his handkerchief, rolled and tied in a loose knot around his neck, always seems clean. I remind myself to tell him to mess it up later so that no one will catch on to his disguise, but I always forget once he arrives.

Occasionally our eyes will meet and we'll both look away quickly, to check if anyone else has seen us. No one ever does.

On the tenth day the yard is unusually quiet during rec time. Drawn by the Governess's voice, I stretch my chain to its limit and squint at the back of the building, where she's called the girls into a line. From here I can see Daphne's red hair in the middle of the pack. It puts me at ease that she's around, for some reason.

A man steps out from the building and says something to the Governess. He wears a suit the color of eggplants and a floppy-brimmed hat, which he takes off as he makes his way down the line.

I cringe and fall back a step.

It's Mercer the Pimp. He comes sometimes after all the paperwork is done from the auction to pick up the stragglers for the Black Lanes. Most of his girls are Virulent, but every once in a while he'll buy a few First Rounders to sell them to his own clients in the Black Lanes. It's everyone's biggest fear.

Two girls are chosen—two who have been here longer than me. Neither of them put up a fight as they're ushered into the building by Pips.

Before Mercer leaves, he lifts his hand and waves. It's not until the other girls turn their heads that I realize he's waving at me. Even at this distance I can hear his laughter as I scram around the backside of the office.

I bite my nails to nothing waiting for him to come get me, too, but he doesn't show up. Someone else does, though. Another Driver, to work at the barn with Kiran. I recognize his silver hair and skinny, warped stature. He used to run the rental barn before Kiran came. He mostly stays out of view, but in the early evening, I catch a glimpse of his ferrety face as he leads a string of sweaty horses back to the barn. I think he must be delivering the animals to the rich city people. He leaves at sundown that night, and in the nights following as well. I don't tell Kiran this relieves me, because now he can keep sneaking over.

I do tell Kiran all sorts of things, though.

I tell him about my capture and Bian's sculptures. About Straw Hair and my anger at Daphne for standing by. About my family. I tell Kiran things I would never admit to anyone else because Kiran is safe to me. A trap for my feelings and words.

I stop being afraid of him sometime after our first week of night talks. I gradually stop thinking about where my weapons are or how fast I need to run to escape. Sometimes we play ball, sometimes we just sit together. Sometimes while I talk he stretches out on the grass and looks up at where the stars should be if the sky weren't so muddied by haze. Sometimes I lie beside him.

But not too close.

I begin to learn each expression of his face, even the slightest ones, and what his gestures say. A raised brow means he's interested. A tightening around the corner of his mouth means something's bothered him. His shoulders hunch more when he's tired. His eyes never lose their gleam.

Sometimes I swear he knows what I've said. He'll nod at just the right time, or open his mouth and then close it again. Or almost smile. But then other times he does these same behaviors for no reason at all. I think they just must be a part of how he listens.

Sometimes I think he's frustrated that he can't understand me, and to be honest, I am too. I want so much to hear the sound of his voice; not just the deep flat tone that I've created in my head, but his real voice, if he has one. One night I tried to teach him to speak. We must have looked like fools—me showing him how to stick his tongue out and say "ahhh," him mirroring me in silence. We both ended up in fits of laughter.

His stayed silent, of course.

It'll be hard not having him to talk to when I get out of here, but the twins and I won't be able to risk any communication with the outside. Not even the people in the outliers. If we're going to stay alive, we don't need to give anyone any reason to come looking for us.

Sort of like the Drivers, now that I think about it.

———➤———

ON MY TWENTY-FIFTH NIGHT I wait for Kiran, as I have every night since his first visit. When I see him emerge from the darkness of the barn, I wait expectantly. Just like every night before this one, he shrugs and shows me his empty hands. His plan for getting me out is failing. He leaps over the stream, hesitating like he always does to check for the Watcher, and joins me behind the office wall.

Something's on his mind. His brows are knitted together, and his lips are drawn in a straight line. Usually he's more relaxed, more confident, at night. Like a mountain lion, I think. Lazing out on the grass, stalking around his turf.

"What is it?" I ask him, holding my arms out questioningly.

He points to a small pile of stones beside the wall. I've placed one there each night so that I know how long it will be until the Pips come back to get me for auction. I figure I've got twenty-eight or so days in here. About that time they'll need to begin prepping me for the meat market.

I count out the stones. Twenty five. My throat grows tight. I hold up all my fingers twice, then once more. "I've been here twenty-five days," I tell him. I'm glad my ma taught me how to count.

He points to the main facility of the Garden and holds his hands out.

How many days before you go back? I hear him say in my mind.

"Three." I hold out three fingers. If Kiran can't get me out by then, I'll be taken back with the others.

Now I can barely swallow.

He slouches on the ground, resting his forearms on his knees and looking irritable. After a moment he points to me, then over the Garden towards the heart of the city. He mimes the snooty look of a Magnate typing on a messagebox as he pretends to look me over. At least, I think he's pretending. His typing fingers slow, and his eyes linger somewhere around my waist before popping back up.

The auction?

"Yes," I manage, nodding. Somehow, I've managed not to think about the auction in several days. He picks up a pebble and flings it across the yard towards the barn. I hear it clap against the wooden siding.

"Your plan to get me out won't work?" I gesture so he understands.

He shakes his head.

"Are you sure?" I wish I knew what he wanted to do, then maybe I could help him. We could work together. As it is, I'm stuck trusting him blindly.

He's still shaking his head. I groan quietly. Breaking me out would have been dangerous, probably even impossible. I know this, but I still can't help but feel like Kiran's not trying hard enough.

It's warmer tonight, and I'm sitting on one of the wool blankets. I don't offer the other to Kiran. If he wants it, he can take it. We've worked out that much over our past three weeks together.

My bare feet, now hard with calluses, stretch out in front of me. My straight legs are about as long as Kiran's bent, and our toes are very close. Almost close enough to touch.

He's looking at my feet, and this makes me look at my feet. I feel the need to cover them, so I try to pull the slinky dress down, but he stops my arm with his large hand. His nails are caked with dirt and when he sees me looking at them his cheeks get a little darker.

"I don't mind," I say.

He hasn't touched me since that day the Watcher slapped me. My skin feels like ice next to his, even through the fabric of my dress. But I'm not cold, he's just *so* warm.

Then he leans forward very slowly and traces his finger very lightly along the twisting scar around my right calf. It's at least a half inch thick and always lighter than the rest of my skin. Like a tattoo of a white snake.

The tickle of his fingertip on my leg sends a bolt of heat right into my belly, and I gasp before I can stop myself. My hand snaps up to cover my lips. The blush burns my face. And then I hold as still as I possibly can, like this will erase everything that just happened.

My voice is a little higher than normal when I finally speak.

"It's from a wire. The Trackers that caught me had one." I can still remember the freezing cold, then the burn. The way the metal tightened, tearing into my skin and flesh. "They gave me surgery for it at the infirmary, but they couldn't get rid of the scar. The Governess doesn't care. It disappears with concealing powder."

Kiran's still staring at my leg. I jerk both knees into my chest and hide them in my skirt.

"I know about doing it," I say.

Something has caught Kiran's attention and he's looking the opposite way. I look over his shoulder to see what he's staring at, but I don't see anything. When he turns back, his face is mild. He's not even irritated anymore.

"I mean, Salma told me. I've never . . . you know. I don't see how anybody would want to. All the jabbing and slobbering and grabbing. I don't know why all the girls at the Garden are so set on getting Promised."

A renewed desire to sabotage the upcoming auction fills me. Kiran's looking up at the sky now, and his hands are clasped together over his knees. I gaze for a moment at his wavy hair, silver in the moonlight, and then pick a fistful of grass just to busy my hands before I do something stupid like reach over and touch it.

"A few years ago I followed Salma down to the edge of Marhallow, to the farms outside of town. She met a boy in the woods, and they . . . Well. They didn't know I was there, but I saw them. So I know how it works."

I don't know why I just told Kiran this story. I don't know why I'm talking out loud about these things at all. I don't normally even think about them. But Kiran's hand on my leg did something to me, and now I'm thinking about all kinds of crazy things.

He's very still for a long time. And so am I. As if waking from a dream, he points to me, and then towards the city gates, with a heaviness in his eyes.

"Why don't I leave?" I ask him, puzzled. He mimics the same gestures.

"You know why I can't leave." I point to the Watcher, then to my heavy metal bracelet and the invisible wall surrounding us.

He reaches slowly for my elbow, cupping one hand beneath it, and slides another finger between my metal cuff and my arm. He's very close to me, and I can see how his skin grows lighter from his neck to his collar, where the sun is blocked by his Driver shirt.

He begins to pull at the bracelet.

First he's gentle. Then he begins to tug, trying to pry the contraption off my arm. Beads of sweat appear at his brow, and he climbs to his knees for more leverage. There's a determined gleam in his eye, almost frantic. I want so badly to believe this thing can be torn off that I try to help him. I try to jerk my hand out, and can feel the bones of my wrist bend and crunch together until they nearly break.

I grind my teeth together, and keep trying.

Please, I pray. *Please let this work.*

We can do this. We can get it off. And then we can run through the barn towards the city gates and pretend that we're both Drivers. We can . . . cut all my hair off, and Kiran can dress me as a boy. It's too dark for the gatekeepers to tell the difference, and too late for them to ask too many questions. We can do this.

The pain from the metal bites at my skin. The tears stream from my eyes, but I don't stop. Kiran doesn't either. He's pulling as hard as he can, until finally the breath bursts from my throat, and I know our efforts are wasted.

My dreams, that had come so quickly, are smashed into the dirt.

"It's not working," I say, already trying to put myself back together. I won't let myself cry. I refuse to. But the look in his eyes is so full of resolve that it's hard not to break down and weep. He tries one last time, before I find myself pushing him back, shoving him away from me so he'll stop.

"Kiran, it hurts!" I say. "You have to stop! *Please!*"

He falls back on his heels. I feel a trickle of blood slide around my wrist, and pinch my eyes closed to fight the burning in my arm. In my eyes. In my chest.

Kiran's hand rests on my shoulder, but I shove it off. I don't want his comfort. I don't want his help. I remember why I don't have friends. Friends give you hope when you shouldn't have it. They make you trust in things other than yourself. They trick you into forgetting what really matters.

"I would have gotten the key a long time ago if not for you," I say. It's not true, but I want to hurt him, just like he's hurt me.

I jolt up to my feet, my aching wrist trapped against my chest.

"Go away," I say firmly. The fire has returned, slicing through my veins. I hate myself for thinking Kiran could get that bracelet off. I hate that he's distracted me from getting out of here for *twenty-one* days. Tam could have drowned in these three weeks. Nina could be starving. All because I've been talking to a mute boy who doesn't even know what I am saying.

How many escapes have I missed? How many times could I have grabbed the Watcher's key, or returned to the Garden, or snuck out through the infirmary? I'm failing them because he's distracting me. No. Because I let him distract me.

"Go away!" I nearly shout now. Brax jumps up from his place at my side and begins to growl. Reluctantly, Kiran falls back a step.

He looks hurt, but his eyes stay on Brax. My protector is

now backing Kiran away from the plaster wall, back towards the barn. Step by step they go, until they cross over the bank, and Kiran's knee-deep in poison water. He trips and falls back, making a splash. Brax snaps his teeth and Kiran rises, sloshing across the rest of the stream.

The automatic office door slides open. The Watcher has heard me yelling, or Brax's growls, or both. He's coming around the corner.

Kiran looks at me one final time before spinning and disappearing inside his safe haven. And seconds later, Brax is gone within the sewer.

The Watcher comes out and stares at me with his horrible, dead eyes. I can't stand it any longer. I fall to the ground, and curl into a ball.

THE NEXT MORNING I wake before dawn, feeling terrible. Kiran's trying to help me, and I shouldn't blame him if he can't. No one's more intent on getting out of here than me, and *I* can't even get out. Next time I see him I'll tell him I'm sorry, but just before I rise to go back to the barn-side, I hear the slide of the doors behind me. A bright light comes from the panel within, and I blink, and open my eyes to shiny silver shoes with black laces standing before me. I don't have to look up to know what I'll see, but I do anyway, because I'm surprised. They're early.

"Get up, girl! *Pip, pip.* I don't see why she doesn't use the bedroll. It's *disgusting* sleeping in the dirt like that. Just like an animal."

I still have three more days. *Kiran* still has three more days. This can't be right.

I look up at another black caftan. The pale, flawless face with the smoothed-out features. He's talking to another Pip.

Slowly I stand, and my head begins to pound. It's time. They're taking me back to the Garden. I must have miscalculated the days until the next auction.

"Is it market day?" I ask. My voice is scratchy.

"Tomorrow," says a Pip, as if I'm some kind of idiot. He places a clean hand with perfectly squared nails on my arm. I shake him off. He scowls, a stream of *pips* emitting from his mouth.

"She didn't learn much," comments the other Pip.

The Watcher joins them outside. I begin to back away from the three of them, the chain trailing me like a snake. I don't know why exactly. It's not like I have anywhere I can go now.

I pass the glass edge of the room and glance one last time towards the barn. And there is Kiran. Sitting on a fence with his hand on the withers of the chestnut mare. He's looking at me as though he's expected that I would emerge from hiding right at this moment.

We meet each other's eyes, and all I can think is that I've disappointed him. But no one's disappointed me more than myself.

The Watcher approaches just as Kiran scoots off the fence. Kiran turns immediately, so that the Watcher can't see that we've had this connection.

"Take my bracelet off," I demand of one Pip. His eyelids are glossy from a shiny charcoal powder.

"Once you're inside," he says.

"My skin's tore open underneath it," I try.

"Then you'll be taken to the infirmary."

"Can't you take it off now? It really hurts." I could run to the barn. The guard would catch me, but I would still have to try.

I can feel Kiran's gaze on me. I suspect he's hiding this, looking the other way, grooming the horse maybe. All of a sudden, more than anything, I want to see his face. His kiran-stone eyes, calm and attentive. Staring up through the night haze to the stars beyond. Maybe that will make me stronger.

I try to think of something he'd say. Anything. In that voice that doesn't really exist. That voice that I've created. I can't.

So I lock my jaw shut. And I throw my shoulders back. And I follow the Pip through the automatic doors, hesitating only slightly as I do so.

Because there's still time before the auction.

PART TWO

THE AUCTION

CHAPTER 8

THE NIGHT BEFORE MARKET is the first time I dream of Kiran.

Maybe this is because since I've met him, we've never been so far apart. Only two hundred more paces really, not *that* far, but it might as well be half the country on account of the fences and sliding doors and walls and security systems. It's the first night I can't sense his presence. Even in my sleep I feel alone.

In my dream I'm on the auction stage. The wood is rough with splinters that jab into my bare feet. The sun is beating down from a clear, haze-free sky. Instead of buildings and factories, the stage is surrounded by trees. The ground below is dusted with pine needles. The air smells fresh.

The Governess is standing before me beneath a silk-draped awning. Beside her is a Pip who is manning a flat, black machine that's tallying my votes. Only there's no one around to vote on me.

And then Kiran appears. He's wearing his daytime Driver gear, but it's clean now, and his golden hair is slicked back with oil—just like a Magnate. With his hands in his pockets, he stares at me, judgment in his bright eyes. He walks to the left, then to the right. He looks me up and down. Up and down again. His expression switches between impressed and disappointed. I want to see what parts of me he approves of, but I'm afraid to look down and see what I'm wearing. It feels too light to be a dress. It feels like I might be wearing nothing.

Kiran walks to the Governess, and they exchange words that

I cannot hear. She hands him an electronic board, and he writes something on it. A look of relief lifts her features as she shakes his hand, and I'm filled with a staggering sense of betrayal. Suddenly there are chains around my neck and my wrists. Heavy, black chains. They are weighing me down, and though I force myself to stand up as tall as I can, I stumble to my knees.

And then I wake up.

THE BUNK I'VE BEEN assigned to sinks in the middle like a hammock, only not half as comfortable. The bars across the bottom of the bed stick into my back, and the sheets smell like the hair glue the girls wear to market. It's too hot in here to sleep. I've stripped down to my underclothes and I'm still sweating.

Today is Auction Day. The day of a thousand maybes. I might finally be able to break free today, to escape the guards, to get out of this cursed city and back to the mountains where I belong. I might be forced up on that stage, too. I might have to stand there in front of a drooling crowd.

I might even be sold.

The farmers in the outliers have market once a week. The high sellers join the city merchants for Trader's Day, twice a month. Those who make enough to pay the fee for a booth will bring their wares to auction, the only event where girls are sold, which is held on the last day of the month. It's a spectacle. Regular work is cancelled, and the party begins at dawn.

Whispered voices float across the room from the side wall. I angle my head towards the sound and hear the groan of a nearby mattress.

"What are you—" I recognize the voice: Buttercup, Daphne's little friend with the slanted eyes. She's shushed, and the mattress groans again.

"Not now, Daphne," she says, bored.

I try to lower my right arm, forgetting that it's been chained to the post. The night-watch Pip didn't want to take any chances, since I tried sneaking out the latrine window after they brought me in yesterday. I might have made it if that little rat Buttercup hadn't squealed on me. The chains make a clinking noise, and the conversation pauses.

"It's just practice," I hear Daphne whisper. "We've been getting quite a crowd outside the rec yard lately." Her voice is high, and a little too loud. Now Buttercup shushes her.

"That's just for show," says Buttercup. "It's not real."

"I know that," Daphne responds quickly.

They're both quiet.

"You don't think . . ." Daphne laughs. "That's witch stuff. That's not me. I'm going to be Promised."

"And I'm not?"

"I didn't say that," says Daphne. "I didn't mean it like that."

"Well what did you mean?" Buttercup's getting sassy.

"Nothing," says Daphne. "Nothing, all right? I just thought you wanted to practice, that's all."

"I don't."

"All right," says Daphne. The mattress groans again. "I'm sorry," she says, and if I'm being honest, I feel a little bit bad for her. For some reason it all makes me think of Kiran, and his hand on my scar, and how I sent him away.

I roll onto my side, trying my best to tuck my right elbow under my head, and wince.

My whole body hurts.

After they brought me back to the Garden yesterday, my legs and arms were waxed, my eyebrows plucked into thin lines, and my hair and nails were trimmed. They didn't bother putting me through the weight shifter because there wasn't really enough to shift, but every other girl with a hint of fat was lined up and molded into a shape the Governess calls "ideal."

The way I look feels unnatural. My feet are still bright red from where a Pip scrubbed the calluses off my feet, and the rest of me is blotchy from a full-body skin scrub. I'm glad I don't have freckles or moles—those girls had to spend hours beneath a laser getting evened out.

The time passes too quickly, and soon other girls are up whispering to each other in excited tones. Those who've been through this before start to snap at each other. A few lie silently, probably nervous about their first time on stage. Most have been looking forward to this day for weeks.

The overhead lights flicker on—all but the one in the center, which has been blinking since before I was thrown in solitary.

My blood buzzes.

I sit up slowly, the grimace still weighing down my face. I wait for my assigned Watcher, offering no help as he lifts my arm to unbuckle the restraint. He sticks like sap to my side as he brings me to the latrine, holding the door open while I go. Even though I know he couldn't care less, it's still humiliating. I only glance in the mirror, disturbed by the way the high arch of my eyebrows makes me look constantly surprised. At least that dreaded bracelet is off my wrist.

Twenty minutes later I'm walked to a line in the main foyer outside the theater so that I can get my one-and-a-half-pill breakfast allotment. All the Garden girls are here now. Fifty or so of us. There are a few new ones I don't recognize who must have arrived in my absence, and several more missing who have been Promised or handed over to Mercer the Pimp in the last twenty-four days. Most of us will go to auction today, but as always, there are a few bitter ducks in the back of the line. The Governess doesn't feel this handful of girls has been conditioned enough yet to make an appearance on the stage. I can hear their whining all the way from where I stand in the middle.

"I hope your new friend doesn't plan on holding your hand

all day. It will kill your bidding," says a girl behind me. Daphne. Her freckles are now completely gone, leaving flawless, pale skin. Her green eyes sparkle. She's talking about the Watcher, who's checking his messagebox an arm's length away.

Heat rushes through my veins. Maybe it's the light on her perfect face, or the way she's always acting like she's better than me, but I forget all about feeling sorry for her.

"Shut up, Daphne."

"It's nice to see you too," she says.

It's the first time we've talked since Straw Hair ran herself into the fence, and I'm reminded all over again how awful it was.

"You could have stopped her," I say under my breath.

"Who?" she asks innocently.

"You know who. The one with yellow hair. The new girl. I know you saw her."

Daphne's ultrathin eyebrows lift. "I don't know what you mean."

"You shouldn't have laughed at her." The Watcher has heard my tone sharpen, and in a warning, winds his printless fingers in the shoulder fabric of my dress. Surely he has orders not to touch me today; bruising can't look good on the auction block. But I suppose there's always makeup for that.

We've reached the front of the line. I tilt back the pills and swallow them with a swig of water. Though it's normally taste-less, today a sour tinge makes my jaw hurt.

I splash the rest of the water on the Watcher's jacket. He tilts his head to the side, just slightly, before stepping out of line to get a towel from a Pip.

"Oops." I breathe, for the first time in a while, as soon as he turns his back.

"You think you're so much better?" asks Daphne as we step away from the table. "Calling the other girls names and getting them in trouble. Don't pretend to be innocent. . . ."

"It was different and you know it," I interrupt. It's not like I enjoy picking fights. Besides, Sweetpea started the last one when she and her friends began making fun of me.

"She was swimming in the pond. It was funny." Daphne shrugs. She's quickly losing status as my half friend/nonenemy, and working towards full enemy. "She should have been happy. Her paperwork had just gone through."

"She was Promised?" I ask.

"Yes. Just that morning."

I picture the boy waiting for her by the fence. Remember how upset he was. He must have known she'd been sold. For some reason that brings a strange ache in my heart.

"You should have stopped her," I say again.

Buttercup walks by with another girl, their arms linked. She giggles loudly, and I see the strain in Daphne's face.

"I'm going to be Promised today," Daphne announces. "And you won't see me crying about it."

"You won't see her crying about it either." I glare after Buttercup, remembering how she told on me for climbing through the bathroom window. My scalp still hurts from where the Watcher dragged me back in by my hair.

Daphne's head whips around to face me. "You've been in solitary too long this time. You're not making any sense."

I give her a look. "I can explain if you want."

She glances back at Buttercup, a little worried, and then back to me. Her green eyes harden like glass.

"You really are a witch," she hisses. "Not just some dense mountain hack like I thought. Your family is probably relieved to be rid of you."

I've shoved her before I've even thought about it. She's flung backwards into three other girls, but doesn't fall. I've got to hand it to her. Instead of crying for a Pip, she wheels back and charges me.

I've fought too many times with Bian and Salma not to see

this coming. All I do is step out of the way and Daphne crashes to the floor. I can see the tears streaming down her cheeks when she gets up. Poor baby.

"You missed," I taunt between clenched teeth. Every pair of eyes in the foyer is upon Daphne and me.

She runs at me again, but this time I stand directly in her way, and just before she hits me, I clasp my hands together and chop at her midsection from the side. It works. I knock the wind out of her, and she collapses to her knees. Before I can jump on her, I'm flying through the air. I thrash my arms and legs, but something is gripping my body like a vice.

The Watcher. He's holding me solidly from behind, and he's squeezing so tightly that I'm forced to abandon my attempts to attack and focus instead on loosening his grasp from my waist.

"Let go!" I shout at him. The pressure is pumping in my head, making black spots appear in my vision.

"What . . . is . . . *this*?" a high voice shrieks from behind. The Governess erupts into the room in a burst of bright yellow-and-red cloth. Her dress is tiny around the midsection, rising at angles over her chest and sticking almost straight out at her hips. The skirt resembles some sort of upside-down wire basket, and her blonde hair is curled into a mountain above her forehead.

"She started it," cries Daphne.

"Shut up!" I say. The Watcher squeezes again and I wince.

"Put her down," the Governess orders. When he doesn't respond, she flails her hands for her Pip assistant. "Tell him to put Clover *down*!"

The Pip approaches the Watcher timidly. He's flustered; his face is slightly flushed.

"Sir," he says, clearing his throat with a stream of *pips*. "Sir?"

Finally the Watcher puts me down, but he keeps his hands clamped firmly on my shoulders.

The Governess marches towards me and leans as close as

she can without allowing her overly stuffed skirt to touch my skintight black uniform. Her made-up face is so severe she's scary.

"This past month has been the best of my career. Why is that? Ha!" All the silent girls surrounding us jump. "Because *you* were out of my hair."

"Hard to imagine, with hair so big," I say, staring back. "I could probably stand out in the rec yard and still be in it."

"Silence!" she screeches. She pulls back, adjusting her dress. "I hope you've enjoyed your time here, Clover, because it's about to come to an end. I don't care if another girl gets one bid today as long as you're sold."

I feel my face drain of color. She smirks, knowing that she's gotten to me.

"After market, I'll be either meeting with your buyer or transferring your ownership papers over to that Pimp, Mercer. Either ways, you'll wait out your time in solitary," she continues. "You and your little friend. I don't want you two near the other girls."

She wouldn't sell me to the Virulent like she's threatening, would she? Mercer the Pimp hardly pays anything for the girls he takes back to the Black Lanes. But I can tell from that crazy look in her eyes that she means it.

Daphne's on her feet now, though still hunched over. Her cheek is swelling from where she collided with the tile floor.

"Sort of beats the idea of *solitary* if there's two of us there, doesn't it?" I say, unable to hide the tremble in my voice.

"I can't . . . not with . . ." Daphne's stammering.

"Maybe you'll kill each other, and then problem solved," says the Governess. "Daphne's out for today," she says in a flat voice to her assistant. I hear a stream of *pips* from him in the background.

"I'm . . . what? *Out?*" cries Daphne disbelievingly.

"Look at your face in the mirror, dear," says the Governess.

"We can't skim that before the show. There's not nearly enough time, what with everything else that needs to be done."

"But I was nearly Promised last time!" shouts Daphne. Her gaze switches to Buttercup, whose mouth has dropped open.

"And you weren't," the Governess responds in a flat tone.

"The Watcher grabbed me," I spout quickly. "There will be huge bruises."

"Any of which can be covered with concealing powder. Don't," she points a long, fake nail directly in my face, "even try it. You're going. And your paperwork will be signed by the end of the week."

With that, the Governess stalks away, leaving both Daphne and I speechless, encircled by the wide, shocked eyes of the other girls.

I'M KEPT WITHIN TWO feet of the Watcher for the next several hours. During that time, my hair is flatironed, greased, and pinned up into an elaborate twist on the back of my head. My scars are all covered with thick concealing powder, and they give me back my Unpromised earrings.

I am ushered into the prep room and seated on a leather stool before a trifold mirror with bright lights. A Pip applies enough makeup to make me look like a Skinmonger. Then I'm shoved into a ball gown the color of salmon meat. It's so tight I can barely walk, and it leaves my shoulders bare and all exposed.

The theme of this auction is *Elegance*. I don't feel elegant. I feel like a prostitute. Like I'm already on my way to work for sleazy Mercer.

They've given me long white gloves that rise above my elbows. None of the other girls going wear gloves, and it's obvious why. The thick fingers keep my nails from scratching at my face, from damaging my clothes, from anything that might disqualify me from the meat market.

The Governess has done an all right job limiting my chances to screw this up.

Reality sinks in very slowly. I'm going to have to go up on the stage. It's only my second time since I've arrived here, due to the good timing of my injuries, and I can't help but be afraid.

I begin to feel sickly by the time we're brought outside into the light. There, we line up, one after another, to fill the horse-drawn carriages manned by men in white suits. Drivers wipe down their horses and comb their long glossy manes. I search for Kiran, but he's not here. The Driver who returns the horses from the city to the rental barn at the end of the day is, though. The silver ferret. He's picking at his scalp, and his nervous eyes are darting all over. They stop on me just for a second before shooting to the ground. I wonder if he recognizes me from my time behind his barn.

I wonder if he's seen Kiran and me together.

Wobbling on my high heels, I'm assisted by a Pip into a decorative wrought-iron carriage holding three other girls. I don't recognize any of them; they're all new and eager. Their chatter grates on my nerves.

The double benches are designed to fit six girls, but I have the extreme fortune of sitting beside the Watcher.

"Must be pretty embarrassing to be carted across town with a bunch of shrieking girls," I say.

"You tell me," he says, not even looking my way. I cross my arms and slouch in my seat.

The Garden's electric fence buzzes loudly, and my pulse goes haywire when the double gates slide open. Our carriage lurches forward. We are the third in line. I look back to the Garden, to its black, chic siding and the tranquil landscaping before it, and I wish I had a stone to throw at one of those perfectly square windows which line its face. I keep staring back; I can't see behind the facility to the solitary yard. I can't see the barn, where Kiran is wiping the sweat from his eyes with his too-clean handkerchief.

Something hurts inside of me, somewhere between my ribs and my stomach. A dull throb that every third or so time turns to a twist. Nerves, I tell myself. I wish I had some maypop tea to calm down.

Because the ache grows stronger when I think of Kiran, I focus on Brax. I remember him as a tiny puppy, his body no longer than the length of my forearm. I remember teaching him not to bite, and playing tug-of-war with sticks in the yard. His ice-blue eyes and his soft silver fur. I try to remember the way his breath sounds through his neck as I rest my head there to sleep. He'll wonder where I am if I don't come back.

I can't be Promised. I have to find a way to ruin this, to throw the bids. If I'm chosen today, I'll be brought to a home in the city's interior, where they'll have high gates and Watchers that patrol the streets. Pips watching my every move. Where I'll be forced to lie with a man I don't even know and bear his children. The fear is so thick I can taste it like blood in my mouth.

"Look," says one of the girls across from me. "The Black Lanes."

She says it like it's some magical place, not the slums just a short walk from the Garden, and touches a ridiculous gold foil crown on her head, like the people here might actually be impressed.

Our caravan of carriages has rolled past the large warehouses and business offices that make up Glasscaster's business district, and we've turned left onto Main Street. The road here is bricked, but there are potholes that show the black asphalt below from the days of car travel. The carriage wobbles over the divots. This area of town is not well maintained by the city.

My gaze follows the girl's pointing finger. The other girls have all hushed.

There are two offshoots in all. They're just called "One" and "Two." We pass Two first, and all of us peer down the darkened way to the bars and brothels and the motel rooms that boast their hourly rental rates.

Trash clutters the street and makes a nice snack for the dozens of hungry rats that scurry from pile to pile. The occasional body is strewn out beside a metal garbage can that still smolders from the previous night—you can recognize the ones with the plague by the blood under their eyes. The city docs have a cure, but the Virulent can't afford it. That's why you see so many of them infected.

"So disgusting," says another girl, scooting closer to the one with the crown. She's got coloring in her eyes—they're supposed to be gold, but they look yellow, like she's gone way too long without peeing.

Disgusting doesn't even begin to cover it. Just thinking of what might befall me if I am bought makes me shudder. I look around for Mercer, but of course he's not here. The neon signs are brighter than anywhere in the city, but today they are dim, and the streets are nearly deserted, because the Virulent who are at least partially sober are going to market.

The girls all sigh as we pass and move through the scattered brick-and-metal factories of the industrial district. Alternating puffs of black and white smoke bloom into an already hazy sky from the high copper towers. This is where they make basic supplies: uniforms, computer pieces, Watcher weapons, meal supplements.

"It stinks," says the third girl.

She's not wrong. The air smells even fouler than in the Black Lanes. Daphne told me once it's the smell of flesh from the facilities where they take pregnant girls to get rid of their unwanted girl babies—a fate decided by the census commissioners and the importance of the girl's owner.

"Hold your breath," whispers the one with the crown. "If

you open your mouth, you'll have bad breath all day." They all cover their mouths with their little nail-painted fingers.

I think I'd prefer Daphne's company to these three.

I picture her sitting alone in the solitary yard and can't help but feel a little guilty. But it serves her right. She was nasty about Straw Hair. She can sit and rot for all I care.

We continue on, passing the residential district of the Merchant class. These inhabitants live in apartments, and we pass a few cars parked on the side of the street. The metal monsters growl and squeal and leak their black oil all over the road. I can see why the Magnates refuse to use them anymore.

"We're here," says Crown Girl.

The other two begin to squeal.

"Sure you don't want to keep holding your breath?" I ask.

The Watcher's hand slides over mine and, quick as a blink, he jerks back my first finger. I howl in pain until he releases the pressure.

"Quiet," he says. I slump back in my seat but keep glaring across the carriage at the other girls. They were the noisy ones, not me.

We've entered the heart of Glasscaster, where the Merchants work in their towering glass buildings. The buildings are so tall they disappear into the haze.

The streets snake off on either side of Main Street, labeled with green street signs. A large, emerald-glass building on the right makes me cringe. The Watchers' Headquarters. Several patrolmen in their black uniforms with their leather chest straps sit astride horses outside the building. Three cars are parked out front as well, but it doesn't look like they've been used in years.

There are more people around now. Mostly men, but many children as well. Some of them are smiling. Some of the kids are waving. They wear terrible costume makeup—fake bloody X's on their faces to simulate the fresh marks of the Virulent. Bian once told me it was like how we would dress up on New Moon nights to try to scare each other, but I don't know why anyone would pretend to be marked, knowing the Watchers are really out there waiting for an excuse to cut up your face.

We pass a woman heavy with child, being dragged forward by an irritable man in a blue suit. She looks up at us and then wipes her brow on her sleeve.

The doctor's offices. The credit lenders. The computer technicians. And, what always interests me, the fine-food stores. People sell actual food here. Eggs, rice, bacon from the pork factory, candy, bread. People pay an enormous amount for real food because it's so rare. Meal supplements are cheap. But a fish filet—one like I could spear in a mountain stream in thirty seconds flat—that goes for fifty, sometimes eighty credits. Most can't afford it. If they could, the mountains would be packed with men stripping the land clean.

The girls squeal again. There, high above the street on a wide, electric billboard, flash images of a pretty actress with long, silver-white hair. Her slender waist is wrapped in the arms of a chiseled man in some strange white suit. She's the actress the girls are always swooning over in the rec yard—Solace. I remember the movie the Governess made us watch, about the girl who poisoned herself when she couldn't please her master anymore. The glamour and lights draw me in, just like the first time I'd seen a movie. But just like that first time, I'm disappointed when the screen switches to a picture of her producer-owner, with Solace standing just behind him in the shadows.

We are entering the town square, and I begin to sweat. The noise is so thunderous I almost clap my hands over my ears. But I don't, I *can't,* because I need to hear everything. I need to know if there's even the slightest chance I can escape. People are shouting. Horses and other livestock are whinnying, baying, shrieking. Music is being pumped in from an overhead speaker system.

Even if I lived my entire life in this city, I would never get used to all these sounds.

Or the smell. Too many people close together. Beer and wine. Animal dung. Vomit. It's enough to make me sick.

Some shouting up ahead draws my attention, and I look to see a small group of men and women holding signs crowding the street. Activists. The only ones brave enough to oppose the buying and selling of girls. They wear red-painted masks to hide their faces from the Watchers, because if they're caught, they'll end up facing a fate much worse than mine.

"Sell goats, not girls!" they chant.

I lean towards the side of the carriage to get a better look, but the Watcher places a heavy hand on my shoulder. It reminds me of my last auction, when I tried calling out to them and they never even heard me. The Governess did though. She had the Pips really work me over with their beaters after we got back.

"What is that supposed to mean?" asks Yellow Eyes.

"The Red Right," answers Crown Girl. "My old house keeper told me they're against the auction because they can't afford it."

The other girls all "ooh" knowingly. I don't bother arguing with them. They won't understand that some people see the ugliness of their world and want to make it better. I understand. But when I get out I'm not sticking around to save this mess. It's too far gone and I've got more important things to do.

A team of Watchers is heading their way, and within moments, the Red Right disperses. A little of my hope goes with them as they melt into the crowd.

In the distance, I see the last part of the city. The worst part. The glass high-rises of the Magnates. The offices of the businessmen who own the Merchants' livelihoods. Mine too, if I'm not lucky today. These are the richest people in all of Isor. Their guarded homes—our prisons—wait in the shadows of those green-blue spires.

There are Watchers up ahead. Some on horseback, some on foot. They've cleared our path with neon-orange pylons. Behind them, some of the Virulent are heckling us with their hideous words.

"She'd earn me double with a scar on her cheek," shouts one woman in a low-cut velvet dress. She's got the plague—her eyes are already bloodshot. Soon they'll weep blood.

"Let's see those legs before you get to the stage!" yells a man.

"Show us what you got," says another, grabbing himself rudely.

I look through the crowd, my teeth now chattering. *Be brave,* I tell myself. Skinmongers, hired thugs, thieves, and other criminals. The scarred faces of the Virulent surround me. They don't need makeup to fake an X on their cheeks, they've got the real thing. And any of the men can place a bid if they've got enough credit.

The carriages roll to a stop behind a wooden platform, and suddenly the journey seems far too short. I don't want to get out. I need to stay within the safety of these iron stems.

I am almost pushed out by the Watcher. One step down, then I'm on the ground. I teeter, my heel stuck between the bricks, before I right myself. It's quieter back here, behind the stage. They'll hide us from the public eye before we're walked out, one by one, and put on display.

The girls congregate into buzzing little groups, and I can hear their giggles cut through the roar of the crowd. Someone's just been hung, out there on that stage where I'll be standing in a few minutes. Someone who robbed a Merchant or defiled one of the Magnates' girls. One of the men from the jail who wasn't lucky enough to be picked to become a Watcher. Maybe that boy who visited Straw Hair is twitching at the end of his rope beyond this wooden barrier. There's nothing like a good hanging to get people in the mood for girls.

Behind us are two or three dozen country people from the outlying towns. With them are cages of chickens and goats, sheep, even cattle. That's where we fit on market day. Between the executions and the livestock sales.

Gradually, Watchers begin filtering down the left side of the stage towards us. They're dragging the still-warm bodies of the deceased. All the girls look away. Even me. It is too much to stand.

"Over here, ladies!" calls the Governess. The Watcher shoves me with the group towards her. "That's it, that's it. Now you all look beautiful, I must say. Just *elegant*!" She sounds so pleased with herself. "Now remember, this day may dictate the rest of your life. Your will to succeed will win you those bids!"

At least the Governess has stolen some of my fear. Now I'm annoyed, too.

"I will be at the auctioneers table where we'll be recording your scores and tallying your bids. Potential buyers will set up your private sessions there. Good luck, ladies! Good luck!" She finishes with a crazed smile. It doesn't look like she's slept in a week.

We are being lined up. I count those before me. Twenty-three. I am the twenty-fourth girl to go. Just like my twenty-four days in solitary.

I hear the announcer make the call for auction.

The first girl takes the stage.

I run through my possibilities. I can't bolt. The Watcher still has one hand on my shoulder. I can't rip my dress or mess up my hair because of these stupid silky gloves. I can't even tear them off because they're glued to my hand with a skin adhesive. I think of the Red Right standing in front of our path on our ride in, but they'd fled when the Watchers approached. They won't do me any good now.

I take a step forward. Number one is finished. She's gotten only mild applause.

The crow of a rooster catches my attention. I look over all the farm animals again and feel sorry for them. Even the goats aren't safe.

Number two gets several boos. I wonder what she's done. My heart beats faster. I wish I could have seen her so that I can do the same.

Number three gets resounding applause. Several encouraging shouts from the audience.

And then someone runs right into me, knocking me away from the Watcher. It's a tall man, holding a horse. A Driver. He must be trying to sell his animal during the livestock sales. But the horse has gotten out of control and is whinnying and spinning in a small circle around his owner.

The man crashes into me again, and I catch myself just before falling. His chest bumps against mine, and the large, calloused hand not holding his animal's lead rope grasps just below my rib cage for support.

Then I see his clean red handkerchief. And the dark eyes, flecked with copper.

Kiran.

CHAPTER 9

MY MOUTH FALLS OPEN. I nearly cry Kiran's name, but before I can, he is whipped away by the chestnut mare I recognize from the barn. Four girls around me are screaming. One seems to be afraid of the horse, the rest of its owner.

I wonder for a split second if Kiran is my salvation. If he's somehow going to throw me up on that crazed animal so we might escape, right through the city walls. But even with the blood pumping through my temples I know that this is the stuff stories are made of, not real life.

Kiran is trying to contain the horse, but I've never seen him, or any Driver for that matter, lose control of an animal. It occurs to me that maybe he's making the mare spook and buck. If this is right, he's a fine actor. Kiran looks like he's about to be trampled.

"No!" I shout as the horse rears back. Kiran's fallen right beneath where the front hooves will land.

She shies away from my waving hands, and the lead, still attached to her halter, jerks Kiran to a stand. But now he's fumbling, and falling again. Right into my Watcher.

The impact is enough to knock the Watcher back a few steps. Kiran collapses into him and they both scramble to stand. The Watcher rises faster, and before Kiran is up, the Watcher kicks him, his black boot connecting to Kiran's middle with superhuman strength. Kiran's mouth flies open as the air is forced from his body and flops to the side, still silent.

Our eyes meet. Mine wide with horror, his pinched tight with determination. I hear his voice in my head.

"Run!"

This was Kiran's plan. He's picked a fight to give me an out. There's no time to thank him. To help, even. That throbbing, stabbing pain is back, right between my ribs and my stomach.

I turn and I run.

I shove through the other girls. My eyes see only flashes of their brightly colored gowns as I tear back towards Main Street into the crowds of townsfolk with their livestock. I search for a hiding place, even one of the painted faces of the Red Right, but come up short. My legs are shaking, and my ankle twists as one of my stupid pointy heels gets caught between the bricks. In the background, another round of cheers roars from the stage.

I kick off my shoes, hating that the Pip has scrubbed away my calluses again. The tiny bits of trash and pebbles cut into my feet. The tight dress is constricting my legs from running full out.

The crowd thickens. I can barely move. The momentum is pushing me back towards the stage and I'm struggling like a fish swimming upstream. Suddenly there are hands around me, grabbing me, feeling me in the hidden places of my body. I nearly scream. The man touching me smells sharply of liquor and sweat. I catch a glimpse of an unbalanced X on his right cheek.

"Gotcha," he slurs.

I fight with everything I can to get free from his hold. I try to kick him, but my legs are bound by my costume. One of my fists connects to the side of his head, but slides right off on account of the silk glove. I bite down, tasting the sweat and filth of his neck and swallow the bile shooting up my throat. He curses loudly, but lets me go.

Then other hands are behind me, pulling me back. These hands are familiar. Heavy. Unforgiving.

The Watcher.

I have no time to think about what to do next; the metal

wire is already whipping out in the Watcher's grasp. He doesn't use it; he simply holds it, and it's enough to carve a space in the crowd around us and raise screams from those closest. The man who had me squeezes through the crowd and disappears. I've ducked, arms wrapped around my body, as if flesh and bone will stop a wire.

The Watcher lifts me with one arm, carrying me on his side like I'm a struggling child. I try to fight him, but my body now feels heavy and sluggish.

Before I know it, he has placed me back in line. I search for Kiran because I want to see if he's all right, but he's nowhere to be found. I'm secretly relieved. I don't want him to see that I couldn't escape after all he tried to do for me.

Thirteen girls are left before me. Kiran's beating, and the running, and the handsy Virulent man all fade from my mind. The nerves are back, and I glance around, looking for any last exits before it is too late.

Right then I know it's safer to be sold to Mercer than to a Magnate. I can escape the Black Lanes—I don't know how, but I will. But once I'm in the heart of Glasscaster the security will be so thick I'll never get out.

I must make sure no one bids on me.

In the final part of the line before the stage is an area where the girls must remain single file, crammed between the partitions and a candy shop. There are only two exits here, back the way I came, or onto the stage. As I enter this final gauntlet, my heart sinks. At least the Watcher is gone; if he stays in line he will be forced to walk across the stage with me.

The line pauses. More cheers. The line moves forward.

Pause. Cheer. Move.

My hands are trembling. I wish I could throw up now, just to soil my dress. At least I don't have on my hideous spiked heels anymore.

I turn to look at the candy shop. The door is open, and there's a boy inside wearing a heavy fur cape that's much too warm for the weather. It reeks of wealth and status. I think for a moment that I could probably push him down and run through the shop to the side exit, but that's just delaying the inevitable; looking past him, I can see at least one other Watcher standing by the register.

The boy is reaching for a high shelf just inside the door as I approach. I look up and see that he wants one of the large colorful suckers that are in a basket up there. One more step and I get a clearer look at the boy's face. He's nine or ten, with short brown hair and pale skin.

"I want one though!" he's shouting back into the store. A closer look reveals a sharp nose, blunted front teeth, and beady little eyes.

"Your father said no," replies a firm but annoyed male voice. Probably a Pip. I can't see him behind the racks of colorful chewy tabs and little decorated cakes. All things I've never sampled.

"You don't have to tell him," whines the boy.

Though there's no resemblance, his age reminds me of Tam. I wonder how tall Tam is now. If he's lost any of his baby teeth. I wonder if he still cries when Nina gets to do things before him.

I'm filled with a burst of resolve. *Do something*, I tell myself. *For Tam.*

"Hey kid," I say. He looks towards me, brows lifted.

"You're not supposed to talk to me," he says. I move forward another space. The girl in front of me looks back warily, but then returns to practicing her smile.

"You're not supposed to have that candy. But I'll get it for you if you want."

"You . . . you're not supposed to talk."

The line moves forward another step. One more and this boy and I will be even. And I'll have only a short time left before it's my turn on stage.

"You have to be sneaky though," I say. "Don't watch me. I'm going to grab one for you."

"Yes!" he says.

"There's just one thing," I add, speaking in my quietest voice, like when I'm trying to entice Tam or Nina into doing something boring that I want them to think is exciting, like cleaning the tent.

"What?" he asks, beady eyes now full of interest.

"I'm freezing. I need that fur you're wearing."

He feels it between two fingers. "Okay, sure. I don't like it anyway. My dad makes me wear it."

"Give it here, then," I say. My voice is a bit higher. If we don't do this soon, I'll miss my window.

"I want the sucker first."

I scowl. "Fine," I say, and pick it stealthily out of the basket. Then I hold it tightly against my side. No one responds. No one has seen what I've done.

"Look at the ground. Like you're not doing anything," I command as he reaches for it. "Then take off the fur."

He follows my directions. I'm a step ahead of him now. There is only one final girl before me. She's checking herself in the mirror and smiling for the cameraman, who waits just before the stage. My heart is thrumming.

He tosses me the cape, I pass him the sucker, and I'm up.

The frowning cameraman waits to take my picture, but I don't let him, because I'm too busy wrapping the fur around my shoulders. I hold my breath. It's wolf hide I'm wearing.

"Sorry, Brax," I mutter. I take one quick glance in the mirror. Curse those Pips and their everlasting makeup. Only a special scrub will remove it. It's not damaged in the least from my sweaty escape attempt. Neither is my hair, which is still swept gracefully behind my head.

And then it's one step up. Then the other. And I'm walking

across the wooden stage, the splinters prickling my bare feet, just like in my dream.

The lights are nearly blinding, but below, I can see two hundred men and even a few women cheering. They've all got miniature texters in their hands so that they can submit their votes to the Governess's counting box, which is dead center before me, back about thirty paces. I see her hand slap her forehead as she sees the modifications I've made to her outfit, and almost smile.

On either side of her booth are two arching rows of grandstands. There, the Magnates sit in their expensive business suits with their associates and servants. Almost every seat is filled for me, and it's no question why. Everyone wants to see the wild girl. Everyone wants to tame her. Everyone wants that healthy boy child they know I can make.

She's not worth the credits, Sweetpea had said. I must make that true, be so undesirable that they overlook my golden insides and realize I'm more trouble than they care to take on.

I'm supposed to walk to the center of the stage and do a slow circle. Instead, I face the back of the stage, looking at the high screens that showcase my statistics. One screen shows a live feed of my picture—the back of my head right now. The next screen shows the black outline of a female body, with lit-up stars next to the different parts. My scores today will be averaged with my past scores. It looks as though my legs have earned seven and a half stars. My breasts are a four—nowhere near the size of Sweetpea's. My waist is an eight. My face is an eight and a half. My outfit has been awarded a dismal two, which I regard with some pride. I'm probably one of the highest scoring girls to not yet have been Promised.

The final board is blank. Typically this would show my breeding credentials.

I turn back towards the crowd now, regarding the booths on either side without much interest. That's where the outlying townspeople sell their wares. Where Silent Lorcan would have sold my jewelry before.

I look out into the crowd, and my heart stutters. I stand tall. I must not show my fear.

I focus on two people directly across from my position on the stage. In the grandstands, in the front row, leaning over the railing, is the boy from the candy store. Next to him is a man in a suit, with a scarf covering the bottom half of his face. His keeper, I imagine, though I don't know why he's wearing the wrapping. If there's something wrong with his face, his Magnate boss should have had it removed with surgery.

I can see even from this distance that the boy's mouth is surrounded by a sticky red ring from the sucker I stole for him. Again I think of Tam. Someday I'll get him a piece of candy. All I have to do is get out of here.

I roll my head in a slow circle and my cheeks brush against the soft wolf's fur. And now I'm thinking about Brax. Sleeping on his neck. When he first told me his name; "Brrrrax!"

I grin at the boy. And bark.

"Ruff! Grrrr! Ruff! Ruff!" Just like a dog. Just like a wild animal. I bark and snap my jaw and bare my teeth. I fall onto my knees and crawl around growling. I bat at my face with my white silk glove. I hear the dress rip at the side seam, and when a piece of fabric falls off, I snatch it between my teeth and shake my head. I slobber. The drool oozes out of my mouth.

The boy is laughing hysterically. He's pointing at me and clapping his hands. This makes me go at it even harder. I make myself as undesirable as possible, keeping my eyes on the boy the whole time. It's almost fun. Almost like it's just us two and we're playing or something.

I hear the screens behind me clang as the power diverted to them shuts off. The Governess has done this no doubt. Though I can barely see her beneath the lights, I can tell she's running out of the booth. The air is filled with resounding boos. The sound makes my soul sing.

My Watcher approaches from the exit side of the stage, and I begin to crawl towards him, growling and threatening to pounce. He hauls me up from the midsection, holding me away from him as I snap my jaws.

I'm brought below the stage to where the Governess is already waiting. Her face is so red it glows beneath her thick layer of makeup. Her whole body is shaking with fury.

"*You,*" she hisses, pointing her long painted nail at my face. "I hope you like the Black Lanes, Clover, because that's where you're going."

While the Watcher binds my hands she tears the fur cape off my shoulders and throws it into a makeshift pen for several sheep. She stretches and flexes her fingers, and for a second I think she means to choke me. Instead she draws back and adjusts the hair piled atop her head.

I swallow, though my throat now feels dry. My eyes narrow into challenging slits. *Just try and hit me,* I think. She shouts orders to her assistant, and he types something into his texter. A few minutes later, I'm brought back to the iron carriage, where I wait with the Watcher through the remainder of the show.

THE RIDE BACK THROUGH town is not nearly as nerve-wracking. In fact, I'm filled with cool, calm relief. I've done it. I've succeeded. There is no way that anyone is bidding on me after that performance. Maybe I'll be sold to Mercer, but if I survived this, I can survive that.

The other girls in the carriage are somber. Now they're the ones who are anxious. They're wondering if they smiled enough. If they showed enough skin, or were mysterious enough to gain the crowd's attention. One of the girls is crying because someone from another carriage ripped her dress in line. I wish some catty competitor had messed up my dress.

No matter. I've done a fine job by myself.

When I think of that little boy, I nearly smile. Mother Hawk sent him to me at just the right moment. He's kept me clear of a buyer, at least for now. If Kiran comes to the solitary yard tonight—if he's not too mad at me for messing up my escape—I'm going to tell him all about it.

We pass through the electric gates of the Garden and halt in front of the building. The buzz when the gates lock shut quickly kills my mood. I may have escaped purchase, but I am still a prisoner.

Inside, we are led back into the preparatory room, where we're given uniform dresses to change into. These are exactly the same as our normal black slinky outfits, except they are pale pink. The Governess thinks that this softer look will add to our post-auction appeal, which is important because over the next several hours the buyers will begin rolling in to take a closer look at the merchandise.

A Pip scrubs my face clean and takes down my hair. I don't like him touching me, but the smell of the jasmine shampoo he uses is so soothing I nearly fall asleep. I feel a little more like myself when my hair curls back up, though I don't like this pink dress at all. In the woods, wearing something like this would attract every predator in sight. Which I suppose is the point.

When the Pip tries to apply my post-auction makeup, I threaten to punch him until he leaves me alone. He scurries away with a stream of indignant *pips*!

We're given a meal pill and lined up in two rows in the foyer, both facing the theater. The girls who have not attended the auction today gather behind these two lines, all sad faces and crossed arms and pouty lips. Daphne is not amongst them. With all that's happened, I'd forgotten she's in solitary.

The Governess appears and she's changed as well. She's wearing a bright red dress that seems to be painted on. It strikes me how old she is. Mid forties, older than most women I've ever seen. She looks like a monster dressing up as a woman, rather than the usual opposite.

Her expression is unreadable due to her newly applied powders and polishes. She's accompanied by her Pip assistant, clinging to her shadow like a frightened puppy. He's got an electronic clipboard in his hands. That list, I know, holds the names of the girls who will now be entering the next stage of the game.

"All in all, a rather pathetic showing," the Governess begins. "I expected more from most of you." She does not even pretend to acknowledge those of us who disappointed her. "Regardless, I have here a list of girls who will proceed into negotiations. When you hear your name, please step forward so that you may be escorted into the entertainment parlor to meet with your caller. Remember that this, for many of you, is your last chance to shine. This. Is. *Crucial,*" she adds. "I can only do so much."

There is a wave of nervous whispering.

"Many of you may be escorted into our private screening rooms following your personal introductions. I've said it enough that you should all know by now, but since you seem to be a bit thick, let me remind you: Certain acts performed within those walls will earn you a ticket to the Black Lanes."

There is a hush over the girls. She's referring to the purity rule of course. We're supposed to tease, but not to let things go too far. If we don't pass a medical inspection, the sale is broken, and we'll be carved up like the rest of the Virulent.

I shudder, thinking about the Governess's threat to mark me if I don't get chosen. I'm not sure she can actually do this; there are laws against it as long as I'm still untouched. Still, it makes me a little queasy. I push these thoughts aside as she passes in front of me, forcing myself to stare blankly ahead.

"Any questions?" she asks. She's not *really* asking, and everyone knows this, so no one raises their hand. "Very good. Read the names."

Her timid Pip assistant steps forward, holding the electronic board out before him. I have nothing to fear. After what I pulled off today, no one will be making a bid on me.

"Lily," the Pip begins. I lower my gaze to her knees, thinking there's still time to kick her as she walks by. There's a proud smile on her face as she removes her left earring to identify that she's a pending sale.

"Daisy." A girl with black hair that reminds me nothing of a daisy steps forward, also to my right. She takes out her earring.

"Lupin. Rose. Lotus."

I slouch back, trying not to smirk as the Pip calls more names. Nine names. Ten. I'm staring absently forward now, bored at these proceedings. I'm thinking about getting that dreaded metal bracelet back on so that I can return to solitary. Maybe I didn't escape, but at least I'll get to play with Brax tonight. When I tell him about the auction I'll have to leave out the part about the wolf cape. He'd hate that.

I make a note to grab the broken knife handle. I'll need that in the Black Lanes for certain. Ugly as the prospect of going to Mercer is, it's better than an unknown future deep in the heart of the city.

"Clover."

The sound of this word shatters the busy thoughts in my mind.

"Last but not least, Clover!" sings the Governess triumphantly. She's almost skipping towards me now. I take a step back, not forwards. The room seems to be getting smaller, and I'm filled with an urge to run.

"What?" I ask weakly.

"You've got a *very* interested buyer, dear," says the Governess.

"I . . . I do?" My voice sounds so small. My chest is rising now. Rising and falling, but how? I can barely find enough oxygen to breathe. Everyone in the room is gaping at me. If our spots were switched, I'd probably be doing the same thing.

"Step forward," she says, more firmly this time.

"No. . . ."

"Step forward!" she shouts with a flash of teeth.

My legs move me forward. I feel like they've betrayed me.

"Take off your left earring," she commands. When I don't move she snatches it and jerks it free. It stings, but I don't even struggle.

Her pleasant expression returns. "This way! Off to the entertainment parlor!"

In complete shock, I stumble from the room, deaf to the gossiping whispers of my peers, one thought resounding in my head: What have I done?

CHAPTER 10

The Watcher has to shove me into the entertainment parlor. I nearly trip as I pass through the heavy wooden threshold; the thick bear rug makes my stance uneven, and the roaring fire in the stone hearth at the back of the room is much too warm. I can feel the sweat already dewing on my brow, sliding down between my shoulder blades.

I scan the room. The Governess is introducing the chosen girls to their prospective buyers. I see a girl named Rosebud fake a shy blush and look to the floor. Lily has already begun to hum softly, working her songbird angle. Another girl I don't know is spinning in slow circles before a man in a charcoal suit. He puffs on a cigar and takes out a messagebox to type something.

Too quickly, the Governess motions me to the far left corner of the room. I pass one of the new girls from last month. She is being interviewed by the assistant of a Magnate, who is asking about her measurements and any food allergies she might have.

I wipe my damp palms on my sides. I can feel the Watcher behind me. There's no chance of breaking out the door.

I freeze when I recognize the man with the maroon scarf wrapped around his face. It covers his hair and everything below his nose, leaving only a thin line where his judging brown eyes are exposed. His hands are tucked loosely in the pockets of his blue pinstriped suit, and as my gaze lowers to the floor, I see the boy from the candy store playing with a remote-control horse. When he presses a button, it whinnies.

The man's head tilts up, and his eyes lock on the Governess.

"Azalea. So nice to see you."

I've never heard the Governess addressed by a name. It strikes me that it's a flower, that she was once a resident here. I don't know why that surprises me; most women in the city have been. I guess it's because she's so independent. I figured she must have gotten in early with her buyer, made him happy, and then earned her freedom as soon as she got old and ugly.

"Clover, dear, this is Mr. Greer." There's no mistaking the tremble in her voice. She fixes a smile on her face. "And *this* is precious little Amir Ryker. You may recall, Clover, that Mr. Ryker is the mayor of Glasscaster."

"A little young to be the mayor," I manage, trying to swallow down the sickness that comes with this understanding: My plan has completely backfired.

The Governess's lips twitch. "You have such a sense of humor!" she laughs. "Mr. Ryker is Amir's father! Amir is the *son* of the mayor."

I must have the worst luck in the history of the world to have attracted the attention of the most powerful man in Glasscaster. I can already see the layers and layers of protection surrounding his house; a prison of guards and alarms and fancy things.

"Well, I'll just leave you two be. Please do not hesitate to wave if you need anything, Mr. Greer." She flounces off across the room to check on the other couples, but it's obvious she's still glancing this way.

It's the craziest thing, but I almost wish she'd come back.

"You're funny," says Amir, standing up. His mouth still bears the red traces of his cherry sucker. He kicks the horse aside. I can't help but feel a surge of resentment that he's not treating an expensive toy with more care.

"That's what I was hoping for," I say weakly.

"Mr. Greer says you're going to come play at my house. We can play on the wall screen if you want. Or a demolition game. I'm good at that."

"I'm sure you are." I'm standing rigid. Every bone in my body seems to be perfectly aligned.

"I'm nine," he says suddenly. "How old are you?"

"Sixteen," I say.

"Do you like elk? It's my favorite."

Even though I've just eaten, my stomach lurches with hunger pains. It's been some time since I've had any kind of real meat. I'm nearly salivating just thinking about it.

"It's fine," I answer.

"Do you like dog fights?"

I cringe. "Not at all."

He frowns at this, and his face reddens. His eyes grow even beadier, like black beans. I'm surprised at how quickly he becomes angry.

"You've *got* to like it. Mr. Greer says you'll like *whatever* I say."

"Mr. Greer lied," I say sharply. I am not about to be talked to this way by a nine-year-old, I don't care who his father is.

"Mr. Greer never lies," says Mr. Greer. I turn towards him for the first time, and there is a strange, satisfied glow in his brown eyes. "Amir, play with your toy for a while, I'm going to speak with the girl."

"But . . ."

"Go play, Amir."

"*Fine,*" he grumbles, and he collapses back onto the floor. He grabs the horse in a pouty way, and begins slamming it about.

"So Mayor Ryker didn't want to see me for himself?" I say quietly, trying to control the edge in my tone. Mr. Greer is sitting on a red velvet chair, and in the dim lighting from the small lamp on the table beside him, he looks positively evil. He motions for me to step closer. I don't want to, but my guard is still nearby, and if I don't play along, the Watcher will surely be summoned.

I take a step towards him.

"Closer, girl. Your name is Clover, is that right?" His voice has a rasp that makes my spine tingle.

I take one more step forward, and balance lightly on the balls of my feet in case I need to back away quickly.

"I am *called* Clover," I say.

"But that's not what you like to be called, is it?"

"It's not my name."

"And what is your name?"

It's a simple answer, but for some reason it feels far too personal.

"What's it matter to you?" I say.

"You're right." He places a hand on my waist. I slap it away, harder than he expects, I think. He laughs. "It matters very little, as long as you come when called."

I say nothing, just glare at him, burning holes right through his hidden face.

"The answer to your previous question is no, Mayor Ryker does not need to see you for himself. He's already got four other girls, three of them First Rounders."

I don't hide my revulsion. "Sounds like he's got more than his fair share. Why does he need me?"

"He doesn't."

"What do you mean?"

Mr. Greer laughs again and attempts to run his hand down my side.

"Don't," I snap.

"I mean that you aren't for him."

My gut clenches as I picture myself becoming the property

of this man. I've never heard of a Magnate buying someone for their servant.

"I'm not for you," I say.

"Oh, I don't know." Quick as a rattler, he grabs my hand and pulls me forward, and I nearly fall onto his lap. In the struggle I dislodge the scarf from his face. He releases me, and I jerk back to a stand. The Watcher is very close now. A warning hand is placed atop his wire.

As Mr. Greer is replacing his covering, the edge of the raised scar on his right cheek draws a gasp to my lips.

"Problems?" asks the Governess. She's standing behind me, gripping my shoulders so hard I wince.

"No problems, Azalea," he says after a moment of strained silence. "Clover and I were just discussing the terms of this transaction."

"Ah," says the Governess. "Some tea, perhaps?"

"No, I don't think so."

No one says anything for what seems like a long time. The Governess releases my arms. "I did tell you she was spirited, did I not?" She laughs at herself, a little too hard.

"Which is why she was chosen," says Mr. Greer. She quiets at his tone.

"I need to talk to you," I say to the Governess. I don't really, but I need to get away from this man. The scar on his cheek's got me spooked; it reminds me of the thugs that snatched me from the mountains.

"Later." Her cheeks quiver a little before she turns back to our visitors.

"I don't feel good," I say.

With a fake smile she smooths down my hair, the way my ma used to do. When I pull back she holds my head in place with her tight grasp.

"You feel just fine," she says. But there's a flash of pity in her eyes. "Shall I go start the paperwork?"

Mr. Greer nods and gives a dismissive grunt, and with nothing more to say, the Governess retreats through the entrance, followed by her Pip assistant. The room is full of girls and suitors, but I'm all alone. Mr. Greer watches me the way fox watches a rabbit.

"You're Virulent," I say to him. I should have suspected as much when I saw the scarf.

His eyes smile. "Which doesn't mean I'm not under the employ of the Mayor."

"I didn't think . . ." I don't know what to say. I may not be an expert on city ways, but even I know it's odd for a civilized man to meddle with the lower class. For gambling maybe. To hire someone to do his dirty work, sure. But to appoint a Virulent as a permanent employee, as a caretaker for your *son* . . . I've never heard of such a thing.

"Of course you didn't," he says, with a gleam in his eye. "A girl's brain isn't meant to take on the burdens of business."

I bite my tongue and fight back the urge to lash out at him. He seems pleased that he's gotten under my skin, so I tell myself to hide my emotions. To show him nothing that will give him an advantage over me.

"I guess you're right," I say flatly. "None of this makes sense."

He chuckles. "You have a sharp tongue. I wouldn't mind getting more acquainted with it. . . ."

"No," I say firmly. I would rather die than become this man's property.

"But not until after you pass your inspection," he finishes. "And we can deliver you to your rightful owner."

"And who might that be?"

"Isn't it obvious?" He turns his head just slightly to look at the boy playing on the floor.

My mouth drops open. "He's a child!"

"Quiet, Clover," he tells me. "I thought you girls were thrilled by such an opportunity. You'll be brought to our home. You'll wait out your days being pampered until he's ready."

"And when will that be?"

"Four, maybe five years. Unless he wants you before."

"You would hold me prisoner," I stammer.

His eyes are smiling again. "Does a prisoner have a bed softer than a cloud to sleep in at night, Clover? Does a prisoner have meat and eggs and wine at her table? Does she have fine clothes and keepers to wait on her? You tell me."

For one measly moment—no, for half a measly moment—it doesn't sound so bad. Better than here anyway. And then I'm so ashamed of myself, I turn bright red and stare at the horse toy the boy is now crushing into the floor.

"Don't worry. If you need practice . . ." Mr. Greer's voice is barely a whisper now. It sends a jolt of tremors through my entire body.

"I would never. Not with you," I spit.

He chuckles. "Such spirit."

I want to gag. Everything about this is wrong. I wish I could jump out of my skin. Disappear.

"I'm not doing this," I tell him.

"That's the wonderful thing about the auction," says Mr. Greer. "You don't have a say in the matter."

He stands, motioning for Amir to follow.

"I want to take her home *now*," whines the boy.

"Patience, dear nephew," he says, motioning the child to the door. Just before he follows, he pauses to whisper in my ear, "Patience for him, but not for the Virulent. I'll be seeing you soon, Clover."

And then they are gone, leaving me in my corner of the room.

I DON'T REMEMBER LEAVING the parlor. I don't remember the Watcher searing the metal bracelet on my wrist. I vaguely recall the Governess debating whether or not she should really place me back in solitary, now that I have such a high-profile buyer showing interest. She must have figured she ought to, because the next thing I know, I am shoved out of the glass office door into the solitary yard.

I am still wearing the tight pink dress that covers my arms and reaches down to my ankles. The evening air is crisp, but I hardly feel it. I hardly feel *anything*. My hair is tucked behind my ears, falling in neatly brushed curls down my back. There is only one beaded earring in my ear.

The sky is fading. It must be close to nighttime. The Watcher has already offered me my dinner allotment, but I didn't take it. I've never been less hungry.

"No!" a girl screams as he's attaching my bracelet to the chain. She's been sitting just outside the sliding glass door on her bedroll, but now stands, red hair disheveled. Latched onto her right arm is her containment bracelet; it peeks out from the sleeve of her standard black uniform dress. There is still a flushed blemish on the side of her face, but the swelling is down.

Daphne.

I look at her, but can't seem to track her eyes. My head is too muddy. I stare down to where both of our leashes connect to the same post.

"Someone chose *you*?" she says.

I don't say anything. I can't believe it either. After everything that I've tried. That Kiran's tried.

Her cheeks pale, like she's about to be sick. The thought of someone choosing me disgusts her. It shouldn't get to me, but it does.

"I would have gone last month if stupid Iris didn't meet with him after me," she says, an edge in her tone. "If you were picked, I'd be Promised for certain right now!"

"I didn't want this," I say.

"Oh, you'd rather stay here, is that it?" Her green eyes look like they might pop out of their sockets.

"No. I want to go back—"

"—to the mountains. I know." She throws herself dramatically back onto her cot. "Such a waste, you are."

"I . . . I am not," I counter, wishing I had something smart to come back with. She only glares at me, and behind the anger I can see the misery. I'm reminded of Salma, fighting with my ma about being brought up into the mountains against her will. It was obviously the safest place for her, but Salma didn't see it that way. And now Daphne doesn't get it either. All she sees is what she knows. The tiny box of a world. A world that has let her down.

"Who is he, anyway? Some plastics worker, probably. Or, no, a maintenance man." She grumbles through several more undesirable positions before I interrupt her.

"Amir Ryker," I say.

She lifts her head.

"Ryker. The *mayor*?"

"His son," I say.

"But his son . . ." She smiles. I can see the laugh building inside of her before it finally breaks free. "His son is a boy. A child."

"I know that." I look at the edge of the office, knowing that around the corner is the poisoned stream and Brax's sewer. And the Driver barn.

Because I'm exhausted, I sit on the other side of the cot.

She quiets as she realizes what this means. "You won't have to be with him, will you?"

"Not for a few years," I say. "That's what his keeper says, anyway." But I think of Mr. Greer's threats and double over, elbows on my knees, face in my hands.

"A servant brought him? Not his father?"

When I don't answer right away, Daphne pinches my arm.

Her chain makes a clinking noise as it draws across her lap. "You have to tell me everything, Clover. You owe me that much at least."

"Don't call me that," I say. "It's not my name."

She groans. "Tell me."

I exhale. The air reeks of oil and waste. The incinerator's been used lately, probably to burn all the excess from the auction preparations.

"The boy came with a man named Greer. He's got an X on his face."

Her eyes widen. "He's Virulent? You're sure?"

"I'm sure."

"Greer is the mayor's brother," she says. "He never leaves their house in the city. I overheard my father once say that the mayor was ashamed of him. I never knew he was marked."

She taps her fingers together like this is prime gossip and waits for me to say more, but I have nothing else to add.

"What is wrong with you?" she asks. "If your paperwork goes through, you'll have the best placement in the city. You'll get whatever you want and you won't even have to share anyone's bed."

I don't tell her Mr. Greer's plans.

"For now," I say. "If I'm lucky."

We're both looking out now, in opposite directions. Her, towards the Garden. Me, towards the city gates.

"You're the luckiest person I know," she says quietly. "You're so blunt you can't even see it. Good thing they've got you chained in, otherwise you might pull the same stunt as that other girl."

I can still see Straw Hair stuck to the fence, her dead body dancing, her yellow hair catching fire. The smell, it's still right there in the back of my throat.

And even now I wonder if she was luckier than all of us.

I feel a growl inside of me, but it doesn't have the strength to rise up my throat. I can't stand being near Daphne any longer, so

I walk away. Back around the side of the office, behind my sheltering plaster wall. The chain drags behind me, catching on the rocks and grass and weighing down my arm. I stumble as close as I can to the poisoned water and fall to my knees. But I still can't pray.

Dark thoughts whisper to me. They say I will never go home. Tam and Nina are dead. Salma has abandoned them. I will be sold and bred and sold and bred until I don't remember that my name is Aya, and I came from the mountains.

At sixteen, I have lived all that I will ever live.

I pull up my dress sleeve and look at the silver bracelet on my wrist. It doesn't even shine in this sorry excuse for a sunset. I think about drinking the poisoned water. Wonder if it would kill the pain inside of me. Or if it would just make it worse, add a new sickness, like the one that's now stealing my hope. I wonder if Straw Hair pondered these same questions.

The sky grows dim, then dark—as dark as it will get here. I hear the bass from the Black Lanes pick up. Auction Day is closing, and the Virulent will make lots of money tonight from any drunken merchants or disguised Magnates who want to gamble or hit the brothels.

I hate them. I hate everyone within these walls. And I hate everyone outside of these walls because they have what I can't. Freedom.

And then, finally, there is peace.

Out of the sewer comes Brax. He trots up the outside of the Garden, past the office, to join me in the yard. His face nuzzles mine, warm and wet and wild. It's his low whimper that finally breaks me down.

I cry into Brax's soft silver neck, and he lets me, panting while my hands fist in his fur. Every so often he licks my face, cleaning the salty tears away, and then I cry some more.

Above my choked-off sobs I can still hear the club music. *Boom, boom, boom.* Mocking me. I can see the man from the auction who grabbed me in the crowd. See Mr. Greer's scar. My ma's scar.

And then I know what I must do.

There is one other way to leave the Garden. Not Promised. Not dead. But marked. With a scar on my cheek. They'll expect me to make a living in the Black Lanes, but I won't do that. I can be strong like my ma. I can pass through the city gates and be reunited with my family before the next auction.

I must fail the medical inspection. And I must do so before the mayor's brother has a chance to lay his hands on me. Maybe it's not what I wanted, not now anyway, but at least I'll get to choose who touches me, and when.

Silently, I stand, telling Brax to stay while I creep around the side of the building. Daphne's sleeping on the bedroll, covering herself with all four of the blankets meant to be shared between us. I can see her chest rise and fall. Inside, the Watcher has laid down to sleep too.

I tiptoe back around the plaster wall, to the hidden place behind the office, and pick a small pebble off the ground. Then, with all my might, I heave it in the direction of the barn. It plunks off one of the paddock fences. A horse snorts and stamps his feet.

And then I sit, and wait for Kiran.

CHAPTER 11

KIRAN TAKES *FOREVER.*

Or maybe time has just stopped since I made my decision. Either way, I'm pacing behind the Watcher office, as far as my tether will let me, thinking that he's not going to come at all, and why would he after I screwed up his escape, and sent him away, and told him such stupid, stupid stories . . . when he finally appears in the back exit of the barn.

His shirt glows pale yellow in the lights from the rec yard fence, and his hair is tousled. There's something soft about the way he looks from this distance. Something not quite real. The edges of him should be sharp against the dark behind him, but they're not. They shimmer, as though he's a mirage. Like the dark can't touch him, no matter how hard it tries.

Then he starts walking towards me, stride long and purposeful, and I see the way the horses flick their ears and stomp their hooves and that golden, shining feeling inside of me gets eaten up by the worries. He hesitates, like always, just before the stream, and when he's sure the Watcher's not watching, he leaps over. From the look on his face, I can tell that there's something he wants to tell me, and it doesn't look good.

For the first time, I'm glad he can't talk.

I stand my ground and tell myself the same thing I'm always telling myself: This is Kiran. There's nothing to be scared of.

Just before he reaches me he stops short. His mouth falls

open in surprise. Very slowly, one hand reaches forward to brush aside my hair, and my neck tingles, because the curls feel foreign to my sensitive skin when he moves them.

His face falls. His hand falls. He's seen the missing earring and knows what that means.

"The mayor's son," I tell him, the shame weighing down my words. "A boy."

Kiran watches me intently, his gaze clinging to my mouth as I talk. A scowl etches deep lines between his brows. There's too much knowing in his eyes.

I can't do this.

I have to do this.

It will be quick, I tell myself. Like pulling out my earring. Like taking a punch. Laying down with Kiran will mean nothing. But it already hurts in my soul, stretching my skin too thin, like I'm made of glass and he can see everything, all of it. I don't want to feel these things. I just want to do this and be done with it.

"Brax, go home," I say. The wolf's jaw snaps shut, and he looks up at me. "*Home,*" I stress, and point to the sewer. Brax whines like a child having a tantrum, then stalks away, boney shoulders rolling beneath his gray fur. He glances back once, and I feel the judgment in his stare, thicker than my own. As soon as he is gone panic spikes in my chest. I lift my chin to Kiran as bravely as I can.

"My thanks for what you did today," I say to him. "I know what it might have cost you."

I think of the bodies carried down from the stage by the Watchers just before the auction and shiver. One of them could have been Kiran.

I tell myself I never asked for his help. Not until now.

"There's another way, you know," I say, unable to look him straight in the eye.

He's still watching; I can feel his gaze on me and wish these last moments before I ruin this—whatever it is—would last a little longer.

I take a jerky step forward, noticing how much taller he always seems up close. We're just inches away now, and the smell of horsehair and leather dusts his skin. I can see each piece of golden hair that's matted behind his ears. And somewhere deep inside of me I know that I will never again breathe in the scent of leather or see the sun's bright rays and not think of Kiran.

His body becomes very still, his kiran-stone eyes seeking mine. And suddenly I don't know. This seemed so easily achievable before. But now it seems wrong. I can't be Salma. I can't lie down with some boy on the outskirts of town and then say good-bye, maybe forever. And that would be exactly what would happen. If I lie down with Kiran, I will be marked sometime tomorrow, turned loose by nightfall, and out the city gates before the sunrise.

I will never see him again.

Something begins to twist inside of me, and I knead my stomach absently, trying to force it down. I'm staring at his bare feet and my bare feet, so close they could touch even if I just shifted my balance. I think about the night he touched the scar on my leg. How strange and soft that felt. And I think that maybe it might not be so terrible if he touched me again, just like that.

I tell myself it doesn't matter. I don't need him to be kind, I need this to be over.

With a sudden burst of recklessness, I yank the stretchy dress over my head. It takes forever to come off, getting stuck around my shoulders, and then around my hair and my earring, and then the metal bracelet. But finally I'm free of it, in just my underclothes, with the cold air biting into my skin. Goose bumps race over my body. My belly button feels like it sucks back all the way to my spine. I crumple the dress in front of my chest.

"Let's get this over with," I mutter.

His eyes go round with shock, and his mouth falls open.

He takes a step back, then forward, then looks around the office. Then up at the night sky. He points at me and turns around. I don't move, because now he's the one who's acting like he's lost his mind.

"Oh," I say. "Can you not do it or something?" Maybe Drivers are like Pips, missing the right equipment, I don't know.

He turns sharply. There's a glint in his eye that makes my mouth go dry, and I swallow. For a moment we just look at each other, trying to figure out what the other is thinking. Trying to figure out how to begin. I never figured there'd be so much thinking involved. Then he reaches forward and snatches the dress, stretching it taut as one sleeve is still hooked around the chain.

I guess he has the right parts after all.

But he only shakes his head, and attempts to hold the dress in front of me like a curtain.

It takes me a moment to realize what he's doing.

"I won't tell on you," I assure him, pulling the fabric down. His stare drops to my chest and lingers before he blocks it again with the dress.

I snort. "They only gave me a four for these," I say, pulling back my shoulders.

When he doesn't move, I step to the side, forcing him to look at me.

"Kiran, come on already, I won't tell. You have my word." I make sure he sees my eyes as I pretend to stich my lips shut.

He holds his hands out, then points at his chest. His meaning is clear.

"Why me?"

My shoulders slump. My insides tie into knots. His eyes are still boring into me, and I can feel the shame heating my cheeks. I'm reminded of all the times I made Salma help me clean rabbits. She always said the same thing, *"Why me?"* Great. Being with me is as detestable to Kiran as slicing up a dead rabbit is to Salma.

"My legs scored seven and a half stars," I tell him. I look down at the slender muscles of my thighs, and he shakes the dress impatiently in front of me.

I take it, half wishing that knife he'd thrown had hit the mark.

"Fine," I say. "I'll find another way." I make it sound mean, but I'm a little relieved.

His mouth is pinched at the corners in anger when he draws an X over his cheek with his first finger, then points at me.

"I know," I tell him. "They'll mark me. But it's the only way, don't you see? I'll never get out of here otherwise."

He points at his chest, and then slices his hands in his *no* gesture.

"I hear you," I tell him slowly, the words sharp. "I get it. I'm not stupid, you know."

He turns away. I stuff myself back into the dress, half livid, half panicked.

"Kiran!" I whisper as he turns. But it's too late. He's already over the stream, stalking towards the barn. He slaps a hand against the side paneling just as he passes through, and even though he can't talk, it sure feels like he's had the last word.

The chestnut mare I recognize from town, and a few other horses, spook at the sound and gallop out into their paddocks, kicking and whinnying. A few moments later the Watcher is outside, staring at me blankly. Then Daphne shows up, peering around the corner of the office wall as though she's about to witness something terrifying.

"What happened?" she asks when the Watcher leaves to go back inside.

"Nothing," I say flatly.

"Did you fall?"

"Go back to sleep," I say. She huffs and stomps away.

I slide back against the wall, but I don't sleep. I shred tufts of grass in my fists and sniffle as the air becomes sharply chilled. I keep thinking about Mr. Greer and the Governess. About the mayor's house, protected in the Magnate district. About how Kiran won't help me even to save my life.

⟶

I DON'T MOVE ONCE during the night. I stay there through the morning, thinking, wishing, looking for something I've missed, something I haven't tried. I bite my nails down to nothing. I screw my thumbs into my temples. The Watcher brings me meal pills in another aluminum bowl, but I don't touch them. All my ideas are coming up blank.

Sometime in the afternoon Daphne comes back around the corner. Her hair has gotten wavy out here in the moist air and sticks out on one side. From the tearstains down her freckle-free, coal-smeared cheek, I can tell she's had about enough of the solitary pen.

"They're here for you," she says.

I don't stand until the Pips make me.

Within the office my bracelet is removed, then I'm led through the door with the key code and down the long, windowless hall-way with the flickering lights. My footsteps are heavy, slower than the pattering of the Pips' padded shoes. The dread turns my guts to water. It feels like I'm climbing back onto that stage again, only this time not for the auction, but for the hangings.

We enter the foyer and pass the entertainment parlor but don't continue down the hall to the Governess's office.

"Where are we going?" I ask the Pip in front, somehow both relieved and even more wary than before. If we aren't going to the Governess's office, maybe the paperwork didn't go through.

The Pip whispers something to the one standing beside him.

"Hey," I say. "I asked you something."

"*Pip.*" He snorts. "So rude." One of the keepers behind me smacks me on the back with his beater, and I siphon in a sharp breath through my teeth. It feels like a fire on my skin. My fists clench at my sides.

They turn and lead me down a white corridor, one I've been down before, and the dread returns in one hard punch.

The medical wing.

My knees wobble, and for a moment I consider letting them give out. Laying on the floor. Making them carry me. But I don't, because no one carries me.

The Pips must sense the change in me because they tighten their ranks. They try to push me forward, but I don't move. The reality of my situation has come crashing down over my head.

It's happened: I've been sold. And now a doctor's here to do the purity test.

"Come on," says the leader. "Don't be difficult. It's not painful."

"How would you know?" I ask. But it's not the pain I'm worried about.

"Come *on*," he says again, and he gives a little nod to the two in back. They both lay in at once, smacking my shoulders, the backs of my thighs. In this thin dress it feels like their blows slice the skin, and they leave traces of heat with every strike.

I move over the threshold and through the doors despite myself. A cool burst of air comes from above, though that's not why I cross my arms over my chest. In the center of the room is a thin metal table and from it extend four angular silver arms. One holds a tray of instruments, one stretches above with a light, and the two at the bottom are capped by half circles that look like horseshoes.

The doctor rises from his desk against the wall and approaches. He's a frail man with tired eyes and a thin black mustache. His long white jacket reaches almost all the way to the gleaming white floor.

"Did you bring the forms?" he asks a Pip, who replies with a nod.

"Disrobe," the doctor tells me. "You can place your clothes on the back of that chair."

I swallow, my heart beating in my ears.

"Take off your clothes," he says slowly. He turns to a Pip. "I forgot she was the one they brought in from the wild."

"I know what disrobe means," I say, already feeling naked. "But I'm not doing it."

Five Pips are watching me. Five Pips and a doctor, all of them barking mad if they think I'm about to strip down to my bare skin. Taking my dress off in front of Kiran now seems a thousand times easier.

I wrap my arms tighter around my waist and glance back at the sliding doors.

The doctor sighs. "A thorough exam is expected as part of every pending sale."

"Well that's too bad," I say, heart pounding in my chest. I take a step back, then another. One of the Pips moves to a corner and presses a button on the wall. He's talking to someone, but I can't hear what he says.

The lead Pip glares at me. "Off with the dress, girl. Don't make us ask again."

"You've nothing to be embarrassed about," says the doctor, although I'm sure he doesn't mean it. "Any disfigurements will be corrected before the sale is complete."

My scars feel huge and foreign when he says this, like they're great, ugly eyesores.

The sliding door opens and I spin to find the Watcher from the solitary yard standing in the outline of white. I back into the table. The metal tray clatters to the ground and the neatly laid-out pieces go rolling across the floor.

"*Pip, pip, pip!*" says the leader. "Now look what you've done!"

The Watcher closes in, one hand on his wire, and I dodge behind the table.

"Stay away from me," I say. "All of you. I don't need any medical exam, all right? I'm pure and my scars have already been lightened. Just ask the Governess."

I keep my eyes on the Watcher—on his hand, still resting on his wire. On the key, strapped in the belt across his chest. If only I'd had that a few hours ago.

A Pip grabs me from behind, and I shake him off. But two more take his place and hold my arms. The doctor is approaching with a syringe, and out of the top of the needle a droplet of clear moisture beads and slides free. I stare at it in dread.

"Hold her still," he says.

I struggle, furious tears burning my eyes. In one heave, I pull free of the Pips, tearing the sleeves of my dress, and charge the door. I try to get past the Watcher, but it's no use. Inhumanly fast, he appears in front of me, and I run straight into his chest. He pins my arms at my sides as if I'm weak as a rabbit, and holds me still while the doctor sticks the needle in my neck.

It burns; flames lick my veins as the poison spreads through my blood. And then I go limp.

I can't move. My arms and legs don't work. I can't even scream. But I feel.

I feel the soft hands of the Pips peeling off my dress.

The rough material of the Watcher's jacket beneath my knees and back as he puts me on the cold table.

The hard metal horseshoes jutting into my ankles as my legs are spread and placed in each arm.

I can't cover myself from their judging eyes. Can't cover my ears to drown out the Pips' snide little jokes. *Ripe for the picking,* they say. *Ripe as a cherry.*

The doctor slides his stool between my knees, and puts his cold hands on my thighs and the places no one has ever touched. The bright light on the band around his head lowers. I watch him study and prod this body as if it's not my own. It can't possibly be my own. It lies there lifeless, stays where it's placed, doesn't fight.

It disgusts me.

"Fertile," he says with a smile. "Very nice."

I want to close my eyes, but can't even do that. The only thing left to do is think of Kiran, and pretend it's just him and me, like I'd planned it last night. But the tools aren't gentle like Kiran's hand on my calf, and I'm thankful more than ever that he can't see me now.

Finally, the doctor wheels back in his chair, and removes the headpiece with the bright, round light.

"Untouched," he says. He pats my knee. "Well done."

CHAPTER 12

I AM CLEANED, RIGHT there on the table. Shaved and scrubbed down with perfumed water, oiled until I'm slippery like a fish, and then sat up and stuffed into a dress I've never worn before. A white gown, like the kind my people wear in mourning.

My head rolls to the side while the Pips prop me up in a chair on wheels and cart me from this room of nightmares. They take me to the front of the building, the courtyard entrance where the carriages line up to take us to auction. Girls stare at me as I'm wheeled past, pouty looks on their faces. Jealousy in their eyes. Lotus is there, the only one of Sweetpea's friends left, and she wipes away her angry tears with her sleeve. I feel a scream, loud enough to make the whole world deaf, building in my chest.

My arm falls off the chair. I watch, unable to lift it, as it swings, slapping against the wheel for nine rotations before one of the Pips notices it and tosses it back on my lap.

Outside the sky is bruised and beaten, gray and purple and low with smog. The Governess and her Pip assistant stand beside a sleek black carriage drawn by two horses. The Driver at the helm is none other than the silver ferret from the barn. Even now, I'm grateful it's not Kiran.

"Don't you look lovely," the Governess says with a smile. Long yellow ringlets trail down to her hips, where a dark blue bustle makes her backside look three times its normal size. She leans forward, and in a strange gesture, touches my cheek.

"I was a little like you once," she says softly. "Always looking for a way to break the chain." She withdraws her hand when the carriage door opens. "We always belong to someone."

By the time Mr. Greer steps out, her fake smile has returned. He's wearing the same sharp suit with the same scarf wrapped around his face, hiding all but his eyes and the bridge of his nose.

I blink. It's the first movement I've been able to do in some time, and it spurs a new burst of determination in me. I try to lift a finger or wiggle my toes, but still nothing.

"Is she all right?" he asks after a moment. My neck is cramping from being at this angle, but I still don't have the strength to fight it.

"She was so nervous," says the Governess with a little frown. "We had to sedate her. You can understand. Going to an estate such as yours . . ."

"Is everything finished?" Mr. Greer interrupts. "I've signed the paperwork. The forms look to be in order."

They are talking about my life. My *life*.

"There's just the matter of payment, sir," says the Governess. It's as sweet as she's ever sounded.

"Ah," says Greer. He removes a small messagebox from his breast pocket and presses a few buttons. "The credits have been transferred."

"Check it," I hear the Governess whisper to her Pip assistant. She smiles broadly at Mr. Greer, rubbing her hands together. The Pip looks down his electric, handheld board and gives her a small nod.

Mr. Greer is staring at me, an unimpressed look in his strange black eyes.

"Put her inside," he says.

I blink. I blink, blink, blink. I will my arms to move, my teeth to bite, anything. But all I can do is blink. I am propped up inside on a cushioned sheet, and just as soon as Mr. Greer gets

162

inside, the carriage shifts, and with the click of hooves, rolls forward.

I am sold.

I am sold.

I hope Tam and Nina are far away. I hope Salma defends their freedom with her life. I hope, if I don't make it out, they think I died the day I was captured. It is better than them knowing I met this fate instead.

And Brax. There is a hard clench in my chest as I think of him. I should have said good-bye. I should have left him food. I should have tried to free him, too.

We hit a bump at the front gates and, jostled, my limp body falls to the floor of the compartment. My skirt flips up, and I can't even pull it back down to cover my bare legs. I stare at Mr. Greer's shiny black boots. He reaches down and for a moment I think he's going to help me up. Instead, his fingertips skim up my bare thigh, stopping just before he would have to readjust his position to go farther. Then he sits back, and returns his focus to his messagebox.

I am sold.

⟶

I WAKE TO THE slam of a door. Draped overhead are sheer linens, hanging from the four posts that support the cushy bed I've been laid out on. I don't remember being brought here, or where I am, and a sudden dose of panic shakes through me because if I don't remember how I got in, I don't know how to get out.

I concentrate, but only fragments of memories return: a house Pip dressed in gray lifting me from the car, holding his head back as he carries me as if I am a dead body.

He arranges me on a bed and turns out the lights. And with nothing else to do but blink, I close my eyes.

Someone else is in my room. I can hear the shuffling of feet on the hard floor and I turn my head towards the sound. My muscles are freed from their hold, but they hurt. The pain shoots straight down my spine through my legs as I roll onto my side, and I bite back against it. The bed is so plush it all but swallows me whole; I have to roll to get to the edge.

There is a face staring straight at mine when I get there.

"You sleep forever," Amir Ryker says.

I cringe. He may be a child, but I can't help hating him for what he's done to me, and hating myself ten times more for giving him the candy in the first place and failing each escape attempt, and for even not being pretty enough to seduce Kiran.

"I'm up now," I say, stretching my tight limbs for the first time in more than a day. The room is bigger than any bedroom I've seen. The floors are pressed wood, and the walls are covered with paintings that change views every time I look away. They unnerve me a little, like the room itself is alive.

"Let's play," he says.

"I'm tired."

"You slept all day, you're not tired."

I see now that the eyes must run in the family—they're beady and black, and they narrow into little slits when he's angry. He reaches for my hand and pulls. I groan, the tight muscles in my arms stretching.

"Where's your uncle?" I ask. I don't remember where Mr. Greer went last night.

"Drunk," he says in a way that makes me think this isn't unusual.

"Fine, okay," I say, standing up. I blink back the dizziness and roll my head in one slow circle on my neck.

Maybe being placed with a child isn't such a bad thing after all. He may be spoiled, but I've got years of experience convincing the twins we all have the same goal. Today's goal: Turn a blind eye on the new girl—me.

"Why don't we play outside?" I suggest. Mr. Greer's distraction is the perfect opportunity to escape.

"Ew," he says. "We'll play hunting."

He drags me by the forearm down an empty hallway with more of the creepy pictures, to a simple room with white glass walls. There's a chest in the corner and he releases me at last to open it. In it is a shiny black bow. My pulse quickens as he removes it.

"Load hunting game," he says.

"You got arrows?" I ask.

He ignores me.

I jump as all four walls around me burst into color. Green and blue—bright, true color. My breath catches. It looks real. It looks like my mountains.

"What is this?" I whisper.

"Shut up," he says.

I breathe in and out, knowing it's a trick, but unable to stop the pang in my chest. The branches rustle in the breeze. I can even hear a nearby stream. Although the room smells sterile, I can almost convince myself I'm home.

Out from behind a tree steps a deer. The dry pine needles crackle beneath his tentative hooves. I hold my breath, watching. Just watching. The way the sun catches every piece of hair, and the fuzz on his new antlers. He is beautiful.

Beside me, the boy lifts his bow, and pretends to draw an arrow. When he releases it, there is a loud "*ping*!" that seems to come from all around, and the deer falls to the ground, knees first.

"Yes!" Amir cries.

I can't look away. It's lying there bleeding, struggling to stand. One front leg straightens, then collapses. It bleats, scrambling to rise.

I have shot animals with my bow before, but only to eat. Only because we needed the meat. Their suffering was always short.

"Kill it," I tell him, a hitch in my voice. "Do something."

He gives me a stupid look. "It's not real, you know."

I shift my weight. "I know, I just . . ." His disregard for the pain of that animal, real or not, gives me the chills. I don't like this game where you pretend to kill for sport. I don't know anyone who would maim a living thing, and take such satisfaction in its suffering. It's sick.

"I'm the best at this," he announces. "I've shot boars and panthers too. They're faster, you know."

I do know. I try to imagine this boy in the mountains, taking down a boar with a real bow. I wonder if he would treat taking a life as a game—if this was just practice to him—or if he would suffer and pray, as I do, feeling the life of another creature drain away.

"Let's play a different game," I say. "How about a hiding game?"

He shrugs and drops the bow on the ground.

"Load hiding game," he says.

"Hiding game, unknown." The man's voice coming through the speakers surprises me. It must be programmed in.

"Load hiding game!" Amir yells.

"Hiding game, unknown."

He kicks the bow, and it slams into the glass wall with a clatter.

"You don't do it in this room," I say quickly. "One person waits while the other hides. Then after a while, the waiter goes to look for the hider."

He looks unconvinced. "What does he get when he finds the hider?"

I reach for an answer, but come up blank. "He gets to hide next time."

"He doesn't get a prize? Sounds stupid." There's another pouting session coming on. His cheeks are already growing red. If Tam ever talked to me this way I would have taken a paddle to him.

"You pick the prize then," I say.

He thinks about this. "The winner gets a new game. All these are easy. I beat them all on the first day."

I try not to roll my eyes. "Sounds fine." Doesn't matter to me as long as I can ditch this kid and find a way out of here.

"And the loser gets marked," he says.

I was heading for the door, but stop and turn as he says this. "What do you mean?"

"I mean marked like the Virulent!" He pretends to slash an X across his cheek, and I'm reminded of the last person who made that move at me: Kiran.

"Pretend marked, you mean," I say, a chill falling over my skin because I'm pretty sure he isn't joking.

His round face falls. "Fine. I guess."

We walk to the door, back into the hallway with the changing pictures. There are flowers in a vase on a thin table, but as I get closer I see that they're made of glass. I wouldn't keep anything glass around this kid. He'd probably throw it into the wall.

"How'd your uncle get that mark?" I ask.

Amir stops. "We're not supposed to talk about that."

I continue on, making a mental map of the layout of the rooms, the curve in the hall. We come to a stairway, but there are still no windows for me to get my bearing. I start to descend, but he grabs my elbow and shoves me up to the next level.

"You can tell me," I say. "It's not like I have anyone to tell."

"I'm going to hide first," he says. He's above me two steps, but has stopped and turned around.

"No," I say. "I thought of the game, I'm hiding first."

He glares at me. "You have to do what I say."

"Make me."

He winds back to slap me. I almost can't believe he's got the nerve. Before he connects, I block his arm and shove him back. He falls with a *thunk* on the step.

And then begins to cry.

167

"You're kidding," I say.

"You hurt me!"

I cringe: That's a pitch I've only heard when Lily the song-stress reaches the high notes. He's faking though; no tears come from his eyes. Nina used to do the same for attention.

"I did not. Get up already," I say, and pull him up. He crumbles, arms thrown overhead. The clattering of footsteps comes from down the hallway and as the boy wails louder, I start to get nervous.

"I'm sorry, okay? I didn't mean it. You can hide first."

"You. Hurt. Me!"

I'm close to punching him. Or dumping him over the wooden stair railing. His body clunking level to level would probably make less noise than this.

The house Pip I met the previous night appears from the floor below.

"Amir!" he calls. "Oh Amir, what happened?"

"He fell," I say.

"She pushed me!" His face is turning purple. I wonder if he might explode. That might be all right, actually.

The Pip shoves by me. "Wait in the preparation room," he says, pointing down the hall. "Go. *Go.*"

I don't know what room he's talking about, but it doesn't matter. I scram the second he gives me permission. But right before I'm clear, he grabs my elbow. His features have been smoothed down so much in the Keeper treatments, his nose is barely a bump on his face.

"Nothing funny," he says. His gaze lifts, and mine follows to the black camera embedded in the ceiling.

I'm being watched.

This hall is much the same as the previous level, though along the wall runs a tapestry, paint on silk. Men on horseback with pointed sticks driving monsters towards a ravine. Creatures falling into an abyss. And then men in long maroon cloaks, holding chains attached to the necks of women heavy with children.

A knot forms in my throat and I reach forward, the urge to rip it from the wall overwhelming. I grab the corner, and clench the smooth fabric in my fist. But before I can tear it, something catches my eye.

On the wall underneath the tapestry someone has drawn a link of chains—a crude sketch in black ink. The chain is broken in the middle.

The Governess's voice—Azalea's voice—is fresh in my ears. *I was a little like you once. Always looking for a way to break the chain.*

I don't know if she was once the property of the men in this house—maybe the mayor's father, or his father before him. I don't know if she's the one who's drawn this. But it gives me hope all the same.

I straighten the tapestry, careful to keep my body between the secret message and the camera on the ceiling behind me.

"You must be one of my new acquisitions."

I startle and spin. Before me stands a slender man with a square jaw and a narrow mouth. He's older than his dark, slick hair and smooth skin might suggest; I see it in his eyes, which are squinting, even in the soft light, giving the impression he's one of those people who's always plotting something.

The mayor. It must be. No one else would refer to me that way.

I glance over the casual black robe he wears, cinched loosely around his waist. It reveals too much of his form beneath. A blush rises in my cheeks.

"I just got here." I don't know why, but I can't meet his gaze. I feel it, though, searing through me.

"Well then. Welcome," he says coolly. "You're finding your room comfortable, I trust."

Hard to remember, being as I was passed out and paralyzed most of the night.

"It's all right," I say. It's strange, thinking I have my own room. I've never had my own room before. Even in the mountains I shared a tent with the family and a cot with Nina.

He's closer than I like, or maybe the hallway is too narrow. Either way, I'm too crowded.

"Such an interesting face." He lifts his cold hand and touches my cheek. There's something about him that makes me feel small.

I turn away. "So you're the mayor, I guess."

"I guess." He smiles. Perfect, white teeth.

"Amir's father."

"Ah." He seems to realize how I've come to his home now. "You must be the girl who barks like a dog."

He gestures down the hall, and I find myself falling into step beside him.

"My son was quite taken by you." His lake-blue eyes sparkle, and it occurs to me Amir doesn't look much like him. "Some might think it's extravagant to purchase a girl for a child."

"Thought crossed my mind," I say, trying to sound smart, like him. "But who am I to judge? If you want to spoil your kids, that's your business."

"You are wild, indeed," he says. "I'm almost regretting not attending the auction myself. We might have fought over you."

I close my mouth. A shadow of regret passes over his face, and he grows quiet, clearly thinking of something. I don't interrupt him.

"There is only one," he continues after a while. "Just Amir." He sighs. "Maybe I do spoil him."

The hall has opened to a large room, ripe with exotic perfumes and soft music, walled by mirrors on all sides. Strewn across the floor are fancy pillows of all different colors, and atop them a dozen or more girls are lounging. When they see us, they squeal and jump to their feet, a flurry of textiles and patterns, and crowd around the mayor.

I'm surprised he has only one kid. From the looks of things, he's not spending too many nights sleeping alone.

A girl who looks a little like Straw Hair with her yellow locks pushes to the front. She's not much older than me and is stroking her flat stomach as if she's just eaten a huge meal.

"It's a boy, Mayor," she says. "It's a boy. I know it. I feel it."

"Wonderful," he says, with barely a second glance.

She is pushed aside by a girl with long gold earrings and skin that's been painted to match. I think I recognize her from my first week at the Garden, but she wasn't such an odd color then.

"Mayor, there's something I'd like to show you," she says in a sultry voice.

But he points to a girl standing near the back. One who looks no more than twelve or thirteen years old, who hasn't grown into her body yet. She's picking at her fingernails.

"You," he says. "Join me for a walk, won't you?"

She gives a little nod and takes his hand.

It's sickening. She looks like a child beside him. She *is* a child.

"Figures," one of them whispers. "Of course he'd take the carrot."

"The what?" I ask.

"Her father just traded her last week," says the girl with gold skin. "Part of some big business deal. He got the mayor's attention by dangling a carrot out in front of his face. Get used to it. Happens all the time."

Disappointed, the other girls return to the floor to laze about.

"Enjoy your stay with us," the mayor says to me on the way out. "You are indeed a fine prize for my son."

I am speechless.

CHAPTER 13

THE CATS WAIT TO pounce until the mayor's footsteps have gone silent.

"What's that smell?" asks one of them, a girl with a purple streak in her hair.

"I think it's fresh meat," says another with an intricate pattern of tattoos winding up her arms. "Yes, definitely fresh meat." She wafts a hand in front of her face to clear the air.

I catch my reflection in one of the wall mirrors. My curly black hair is messy from sleep, and my eye makeup is smeared a bit. My white dress is wrinkled. It looks like I've just rolled out of bed, though not in the way they're thinking.

"How'd you like me to break your nose?" I ask Tattoos.

Her little smile flips upside down as she scoots back to make room for me.

"You must be new to the city," says Purple Hair. "I remember when my brother brought me from my little waste of a town in the outliers. . . ." She forces a laugh. "If he hadn't tricked me and told me we were going to the fair in Anders, I would have scratched his eyes out. Traitor."

"Didn't turn out too bad, did it?" asks Tattoos.

Purple Hair shakes her head, then narrows her eyes at me. "What town did they haul you in from? Somewhere up north, am I right?" She laughs again, like this should be funny.

"No town," I say.

Tattoos's brows rise. "Born and raised city? I hadn't heard the mayor was pulling stock from the locals. The census must be low."

"Free," I tell them both clearly. "And wild." I smile as fiercely as I can.

I kneel on a flat blue pillow and snag one of the little treats on a silver platter in the center of the room. It's sweet and warm, creamy too. I sort of hate that it's the best thing I've ever tasted. But the memory of the young girl walking out of the room hand in hand with the mayor makes the food curdle in my stomach. Just a few more years and that could be Nina.

The guilt is thick on my skin, weighing me down. I should have tried to stop them, but what good would it do? It wouldn't change anything.

The girls stare at each other, then at me. There's no mistaking the jealousy there.

"Lucky you," says Tattoos. "You've got it made."

I don't ask what she means.

"I have to get out of here," I say, more to myself. This place is a palace of nightmares. I know they'll probably tell on me, but I don't care. I'm already sold. Things can't get much worse.

"Sure, all right," says the girl with the purple streak. One bony shoulder sticks out from the neck of her shirt. When she sees I'm serious, her eyebrows hike up beneath side-swept bangs. "Why would you want to?"

"That's not your problem," I say.

"There are walls," says Tattoos. "Walls ten stories high. And Watchers manning the gates. And sensors all over."

"You don't know," says Purple Hair. "You haven't been off this level since you were brought here."

"Neither have you," the other argues.

"But I heard the mayor talking about it. In bed." Purple Hair smirks.

The blush rises in Tattoos's face. "Funny," she says. "The mayor never has the energy to speak after I'm done with him."

A groan rises in my throat. These girls have no idea how pathetic they sound, each fighting for a position as the most valuable slave. They've forgotten, or maybe they never learned, that their worth is not determined by how much a man wants them. If I weren't so preoccupied with getting out of there, I'd feel sorry for them.

A house Pip enters and begins to trade out the trays for something new. Before he can take ours, I cram another two of the cream treats in my mouth and rise. Obviously I'm not getting anywhere with these two. They continue tossing insults as I exit the room.

THE SCANNERS ON THE ceiling track me as I emerge the way I came. It's quiet here, but for the buzzing as they shift positions. I'm surprised I was allowed to leave at all, but none of the serving Pips raised a finger to stop me. I keep checking over my shoulder to make sure they're not following.

The doors on either side of the hallway are all locked. Finally I come across one that's already cracked.

The room is small, making the round bed in the center seem overly large. A centerpiece, with its cushy red blanket and mountain of pillows. On the opposite wall is a window, and I race to it. Outside the sun is beginning to set, reflecting off the gleaming green buildings. We're high. Too high to climb down. I place my hand on the glass lightly, hating this thin barrier separating me from my freedom.

And then the alarm sounds.

The high ringing stabs into my temples, and I jump back. Behind me, the heavy wooden door slams shut, as if moved by a ghost. Fear grips me, and I do the only thing I can think of: I dive under the bed.

My breaths are heavy and too loud. Footsteps patter outside the room and come to a stop outside my door. As it pushes inward I see the small black slippers of a house Pip.

And then his shiny, made-up face as he lowers.

"Nice try," he says in a high voice with a little *pip*. "If you think you're the first to have tried to go out the window, you'd be a fool."

"I was just admiring the view," I say.

"The last one to admire the view got a nice close look at the ground below," he says, snatching my hair and pulling me forward. He's surprisingly strong for how delicate he looks. "That's when we installed the alarms."

There's not much to say to that.

——————▶

I'M THROWN BACK INTO the room I woke up in. For a moment I just stare at the door, willing it to reopen, but it does not. There aren't any windows here. Just four walls adorned with strange rotating pictures of shapes: triangles and squares and circles. They make me dizzy. I wonder who thought this was art. Looks like a three-year-old drew them.

Frustrated, I turn, but my eyes stop on the bed.

A man is stretched out on the covers.

"Mr. Greer." The blood inside me has turned to ice.

He sits up fast, and I fall back into the door, surprised. He's not wearing his head wrapping today, and the red scars across his cheek are bold and angry. Most of the Virulent marks are fairly neat, but his is jagged, as if someone carved it with a sharp fork.

With a groan, he rubs his temples with his thumbs.

"What are you doing here?" I ask.

It takes him a while to answer.

"Checking on you. You were so . . . *boring* the last time we met."

I was drugged actually, but I don't correct him because it's clear he's still drunk. The whites of his eyes are bloodshot, and as he rises he stumbles and catches himself on the bedframe.

"You should go walk that off," I tell him.

"I can think of better things to do," he says.

There's evil in him. Dark, ugly, evil. It makes me shake down to my very boots. Carefully, I step to the side, and he follows. Mirroring me like we are dancing. Then he lunges, and I dodge out of the way.

"Still want to play a hiding game?" He grins and rolls up his sleeves.

We've almost traded places—him near the door, me near the bed. I search for something to defend myself with and grab a pillow.

"Spying on me, huh?" I say. My heart is galloping.

"The walls have ears." He steps closer, and I throw the pillow at him. He bats it out of the way.

"Then I'm sure it'll get back to the mayor that you're in here now," I say. "He got me for his son, you know."

I hate saying the words, but I'm willing to say almost anything if it keeps him back.

"His son," Greer spits. "His *son*. Do you know how many girl children the mayor has had destroyed? More than you can count, I'm sure."

The words bring a sick feeling to my belly. He stops moving finally and stares at the shapes changing on the wall, mesmerized. I edge past him back to the door, and even though I know it's still locked, I try the handle again. It doesn't move.

"He can't make a male," says Greer after a long pause. "He lacks the necessary *fortitude*."

"Looks like he managed somehow," I say, trying to keep him talking about something other than me.

"Of course," he says. "Of course he did. How else could little Amir have been created?"

The truth is plain as day in his face. In his black, beady eyes that match the boy's almost perfectly.

"There are treatments for that, I'm sure," I say, delaying.

"Oh surely," he agrees. My throat ties in knots. I think of the medical exam, the powerlessness I had on that table. It will not happen again.

He turns towards me. "There are treatments, but then word would get out of the mayor's little problem. The leader of our great city can't have such a fatal flaw, wouldn't you agree?"

He's getting close again. Too close.

"Does the boy know?" I ask.

Greer looks impressed—as if he's surprised I'm smart enough to have pieced the puzzle together.

He runs his finger down the jagged length of his scar. "A fine payment for services rendered, wouldn't you say?" The finger moves over his thin lips. "I wasn't supposed to tell. It slipped out."

"The walls have ears," I say, voice trembling.

"Yes," he says. "But not in the bedrooms. The mayor will have his privacy there." He spreads his arms. "Here."

My heart sinks.

"There's a legend about it, you know," he says. "About two powerful men sharing one woman. It nearly destroyed the Brotherhood."

"I've heard of it." My mind flashes to my ma's old stories of the Red Years.

"She tricked them," he says. "But she also reminded them of the truth: that a dog may eat a man's food and sleep in a man's bed, but that does not make it a man."

My jaw tightens. He laughs, and the sound sinks its claws straight into my bones.

"You know Amir's mother was wild as well. We captured

her from the Drylands. She was exotic. Wiry hair, skin like cinnamon. My brother kept her even after she conceived three girls. He just knew she'd give him a boy." His mouth quirks in a twisted smile. "And she did."

Greer's moving closer, stalking me like a predator. The door is firm against my back. I might be able to get by him again, but where would I go?

Blood pumping, I lower, fingers bared like claws. He smiles and loosens the silk tie around his neck.

Just then, the door handle turns, and Amir steps inside.

Greer straightens.

"What are you doing here?" Amir asks him. I've never been happier to have that kid around. He's calmer than the last time I saw him. His face is pasty white, but for an orange smear on his cheek. Looks like he's gotten a little treat for being such a pain.

"Just making sure your new pet has settled in," says Greer.

"Oh," says Amir. He turns to me. "She can't have any dinner."

"Why is that?" asks Greer, kneeling before his son. I wonder if the child knows who his real father is. Greer didn't really answer my question before.

"She was bad earlier. She needs to be punished."

I cross my arms over my chest.

"I see," says Greer. "Well you can play with her tomorrow. I'll be going on a hunting expedition."

"Where?" I ask, fear cooling my fight.

"Somewhere in the hills, I don't know. A scout said he found a nest of undocumented females living in the wild." He rises to meet my eyes. "You wouldn't know anything about that, would you?"

I shake my head, but the words have all dried up inside of me.

Nina. Salma. Tam. Are they safe? There are other families hiding in the mountains, but all I can think of is mine.

Nina, holding hands with the mayor.

Tam, made into a Pip.

I try to shove past them, but something sharp bites my waist. I jump back. The boy has a little silver box, and when he presses it to my skin, it shocks me.

"Bad girl!" he yells.

They slip out the door before I can charge through. And then it is locked again. And I am left alone.

I DON'T SLEEP. I pace until my heels ache and my skull can't hold any more bad thoughts.

Finally, there's a click in the door. The handle jiggles a little, and then the door opens and Amir is standing in the space, holding his nasty little metal shocker in one hand.

"Did you think about what you did?" he asks me.

I nod.

"Good," he says.

When I move towards him I see the house Pip standing in the hall. He's holding a silver tray and in the center, on a white lacy mat, are two meal pills.

"Put it on the ground," Amir tells him.

When he does, Amir points at it.

"Eat."

"I'm not a dog," I say. My throat is parched. It has been too long since I've had water. When he pours some in a little cup beside the pills, my tongue seems to grow thicker in my mouth.

"No talking," he says. "Bad girl!"

He jams the silver box into my belly and presses the button. It sends a bolt of lightning straight through my insides. My face screws up in pain. For moments after, I'm still twitching.

I want to take that box and smash it to pieces. Or maybe shock him with it, give him a little of what he's doling out, see how he likes it.

But I don't.

Memories of the Garden are pouring back over me. All I did was try to get out. I never played along and this is where I ended up. But all the girls who did—who followed the rules and did what the Governess said—they all got what they wanted. They got chosen.

I kneel. Something inside of me breaks, but I do it anyway. I bend over, grab the cup with my teeth and swing it back. Water streams from the corners of my mouth as I gulp it down greedily. I shove the meal pills in my mouth too. My stomach is gurgling now, and I can already feel the pills start to expand.

I don't know the person who is doing this. She is weak. Desperate.

"Good girl," he says, clapping his hands together. "Let's play a hiding game."

He makes it sound like it's his idea.

"You hide first. If I catch you, you're getting marked!" With that he runs away into the room next to mine and slams the door. The Pip remains in the hallway, a pointed stare on me.

I rise to my feet and step by him.

I walk slowly down the hall to the stairs, feeling the sensors in the ceiling above me adjust as I walk by. The Pip stays where I left him, still with that snooty look on his face.

Slowly, I descend the steps. One floor, then two, and another window appears on the stone wall. Trying to keep a cool head, I make my way towards it, careful not to touch the glass.

I'm still several floors up, but through the green-tinted glass I see a courtyard. A fountain sits in the middle of a garden, shooting streams of water into the air. Surrounding it all is a high stone fence.

Horses, led by men in day suits, move from a silver-roofed barn towards a sloped, twisty iron gate that opens as they approach. Drivers move amongst them—hunched, carrying the weight of this low, coal sky on their shoulders. They tend to their stock and hold them still while the Magnates climb up into their fancy saddles.

My heart races. Frantically I search for Kiran, straining my eyes, but none of them look familiar. The mayor probably has his own Driver staff. Why wouldn't he? He has everything else.

Despite this, the open gate renews the urgency within me, and before I can stop myself I'm padding down the stairs. I descend two levels, and then a third. Finally I reach a wide, open room, fancier than any I've ever been in, with green-glass walls. There are five Pips cleaning these, and two more dusting the cozy chairs scattered around the room. They all look up as I step into the room.

Somewhere above me, in the distance, I hear Amir's demanding yell: "*Where are you?*" It's like someone's pulling the tiny hairs on the back of my neck.

I'm on the ground level. Out the two sliding doors, directly across from the stairwell, are the horses, and the gates are already beginning to close behind them.

I spot Mr. Greer in the shadow of the barn, talking to the mayor, who is wearing a long gray suit jacket for the occasion. Something's not right between them; the mayor's posture is stiff and his arms are crossed over his chest. He throws his hands up and walks away, and after a moment of staring at his back, Greer turns away as well. He nearly runs into a Driver attempting to load a carriage with supplies, then stalks around the side of the house, his maroon scarf waving in the breeze until he is out of view.

My gaze returns to the carriage. From where I'm standing, it's hard to see what was in the box the Driver loaded in the back compartment, but that doesn't matter. What matters is that he's preparing to leave. He's made his way to the front and has begun adjusting the straps that attach the contraption to his horse.

Maybe he's following the hunters into the mountains with extra supplies. Maybe he's just going back to the city. I don't care. All I know is that there is room in that back compartment for me to hide and if I get there quick enough, I'm going with him.

I move for the door, but stop short as a few men in lavish embroidered coats enter the room through the sliding doors from outside. Magnates, like the hunter who captured me in the wild.

A Pip rushes to their assistance.

"Come with me," says one of the cleaners, grabbing my elbow. "You aren't supposed to be down here." His little mouth is drawn in a tight frown.

I am dragged from the entryway, away from the carriage, into a shiny silver kitchen manned by Pips who prepare food—real food. Savory-smelling meats and soups that make my stomach grumble. Distracted by their tasks, they barely glance up at me, much like the serving Pips from the preparation room upstairs. I feel panic swelling in my chest. I hadn't counted on this moment to escape, but now that it's passing, I can't help feeling as though I've let something crucial slip away.

The cleaning Pip backs me into a corner and tells me to stay out of the way. When he leaves, he shuts the door behind him. I want to scream. I tell myself to focus—Amir is still looking for me. I need to think, plan my next move.

On the far side of the kitchen is a sliver of gray light, and my panic turns to steel. There's a slider door on the other side of this room. It must open to the outside, behind the house.

All that stands between me and the outside are the Pips, who chop strange-looking vegetables and arrange decorative morsels on serving trays. There are at least ten weapons nearby. Knives. Forks. Even that steaming basin on the stove can be used to my advantage. If I can get my hands on something, I might be able to force my way through, but too much of a stir will surely bring more Pips, and maybe even one of those Watchers guarding the gate.

I step forward and my ears register a buzzing from above as the scanner eye on the ceiling shifts positions.

The Pips are still focused on their duties.

One deep breath in, and I start to walk. I keep my head down, but my eyes moving and my hands ready. I make it past the first Pip, who hardly gives me a sideways glance. Another two give me dirty looks, but don't stop what they're doing. Maybe they think I'm too stupid to try to escape. Another scanner buzzes as it points my direction. My heartbeat is thumping in my ears.

I tell myself to slow down, but I can't. I walk faster, and when a Pip makes a sudden turn away from his station, we collide. Small yellow pastries fly off of his tray across the floor, and in his anger, he throws the metal sheet at me.

I block my face, but before I can lower my arms, he's got me by the wrist and is dragging me outside.

"Stupid, stupid, *stupid*," he says, following up with the longest stream of *pips* I've ever heard. I trip over the threshold of the door, but catch myself before I fall. When I look up, I see gray sky and wish I'd decided to grab a weapon.

I don't need it. I can take one single Pip on my own. I have to.

He winds back to hit me in the face, but stops short. He's looking at something over my shoulder, and when I glance back I'm sure I'm going to see either the kid or a Watcher. But it's neither. It's a tall, thin man in a black velvet coat and a maroon scarf wrapped around his head.

He stops a little ways away and gives a curt nod to the Pip, who seems to take this as a dismissal and reenters the kitchen.

There are no scanners back here, no eyes watching me. We are blocked from the front of the building, between the perimeter wall and a trash incinerator. Alone.

The dread rises up and crashes over me.

"You didn't get to go?" I ask, unable to hide the tremor in my voice. He's changed since I saw him just moments ago; his coat must not have been suitable for the mayor's Magnate friends.

He stares at me. Just stares. His hands are rubbing down his chest—the drink must be starting to wear off. After a moment, one hand lifts to the side of his face as if he's going to take off the scarf, and though I've seen what lies beneath it, I'm petrified for him to do this.

Before he can speak, I lower and try to run past him.

Quick as a flash, one hand shoots forward and his strong fingers wrap around my forearm. He pulls me towards him.

I lock my knees. My feet slide over the walkway. I try to pry his hand open and see that his knuckles are smeared black with polish of some kind. His mayor brother must be pretty upset if Greer can't even find someone to shine his shoes.

Without thinking, I attack. My fist wheels around and knocks him in the jaw. One of his hands flies to his face while the other slides down around my wrist. I wriggle free and try to kick him, but he grabs my leg, yanks it, and I slam to my back on the ground.

I will not let him better me.

My legs are flailing and I'm trying to push him back, but he's on me now, pinning me down with his body weight.

"No!" But the word is no louder than a breath. I struggle, harder than I ever have, and he releases me suddenly. His hand has flown back to his face, to the wrap, which is beginning to sag. I must have hit him hard.

"Stop, *stop*!" he hisses. I freeze. This voice isn't low and graveled. It's sharp, and warped by an accent I've never heard.

This isn't Mr. Greer.

I swipe at the scarf and jerk it down. Suntanned skin, smeared with dirt across the jaw. Lips drawn tight. And here, up close, those eyes I would recognize anywhere.

"Kiran?"

He scoops me up to standing in one swift motion.

"Come on, Aiyana," he says. "We've got to go."

CHAPTER 14

"You can *talk*?" I say.

Without thinking, my hands clasp his face and pull his jaw back open, as though this will somehow make him speak again. His skin is dirty, but the space around his eyes that shows through the scarf has been recently scrubbed. He forces his mouth shut and winces.

"I didn't make it up, I know I didn't," I tell him. "Say something."

"We don't have time for this." His hurried words are warped by a strange accent so different from my own. They seem stretched, pulled. My smile must be a mile wide.

And then it vanishes, like ashes in the wind.

"Oh no." I swallow, but the lump won't go down my throat. All the things I've told Kiran fill my mind. The secrets, the stories about my life. I've laid it all out for him to listen to in the way I listen to Brax whimper: knowing what he feels, but not what he says.

"Why didn't you tell me?" I ask weakly.

"I couldn't." He glances to the side.

I want him to say more, but this isn't the place.

"Your voice is all wrong," I whisper. It isn't at all like I heard it in my head.

"Sorry to disappoint." He snorts, and I quiet him with my fingers over his lips.

They're soft and warm, and I draw back immediately because I didn't mean to touch him just then.

"I saw a carriage in front of the barn," I whisper. "You can hide me inside."

His brows raise as if he's impressed, but then he shakes his head. I take this to mean he has a better plan.

He's here. I can hardly believe it. Here, at the mayor's huge house, surrounded by men who could have him hanged for impersonating one of them. I think back to how he tried to help me at auction, too. Nobody's ever done anything like this for me.

I can feel the heat creeping up my neck, and suddenly I'm thinking about the way I acted the last time we were together. I take a step back so I can breathe, and look up the side of the house for any outside scanners. I don't see any, but know we should keep quiet all the same.

"*Where are you?*" calls a voice in the distance. Amir is outside.

"We have to go," I say. "Now."

My fright reflects in his eyes. He adjusts the wrap over his face—now that he's standing before me it's obvious he's taller than Greer. I hadn't thought to look too closely once I saw the wrap on his face.

We creep along the side of the house, keeping to the language we both know well: points and nods and the little gestures that we've learned over the last month. With my heart in my throat, I let Kiran take me by the arm and lead me straight around the corner into the open courtyard before the barn. The house Pips that scurry around outside pretend they're not watching, but they are, I can feel their eyes upon me. I look for Amir, but he must have gone back inside because I don't see him. I keep walking, one step at a time, out of the shadows of the house and into the dim sunlight.

Kiran's moving so fast that I'm struggling to keep up. It's cooler here than behind the kitchen and the air smells different, like the cleaning products they use at the Garden. The grass smashes beneath my boots, too soft to be real, more like hair than the real thing. I step on the hem of my dress and would go sprawling if not for Kiran's firm grip pulling me back to a stand.

The other Magnates have all gone now, along with the carriage I'd planned on sneaking out in. The iron gates are closed, and two Watchers are activating some kind of security system that buzzes to life, then makes the air shimmer just beyond the property's threshold.

We head to the barn, and my eyes are drawn to the support beams, where horses, rearing up and pawing the air, are carved into the wood. The sweet, musty scent of hay greets us. Soon we cross under the threshold, and I immediately scan for sensors on the ceiling.

My pulse is racing. We are just a gate away from the city.

Inside one of the stalls is the chestnut mare I recognize from the Driver barn. She snorts and paws the ground as Kiran approaches, as if she's been waiting for him to return. He slides the door open and we duck inside, and the way she greets him, nuzzling his neck with her soft nose, makes me miss Brax terribly.

"How'd you get in?" I say quietly, standing clear of the mare's front hooves.

He points behind him, down through the breezeway, but then seems to remember he can talk.

"There's a separate entrance for the animals." He clears his throat. "The mayor had extra stock brought in for today's hunt."

I stare at his mouth as he talks. It's still so strange to me. The questions are building, one atop the next—Do all Drivers talk? Why hide it? Why didn't Kiran tell me earlier?—but we don't have time. Mention of the hunt has me ready to run.

"Can we get out that way?"

"I can," he says in a way that makes me realize that I can't.

He's already adjusting the wrap back on his face. He nods in the direction of the front gates.

"How?" I ask, remembering the Watcher guards.

He points to the scarf wrapped around his face. It's drooping on one side so I reach forward to help him. The back of my hand skims over his, and he pulls away. I guess it's too much to think that he's forgotten what happened in the solitary yard.

When the scarf is fixed, I step back. "The mayor's brother—have you seen him?"

He gives a small cough. His voice is a little rough when he answers. "Drunk," he says. "He's laid out by the delivery gates."

I remembered the argument outside with the mayor. Bet that didn't make a good impression with his fancy friends.

"Wait," I say. "You stole his clothes?"

Kiran shakes his head. "I brought 'em."

He planned this. He came here for me.

"Aiyana," he says, and I grow even warmer. It's been so long since someone said my true name. "You can't tell."

"About the talking. I know," I say. But I don't really know. I don't understand any of it, though I want to. I expect a full explanation as soon as we get out of here.

Soon the chestnut mare is saddled, and Kiran is pulling me up behind him. I sit sideways on account of the dress, and hold on tight around his waist so I don't go spilling over the other side.

He's all muscle. Long, lean muscle. I can tell even through this suit he's managed to find. He sits rigid, and I do too, careful not to press my chest against his back. But it doesn't matter. It's as if Kiran is his own shock box, just like the one Amir has, only this one doesn't hurt, it just makes me tingle straight through.

"What will you say?" I ask.

He shakes his head. I feel his heart thumping in his chest and know he's afraid. If the Watchers catch us, we're as good as dead.

He makes a clicking sound, and the mare steps forward into the light. He's left the carriage of supplies back against the side of the breezeway. I stare at our shadow, feeling the movement of the horse's hindquarters beneath my legs.

As we approach the gate, I pinch my eyes shut.

"Sir," says one of the Watchers. "I thought you were staying in today."

Kiran says nothing. My fists, filled with his shirt, are trembling. He stares at the Watcher, stares like he's a Magnate. Like nothing in the world scares him. But I know better.

After a moment the gate makes a quick clicking sound, then slides open.

We ride straight into the heart of the business district, leaving those Watchers behind to pay the price of my escape.

THE MAYOR'S HOUSE SITS at the end of a street, between two buildings made of green glass and brick. People live in these monstrous homes. I wonder if they have their own staff too, and a roomful of girls to choose from.

I keep looking back. Maybe it's real, maybe it's my imagination, but I can still hear Amir's voice calling, "*Where are you?*"

"Faster," I say. I see the twins kneeling beside the brook, running across the meadow, leaping into my arms. I can *feel* them.

Kiran makes no move to hurry.

We ride out of the residential area onto the main street, where men on horseback or in carriages pass by. The tall glass buildings on either side stretch straight into the clouds, smooth and cold and breathtaking.

Kiran veers down a small road between the buildings. We're the only ones around now. Finally, I exhale. I'm shaking a little, and all of a sudden feel a giggle swell inside of me.

"If I'd have known it was that easy to get out, I would have made sure I was sold months ago," I say, feeling giddy enough to jump off the horse and dance right here in the street.

"Easy?" he says so quietly I have to cock my head to hear. "You're funny."

"*Yoa,*" I mimic.

"Keep it up and I'll take you back."

I freeze. He's joking. At least I think he is.

"Don't," I tell him.

We come to a small alley where a plain, single-rider carriage waits. It's made of cherrywood and flaking on the side. Obviously a rental. Kiran offers his arm, and I swing down. He doesn't need to speak the words to tell me he's planned this, too. I shimmy between the side of the building and the carriage and slide inside. Through the punched-out window I watch as Kiran shucks the scarf hiding his face and tosses it under the wheels. He takes off the coat, revealing the dirty button-down shirt beneath, and stuffs it in beside me. Then he kneels, dips his hands in a puddle, and smears his cheeks with filth water—yellow and shiny with greasy spots. It stinks like waste.

I hear footsteps nearby, and Kiran freezes. I bite my tongue, holding back the urge to tell him to hide. It's too late.

Two men in suits approach. Kiran keeps his head lowered and wipes his hands on his pants. They don't look at him; they look everywhere but at him, and they keep to the far end of the alley as they pass.

He stands suddenly, not fully upright, and one of them gives a scared little shout. Kiran tilts his head towards the mare, as if to offer his Driver services, but they hurry on without a backward glance.

I should be happy they're gone, but instead I'm angry. They didn't even look at him.

He stays low and slips beside the carriage, hooking it up to the mare.

"Kiran," I say. He twitches, but continues to work, fastening leather straps, setting the long wooden carriage arms into the saddle's hooks.

"Kiran," I say again. "Thank you."

He stops, just for a moment, and gives a small nod.

Then he mounts the horse, and we pull out of the alley. I sit back in the seat, as far back as I will fit, keeping clear of the window. Every once in a while I catch a glimpse of Kiran, his head lowered, his back hunched. He looks like an old man.

I'm ready for the fresh air, the mountains, my family—so I'm surprised when we pull under a shaded overpass and back into a small space that smells like hay and manure.

I poke my head out of the window. We're in another barn, this one rickety and packed with gear: walls of blankets, gleaming saddles on racks, barrels of water. Down the aisle, the dirt floor has been raked clean and the metal stall doors shine in the afternoon light coming through the entrance, but where I am is more like a scrap heap.

Kiran unhooks the mare and without removing her tack, ties her lead to the outside of a stall. He returns, bright eyes shining through his mask of muck, and nods upward.

I slip through the door, quiet as I can, and climb the ladder against the wall to the loft over the stalls. The ceiling is low here; I have to crouch to move away from the ledge. Near a small open window is a bedroll. Plain, canvas, with a red horse blanket folded at the bottom. At the head is a jug of water and a tin box.

Kiran crawls up behind me and opens the box. Inside is jerky—real jerky—and flatbread crackers. My mouth waters and my stomach grumbles.

It's quiet but for the movement of the horses—no one else is here—but that doesn't stop Kiran from moving so close, our knees touch on the blanket. He leans in, and I'm watching his lips as he says, "Stay here. We'll leave after dark."

"*Dock,*" I repeat with a nod.

He smirks and shakes his head, but before he turns away I grab his arm.

"Why didn't you tell me?" I ask.

His jaw is working under the skin as if he's chewing the words to a pulp before he says them.

"It keeps them safe," he says finally. "Our girls." Only when he says *girls,* it sounds more like *gells.*

Then he disappears down the ladder.

I've never seen a Driver woman, but I know they must be out there. As far as I know, no one in the city wants them because they assume the women are just as strange as the men who come to rent the horses. I guess they've done a good job making themselves unauctionable. I wish I'd thought of that a long time ago. I'd have rolled my whole family through the mud every morning at dawn.

I'm anxious to go now, but Kiran knows the city better than I do. If he says we need to wait, I'll do it. He's been right so far. Tam and Nina will be safe.

Please let them be safe.

I rip off a piece of jerky and stick it in my mouth. It's boar. I can tell from the rough texture and the smoky taste. Soon I'll be having a lot more of this, I tell myself. I crawl closer to the window, careful not to let myself be seen, and look out.

Below, just beyond the stables, is the poisoned stream, and just past that, the solitary yard.

I almost choke.

I should have figured Kiran had brought us back here, but I was too busy preparing for the outside. It makes the meat a little less tasty, looking at the facility that kept me prisoner all this time.

I glance down at Kiran's bedroll, and then across the space. He could see me the whole time. He might have laid right here and watched me sleep. The thought makes my throat dry, and I reach for the water jug below the window.

The night is hazier than usual on account of the thick smoke in the air from last night's celebrations in the Black Lanes. Someone moves against the back wall of the office—my place during my time there. My heart leaps—I hope for a moment it's Brax, but Brax doesn't have orange hair.

Daphne.

She's sitting in my spot, and as I shift to get a better view I can see that she's digging. She's pulling up my bottle of supplies. I know I don't need them anymore, but that doesn't mean I want *her* to have them.

Her hair is swishing; she keeps looking up and checking the corner, waiting for the Watcher. It's like viewing myself in a way—how many times did I do the same thing? A piece of silver glints in the failing light, and I know she's found Kiran's broken knife handle. She has no idea what to do with it, and even if she did, she's not crazy enough to attack a Watcher. She's helpless, and as I stare down at her something begins to boil inside of me. Soon my hands are gripping the window ledge so hard they're turning white. I feel the panic she must feel now. I feel it as if I'm the one trapped down there behind that invisible wall. I feel her helplessness and it disgusts me.

The Garden trapped me like an animal. The Governess sold me like livestock at an auction. And the mayor and his family would have made me their whore.

I am shaking with rage.

Daphne's all hunched over herself, and I squint to see what she's doing. It doesn't take long to figure it out: She's trying to break the chain off her solitary restraint.

It doesn't make sense. Daphne wants to get back in the Garden, she wants to be sold. Surely she knows a stunt like that is going to earn her more time out here. But that doesn't stop her; her moves become more frantic, and soon I see the reason for her rush.

The Watcher rounds the corner of the building.

He's so big he makes her look like a mouse. In the failing light, he doesn't even look human—so much muscle there's hardly any neck, bald head gleaming. The silver wire and key to her bracelet stand out on his black jacket.

Daphne doesn't stop trying to break the chain. In fact, she's going at it harder now. I'm sweating just watching her.

Stop, I think at her. I want to scream it. Solitary's messed up her head, that's the only explanation. The Watcher is going to give her the beating of a lifetime, and she's doing nothing to defend herself.

Suddenly, I'm thinking of Straw Hair, running towards the fence. I'm yelling at Daphne to stop her, but she and her friends do nothing, as if they're rooted to the ground. Again, that heavy, helpless feeling comes over me, like a wet blanket on my shoulders. I want to stop Daphne like I wanted to stop Straw Hair, but I can't. If I leave here, I risk everything. My life. Kiran's life. My freedom.

I blink, and when I open my eyes the Watcher has Daphne by the forearm. He lifts her with one arm, and her feet fly out from beneath her. Then he throws her down and kicks her. It's not as hard as he can, but hard enough that her cry is cut short.

The water jug spills across Kiran's bedroll, breaking my trance. My fingers ache from squeezing it so hard. I can't even right it. My eyes are stuck on the scene before me, and I'm sick with anger.

A dog may eat a man's food, and sleep in a man's bed, but that does not make it a man.

The Watcher kicks Daphne twice more. He doesn't have to, she's already down. She's not even moving.

"Stop." A strained whisper comes from my lips.

I've known Daphne as long as I've been in the city. She's not one to be daring, unless it involves drawing the street crowd with her kissing act. Most of the time she keeps to someone else's shadow. So I'm shocked when she snags the knife handle out of the dirt and jams it straight into the Watcher's foot.

At that moment, half of me is cheering. The other half is horrified.

Very slowly, the Watcher removes the metal from his boot, balancing easily on one foot. When it's clear, he grabs the slack in Daphne's chain and gives it a hard yank. The handle is in his hand, and I know that means the broken shard of metal is sticking out of his fist.

Daphne screams.

I'm halfway down the ladder before my head catches up. I can't cross the stream. I can't be seen. I'm nearly free—out of the Garden, out of the mayor's house. Helping Daphne is as good as soaking myself in water and running for the electric fence.

I don't even like her. Not really.

She's only a half friend.

Her scream stops short.

I jump the last three rungs down, and now my feet are on the barn floor and I'm running for the back exit I know is just below the loft. Kiran is racing towards me from the opposite side, but I reach the turn first, and streak out the back door. My white dress, now smeared with dirt and speckled with horsehair, catches on the paddock fence and rips from the thigh down.

At the edge of the stream I see them: The Watcher is facing away from me, and Daphne is shoved up against the office wall. In his raised hand shines the broken knife.

I slide down the gravel bank and leap across the stream, landing with a splash just short of the other bank. Blue water dyes the body of my dress and makes the fabric stick to my skin. I rise just as the Watcher is turning, his giant hand still holding Daphne's shoulder.

I have no weapons. I have only my fists.

What have I done?

I should run, but the Watcher is reaching for the belt across his chest. I hold my breath, fearing the wire, but instead he removes his messagebox. I know he means to send an alarm to the Garden, maybe even to the other Watchers, and I can't allow that to happen. I need more time. Time to get to the gates.

I charge him. He can't hold both of us so he throws Daphne down, opening both his arms towards me. My diversion has worked; he can't finish the code before I collide into his brick-wall body.

I go for the lower gut. Watchers have muscles like steel, but they're still slightly softer below the reinforced bones of their rib cage. I aim for that spot and pummel it with my fists until he heaves me clear off the ground.

I think he's going to toss me against the wall, so I splay my limbs out in all different directions in order to make myself as difficult to throw as possible. The world tilts, I'm upside down. I kick hard, and my knee slams into his face. His nose breaks with a *crack*.

In the background I hear a faint gasping and realize Daphne's been freed. My plan was to help her, but now all I want is to get away.

"The key!" I say. "Get it!"

Daphne swipes down his chest and rips the entire belt free. She scrambles across the ground at his feet, but I can't see if she gets the key to her bracelet because the Watcher is once again reaching for my throat.

He doesn't get me. I thrash hard, and he ends up rolling me into his side, my legs behind me, my upper body beneath his arm, the way he would carry a bundle of sticks. He's pinned my arms against my sides, and though I struggle, I can't break free. There's a *thunk* and the Watcher goes suddenly still. A rock falls into my path of vision and hits the ground.

I jerk my head back and see Kiran. He's standing on our side of the stream, arms braced before him, fists ready. His shirt is damp from the water, plastered to his his chest. In the moon-light he looks like a wildcat, muscles lean and taut, body ready to pounce.

The Watcher's hold on me loosens, and I can work my hand free and hit him again, anywhere I can. He's bleeding from where Kiran's rock smacked him in the eye; a drop splashes onto my face.

Kiran throws himself at us. He must have figured the best plan was mine; take him by surprise, hit fast and hard. There's not much use going for the face. If Kiran leaves his body exposed and the Watcher hits him, he'll end up broken in half.

In one move, the Watcher shoves Kiran back and drops me. I hit the ground flat on my back. The air is knocked out of my chest, and though my mouth gapes, I can't swallow a breath. Stars burst before my vision. Finally the air comes through.

All my thoughts turn to Kiran.

I flip over just in time to see him. He's tall, but still a head below the Watcher. There's a moment when they square off, staring at each other, and then the worst happens.

In a flash, the Watcher grabs his wire, and snaps his wrist towards Kiran. The metal extends through the air like a striking snake. Kiran's fast, but not fast enough. He dodges to the side, and the metal snake latches below his arm, smacking against his ribs.

There is no time. Soon, the wire will coil around Kiran's body. It will freeze at first, then heat gradually, until it burns and tears through his flesh, his ribs, into his organs. I crawl towards the only thing I think can help. The broken knife handle.

And then I'm up, running back towards the Watcher. With a heave, I leap onto his back and gouge the knife down hard.

It connects. I hear the tear of flesh, made callused by skin treatments, and then the broken blade slides into something soft. I fight back the nausea scratching its way up my throat. This is different from killing an animal. Different even than killing a man, I imagine. I'm trying to kill a monster.

I fall off and stagger back. He falls on me, grasping my throat. The handle is sticking out of his neck at an angle. Blood is spraying out in the pulse of his life force. His thick hand squeezes my neck, and I can feel my windpipe close and bruise. The breath to my brain is cut off. I begin to panic and flail.

Out of the darkness springs a silver beast. With a ferocious snarl, the animal latches onto the Watcher's calf, tearing through his skin in one bite. He whips his head from side to side, trying to rip the flesh from the Watcher's leg.

I am released. I suck in a hard, ragged breath, and peel the handle of the wire out of the Watcher's grip. Struggling, I press a red button, praying that this is the release. It works. The wire retracts from Kiran's body in a whir of metal and blood.

Kiran falls to his knees. The wound is not fatal, but it's deep enough to have begun to eat through his skin. The wire never made it around his core; it locked, like a hook, only around one side of his rib cage. I don't see bone, and for that I'm thankful, but the blood has stained his shirt and is draining in long lines down into the gravel below.

The Watcher is swiping at Brax, but the wolf is edging him back towards the office. Pride flushes through me. Brax has just saved our lives.

Frantically, I search for Daphne, but she's missing. She must have run around the other side of the office. At least she's free; the chain with the metal bracelet is strewn across the dirt.

I try my best to haul Kiran to his feet, and though he's dazed at first, his eyes clear a little as he stands. His jaw is working beneath the skin. I know it's taking everything he has to stay silent.

He staggers into the poisoned stream. I hesitate, glancing back, but Kiran grabs my hand and we slosh through together. It doesn't register immediately that I am afraid, but that's what it is. I'm scared. More scared than I have ever been.

Brax cries—a short, high whine. From behind me comes a *thunk,* like a tree falling to the ground.

"Brax!" I shout.

The Watcher is on his knees crawling after us, the wound in

his neck leaking crimson in a slow drip. One eye is round and crazed, a black circle in a sea of white. The other is mashed to bruises by Kiran's well-aimed rock. Behind him, Brax shakes and slowly rises from the ground.

The Watcher makes it to the stream. Kiran and I pause on the opposite shore and watch him with bated breath.

A groan gargles out from the giant's throat. And then he falls face first in the water and lies still.

CHAPTER 15

I'M RIGHT ON KIRAN'S heels as we charge past the white-fenced paddocks into the barn. The horses within lower their heads and stomp their shod hooves. Only when we stop do my knees threaten to collapse. I grasp a stall door before they give out completely, and open my eyes wide to hold back the hot tears threatening to break free.

"We have to go," I say weakly. "Now. We have to go now."

He must be hurting, but you couldn't tell by the look on his face. It's completely bland, untelling, but his eyes are dark, like a shadow passing over the sun. He unlatches a stall door and disappears within.

The clomping and nervous whinnies from the horses are like screams to my ears. My head jolts towards each noise and soon I've spun in a circle, overloaded by my senses.

From outside comes the patter of footsteps, and I duck down, bracing myself to fight once again. Kiran springs back to my side.

Daphne rounds the corner of the hallway into the barn. Her orange hair is a mess of dirt and grass, matted on one side with blood, and her chest is heaving. She's been crying too; her pale face glimmers like the moon.

She looks from me to Kiran and back to me. Her arms cross over her waist. She's holding the plastic bottle in one hand—my supplies. I snatch it from her, and it crinkles in my hard grip.

"You're running?" she asks, like she's confused. "With a *Driver?*"

"Get out of here," I growl. I helped get her free, now she's on her own. The farther away from me the better.

"If you leave, I'll be blamed for what you . . . and that animal did."

She's talking about Brax, but she's staring straight at Kiran as she says this. He glances my way. She's obviously figured out there's something different about him, but she doesn't know the half of it.

"I don't know why I helped you," I mutter. "I don't know what I was thinking."

Kiran gives a little snort, which doesn't help.

"A dead Watcher," she says, almost to herself. "No one's going to buy me now. They'll think I did it, you understand? They'll look for me. I won't even be able to hide in the Black Lanes."

Kiran points to a saddle blanket and I hand it to him.

"Take me with you," Daphne says.

Now I'm the one who snorts.

"Please," she says, stepping closer. When Kiran moves, she jerks to the side and breathes in sharply.

"Please," she begs now. "I can't stay here. I'll be hanged." She grabs my sleeve, but I shake her off. Big tears are rolling down her cheeks.

Kiran is throwing a saddle on the chestnut mare. This one isn't shiny like the others; the leather is dull and well worn.

"You should have thought of that before you stuck your guard." I want to throttle her. If she hadn't started that fight, I never would have gone outside. I never would have stepped in. That Watcher would still be alive and I'd be free right now.

Maybe Daphne had it right letting Straw Hair go to fry like that. Right now I wish I'd just left my half friend to defend her own self.

I toss Kiran the plastic bottle to stuff in his saddle bag and when I turn back, Daphne's practically crawling all over me.

"They would have marked me," she whispers, clawing the front of my tattered dress. "I can't be sold. I won't pass."

I shake her off.

"What are you talking about?"

Her hands pull down her face. "Last auction I was almost sold." She closes her eyes tight. "Almost. He chose Iris instead. After we met."

She doesn't need to say anymore. She broke the purity rule. And judging by the tortured look on her face, it wasn't by choice.

I push past her as Kiran leads the mare out of the stall, and she crumbles into the side of the barn. She's bawling with full force now, holding her arms before her like a child begging to be picked up.

"Clover, you can't leave me."

"Go," I tell her, one last time. I turn back to Kiran, who's watching Daphne's display with his brows knit together.

Then I look lower and see the dripping band of blood from the wire that was hooked around his left side. It looks like oil in the dim light. Thick black oil.

"Your side." I rush to him, and he looks down, as though noticing it for the first time. When he lifts his arm, his face warps into a cringe. The shirt is stuck to his skin. He peels it away slowly. The wound is so deep I can feel it in my own side, as if I'm the one that's been hit.

I skirt around him into the storeroom just past the stall. There are three saddle racks, one atop the other on the side wall; five or six large containers filled with grain and pellets of some kind; and a floor-to-ceiling shelving unit directly to my right. There I find bandages for the horses; I grab one and hurriedly unwind a long piece of four-inch-wide felt.

"I'll bind you up for now, but it won't hold for long."

Kiran shrugs away from me as I make for his chest with the wrap. He's grabbing a Driver jacket off the peg on the wall and preparing to pull it on over one arm.

"You're going to bleed through," I tell him.

Kiran slows and then, sighing painfully, lifts his arms so that I can wrap the bandage around his body. When we're on the outside, I'll make a poultice to pack the wound, though I know something as deep as this is better suited for city doctors and their stitching kits.

"You're talking to the Driver," Daphne says, as if I didn't know. I ignore her.

"Ignore her," I tell Kiran. "She's not coming with us."

"You haven't been listening!" she cries. "They're going to hold me responsible! I have to get out of the city!"

"She's right."

My fingers freeze. "*Kiran,*" I say between clenched teeth.

Daphne stumbles back so hard she hits the wall.

"He can speak!"

"What a surprise," I say, trying not to pay attention to the fact that it took him weeks to talk to me, but only minutes to speak in front of Daphne. I finish bandaging him a little more tightly than I probably should, and bind it with the tie attached to the end.

Kiran shrugs painfully into his long, dusty coat and stuffs something from the pocket into my hands. When I look down, I see a wadded bunch of fabric. Something pale yellow and lacy.

I swear my whole body goes red.

"It's a dress," he says. "I've only got one."

I take it and shake out the outfit. Even though I'm not yet in it, I can tell that it's going to be snug.

"Did you get it in the Black Lanes?" I frown, thinking of the brothels we passed on the way to the auction stage and not sure I want to know how Kiran got this.

He nods.

"What am I supposed to wear?" Daphne asks.

Before Daphne can steal it from me, I strip off what's left of the white Promised dress and shove the yellow one over my head. It's dirty and wearing thin in places, and so short it barely covers my hips. Strips of lace cover my shoulders, which are otherwise bare. There's no mistaking me for a Garden girl now; I look like one of Mercer's girls who work in the Black Lanes. Kiran glances at me, then quickly looks down. His fingers fumble as he pulls a flat black square the size of his fist from the saddle bag.

"Costume makeup," he says.

"Hurry," I say, remembering the way the city folks dress up like Virulent on auction days.

Daphne's still going on and on behind us.

"If you leave me, I'll tell everyone what you did," she says. "You ran away from the mayor, didn't you? I'm sure they'll be looking."

I've had enough of Daphne's sniveling and scheming. I lunge at her, ready to strike, but before I can bring my arm forward, something catches my hand.

"Easy," says Kiran, releasing me when I turn to glower at him. "How are we going to get your friend through?"

"We're not friends," I tell him.

"We are too," says Daphne quickly. "Clover, don't lie." She's just saying it so I won't leave her.

"I really am going to hang tonight," Kiran mutters dryly. He pulls me close to his face. "Accept it. Plans have changed. Move on."

I feel my fists bunch at my sides. He's right. We have to take Daphne because if I believe nothing else she says, I know she's truthful about turning us in. I need to keep a close eye on her wagging jaw. I look down at the ground to pull myself together, and groan when I see nearly to my navel through my four-star cleavage.

"Let me wear your dress," Daphne tries.

"It won't fit you," I tell her. She's bigger than me—taller, and curvier. As it is, I can barely twist without popping the seams.

With a short whine, she runs to the supply room, giving Kiran and the mare a lot of room as she passes. When she comes out, she's got a horse blanket over her shoulders. I'm not sure what she plans on doing with that.

Kiran twists the makeup box, and it opens with a pop. He pulls a red marker the size of my pinky from it and gives it a squeeze. Thick ooze drips out to the ground. With one hand firmly on my chin, he begins to trace an X shape across my right cheek. The thick clumping of the makeup covers my skin. It's meant to look like flesh. It certainly feels heavy enough.

I close my eyes and summon every amount of strength I have within me. It comes from the ground, right up through my feet, my legs, my body. I breathe deep and think of my ma. How strong she was to leave this city. How she went right through the gates, and the keepers let her go because she was marked. I was already in her belly then, so really, it's my second time through.

Kiran finishes the X on my cheek and nods grimly.

"I guess that will have to do," he says, and I wish for the first time that I had a mirror to see how I look. I hope the gatekeeper doesn't examine me too closely.

"Me next?" Daphne asks, dropping the blanket.

There's no way around it, she's coming with us.

"If they ask, we'll tell them you're plagued," I say. I nod to Kiran. "Quick. Mark her. Just like you did me."

He moves towards her, but she shies away.

"Clover, you do it," she whispers.

"Shh," he hushes gently. As though she's a spooked horse and not a leech. Slowly, he moves towards her, hands raised. When he's close enough, he reaches to hold her chin in his hand, and my blood turns fire hot.

"I can do it," I tell him, reaching for the marker.

He doesn't give it to me. Daphne's fallen under a spell—she's perfectly still. Not even her tears fall. But she doesn't look at him. She stares at me until he's finished the job and backed away. Then her hand rises to feel her cheek, just below the makeup, where Kiran touched. She's probably trying to see if his skin burned her or something.

"All done." Kiran adjusts the bandage around his waist; the blood has already begun to soak through. I gently press my fingers into the wet fabric and smear a little red below Daphne's eyes.

"Disgusting," she whispers.

"Because it's blood or because it's mine?" Kiran asks without looking up. I feel myself smirk. Daphne's cheeks blossom pink.

"Let's go." No one has followed yet. No more Watchers. No Pips either. Through the nearest stall I can make out the Watcher, still lying motionless, halfway in the stream, and a shudder rakes through me.

Kiran glances down the breezeway, chewing the corner of his lower lip.

"What is it?" I ask.

He shakes his head. "Aran will come tomorrow morning to get his horses for the village. He'll see I'm gone then and tend to the others." I get the distinct impression from the guilt in his voice that he's reassuring himself, not me.

"Will you be in much trouble?" I whisper, picturing Ferret Face with his greasy hair.

Kiran places the silver bit of a dark-leather bridle into the mare's chomping mouth and clicks softly to urge her forward. She begins sniffing my hands and my hair, shoving her giant nose into my chest, and I coo despite myself.

"Yes," says Kiran.

"We could go for it on our own," I offer.

"You can't ride," he says. "You'll fall off."

I remember the story I told him about trying to ride Silent Lorcan's horse while he was out with my ma. I ended up on my back with a broken arm. It's strange hearing him mention it as though we hadn't been having a one-sided conversation at the time.

"I can ride," says Daphne. "My father rented horses sometimes."

"That's all nice," says Kiran. "But Dell's my girl, and she's not going anywhere without me." He places a flat hand beneath the mare's forelock, and she dips her large head and nibbles on his shirt.

"Up you two go." Kiran backs to the side of the horse.

Daphne pushes herself in front of me. She grabs the saddle horn in one hand and bends her knee. Kiran pauses, then with a small snort bends, and lifts her up over the mare's back with a wince.

"I'm not that heavy," she says, injured. "My body scores always come in above an eight on Auction Day."

"He's hurt, you idiot," I snap.

I grab the back of the saddle and try to hike my foot high enough to reach into the stirrup, but the dress starts to rip at the seams, and I fall backwards into Kiran. He catches me with another grunt, and I feel a pang of regret for having accidently elbowed him right in the ribs.

I'm just about to reach for a bucket when he grabs me around the waist and hikes me up onto the back of the animal. If it weren't for the sharp twinge in his eye, I would never know he's in pain. He's used to keeping his lips sealed.

The dress slides up my thighs, stretching across my skin. I tug the lace down as far as it will go, which isn't far.

I hold onto the back of the saddle, remembering how much more secure I felt with my arms wrapped around Kiran's waist.

He pulls the side rein and leads us out of the barn.

THE NIGHT IS THICK with smog and cold enough that the breath clouds in front of my face and my bare legs and arms get bumpy. I wish I had a coat or, even better, pants to cover my skin. I hate being so exposed, especially now, when I already feel like everyone's eyes are on me.

I'm sitting behind the saddle, directly on a thick wool pad separating me from the horse's rump. I grasp the back lip of the leather until my fingers hurt, but I'm so unaccustomed to the strange cadence of Dell's gait that I nearly slide off at every step. I make a conscious effort not to squeeze my legs too tightly; Kiran says that can make her go faster, and if we get away from him, it's just me and Daphne.

I've never seen the front of the barn before; it's out of view from the solitary yard. The face is made of plain, weather-stained white boards, and it has two triangular rooftops. There's a swinging sign outside, held onto its outstretched arm by rusty chains. It shows a picture of a horse. Nothing showy. No words.

The stone path is narrow enough for only one car or carriage and reaches out into the main bricked street, where an alley cutting between two business offices connects us to the city gates. We're not far from the high stone wall surrounding the capitol. I can see it looming in the foreground, gray and ominous. The last barrier to my freedom.

"The wall was meant to exile women from Glasscaster," says Daphne quietly. "Now it separates the men from the beasts."

"One of those beasts is going to be you, you know," I say.

She fidgets, her posture perfect. "They built it during the Red Years. After they rounded up all the women and sent them away. They fought back, did you know that? That's when the Magistrate started making Watchers. No one could stand against the Watchers."

I didn't know that. "You sure got a lot to say."

"I'm nervous," she says.

"Well keep it down."

She leans back. "How come that Driver can talk?"

I look down at Kiran. He's walking stiffly, leading Dell as if she's always so calm and trusting, not wild like he made her act behind the auction block.

"He's a man, Daphne. That's how come."

"How do you know you can trust him?"

"Because I know."

Something rustles behind us. The sound sticks out from the thump of the Black Lanes in the distance, Dell's shod feet on the bricks, and Daphne's chatter.

Kiran's heard it too, and he slips his hand into his Driver coat around his back. I catch the glimpse of something metallic. Something he's added since we left the Garden.

His eyes meet mine for a moment, then he glances over to the saddle.

"What's wrong?" says Daphne, her voice hitching.

I hush her and slide my hand beneath the back lip of the saddle, where Kiran directed me. It's a tight press, but there, right between the wool blanket and the leather seat, is a firm, narrow strip of rawhide. I pry it loose, careful not to throw my weight too much and slide to the ground.

My hand emerges with a narrow sheath, and within it, a thin, iron dagger, no longer than my hand. I hide it beneath the bunching yellow lace around my waist.

The noise continues. Rustle, then pause. Rustle, pause.

Acting like I'm straightening my skirt, I glance back, and sure enough there's something lurking in the shadows—crouched low, following us. My pulse races, and I strain my eyes. The figure steps into the light. And he doesn't stand, because he can't.

"Brax!" I cry, louder than I mean to. I push off the back of Dell, and hear another seam pop in the side of my dress.

Brax races towards me, whining high like I've never heard him do before. He must know I'm leaving for good this time.

I bury my face in his soft neck, and he paws closer into me, punishing me for leaving, begging me not to go.

"Thank you," I tell him, an ache in my chest. "I won't ever forget what you did."

"Kill it!" I hear Daphne order Kiran. "It's biting her!"

I stand up sharply. "Shut up!"

Kiran motions me towards the wall, but there's pity in his eyes. We have to go.

I give my friend one more hug. One last hug.

"Brax, you have to go home," I say.

Brax doesn't move.

"Home." I point towards the Driver barn, towards the sewer where he lives. He whines again and turns the direction I've pointed, as though I've thrown a ball for him. A second later, he spins back, realizing he must have been tricked. His mouth is open, his tongue lolling out. He crouches low and pounces up towards me in our favorite game. But I push him away.

Kiran comes up beside me.

"The gatekeepers'll shoot him," he says in a low voice. I figured this. I don't need him to say it out loud. I bite the inside of my cheek to keep from telling him so.

"Home, Brax." My voice breaks, right along with my heart. Brax is my best friend. He's kept my soul alive these past months, kept the mountains alive in my mind. His ice blue eyes are burning me now, the question in them clear.

Because I don't want you to die, I want to tell him. Because I don't want to see you shot like Bian.

Brax steps closer, tentatively this time.

"No!" I grab a pebble off the ground and throw it at him. "Go *home*!" He yelps when it hits him, and edges back. I want to break down in sobs, but I can't. I pick up another pebble, and this time when I throw it, he growls at me. Dell sidesteps, and Daphne tries to calm her.

The next pebble hits Brax in the neck and with a yelp, he turns and finally scampers away. A weakly thrown pebble is scarier to Brax than a full-grown Watcher. I cling to this thought because it's so much easier than the fact that he's running away from me in fear.

When I turn back towards the horse, Kiran is standing very close.

"It's better—"

"Don't," I tell him. Without waiting for his help, I shove my foot into the stirrup, and heave my body upward. Kiran does end up hoisting me most of the way, but I don't look at him, not even when I feel his stare.

Brax will live because of me. I couldn't save my ma. Or Bian or Metea. But I'm going to save the twins and Salma. And I saved Brax.

We move on to the edge of the alleyway, and by the time Kiran leads us around the corner, my tears have dried, and my body feels like stone.

Kiran has hunched, his chin buried in his handkerchief. I see the gate station up ahead where there'll be one or two Watchers on guard through the evening. There is a scanner just above the booth, arcing in slow half circles towards the alley, and it makes the breath catch in my throat.

I've only been here one time—when they brought me to the Garden. I'd been bound by the hands and carried in a black jailer's carriage that was complete with thick metal bars. But I recognize this place as though I've visited it every single day.

I steel myself as we approach the decider of our fate, and lean forward to whisper in Daphne's ear, "If you say a word about Kiran talking, it'll be your last."

She sits as stiff as a board.

And with Brax torn from my heart and the dead Watcher seared forever into my memory, she had better know I mean it.

CHAPTER 16

THE INTERSECTION OUTSIDE THE city gates is silent and cold as death. Crumbled pieces of trash stir in the gusts of wind that sneak between the rungs of the heavy steel exit. A large rat with matted fur stalks us. When Dell stomps her front hoof, the creature slips between the iron grates of a sewer and disappears into the darkness below.

Beside the gates is a green-glass box with a Watcher sitting inside. This is the last barrier. The final test.

There's a pressure in my chest; it feels like someone's sitting right on my ribs. My life waits just outside. I can feel its grip on me, pulling me right off the back of this horse. I keep my eyes down—I can't even look through those narrow metal rods. If I do, I will ruin everything. The desperate truth will show on my face, plain as day.

Kiran leads us to the glowing pool of an overhead streetlight. He hesitates at the edge, ever so slightly, as though the brightness will burn his eyes, and once again I marvel at how perfectly he plays a coward. We stay just outside the beam, keeping to the shadows.

"Hold," comes a deep voice from within the booth.

My grip on the small dagger beneath my dress skirts is slippery with sweat, but firm.

A Watcher steps out into the light.

I stare at him for a moment. He's wearing the traditional

Watcher uniform. Black jacket, high-laced boots. The leather strap running across his chest that holds a messagebox, a wire, and whatever other torture piece he's been issued. His smooth, hairless face is so similar to the Watcher from the solitary yard, I can't help but imagine him with a rock-bruised eye and a knife handle sticking out of his neck. It's enough to make my stomach churn.

In the silence, I realize everyone is waiting for me to speak. Kiran, as far as the Watcher knows, is mute, and if Daphne talks she's likely to ruin everything.

The pressure in my chest grows tighter.

"Evening Watcher," I say, adding a little gravel in my tone. Kiran's act has inspired me. I need to play my part: Skinmonger. Virulent. I can feel the thick makeup on my cheek and the sweat dripping down my face that threatens to smear it. Better make this quick.

The Watcher moves closer and looks directly at me. His pupils take up most of the space between his lids; I've heard it's another modification they've made to help him see in the dark. I hope he can't see too well, otherwise he'll know the mark is fake and we'll be done for.

"Won't you open the gates for us?" I ask before I lose my nerve.

"It's late," he says. "Why aren't you working?"

Good. He believes I'm a Skinmonger. I push myself to continue.

"My cousin. She's plagued," I say. "Doesn't have much longer." A camera like the one in the rec yard at the Garden makes its slow trip our way, and I look down momentarily to avoid giving it a clear view of my face. Daphne begins to cry softly and hides her face in her hands. She sags back into me, and I hold her upright with one arm around her waist. For the first time tonight, she's doing something right.

The Watcher's blank stare sends chills racing over my skin.

"Looks all right to me," he says.

"On the outside maybe," I say. "Her insides are all rotten though."

The guard takes a step forward. Kiran jerks back fearfully, but holds his ground.

"So patch her up," says the Watcher.

I shiver. I feel Daphne shiver too. I've heard the girls whisper about such places. Death houses. For the right price, the docs there claim they can put any Skinmonger back on the market. But they don't call them death houses for nothing. The girls that go in don't always make it out.

"And then someone will have to call a Watcher up to get rid of the body," I argue, trying to think of how the Skinmongers talk at auction. "Look, my cousin's sick, and she's going to die. I can't afford to lose a week of business while you Watchers take your time cleaning up." My heart is pounding so hard I think that his sensitive hearing must have picked up on it.

He stares some more. Long enough that I think we might have to make a run for it.

"She's only Virulent, what do you care," I mutter.

Finally, he asks, "Any weapons?"

You can't bring weapons through the gates, but that doesn't mean you can't get one from an arms dealer in the Black Lanes.

"No," I answer.

"Apparatuses?"

"Appa-whatuses?" My brows rise.

"Computers. Messageboxes. Texters."

"Do I look like I can afford any of that?" This is the first real thing I've told him.

He takes another step forward. I grip the knife handle. My mind shoots to what kind of weapons Kiran must have on him.

"You going to search me?" I say. It sickens me to add that sultry edge to my voice, but I can't let him get too close.

The Watcher stops and though no disgust dawns on his face, I can tell he's rethought getting too close to two Virulent, one of them plagued.

"Gates reopen at dawn," he says, turning his back on us suddenly. "You can return then." He disappears within the glass guardhouse.

A moment later there is a clicking noise, and the gate rises high, straight up into the air, so that we can pass through. A wave of sick rolls over me as I remember the carriage that brought me through here. I can still hear the way the gate closed steadily behind me, mocking my freedom.

And then Kiran is leading Dell through, and I am staring ahead into the darkness, the real, true darkness beyond the city walls. I feel the tingling of something so much more shattering than pain, but so much brighter than joy, climbing up my body. The combination steals my breath. It makes me tremble like the very ground beneath us is shaking.

We are nearly even with the guard box, not yet outside the gates, and I'm beginning to think we've done it when the Watcher steps outside the automatic doorway again, this time searching the area behind us as the camera above his head is doing.

"Have a fine evening," I say in a hurry. I look over my shoulder back down empty Main Street and around the alley, the way we came, my blood turning to ice. Someone's after us. We weren't fast enough.

Kiran keeps walking. Slowly, so as not to make it seem like we're bolting. But that's exactly what's going to happen if someone's after us. He's getting ready to pass the Watcher.

The Watcher very slowly removes the wire from his chest strap and grips the handle. In front of me, I feel Daphne choke on her sobs. Without thinking, I squeeze her tighter against me. I tell myself I'm going to use her as a shield, but the truth is I feel safer when we're close.

I grip the knife in my hand, hard. We just need to get by him. Once we hit the gates, we can run.

But Kiran's injured and on foot, and Dell can't carry all three of us.

The guilt comes fast and hard; a punch to the gut. I am the reason the solitary Watcher is dead. I am the reason Kiran and Daphne are in danger right now. If they're harmed, it will be my soul's penance in the next life.

It should be the two of them on horseback and me on foot.

Just when I am about to jump, I hear something. A soft but steady pounding against the stones. I hold my breath. The Watcher lifts his wire. And a shot of gray whips by.

Brax.

He is gone, outside the fence, away into the night for his first taste of freedom.

The Watcher jerks around as though he will attempt to follow, but holds still.

"Was that . . ." asks Daphne between hiccups.

"A stray dog." I force a laugh but my heart is singing. Brax has returned to me, and we will escape together.

"Go on your way," the Watcher orders. With Kiran at the lead, we walk straight through the gate. It closes with a loud clang. I don't turn around to check. I will never look back again.

Ten paces. Twenty. Fifty. The night blackens the farther away we get from the city smog. I look up to the sky and pray that the darkness will eat me whole, that the city will forevermore be blind to the mountains. That this is finally over.

My family, I am coming home.

WE MOVE ON IN silence for some time, the gates folding into the greenish-black city smog behind us. Kiran keeps one hand on Dell's neck, leading her this way. Daphne is still sniffling. I feel like my soul has left my body and I am floating above, through the darkness, finally free.

Kiran glances over his shoulder at me.

"Be mindful up ahead. We're entering the Witch Camps."

I have only vague memories of passing through this place during my capture, but even then, on that rainy afternoon when I was locked behind the bars of my prison carriage, I remember the cold breath of fear on my neck.

"Why do they call it the Witch Camps?" I ask Daphne. I hope this stops the crying, which is starting to cut into my joy.

She wipes her nose on her sleeve. "This is where the women were taken after they were rounded up by the Magistrate." She hiccups. "Before the Watchers destroyed them."

That definitely cuts into my joy.

After the Red Years, the Witch Camps became a dumping ground, a place for things that were abandoned in an attempt to return to the simple life. Cars, trucks, wrecking machines, old-fashioned wagons, all strewn across the land, left to rust in the damp haze.

It's also where they toss the plagued, and the Watchers and Pips that don't take to the treatments.

The central road remains clear, but on either side, junk is piled high. Broken, smashed, useless. A reminder that anything left outside the gate will certainly perish.

The bare skin on my legs and shoulders prickles. My ma once said that this place was full of souls stuck with no one to sing them to the next life. I think she was right; I can feel them now. Slipping from the damp ground like steam.

Panting up ahead catches my attention. It's Brax, coming through the darkness like a silver ghost. He doesn't look up at me. I know he'll punish me a bit longer for what I've done.

That's all right; I'm just glad he's made it. He walks by Kiran's side as if the Driver's an old friend.

I'm still watching Brax when he lowers his head, and I can feel the hair on the back of my neck rise just as Brax's does. He starts to growl, a low menacing sound, and to creep forward, ready to pounce.

Kiran's knife is out, and now mine is too. I don't know what's got Brax's guard up, but I'm in a better position to fight from the ground. Using Daphne to steady myself, I throw my leg over the horse's hindquarters and land silently.

"What is it?" I ask Kiran. He shakes his head, unknowing.

We sneak forward.

"Where are we going?" Daphne asks.

"Quiet," I tell her.

"Well, we can't stay out here."

"I'm going to gag her," I whisper to Kiran. He doesn't respond. His eyes are still searching the darkness.

We approach a barricade of old car frames, stacked up ten high and smelling strongly of rust. There is a sudden movement behind it, and all of us, Dell included, freeze.

Brax's lips pull to reveal sharp yellow fangs.

Out of the darkness comes a great towering figure. A Watcher, lumbering towards us. An alarm screams in my head. My muscles brace to run, but Kiran motions for me to hold.

The Watcher isn't wearing a uniform. At least, not anymore. He's wearing the dark pants, but the jacket is torn off and there's no strap or weapons on him. The lights from the city reveal knotted welts that gleam in silver crisscrosses over his chest. His hands are stretched in front of him, and he's groaning softly.

He's blind.

But that doesn't calm my heart as he ambles an arm's length away across the lane, towards the skeleton of an old construction machine.

I wonder how long he's been out here in the Witch Camps.

He's obviously failed to adapt to his treatments, but unlike the other deformed test subjects, he can't hack it in the Black Lanes. I can't imagine how he survives.

I don't have long to consider it. A moment later there's another body moving our direction, though this one is much smaller. As it approaches, I see it's another Watcher, but he's bent over his midsection, like he can't stand all the way up. He walks on his hands and his feet, like an animal.

His back may not be able to support his chest, but his arms are great trunks and his legs are twice as broad. As he comes closer I can see that his midsection's no bigger than Kiran's.

He stops. His gleaming bald head wrenches back at an impossible angle. He can see us. The breath hitches higher in my throat. He begins to scuttle towards us faster, faster, but without a sound. That's because half of his jaw is missing. The wound looks recent; blood is still dripping on the ground.

"Oh!" Daphne cries. "Let's go. Now. Let's go *now*."

She's right. Together, we veer off the path, away from the blind Watcher and around a pile of old metal wheels. Kiran is still leading Dell, and I take up the rear, dagger braced before me. Then we're running as fast as we can through this maze of potholes and machinery. The monster can't make a sharp turn and he stumbles with a cry that sinks its teeth into my bones. Soon he's up again, using his arms just as he does his legs. He's a beast, loping on all fours.

For a moment, I'm frozen. Scared stiff. And then Brax is beside me again, snapping viciously at the half Watcher as I twist my fingers in his coat. We pull backwards, both running sideways.

"Hey! Look up, look *up*!" I hear Kiran shout.

I spin around, just in time to see the blind Watcher. It's too late to stop. I slam into him. Brax is barking, the sound of it firing between my temples. I spin off his solid body before I fall, and catch myself just in time to run again.

The bent-over Watcher can't stop. He plows into the blind

one seconds after me, strings of saliva and blood swinging from his missing jaw. The blind Watcher's hands slash through the air and connect, and in an instant he's wrapped his arms around the other's shriveled waist and is squeezing.

A gargling scream. The crackling of bones. And then silence.

I turn. But not before I see the blind Watcher open his mouth, and bite into the flesh of the dead monster's shoulder.

I CONVINCE KIRAN TO ride ahead and scout our path. He sits in front of Daphne on the saddle. Maybe she was prissy about him being a Driver before, but that's gone now. She holds tight to him as they gallop away. Brax stays by my side and together we run hard in their tracks, winding through the piles of machinery, alert to what might lurk just around the bend.

We find nothing. Nothing but an open field marking the end of the Witch Camps.

My heart collapses in my chest, and for the first time, I feel a sense of relief. Kiran and Daphne emerge a moment later behind me. They've doubled back after clearing the way and now are leading onward, over the wooden bridge crossing a deep ditch, and into the mountains.

PART THREE

THE MOUNTAINS

CHAPTER 17

I CAN'T MOVE FAST enough.

The city sticks to my heels like a long-stretched shadow. Always there, right behind me, a black reminder of Pips and cold silver tables and a Garden full of flowers. The wood in the trees makes me think of the auction stage. The rustles in the brush of a boy playing a hiding game. The mountain streams remind me of a Watcher's body, head under water. All things I wanted to leave inside those tall iron gates.

We must go faster.

Brax and I keep a steady pace up a steep embankment lined by prickly pines. The ground is muddy beneath my feet, and I tear off my boots, needing to feel the soft earth ooze between my toes. The boulders are rougher to the touch and larger than I remember. The black sky above is as dark as tar.

I imagine Nina asking where I've been while Tam throws his arms around me. He won't care that I've been gone once he sees me again. He's quick to forget heartache. Nina will follow his lead and once we've resettled in a new camp, I'll coax Salma into making me fry bread and teach the twins to knife fight. They'll be old enough now.

Just before dawn I turn around and find that Kiran has fastened Daphne's hands around his shoulders with his handkerchief while they ride. She's fallen asleep somehow, and her head is flopping to the side. With the makeup and Kiran's blood still sticky on her cheek, she really does look plagued.

I'm tempted to dump her here, but we can't slow down yet. If an alarm at the Garden or the mayor's house has been sounded, they'll search the city first and then send a crew of Trackers into the mountains. I want to be as far away as possible before that happens.

Up and up we go. Higher into the mountains. The air is biting; my breath forms moist clouds in front of my face, but I barely feel it. I'm sweating clean through the yellow Skinmonger dress; even my bare shoulders feel warm now.

With the sun just cresting the mountains, Kiran whistles for me to slow down. Dell's girth and breast piece are lathered with foamy white sweat. She snorts in a pouty way, no doubt frustrated with Daphne's extra weight. Now that we've stopped, I feel it too. I'm bone tired; the muscles in my legs are wobbling, threatening to give out.

Kiran leads us southwest, off my course, to a small pool that sparkles in the gray morning. He's woken Daphne in a soft voice and is easing her down to the ground. Her legs give way and she stumbles, backing into a tree for support. She looks terrible: eyes blackened by smudged makeup and swollen by tears, the fake Virulent mark smeared across her nose and mouth, her hair slicked back with sweat and dew. She must realize this because a second later she turns away and begins to scrub her face clean with the neck of her dress.

Kiran beckons me over to a tree split by lightning down the middle. He swipes away a cobweb covering a hole and then pulls out a bow and a packed leather quiver hidden inside. I smile. It may have been a while since I've hunted, but I know just how it will fit against my shoulder and the *ting* the sinew will make when the arrow flies.

I hold out my hand expectantly, and he lifts a brow.

"Yes, I know how," I say before I remember that I don't have to answer his gestures anymore. He has a voice and can speak for himself.

"Your hands are soft." It's not a compliment. You can't notch an arrow without callouses on your hands; they'll be all blistered and useless in no time.

"I'll manage," I tell him.

He hands it over and retrieves another for himself. The past hours have put a strain on him; his face is pale and damp, except for twin pink blotches staining his cheeks.

"Let me check that cut." I reach for the bandage, but he backs away.

"It's all right."

I'm sure it's not, but I don't press it. We don't have time to clean it properly anyhow.

Daphne's touching the pond with the toe of her shoe, as if something might rise up and bite her.

"We can't leave her," Kiran says in a low voice, now reading *my* face.

"We most certainly can."

"She knows about me," he says.

"Well, whose fault is that?"

His golden eyes harden.

"She's not gonna make it out here."

I feel my shoulders creep up. "What do you care?"

He breathes in, nostrils flaring. "I've got a soft spot for fragile women."

I narrow my eyes. "Who you calling fragile?"

He laughs—it's the first time I've ever heard it, and there's something crushing about the fact that he's doing it at me.

His hands raise in surrender. "I didn't say I have a soft spot for you, don't worry."

My neck gets all warm, and I look down at the bow, mad

that he's making fun of me. I expected it from Daphne and the other girls, not from him. I'm pretty sure I liked it better when he couldn't talk.

"She's *not* fragile. Trust me." But even though I say this, I know he's right. I couldn't leave her to the Watcher's beating and I can't leave her to the mountains. They can be twice as vicious as the city if you don't know how to survive them.

A twig breaks, and I turn to see my half friend half hidden behind Dell. Her nose turns up. From the look on her face it's clear she's overheard.

"Leave then," she says. "I'll be fine."

If only she were right. "You won't be," I tell her. "You'll come with us until I can take you to one of the outliers." Marhollow, maybe, where my ma was raised.

"Us?" she says. "The Driver is going with you?"

I hesitate, unsure what to say to this. I did think Kiran would help me find my family. I don't know why; he has his own people up here in the mountains. But the thought of us splitting up hollows out my stomach. He's the only one who knows everything that's happened these past few days, and as long as he's around, it feels like we're sharing that load somehow.

I wish he would say something, but he's busy pretending like he hasn't heard.

"The *Driver* has a name," is all I can think of to come back with. The cold is beginning to get to me now. The sweat-soaked dress is freezing against my skin.

"Oh," she says quietly. "What is it?" She's looking up at him through her lashes, and picking at her fingernails.

"Kiran," I say.

"Varick," he says at the same time.

"*Varick*?" I turn and stare at him. And then shut my gaping mouth.

Of course Kiran—*Varick*—has a real name. Kiran was just something stupid I made up when he wasn't talking. Suddenly

I'm angry with him; he's kept this a secret on purpose. Maybe I *should* be on my own. Daphne knows as much about him as I do.

Varick? It doesn't fit him at all. Varick has such a crude, harsh sound to it. It's not a name meant for someone who watches stars and plots escapes and speaks to horses. It certainly doesn't match his gold-flecked eyes.

"Here." Without meeting my gaze, Kiran hands me some more supplies from within the tree. Men's pants, like the kind he wears. An oversized Driver's shirt. I duck behind a boulder to change; I have to cuff the pants four times to make them short enough for me.

"Leave the dress in its place," he tells me. "I'm sure the next Driver through will appreciate it."

"*Driva,*" I say under my breath. Luckily, I can tell he's being funny, so I wind the dress into a yellow ball and stuff it into the saddlebag.

"You're not really planning on going it alone," Kiran says, one brow rising beneath his messy hair.

My heart settles. But then he walks over to Daphne, gives her a small, lopsided smile, and hands her the reins. She smiles at the ground.

So glad everyone's getting along.

Brax pads up beside me and drops a dead sparrow at my feet.

"Thanks," I mutter. He lowers and begins to pull out the feathers with his teeth.

"I won't be a bother," Daphne says.

I seriously doubt that.

"Fine," I concede, because somehow it seems easier right now than parting with them. "But keep up. Both of you," I add to Kiran, because I don't want him thinking I won't leave him if he takes too long tending to his new pet. He shoots me a cocky grin, and I'm really beginning to think I've made a mistake.

THE SUN IS PERFECTLY round, glowing white against a pale, cloud-stretched sky. Every time it's blocked by a tree, I feel a twinge of panic and look up, just to make sure it's not been swallowed by the city's haze.

We follow it eastward, cutting through the warped, wind-blown trees. We twist along the mountain trail above a shale ravine, climb higher, deeper into the forest, over the creeks, through a meadow of flowers—real flowers that make me think of the girls at the Garden. Daphne and I ride Dell while Kiran walks beside us. He's insisted that I take a break, and I'd be lying if I said my blistered feet weren't grateful. Daphne's asleep again behind me; her chest is warm against my back. She's drooling down my arm. I'll take her spit over her crying any day.

"You look tired, Aya," says Kiran.

I sit up fast enough for Daphne to blink awake. She settles back against my shoulder and is snoring a moment later. One of my feet has fallen out of the stirrups and I put it back in. I wonder how far I was leaning before Kiran said something.

"Why do you call me that?"

"It's your name, isn't it? Aiyana." He glances back. "I could always call you Clover."

He thinks he's funny.

"Aya's what my family calls me, that's all."

They're close—closer than they've been since I was taken—but still seem just as far away. I tell myself we're almost there, but it still doesn't seem possible. The mountains feel bigger than before, and the weather has changed even the familiar parts. I feel like an outsider in my own home.

Kiran's moving more slowly than before, but his color does

seem better. This eases my mind a little; the wound must not have been as bad as I thought.

"Nina and Tam," he says, the names so different when he says them. "And Salma."

I inhale. "That's right."

For some reason the questions I want to ask Kiran get stuck in my mouth. There's a hundred different things I want to know about him, but it's hard to get them out.

"What about you? *Varick*." I try it out, but it still doesn't fit. "What's your family like?"

He places a hand on Dell's withers. "They're like me."

Nothing more is offered.

"That's all?" I say. "'They're like me'?"

He shrugs. Keeps walking.

"There are rules," he says. "If my people knew I'd broken them, there'd be consequences."

"I'm not going to tell anyone." I shove my hair back behind my ears. The fresh air has made it impossible to tame.

He thinks about this. "What do you want to know?"

Same pace, same slow rhythm. It's like he hasn't got any worries in the world. It calms me a little, actually.

"I don't know." A frown pulls at my mouth. "Anything."

He waits a while before responding. "You know more than most."

It isn't good enough. I want us to be even. It's only fair after everything I've told him.

"Ask me something then," he says.

I glance over the Daphne lump on my back. No one's following us, at least not that I can see.

"How come you tried to knife me?"

"Ah." He scratches his head. "It was my first time in town. Guess you could say I was a little edgy." He shoots me a wicked smile that makes my insides go all soft. "For what it's worth, I'm sure glad you ducked."

"Me too," I say. "Why'd you come? City folks treat your people worse than the Virulent." I remember the way the men avoided him in the alleyway after Kiran helped me escape the mayor's house.

"Same reason anyone does," he says. "They have things we need. Gadgets. Medicine," he pauses, as if thinking of something. "Taking a heap of nasty in town is better than letting our people die without reason."

He stops just as he says this, and I know we're both thinking of my ma. City medicine might have saved her from the fever. But instead we only had what the mountains provided: herbs to make tea to help her sleep forever.

The mountains can be cruel.

He's turned, and takes a step towards me. "I didn't—"

"Why didn't you tell me you knew what I was saying?" I say, my voice sharp enough to make Dell's ears flick back.

"I told you why. It—"

"I know, it keeps your girls safe. So why help me at all then?"

"Because . . ." he scratches the side of his head. "Because you and me, we're alike."

A mean laugh tumbles out. "Not that alike. I wouldn't have lied."

"You don't understand."

"I understand fine."

Dell's stopped, and I squeeze my heels around her ribs to urge her forward. She turns her massive head to look back at me. It's clear she isn't moving without Kiran's approval.

I sigh. Maybe it stings a little, but I know why he didn't tell me. I wish someone had done that for me. If it meant keeping Nina off the stage, I wouldn't say another word my entire life.

"You can keep calling me Kiran if you like," he says quietly.

My gaze slides up and meets his, and for a moment everything else goes away—the city, the birds chirping in the trees, everything. My breath catches. It feels like it's just us two, like we're the only ones in these mountains. And I feel it happen—silent and soft as a feather, a piece of my soul becomes his.

"We have to keep moving," I say, tearing my eyes away. "I'll walk."

"I'm fine—"

"I'll walk." I need to move my legs again, they're cramping up. And I need some space. With everything that's happened, I'm not thinking straight.

I belong to no one. Kiran's all right, more than all right. I owe him for what he's done, but that doesn't make him entitled to own any part of me.

As I move, Daphne's cheek slides off the back of my shoulder and she jolts awake.

"I need a pill," she says after a moment. "I'm hungry."

Kiran's holding Dell's headstall, smoothing her forelock over the star between her eyes and whispering something I can't make out.

"There's one in the bottle," I tell her, sliding to the ground. She's sitting behind the saddle and fishes the dirty, crackling plastic out of the leather bag.

"There's something all over it."

I don't have to look back to know she's making a sour face.

"Bloodroot," I tell her. "I found some in the solitary yard and dried it."

"Of course you did," she mutters.

Brax emerges from a nearby brush, feathers still stuck to his damp jaw. His tail curves happily. I knew he'd like it out here.

"Daphne is what they call you?" I hear Kiran ask. "Like the flower, right?"

"We're all named after flowers," she says tentatively as he checks Dell's girth.

"Not all of us," I say. Some of us are named after weeds.

"They got it wrong," he tells her. "They should have called you Strawberry."

Her cheeks glow to match her red hair. Mine do, too.

"*Strawburries* are plants, not flowers," I say. I don't know why he's being nice to her. She hates Drivers.

"You can . . ." she swallows, and deliberately lowers her voice to a more husky tone. "You can call me whatever you like."

She moves her leg so that it skims his arm while he tightens the leather strap around the horse's ribs.

I snort and look to Kiran for proof that she's being ridiculous, but he's grinning like a fool.

Brax's growl distracts me. He's lowered to a crouch, staring behind us into the shadowed woods. Kiran and I share a quick glance before he unhooks the bow from over his shoulder.

"What is it, Brax?" I whisper, straining my ears.

"What's going on?" Daphne says.

I lick my dry lips, listening, hearing every bird whistle, every crackling branch. I pull the bow from over my shoulder and notch an arrow. I've only got three—the loaded quiver is with Kiran—so I better make them count.

Like thunder from across the skies, the sound reaches me. Hoofbeats. Moving fast.

I look to Kiran. He tilts his head north, in the direction of Glasscaster.

Trackers.

His hand is on my arm then and he's trying to hoist me onto Dell, but I squirm away.

"You can ride," I say. "If they see the horse we're done for. Take Daphne and get out of here!"

"Clover?" Daphne's voice is thin. Kiran looks at me for a long moment before removing a handful of arrows from the leather quiver over his shoulder and shoving them in my direction.

"Stay high," he says. "Don't shoot one unless you can shoot them all."

An instant later he's thrown his leg over Dell's withers, and they're gone.

I DON'T BOTHER RUNNING after them. I make for high land, just as Kiran said. On the way I snag an armful of dead leaves and shake them over my path, walking backwards. I hope it's enough to cover my tracks. Then I find a high tree, thread my arm through the bow, and get to climbing.

"Hide, Brax," I order when I reach the lowest branch. He whines up at me, and then lopes away. I wish he would go farther, but I can see him, twenty paces off, ears perked towards the north and the oncoming danger.

They arrive quickly, before the fear has time to poison my blood. Three men on horseback. All Virulent thugs. I can see their X's from here. I look down on them from my position three stories up, in the split in the tree trunk. My arrow is notched and ready to fly.

I will not be taken this time. Not when I know what awaits me in the city.

One's wearing checkered pants and has grease smeared on his shirt. The other two are in dark gray, with knit hats covering their hair.

"Prints turn that way," says Checkered Pants. Looks like he's the leader.

One of the others dabs at his mouth with the collar of his shirt.

"I should be sleeping," he grumbles.

"Then go knock off," counters the third. "I'll take your share of that reward Gray was talking about."

"Greer," corrects Checkered Pants. "The mayor's going to

stretch his neck when he realizes his kid's favorite toy went missing."

My heart trips in my chest. If I hadn't been convinced they were searching for us before, I am now. And not just us. *Me.*

My hand falters, but I lift it again, steadying my breath. The quiver is just over my shoulder, but I've already stuffed a dozen extra arrows into the waistband of these Driver pants. Kiran's words echo through my head. I might be able to strike them all before they know what's hit them, but I'm safer hiding if they don't know I'm here.

The vision of the Watcher, the blood draining from his neck, fills my mind, and the sweat rolls down my forehead and burns my eyes. I'm not sure I can do it again.

"What's that?" says one of the men in gray.

"A dog," answers Checkered Pants. "Kill it before its pack comes."

Brax. I bite down hard enough for my teeth to crack.

One of the Trackers pulls a black gun from his waistband and aims it into the brush. I can't see Brax. I nearly fall out of my hiding place trying to follow the man's sight line. In the silence, I hear a low growl and know they've found my friend.

I draw back the arrow and the string stretches with a morbid creak.

The Tracker fires one shot. Two. I nearly drop the bow right onto the man below me. My lungs collapse. I can't find the air.

"Get it?" asks Checkered Pants.

My shaking hands restring the bow, preparing to avenge him even as I'm refusing to believe he's dead.

"Scrammed," says one of the others. "Scared him off. He won't bother us no more."

"We'll pick up the last set of hoofprints and start again," says Checkered Pants. "I want to catch her before the weather turns and we lose our trail."

A few seconds later they disappear, riding at an urgent trot towards the south.

I want more than anything to get down from this tree; I need to warn Kiran that they're on his tail, I need to find Brax and make sure he's all right. Right now the tree feels just as much of a prison as the solitary pen at the Garden did. But I can't get down. Not yet. I have to wait a little longer. Just a little longer, until I'm sure they aren't coming back.

Until I'm sure this isn't a trap.

I count to one hundred and am just about to climb down when I see Brax.

He's come to the bottom of the trunk, panting. He's not injured. There's no sign of blood on him. My stomach feels as though I've just fallen from this very tree I'm hiding in. He paws the trunk, crystal blue eyes trained on mine.

He's telling me the way is clear.

I swing down, feeling the sting from a dozen cuts I gained on my hasty climb up. I grab him by the scruff of the neck.

"Next time hide, you idiot."

He licks my face. His breath stinks worse than ever.

That's when I hear the scream.

I recognize the voice; I heard it just yesterday in the solitary yard.

Daphne.

I'm running before I can think to stop. I try my hardest to focus on the origin of that cry—how loud it was, exactly where I turned when I heard it—because Daphne doesn't make another sound.

I should have killed the Trackers when I'd had the chance.

"Brax, find Kiran," I say. "Come on, boy."

He spins on his hindquarters and runs. I follow, racing after him, forgetting my need to stay silent. Kiran saved my life. He's out here because of what I did. I can't let anything happen to him.

And Daphne. Crazy as she makes me, I can't leave her now.

Brax runs though the brush, opposite the direction of the Trackers, away from where Kiran and Daphne rode off. Either they switched course, or we're going the wrong way.

We do not search long.

The woods open to a clearing facing a steep shale cliff. Daphne and the horse are pressed against it, held in place by a large black bear.

He roars, bouncing from all four paws to his hind legs as he lumbers towards them. Tufts of fur, shed in preparation for the warm season, shake from his thick coat. Standing, he's as big as a Watcher. I cannot see Kiran.

He's not with them. I creep behind the bear, knowing I'm downwind because otherwise he would have charged me by now. He's young and small, only three times my size, but he'll have claws as long as my fingers and teeth strong enough to rip me apart.

Daphne's trying to hide herself behind Dell, who is stomping her hooves and snorting. I can see the whites of the mare's eyes from here. If Daphne isn't careful, the horse is going to trample her.

I move closer. Now I'm just fifteen paces away and I can hear the rumbling growl coming from the bear's chest. The fear coming off Daphne and the horse is drawing him in. I can almost taste it from here.

There is something on the ground between them. A lump in the fallen leaves.

A body.

"No!" I slap a hand over my mouth.

It's Kiran. He's lying motionless. My mind races to try to figure out what happened. Has he been shot by the Trackers? Has the bear already attacked him? Was he thrown from Dell?

There's danger in making too much noise—I can easily bring

the Trackers back our way. But the best way to fend off a bear is to be a bigger bear, and so to save Kiran, I have to do it.

"Get ready to run," I tell Brax, and fit an arrow to the bow.

I take the deepest breath I can, and roar. I catch the bear off guard, and he spins from Daphne, from the crumpled form of Kiran, towards me. He rises up to his full height and his chest is so broad he blocks my view of the horse behind him. Black lips pull back over sharp white teeth. The muscles in his neck ripple beneath the skin.

The air locks in my throat, and my great roar ends in a whimper.

It's not working. He won't move. I raise the bow.

If he doesn't change his mind soon, I'll have no choice but to shoot him, and I know where that road will lead. The first arrow would just be an irritating prick into his thick hide. I don't know if I'd have the chance to fire again before he'd be on me.

Finally, the bear drops down to his front feet and ambles away.

With the blood still hammering through my ears, I run to Kiran, praying that the Trackers are so far away they haven't heard me. I search for a bullet wound for evidence of a bear's swiping paw. When I pull back his coat, I suck in a sharp breath. The wire wound has gone straight through the cloth, straight through his coat. It's left a dark, wet stain all the way down to his hip.

Daphne's weeping.

"He started bleeding a lot," Daphne says, and when she holds out her hands, I see they're smeared with red. "He didn't say a word, he just fell. He's dead, isn't he?"

CHAPTER 18

KIRAN IS NOT DEAD. He can't be. He was just talking to me as if nothing was wrong.

I put my hand on his brow. His skin feels like he's slept too close to the fire. Dead people aren't feverish. And he's still sweating. Dead people definitely do not sweat.

My eyes blink out of focus, and suddenly I am looking down at my hand atop my ma's forehead. Her curly black hair sticks to her brow and her breathing is much too shallow. Even all these years later I can perfectly recount the last moments before her death.

I banish the thought from my mind. I will not let Kiran die.

"Wake up." I slap Kiran hard across the jaw. His eyes flutter open, whites with no golden iris. My stomach lurches, and then sinks. Brax has begun to growl again, and Dell's ears have pinned back to her head.

The Trackers are coming.

"Not now, Kiran," I say. "Just hold out a little longer."

He doesn't move.

"Leave him, we need to run!" shouts Daphne.

"Quiet!" I nearly slap her, too. Kiran is the only reason she is still alive. Without him, the Trackers would have found her and who knows what they would have done with her.

The thoughts scream in my head, one clawing over them all: We need to hide.

"Water," I say. "A stream—did you see one near here?"

"I don't know. I don't *know*!"

"Think!" I grab her shirt and pull her down close to me. "Think, Daphne," I say more calmly. "Did you ride through water?"

She closes her eyes tight, then nods. "Back that way." She points down the shale cliff.

"Help me move him." I stuff my arms beneath Kiran's shoulder, hook them under his armpits. He doesn't make a sound. I tell myself that's because of Driver habit, not how injured he is.

"He's dead!" Daphne backs away.

"He's not dead, you idiot. He's sick." Because of me. Because I was stupid enough to save Daphne.

She approaches slowly, wiping her hands down the sides of her dress.

"Help me get him over the back of the horse."

I stand with a groan, hoisting him up against my chest. Kiran may not be bulky, but he's long, and his body is hard to maneuver. After a moment, Daphne grabs his waist and lifts from beneath, and somehow we manage to lay him facedown over the saddle.

A hiss escapes through my teeth. I know it must be tearing at his wound, but we have no choice.

Daphne takes Dell's reins and leads her against the cliff through the brush. I hold Kiran's legs, steadying him over the back of the horse.

The hoofbeats pound in the distance. Head low, Brax slinks off. I don't want him to go, but I can't make him stay now.

"Quick!" I whisper. Daphne begins to run, pulling Dell at a trot. Kiran is jostled all over, but I hold on tight, not letting him fall.

Finally, the gurgle of water sifts through the trees. I direct everyone straight into the shallows and while they wait, backtrack fifty paces to cover our tracks. We've travelled mostly on shale, and there are few prints to hide. When I'm done we move upstream, downwind, so that our scent blows away from the Trackers and our path is swallowed by the current.

The hoofbeats fade and then disappear.

"There," I say, pointing to the mouth of an old fox den just off the shore. We make our way over, and I'm relieved to find it empty. A roof of tangled roots hides us from above, and the water has worn away the entrance, making it wide enough for the three of us to squeeze in.

Dell snorts and prances nervously while Daphne and I slide Kiran off her back and lay him down in the cave.

"Water," I say to Daphne. "Bring me the bottle."

While she retrieves my things from Dell's saddlebags, I remove Kiran's shirt. With the thin metal dagger, I saw through the felt wrapping, soaked with his blood.

It's the smell that hits me first. Sour enough to bring the bile up my throat. The skin has turned white around the wound, and though the worst of the bleeding is over, it doesn't look good. The puckered lips tracing around his torso haven't even closed. It's infected.

"No. Not now," I whisper. The Trackers are near and my family is close and I'm finally, *finally* free, and now the one person I owe everything to is hurt. It's the stupidest thing, but I'm so mad at him right now I could scream.

Daphne brings me water from Kiran's canteen, and I dribble some in Kiran's mouth.

"Swallow," I order. He doesn't listen. The water leaks down his chin.

"Hey!" I give his shoulder a little shake. "Quit it, Kiran. This isn't funny." I don't know why I say this; I know he isn't playing. I'm just sick that he hasn't woken yet.

"I should have been sold." Daphne's sunk against the far wall. She's filthy. Her arms are wrapped around her knees and she's rocking like a child. "I'd be living in a nice house right now, with food and blankets and a warm bed, if not for that buyer."

"Shut up, Daphne."

"My father will take me back. I was the favorite of all his girl children. You have to bring me back to the city."

"Shut up!"

"I shouldn't be here." Her voice cracks. "I shouldn't be here. I shouldn't be here."

I'm on my feet in a flash, and before she knows what's hit her, I've tossed the rest of the water in her face. She sputters, her wide green eyes looking up at me like I'm crazy.

"Go then! Get out of here!" I say. "I hope they catch you."

I fall back to my knees and begin digging through my supplies. Meal supplement pills. Bloodroot to make a sleeping draught. Purslane for a headache. The needle and thread I stole from the Pips—that's helpful. I need horseradish to make an antiseptic. And I need it now.

Daphne's risen and is pacing, and I can see the struggle darkening her perfect, freckleless face. She wants to leave, but she's too scared to chance it on her own.

I tear out of the cave, keeping to the streambed. While filling the canteen, I scan the water's edge for small white flowers. We've passed a hundred of the plants since entering the mountains, but when I need one, it's nowhere to be found.

A crackling of twigs behind me startles me, and I jump. It's just Daphne. She's following me like a little kid.

"White flowers," I tell her. "Small, about this size." I make a tight circle with my thumb and first finger.

We comb the water's edge together. She pulls up all sorts of plants and weeds, but none of them are right. Finally, I spot the right one. I tear three green stalks from the ground, shake off the bugs, and run back to the cave. Outside, I grab two rocks: one flat, the size of my hand, and another oval shaped, then set to work, grinding the stalk of the plant into the rock until it creates a soft milky residue. When it's done, I pour water over Kiran's wounds, trying to clear out the bad blood. He shivers, and I cringe—the sun is beginning to fall, and soon it will be cold.

"Look!" Daphne points down at his face from over my shoulder. "He's trying to say something."

His lips are moving, just a bit. I tilt my ear over his mouth, but there's no sound.

"Fever dreams," I say. Just like my ma had near the end.

With the horseradish ready, I take a deep breath. I need to remove the infected skin, otherwise it's going to spread. I saw my ma do this once when Bian cut his knee, but that was ten years ago or more.

If ever I needed Mother Hawk it's now.

Even though there's Trackers still out looking, I light a small fire on dry leaves. The blade is sharpened, cleaned. Time is going too fast. I wish it would slow down. I wish I didn't have to do this.

Daphne argues weakly before crawling away.

I set my teeth, and carve into Kiran's skin, removing the graying crevice of flesh. With a blanket from his bag, I wipe away the blood. He wakes up briefly, mouth open in a silent scream, and then falls unconscious. Beads of sweat mixed with tears drip into my work, and I wipe those away too. Thankfully, the infection is not everywhere, and I am rid of it quickly.

I thread the needle with focused hands and sew the wound shut, leaving big spaces between each tiny X to ensure I have enough thread to go the entire length. Fresh blood blossoms over his pale skin. I slop the horseradish poultice over the entire area. Some honey would be a good sealant, but I don't have any. Another quick trip to the stream, and I've cleaned the wrapping and wrung it out.

I hesitate before turning back to our camp. My stomach twists. My skin crawls. The blood runs cold, numbing my fingers. I stuff the extra length of my shirtsleeve into my mouth and scream, and then fall to my knees and puke. My muscles bunch and quiver, wrenching too hard around the bones. I think of the Watcher and how we killed him. Kiran and Brax and me. And if Kiran dies, no one else will ever remember what his blackened eyes looked like the moment he realized he was done for. No one will hear that gurgle as his face plunged into the water. Hideous secrets I will be forced to bear alone with my silent wolf friend.

The only way I can move past the shakes is to remember that Watchers are no longer men. And Kiran's not dead yet.

I rinse my mouth out and return.

Then I wait.

———➤———➤

KIRAN BARELY MOVES AS the sun dips below the horizon. With nothing more I can do to help him, I search the surrounding area and find Brax already on the prowl. It seems we've escaped the Trackers for now, but that doesn't mean they won't be back.

I am torn in half. I will not leave Kiran to die, but I need to find my family. If something happens to them while I'm this close, I will never forgive myself. If Kiran dies, I will never forgive myself. I snatch a stick off the ground and break it over my knee. I break the halves, and then the halves, until my hands are blistered and my hair is damp with sweat and there is nothing more to break.

When I return, Daphne's curled in a ball against the wall, sniffling again.

"You should try to get some sleep," I tell her.

She doesn't answer.

"Daphne, it's going to be okay. I've gotten out of worse scrapes than this."

It's not true—the last scrape I got in that was this bad, I ended up at the Garden.

She rolls over and faces the opposite way.

"You hungry?"

Silence.

I stare at the back of her head. Her red hair is a nest of sticks and mud and bits of leaves, but she doesn't even bother to clean it up.

"Want a meal pill?"

"There's only two left." She sounds miserable. "We're going to starve."

I'm relieved she's talking at all.

"You don't have to worry about that," I say, more to myself as I blot the sweat from Kiran's brow. "I've got the glass arrow."

It's an echo of the past, something my ma used to tell us when we were little. I use the water to wipe the dirt off Kiran's face. It's the first time I've ever seen him so clean and I feel a little bit like I'm looking at him without his clothes on. His skin is smooth, pale in the reflection off the water. He's got light freckles on his cheekbones I never noticed until just now. His lips are parted just a little. I skim the edge of his mouth with my fingertip, gently, and then draw back quickly and make sure Daphne didn't see.

"What's a glass arrow?" she asks without turning around.

I sit back on my heels.

"It's just a story my ma would tell." It was like saying, *Don't be afraid, I'll take care of you,* but I don't tell Daphne that.

"So let's hear it."

I take a slow breath, suspecting that this will end in her making fun of me. But for some reason, I tell her.

"Once, a long time ago, when the grass was grazed too thin and the game was scarce, Fox and Deer sang to Mother Hawk for food to end their families' suffering."

She snorts in her snooty way, but I keep going.

"She flew down from the sky with an arrow made of green glass and told them that she'd give it to the winner of a race across the country."

"What were they supposed to do, eat it?" Daphne rolls onto her back, staring up at the woven roots overhead.

"Fox thought the race was a waste of time and went to the lowlands in search of food. So Deer ran the path Mother Hawk had chosen alone. Into the mountains, across the sky, and back down into the valley. When he was through, Mother Hawk gave him the arrow to do what he would. He gave it to Fox, who placed it in the bow, drew back, and pierced Deer through the heart."

"Deer wasn't too smart, was he?"

"Just listen."

Daphne's breathing is slowing.

"Deer's blood seeped into the ground, and from that place grew enough grass to feed his family for generations. But Fox and his family starved."

"Why didn't the deer just kill the fox?"

"A deer can't live off a fox," I say, quoting my ma. "But a family can live off one sacrifice for a long time."

"So give this magic arrow to me," she says after a while. "I'll shoot you and eat you."

Daphne doesn't get it. She wouldn't. She knows nothing about sacrifice.

She's quiet, but just when I think she's fallen asleep, she speaks.

"I wish I was ten years old again."

"Me too," I say before I think about it.

"Everything's wrong out here. Even the sky. It's like . . . there are holes in it. Bright spots."

"They're called stars." Pity softens my words. I can't believe she's never seen stars on a clear night.

"Why do they do that?" She fans her fingers to represent the glow. "It can't be normal."

I take a slow breath. "My ma said they were the souls of those who have passed, waiting to return to their new forms." I eye her through my lashes, wondering how she will attempt to make me feel foolish.

She's staring at me. "Your birth mother? Not a Keeper?"

I nod.

"You think she's one of . . ." She points to the sky.

Unsure how to answer, I only shrug. Sometimes I think she's up there. Watching. Waiting to return. Sometimes I think she's already back in her new body, spreading her wings and soaring over the mountaintops, free from disease and the hunters. Free from me.

Sometimes I wonder if her stories were always just stories, and she is part of the earth, nothing more.

Silence. Daphne is looking back up at the sky.

"It's kind of pretty I guess."

I want to tell her I think so too, but she's already asleep.

⇥⟶

NIGHT COMES AND KIRAN'S fever rages on.

So I pray.

Really pray, for the first time in weeks. Inside, I am empty, and the song does not come easy, but I do it anyway. For Kiran. For myself. Because I can't do this by myself, and Mother Hawk is the only one who can help him now.

I sing into the night, and as Kiran begins to shiver, I press my forehead into his chest, and weep.

"Please wake up."

As if in answer, he rouses suddenly and stares straight into my face.

"It dudn't work. The songs," he says. I am off my knees before he finishes the thought, already pouring more water into his mouth. He sputters, jaw working as if I've offered sludge.

I try to keep him quiet, but he keeps talking.

"I used to sing, too. Long time ago. But no one could fix her."

I want to ask who he means and what happened, but he's blinking fast, fighting to stay awake.

"Quiet now," I tell him.

"Diyou cud me?" he slurs.

"I had to take off the infection." I don't ask if it hurts; the pain is sharp in his eyes. "You need to rest."

"I dream of you, Aya bird," he says. And then he's out.

When I turn back around, Daphne's standing behind me. The smile I hadn't known I'd been wearing fades immediately. She sits back down, giving me a strange look, and stares back up at the sky.

KIRAN TAKES A TURN for the worst just before dawn.

His unseeing eyes stretch open, and the sweat soaks through his clothing. The fever dreams take him. He begins to say a woman's name: *Kyna*. With a pang to my heart I wonder if he loves her—the hint of a smile dawns on his mouth when he says the word. He tells her not to worry. He'll come back.

I mop his brow and force more water down his throat. I change his dressing and apply a new poultice. I talk to him, remembering how Metea said this soothed my ma when she was having visions. I tell him all the best lies: that we're safe, free, fat and happy.

Just as the red dawn is breaking, he sits bolt upright, staring at something behind me in the bushes. His breath grows shallower and his limbs are wild as I force him back down.

My heart twists. My face is wet with tears.

Kiran is dying.

I squeeze his hand, sending all my strength down his arm. I don't even know if he can feel me near.

"What's happening?" asks Daphne.

"I don't know what else to do!" My cry doesn't distract Kiran from muttering something else I can't make out. "I can't fix him. I'm not a doctor. He might be dead by the time we get him to a town."

Every part of my body has grown tight in my desperation. I am failing Kiran. I have failed my entire family.

Daphne grows very quiet.

"Kyna needs a doctor," Kiran says. I can't tell if he's mimicking me, or if he's talking to spirits. I clap a hand over his mouth to keep him quiet, but his words have sparked something inside me.

"Where is the doctor?" I demand. "*Where?*"

"Three . . . three rivers crossing."

I ask him where, but the answer is already waiting. I know a place, not far from my mountain, where three rivers collide. I could see it on the clearest days from the meadows near our camp. Is it possible Kiran and I have lived only a valley away our whole lives?

"Do you remember the snowy peaks above our home?" I ask, pretending to be Kyna, the person he keeps talking to.

"I'll carry you to the top," he mumbles. He's jostling from side to side, and fresh blood breaks through his bandages. I hold him down.

"Do you think his people have a doctor?" Daphne asks.

"Be still," I beg him, laying my body across his.

I can't leave Kiran. He doesn't deserve to die alone. And my mountain is still a day's ride away, which means his camp is at least double that. I could run or ride Dell, but that would leave Kiran and Daphne defenseless if the Trackers return. The woods are dangerous enough anyway, the bear already proved that. And anyhow, what if I find a doctor, and by the time we return, Kiran's already dead?

"Stop it," Daphne tells me, worrysick.

I grind to a halt, realizing that in Kiran's calm, I've risen and begun pacing, tugging on my hair and talking to myself.

"I'm going," I say.

If there's a chance that his people can help, I have to find them. If not, I will find Kyna, and bring her back to comfort him.

Or bury him.

I can't think that way. I don't have enough time to dwell. These next moments are too precious to waste.

"I'm going too, then," Daphne says.

"You have to stay with Kiran."

"Wait," she says. "Clover, no."

"I think I know where his people live. It's near my camp. I'm going to find my family and bring back a doctor."

"He doesn't love you!"

I'd been reaching for my bottle of supplies, but stop abruptly at her words. She's staring at me, arms outstretched, green eyes sharp.

"He loves Kyna. Not you. Don't kid yourself that if you save him, he'll choose you."

I stand perfectly straight, and focus hard on controlling my voice so it doesn't shake.

"There are bigger things in life than being chosen."

I'm grateful for her sulk then, because it gives me the time I need to grind the dried bloodroot that I'd gathered so long ago in the solitary yard. Of the three stems I have, I only use one. I need Kiran to sleep so that his body can heal. I'm going to knock him out so that he stops twisting open his wounds.

I go over how much I need. Too little won't touch his pain. Too much will kill him.

Oh please don't let me kill him.

THE TEA STEAMS FROM Kiran's tin cup, misting with the fog. Rain is coming, I saw it in the red dawn, felt it tightening the curls of my hair.

My hands shake; Metea's voice whispers in my ear.

"More, little girl. Just a bit more, sweet girl."

It was too much. Even then I knew it.

When I told her so, Metea held me tight in her arms and said, *"She's ready. Help her let go."*

I remember holding the cup, tilting it back as Metea held my ma's head up. I was the one who had to do it. Her blood. Her only child. So that her soul could be freed from her failing body.

"You must be brave, Aya."

"Drink," I tell Kiran, propping his head up against his saddlebags. He's tossing from side to side, and between that and my trembling hands, I can barely get the warm liquid in his mouth.

But I do.

It doesn't take long—moments is all—and Kiran becomes deathly still. I place my fingers gently on his throat to feel his pulse. It's so slow each space makes my own heart skip a beat.

A light rain begins to fall, and Kiran's eyes drift close. His mouth goes slack. He looks dead. I check his heart three more times before peeling all the extra weight off Dell's back. I place the knife beside Daphne, along with the remaining meal supplements.

"I'll be back with the doctor."

"So you've said." She doesn't believe me, I can tell.

I kneel beside Brax, rubbing his ears.

"Take care of them," I whisper, then climb a large rock and mount Dell. As I turn away from the camp, towards my mountain, his howl splits the heavy air. It sounds like the forever kind of good-bye.

I dig my heels into Dell's sides, and hold on as tightly as I can.

RIDING DELL IS A rush unlike any I've ever known. Kiran dreamed me a bird and he must be a seer because now I'm flying.

My legs tremble, latched on tight to her barrel body. My fingers ache from holding onto her mane so tight. I lean down over the saddle horn and keep my head low as the forest whips by.

Dell is a mountain horse; she knows this land. She doesn't shy from anything—leaping over fallen trees and the streams that are swelling with the pelting rain. She keeps her head low and runs full out on the straightaway, chomping on the bit. It's as if she knows Kiran's in trouble.

We slow when the land makes us, but that's it. Noon passes. Dusk falls. The rain doesn't cease. The leather saddle becomes slippery, burns blisters between my knees, and it's hard to stay on. I keep my eyes trained east, and when I see the line of jutting peaks loom out of the gray before us, my hope soars.

I am almost there.

The only way I know to Three Rivers is past my camp, so that's the way I go. At last the woods become familiar. We pass a long, narrow rock I used to balance on as a child. The walk-up trees, bent so severely by wind that you can run halfway up their trunk. My hearing's honed not just for Trackers now, but for children's voices. I sniff the air for the smell of wood smoke, but the rain drowns out everything.

The sky grays, making me wish I had a Watcher's night vision. I look out for traps and snares, hoping the twins have kept them up like I taught them. But we come across none.

I urge Dell on faster. We come to the cave where I'd taught them to hide, but there's no sign anyone's been there for months. We head through the meadows. No tracks. No snares.

We reach my tent. And it is standing. But barely. One side has collapsed; the broken wooden bones sticking out on the ground from under the torn hide patchwork.

"Salma!" I shout.

There is no answer.

"Tam! Nina! It's Aya! I'm home!"

Nothing.

"TAM! NINA!"

I shove off Dell, swaying on weakened muscles from so many hours in the saddle. And then I'm running. Running to the rawhide walls, stripped down by the weather. To the one-time circle of stones around our fire, scattered by the rain and wind. To what remains of our supplies, left in ruins by the raiding animals. A few rusted knives, a steel pan, and even our old cast-iron kettle. Each is tied to a memory. Metea making tea. The crackle and hiss as Salma fries elk over the fire. The laughter of the twins. Memories as thick as the spirits haunting this place.

I yell until my throat goes dry. Until I can yell no more.

They are gone. All gone.

I fall to the ground, barely noticing the sound of the arrow as it whizzes through the air. It's not until the point embeds in the mud beside my wrist that I realize I'm being attacked.

CHAPTER 19

I SPRING TO MY feet, loading my bow with an arrow even before it's readied in my hand. I search in all directions, but see no one. Like a fool, I've left myself completely exposed while whoever is trying to shoot me hides in the dark.

I don't wait. I run to an outcropping of trees. We're on my land now, and I know the best hiding places. But another arrow comes out of nowhere and plunks into the stump beside my head.

From behind a trunk, I squint into the night. They're likely not Trackers—they'd have guns. Could be Magnates on a hunting party, like the one that caught me. He'd used a spear on Bian. Maybe these Magnates carry bows.

From the darkness comes a whinny and the clatter of shod hooves over rock. Dell's spooked, and for a moment, I consider going after her. She is my only means of escape. But another arrow comes, this one skidding through the dirt on the opposite side of the tree.

I'm stuck. The only way out is up.

I loose one arrow in the general direction I think they're hiding and jump for the lowest branch, still high above my head. I reach it on the second try, but have to swing hard to pull my legs up. A cry tears from my throat; my heels grab, but the bark breaks free and my fingers are slipping.

At the scurrying sound below, panic pumps into my veins.

My attackers are in the open. I've got to get up *now*. Then I'll be hidden in the brush, able to pick them off one by one.

But something hooks around my hip. For an excruciating second I think it's a wire, but no burn comes. It doesn't rip through my clothes. It's just a rope; enough to throw off my balance. I bite down hard, and hear the strain echo from my throat. My legs fall from the branch, and I hoist them up again, arching my back with all my strength to stay as far away from the ground as possible.

A whoosh of breath. Another rope striking my back, and this time it does sting. Then a hand fisting around the slack at the back of my pants, yanking me down. I fall in a heap, the air fleeing from my lungs.

I open my eyes to a metallic arrowhead, aimed right at my face.

Breath suspended, my gaze travels down the narrow wooden shaft to the weathered knuckles holding it, to the gray beard peppered with leaf crumbles, to the long, stringy silver hair, and the faint scar, running from chin to collarbone, glowing a pale blue in the moonlight.

He drops the bow as though it is burning his hands, and stumbles backwards in silent surprise.

"Lorcan?"

His mouth is open now, and my mind fills with a sudden memory of the first night Kiran crossed the poisoned stream into the solitary yard to give me the broken knife handle. He'd wanted to talk to me, it had been so clear on his face.

One dirty hand rubs absently at his scar. I know that feeling. The knot-stuck-in-the-throat feeling. It strikes me that I haven't seen Lorcan in years. He's so much older now than he was the last time we traded. His skin is pulled too thin over his face. He hasn't bathed in some time either; I can smell him ten paces away.

"What are you doing here?" I ask.

He looks behind him, to my fallen tent, and suddenly I'm furious.

"Tell me!" I demand. "I know you can talk!"

His eyes widen. A long beat passes, then he touches his throat. Just one finger down that long, straight scar. My ma used to tell me he had his voicemaker taken out because it was broken. I'm not so sure that was true now.

"You promise you can't? Don't lie," I say. I've had enough of that.

He touches his scar again and opens his mouth. Just a breath of air.

I don't know why, but I believe him.

"Salma and the twins, are they alive?"

He nods slowly.

"Did they move on?"

Hesitation. Nod. I sigh, relieved that they are still safe.

"You'll take me to them," I say. "But first I need you to take me to the Driver camp."

Lorcan's mouth drops open. He shakes his head adamantly.

"It's okay!" I tell him. "I know a Driver who's sick. He needs a doctor."

Another vigorous no. He points to the scar on his neck, his eyes wide with warning.

I stand too, now that my legs have regained their strength. "If you mean that they can't help him because they couldn't help you . . ."

He grabs my arms so hard I yelp. When he releases me, he points again to the remnants of his injury.

At first I don't know what he's trying to say, but slowly it dawns on me.

"There are rules," Kiran had said. *"If my people knew I'd broken them, there'd be consequences."*

"It was *your* people that did that to you?" I ask Lorcan.

He nods. And the stone-cold look in his eyes tells me they'll do the same to Kiran.

"I'll make them see. They can trust me, just like he trusts me. They wouldn't let him die, would they?"

Lorcan says nothing, and it hits me with one cold blow: They would not save him if they knew what he had done.

The Drivers can't help us. It's up to me. A chill travels down my body, and I'm sickened because I know I'm not enough of a healer to save him.

I do not understand these people. They hide in the shadows and slice their own members' throats in the name of protection. Kiran is not that way. I would trust him with my life.

Just as he is trusting me now.

"I have to go back," I say. There is no more time to waste.

Lorcan taps his chest twice, then points to me. Looks like he's coming, too.

DELL DID NOT GO far, and once she's gathered, we're off, riding at a brisk pace through the morning, following the trail of broken limbs and trampled brush I'd left in my hurry. It shames me; even a half-blind Tracker could have followed that. I must be more careful.

A motion in the woods freezes us, and before I take another breath our weapons are both drawn and aimed. I don't have time to worry—it's an animal that approaches, not a human. I'd recognize that flash of gray anywhere.

"Brax!" I call. "What are you doing here?"

He's whimpering. Concerned, I dismount and run my hands down his muscled legs, beneath his feet. I feel his stomach for any wounds, but find nothing. Lorcan's watching from his palomino stallion, eyes curious.

The dread slides over me. Something's happened. Brax has come to warn me of danger back at the camp. Trackers. Bears. Something.

"Dog!" I hear a girl whisper shout. "Here, doggy dog! Mangy old mutt!"

I dismount and run towards the sound, only to find Daphne crashing through the brush, more disheveled than ever. Her red hair is wild as flames and her uniform dress is shredded to her hips. Mud covers her front. The telltale signs of a fall. The instant she sees me she screams in surprise, then covers her mouth with both hands and shuts up quick.

"You scared the life out . . ."

"What happened?" I interrupt. "Where's Kiran?"

And then it hits me. She's left him because he's dead. I step back and keep stepping back until I run into Dell. I don't want to hear what she has to say.

"Riders," she sputters. "Drivers. I was . . . at the creek and . . . and they came and found him. I thought maybe you sent them, but they didn't look happy so I ran."

I feel my jaw lock into place. I turn as Lorcan approaches and all I see when I stare up at him is the glowing scar down his throat.

"How many?"

"I don't know. Five or . . . or six. We can't go back there, Clover. They were mad. Really mad."

But I barely hear her. I hardly register the feel of my foot in the stirrup or the strain in my arms pulling me up into Dell's saddle. The next thing I know I'm leaning low over Dell's neck, urging her to give me everything she's got left.

EVEN AT DELL'S fastest, we don't close in on the cave where I left Kiran until late afternoon. The mountain wind has cleared the area of the misting rain, and the sky is untouchable, infinitely far. I slow to a walk, taking my cues from Brax, who pads silently just ahead. When he lowers and the hair on his neck rises, I slide down.

I smell the smoke before anything. It's strong, from a fire larger than I would have made. My stomach tightens. They're not afraid of drawing attention like we are.

I'm alone. Lorcan hasn't followed, or if he has, he's a ways behind me. Maybe he's with Daphne. Maybe not. I have no help if this comes to a fight. Not that Lorcan would help me anyway, considering how they cut his voicemaker out.

None of this matters. I'm not leaving Kiran to be butchered like the half-dead Watchers in the Witch Camps. I tie Dell's reins to a low-hanging branch and leave her a hundred paces away.

Bounding over the creek, I approach the camp. There's a hidden place facing the shale wall, close to where I challenged the bear. That's where I'm hiding when I see them.

Five Drivers. All dressed in some mix of the same thing I'm wearing: Breeches, boots, a button-down shirt, a handkerchief. Their faces are clean, unlike the Drivers in the city. They've got nothing to hide out here.

The closest is a boy not much older than me. His hair is wavy and he hasn't shaved, but it doesn't look like he needs to all that often. His nose has been broken at least once—it's crooked—and that tells me he doesn't shy away from a fight. He's casually guarding the edge of the stream with a long bow.

Twenty paces to my left are seven saddled horses, tethered to trees. Seven. Which means that there are two Drivers I can't see from where I'm standing. I look back to the animals. My heart pounds so hard it hurts my chest. I begin to creep towards them, preparing to set them loose. I'll have to bolt once the chaos ensues, but hopefully it's enough of a distraction to steal Kiran away.

I adjust my position and from here I can see behind the boulders, to where my friend still lays. There's another Driver hunching over him. The sixth.

A girl.

I stare at her a moment, in awe. I've never seen a Driver girl before. She's got long honey-colored hair, plaited down her back, and she's wearing a buckskin dress not well suited for riding.

She's holding something in her hand. The sun catches it, and the metal reflects into my eyes. A knife.

She's going to cut his throat. She's going to take his voice-maker. Just like they did Lorcan.

I don't wait another moment. The muscles in my legs quiver, and I jerk to a stand, but before I can run something thin and rough flies over my face and ratchets around my throat. My hands drop the bow, swooping up to pull it loose. My body bucks, and I crash against someone behind me. My heel connects with his shin, my elbow sinks into his side, and I'm rewarded by a grunt and the loosening of the cord.

Growling. A sharp wince. Brax has him by the leg. In one last effort, the Driver boy shoves me hard into the stream, right in front of the clearing before the cave and his people. I'm surrounded. My eyes glance from face to face. A driver with bushy eyebrows holds a dagger in his left hand. The boy guarding the clearing has an arrow aimed directly at my heart. The one with the rope is older—maybe twice my age—and has spots on his skin. He's where I'll start; he's already breathing hard from my hit. There is a girl I'd thought was a boy earlier. She's got a bow too. No one else holds a weapon.

I'm not completely unarmed. I have Brax, crouched beside me, growling and snapping his jaw.

"Stay away from him!" I shout, careful not to use his name so they won't know he's talked to me. "Don't you touch him!"

They don't look to each other. They keep staring at me, playing perfect mute Drivers.

The girl with the buckskin dress draws my gaze. Her lips are pulled down in a thin frown, and when she moves through the parting crowd, I can see she's limping. Boards have been fastened to her ankles to keep them perfectly straight. She hunches over a crutch latched to her right forearm. The knife gleams from her right hand.

A shuffle to my right. I spin, ready to defend, but the wavy-haired boy does not move any closer. He's still holding the loaded bow, though now it's aimed at the ground. He's staring hard at me as though trying to read my mind. I can see his teeth grinding in his sun-weathered jaw.

The air seems to be thinning. I am aware of every movement of those around me.

"Leave them be."

I jerk back towards the strained sound.

Kiran's conscious, leaning against the shale cliff behind the girl with the boards on her legs. A sob bursts up my throat when I see he's okay, and that his face is flushed with life, not illness. His shirt is open and his wound has been redressed.

"Kiran," I whisper. He sends me a weak smile and I nearly buckle to my knees. I don't care how he's better, I'm just glad he is.

The girl's eyes twitch in response to his words. Her mouth drops open in silent question. Absently, she worries the metal shank in her hand.

"She's one of ours, Kyna."

Kyna, the one he spoke of in his fever dreams. I glance to the braces on her legs. *I've a soft spot for fragile women,* he once said when he'd spoken of Daphne. I wonder if he was talking about this girl. Kyna.

Whispers. The Drivers are speaking to each other. It takes a full beat to realize he's talking about me.

"She's got Driver blood?" Kyna asks. Her voice is like his, but higher. It takes me a moment to decipher the words.

"No, I don't," I say. My ma conceived me in the city; it's why she was marked. My father was some faceless buyer. A Magnate.

"She says she's not," says Kyna.

Kiran must be lying. He's probably told them this to free me.

"She doesn't know," he says.

"It's the outcast!" someone calls from behind me.

The eyes of every Driver, Kyna included, whip back to beyond the fire, to where Lorcan approaches, knives braced in both hands. They do not threaten him with their weapons, but seem frightened all the same.

I flex my fingers then pull them into fists, stronger with Lorcan near, but surprised by his presence. I hadn't even heard him sneak up.

"What is going on?" Kyna rubs a hand over her forehead. "What is he doing here? And how do you know she's like us?"

"Her stories," he says. "She talks about the outcast. She calls him by name."

"I . . ." I shift from one foot to the other, not sure what I'm supposed to say to get us out of this. "It's Lorcan," I finally say.

"Who told you his name?" Kiran asks.

"My ma."

Kiran takes a slow, pained breath. "She wouldn't know who he was unless someone told her, and the only one the outcast ever said he told was the girl he met in the city."

They all seem to know who he's talking about. Grim looks are exchanged, and all of a sudden I feel like I'm on display, like I'm on the auction stage again.

Shades of doubt slide over me. If Lorcan was my father, my ma would have told me.

"Of course," I say. "Lorcan's my father." I'm just playing along, but all the memories are flashing before me. Lorcan teaching me to use a bow, to set snares. His long walks with my ma. The worried anger when I'd broken my arm falling from his horse. The blueberry pie on my birthday.

I turn to glance at Lorcan and find he's already staring at me, his hand on his throat. His mouth opens and he works to swallow. And then, so quiet I barely hear it, he croaks out one single word:

"Mine."

I stare at him. That one word—the only word I've ever heard him say—changes everything. I don't care what kind of game we're all playing anymore.

"I'm not yours," I say.

"Would it be so awful?" Kiran mutters.

"Yes!"

He doesn't understand. It's okay for a Trader to come and go as he pleases, to have no obligation to help or stay. It's not okay for family. What would have happened if I had disappeared whenever I wanted? Who would have been there to do the hunting, to keep the twins safe?

I'm trying to meet Kiran's gaze to figure out what I should say next, but he won't look at me. He's staring at the ground, and even from here I can see his jaw flexing under the skin.

Kyna adjusts her place on the crutch, and in her hand I see a spoon, not a knife. She pulls a bottle filled with green syrup from her hip pocket. Medicine.

"You're a doctor," I say.

In Kiran's fever dreams he had said that Kyna needed a doctor, but he'd been delirious. Maybe he'd meant that she *is* a doctor.

Her brows rise. "I'm as close as he's going to get to one out here."

My shoulders fall. I'm no doc, I know that. But when she says this it sounds like I didn't help at all.

"So she's the half-breed," says Kyna, as if she's settling something.

The word stings.

Kiran looks up at me then, but there's no hint of the boy I know. His amber eyes are hard and uncaring, and they make me feel small.

"Yeah," says Kiran. "She's a half-breed."

That piece of me that belonged to him is crushed in his fist and thrown aside.

I lift my chest and narrow my eyes. I stand strong so they can't see how much it hurts to belong to no one. Because it *shouldn't* hurt. No one owns me. Not before, not now. Not ever.

The girl in the boy's clothes laughs cruelly.

"They snipped her da's voicebox because of her ma," she says. "And they sliced her ma's face because of her da. That's some love story."

I look back at Lorcan, hoping this isn't true, that he wasn't the reason my ma was cut. And when I think of how I asked the same of Kiran it makes me a little light-headed.

"Time for you to move on, Aiyana," Kiran says.

He might as well have slapped me across the face because that's what his words feel like.

His friends are all watching me. Staring at me. The freak. The outcast.

Kyna approaches him and slips beneath his arm as though she always belonged there. She watches me curiously over her hunched shoulder. The joke's on me, and she feels guilty. Well I don't want her pity.

Kiran's found his people, now I need to find mine.

"Yeah, all right," I tell him. "You were just slowing me down anyway."

Kiran's face is expressionless, like it was so many nights in the solitary yard. I can't stay any longer. I turn and walk back into the woods, soul sick that I will always remember him that way. With a face of stone.

CHAPTER 20

DAPHNE'S WAITING WITH THE horses. Her face is drawn tight, and even after just these couple days, her freckles are beginning to return. They make her look younger. She stands beside a fallen tree trunk, biting her nails and keeping her eyes on Lorcan.

"Is your Driver alive?" she asks.

"He's not mine," I say, still burning. "Why would you say that?" I untie Dell's reins from the tree limb, knowing she'll find her way the hundred paces back to him.

Daphne's arms drop. "So he's not coming?"

"No he's not coming," I snap. "We don't need him."

Lorcan lifts his brows at me, and I glare back.

"Is it true?" I ask him. There's still a chance that he'll say no, and maybe then at least one thing will be righted.

"Is what true?" interrupts Daphne.

Lorcan stands with one hand on the withers of the palomino, his stare deep enough to go right through me. I wish I had a shield so I could stop him from trying to read my mind. I don't want him to wonder what I'm thinking. I don't want him to know how I feel. I don't want to know him at all.

He inhales slowly.

"*Mine.*" It's just a breath. I doubt Daphne even hears him.

"Stop saying that!" I cover my eyes with the heels of my hands.

Kiran is gone; the second his people showed up he turned me

loose like I wasn't anything to him. And now Lorcan's trying to claim me as kin. It's like these men think I'm their property. It's like they don't know me at all.

A hand covers my shoulder. I shake it free, burning Lorcan with my glare.

"I'm not yours." My voice is trembling. "You aren't my family. You don't even know what family is. You weren't there when we were hungry. You weren't there when she got sick."

I lean closer, but he makes no attempt to back down.

"I couldn't heal her!" I shove him, but he only rocks back on his heels. "Metea and me, we did everything we could, but it wasn't enough. So I had to end it. *I* had to watch her die. *I* had to dig her grave. If you had been there you could have brought your Driver doc and saved her. But you weren't. You let me kill her."

My words are muffled into his jacket, and his wiry arms close like a vice around my shoulders. I lost my ma four years ago, but it feels fresh, like Lorcan just ripped that wound right back open. I hear a sound in his throat. Halfway between a choke and a sob. And I'm crying too. I want this nightmare to be over, but it just goes on and on.

"If I was yours you would have come for me at the Garden." I push away from him, and he slumps forward like I've punched him in the gut.

"Where are they?" I demand. "Where is what's left of my family?"

Very slowly he lifts his hand and points north.

"They wouldn't have moved that way," I say. "That's the direction of Glasscaster."

He nods somberly.

"You said they moved, not that they were taken!" My knees are feeling even weaker.

Lorcan shakes his head and points again towards the city.

Daphne moves behind me. "What if they weren't captured?"

I turn on her, and she jumps back a step.

"That's stupid. They wouldn't do that. Salma knows better."

Lorcan's chest rises and falls in a slow breath.

"No," I say.

Daphne is smoothing down the front of her dress. "Remember Rose and Lily? Both of them were from the outliers. Their fathers turned them in when they were of age for auction. Maybe your family did the same."

The look on Lorcan's face tells me it's true.

I don't believe it. I can't. But it must be true because everything I'm afraid of is. My mind flashes to Salma, to all the times she resented our home in the mountains. Without me to stop her, would she have gone to the city? Looked for work? Turned Nina in to the Garden?

Everything I know is shattering apart.

"Clover." Daphne's voice is as gentle as I've ever heard it. "Where else would they go?"

She stands before me, red hair matted and wild, face smeared with muck, and for the first time maybe ever, I'm really, really glad she's here.

Lorcan hands me the reins to his horse. I don't say good-bye. I don't even look at him. By the time Daphne and I are in the saddle, he's gone.

DAPHNE AND I RIDE north until the mountains begin their steep decline. I don't know why she's come with me, but I don't ask. The truth is, I want her to stay. It's better than being alone.

At night we make camp against a landslide overlooking Glasscaster. From here we have a clear view of the Witch Camps and the sinister gray-green smog that blankets the bright lights of the Black Lanes.

The city spills out into the distance, impossibly big. My family is somewhere inside those walls. There are as many places they could be as there are stars in the sky. It's almost funny. I never worried about finding them in the mountains, but in the city, I'm overcome by the feeling that they are truly lost.

The crack of a branch behind me makes me turn, and I blink as a red-haired girl with her arms crossed comes into focus.

"You should get some sleep," Daphne says.

Her saying so reminds me of how exhausted I am.

My feet drag as we walk back to where the palomino is tied, and I can barely keep my eyes open as I build a small fire. The camp is secure, we haven't seen any other tracks since noon, but that doesn't stop me from walking the area with Brax.

When I return, Daphne's sitting beside the flames, twisting her neck from side to side, trying to place each rattle, yelp, or whir of the forest's song. The hardest part of a new place is the not knowing.

"Did you eat?" I ask her, looking down at the charred jackrabbit I left to cool on a stone beside the fire. She stares at it, then lunges forward and digs in like she's famished.

I blink, realizing that she's been waiting for my permission. Daphne has never lived anywhere someone wasn't telling her what to do, when.

After a while she stops and wipes her mouth clean. Her shoulders sag and she won't look me in the eye. At an owl's hunting cry, she jolts to a stand. When I don't move, she sits.

"When I first came to the Garden, I thought there was a monster outside," I say. "I swore I heard it stomping down the streets."

She smirks. "What was it?"

"Music," I say. "From the Black Lanes. It took me a while to figure it out."

She gives a small laugh.

"Maybe he . . . the old Driver can help you find your cousins," she says as she scoots inside the bedroll from Lorcan's saddle. I notice how careful she is not to say the word *father*.

I shake my head, trying not to think about how we left him with nothing—no horse, no supplies.

"He seems decent," she adds.

"He's not."

It never mattered what kind of man he was before, but now all I can feel is betrayal when I think of him.

"Well at least he didn't sell you to the Garden."

I face her, surprised, and find her picking the leaves out of her hair. My feet tuck under Brax's belly while he happily tears apart a fish he pulled from a nearby stream.

"I thought that's what you wanted. A nice home. People to look after you."

She shrugs. "Maybe I want something else."

She tilts her head up then, and I remember the night before auction when Buttercup turned her away.

"Someone who'll fight for you," I say.

She nods. "Who doesn't care who you are."

The crickets have begun to sing, but Daphne doesn't even flinch. I wonder if things would have been different if Kiran hadn't known, or cared, who I was.

"I bet it was hard giving you up." I don't know why I say this. I don't know anything about her father.

"My birth mother was my father's forever wife," she says quietly. "He kept her and sent me away. I lied when I said I was his favorite. He was capable of love, he just didn't love me."

Daphne once told me how rare it was to become a forever wife. I don't think she ever really thought it would happen to her. In that moment, I feel worse for her than I ever have.

Images of Nina on the auction stage plague my dreams, and when I can't sleep anymore I sit on one of the logs by our fire and stare ahead, watching how the leaves that dance in the breeze are sucked into the flames and twist into tiny glowing flowers. Lilies, sweetpeas, daphnes. They flash gold for just an instant, just long enough to catch your eye, before burning to ash and disappearing forever.

DAPHNE AGREES TO KEEP watch while I sleep through the early morning, and when I wake, she's braiding strands of tall grass beside me. Rubbing my eyes, I squint over at her work and a grin spreads across my face.

"What?" she says, lowering her hands.

"That's it!" I count out the days in my head since the last auction. Trader's Day is only four nights away; all those who made enough in the farmer's markets in the outliers will be there. If the girls have been captured, they won't be sold until the auction in two weeks. I'll be able to find them by then.

I hope.

I'm going to make jewelry, like the kind I used to trade with Lorcan. I don't have the booth fees to get past the city-gate guard, but if I can make enough pieces to sell, maybe one of the other merchants will let me go with them if I promise them all the profits. If not, I'll have to steal the credits—and right now, I don't care if it's honest or not, I'll do it. I look enough like a Driver; I've got a horse. If I muddy up my face enough, they won't be able to tell I'm a girl.

I'll get them out the same way Daphne left. We'll make them all look like they've got the plague.

For the rest of the day I teach Daphne how to make simple snares from whittled branches. When the first catches a rabbit, I show her how to clean the kill and scour the pelt of flesh and hair, and then soften the skin with the animal's brains.

She vomits twice and then tells me to do it on my own. So much for being helpful.

By sundown we're cooking rabbit stew in Lorcan's pot, and I'm cutting the hide into long strips that can be braided into a necklace. I tell Daphne we'll need to gather precious stones tomorrow, and she only snorts and says, "We'll see."

It helps to have a purpose, but my thoughts keep pulling back to my family. I don't know how long they've been in the city or what's happened to them. I don't know if they're still together or if they've been pulled apart. Nina could be at one of the dorms preparing to come to the Garden. Tam could have already started treatments to become a Pip. Thoughts of Salma working the Black Lanes make me ill.

I think of Kiran, too, much as I wish I could shut him out.

Just after nightfall, Brax rises abruptly and sprints south. His instincts are just as good to me as the security fence at the Garden. There is no doubt in my mind that someone's broken our perimeter.

Daphne and I are on our feet in an instant, stamping out the fire and preparing to escape. As soon as she's mounted, I'm kicking through our tracks and cursing the Drivers that took back the bow. I only have twin knives from Lorcan's pack.

I keep my ears trained after Brax, but hear nothing. It starts to worry me; he would've given me a signal if Trackers were coming—a growl or a bark. He knows the difference between what's dangerous and what's not, and his silence worries me. Daphne mounts the horse, reaching for my hand to pull me up, but I keep staring in the direction Brax ran off.

"What are you doing?" Daphne whispers. "Let's go!"

"I'm going to go check it out," I say. "It might be an animal."

"A bear?" Her green eyes are as round as saucers.

I doubt it, but I'm not sure. I don't tell her this though; the last thing I need if we have to move fast is a panicked Daphne.

"Be ready," I tell her, and with a knife in one hand and a palm-sized rock in the other, I creep around the boulders guarding our southern side.

I can make out the outline of a horse by the water. If it's a Tracker, he's come alone or his friends are somewhere nearby. Silently, I move on, keeping low and moving fast.

It doesn't take me long to find our intruder. The night shadows leave only a silhouette; a figure crouched low over an animal lying still in the space between two trees. From here I can hear Brax panting. My blood runs cold—whoever it is has hurt my wolf.

Without another thought I launch the stone with full force.

A hand snaps up. Even in the fading light he catches it.

There's only one person who can do that.

"Kir . . . *Varick*?" A moment later I remind myself that we're not friends or anything else and steel myself for a fight.

He's marching through the mounds of rotting leaves towards me, a bow in one hand, the arrows slung over his shoulder. I'm still not used to seeing his face so clean. Brax the traitor trots behind him, tongue lolling out of his mouth.

"Don't call me that," Kiran says, flexing his hand. I wonder if he's hurt himself with that catch. I hope so. It was one of my better throws.

"It's your name," I say.

"Not to you, it's not."

I groan, tired of these games I can't figure out, even as my stomach fills with the flutters.

"You're better, I see." I move back as he comes close. I don't trust myself around him. He makes me lower every guard so that I'm defenseless when he casts me aside.

"Getting there," he says. "Thanks to you."

My heart squeezes. "What do you want?"

I hear the slow clip-clop of hooves, and in the growing dark my senses are baffled—has he brought his whole gang with him? Or worse, have Trackers found us? In a flash, I've stripped him of the bow and a handful of arrows from the quiver over his shoulder. He winces, letting me know that the ribs I just grazed haven't been completely healed by the medicine.

"It's just your father."

It takes a moment to sink in. I'm not used to thinking of anyone, much less Lorcan, as bearing that title.

I lower the arrow. "He's not my father."

"Just because you don't want it to be true, doesn't mean it's not," he says.

I turn away, but he grabs my arm. I jerk it out of his grasp.

"Why are you following me?"

He's close enough that I can see the flash of his copper eyes.

"I ran into Lorcan in the woods. In not-so-many words he told me your people are in the city."

"I don't have people," I say bitterly. "I'm just a *half-breed*."

The corner of his mouth twitches. "Better than being a full-blooded Driver I suppose."

His words hang between us for several long beats. Kiran's message is crystal clear: He thinks I'm angry not because of *who* my father is, but *what* he is. As if I haven't always been an outcast, regardless of bloodline.

"I don't care that I'm part *Driva*," I say.

He laughs, clearly not believing me.

"It's better than being half Magnate, isn't it?"

He hesitates at this.

"Besides," I say. "I need to be more than part Driver to get back in the city."

It takes him a moment to realize I've already planned my disguise, and when he does, his eyes go round.

"You're not going into that city by yourself," he finally blurts.

I straighten. "I'm not one of your fragile women needing protection."

Again with his I-don't-believe-you laugh. I cross my arms.

"And that's all that matters, is it?" he asks. "Believe it or not, Aya, your family isn't the only one in danger here. Do you realize the harm you could do going into that city? What if you speak? What if that temper runs away with you and you pick a fight? You're not an auction girl anymore, you're a lowlife. A Watcher can kill you without thinking twice. And anyone that sees will only remember that a Driver overstepped his boundaries. In the best case we'll lose business, in the worst, we'll all be hunted."

I step closer. "Just like I was?"

He steps closer. "Yeah, but this time if you get caught, they don't set you up at a high-security resort. They get rid of you, right there."

How dare he act like my life's been easy? I lift my arm to punch him, but he catches my wrist with his good hand.

"This is exactly what I'm talking about."

I shove away from him. "You're picking fights on purpose."

"You think they won't? You walk through those gates and you're *nothing*." His voice grows heavy, and I know that his own city experiences are filtering through.

"I'm not nothing," I say. I'm a cousin and a mother and a father and a sister all in one. "Even if you see nothing but a half-breed. . . ."

"Aya, you *are* a half-breed," he says.

The word lashes out like a whip.

He moves closer, gaze holding mine, hands beneath my elbows. "Half girl, half bird. Always trying to fly away." His mouth quirks in a tiny smile. "Once I dreamed you had wings."

I can see his temper settling in his eyes, just like I used to, before I knew he could talk. Mine is falling too, and in its place, a strange, nervous feeling forms in the base of my stomach.

Half girl, half bird. I wonder if this is a compliment. I'm not sure what to think after he humiliated me in front of his friends.

"It's not the first time someone's called me names." I do my best to hold my chin up. "I'm not crying about it. I just thought you were different."

A twisted, hurt look pinches his brows. He takes a step back, and smooths out the front of his shirt.

"You really don't care?" he says, bewildered. "You don't care who you are? Who *I* am? That doesn't bother you?"

I shake my head.

"I told them because I thought it would protect you," he says softly. "My people can be . . . strict about the rules. I never meant to hurt you."

I search his eyes for truth and find it. I wish I could tell him he didn't hurt me, that they're just words and my skin's thick enough that they just roll off, but these would be lies. The girls at the Garden couldn't knock me down, neither could the Governess. But Kiran's harsh words are like knives.

"Would you have told me?"

He runs his knuckles over his chin. "There's a lot I wanted to tell you."

"So tell me."

His mouth opens, but not a sound comes out. It reminds me of all the times I tried to make him talk to me in the solitary yard. I was okay with him being mute then. Now I'm not.

"That's a lot, you're right," I say.

For a moment he chews his bottom lip, running a hand through his hair. Then he says, "I'm coming with you into the city. Do me a favor and don't get sore about it."

This is probably the only apology I'm going to get. I should object, but I don't, because when it comes down to it, I don't want him to leave.

"Great, I need someone holding my hand," I say.

He laughs. "Was that a joke, Aya?"

"Shut up, Kiran."

I smile at the ground.

Grasping his injured side with one hand, he bends slowly to retrieve the bow I kicked. "You know, Drivers got to look out for each other. There's your first lesson, half-breed."

I scoff, wondering how he flipped the term to become endearing when it had sounded so ugly just a day before. But then, the day before, he'd thought I felt *Driver* was an ugly word, too.

"Does Kyna know you're here?" I ask.

He stills and his eyes grow sharp. I know that gleam—it's the kind I get when someone says something mean about someone I care about. I don't know why I brought her up at all; as much as I want to know what she means to Kiran, I don't want to know, too.

He breaks my gaze and digs the toe of his boot into the dirt.

"You don't have to worry about Kyna," he says. "I told her everything."

I don't know what *everything* entails, but it worries me all the same.

"Are you in trouble because of me?" There are many questions inside of this one that I'm too scared to ask: Will the other Drivers punish you for helping me? Will they make you an outcast? And the biggest question has the smallest voice: Is Kyna angry because you're here and not with her?

"You're one of us," he says. "I haven't done anything wrong."

It's not exactly the answer I was looking for, and when my face falls, he moves closer.

"What is it?" he whispers.

I breathe in, out, in again. Looking for just a few seconds of courage to say what I want to say.

"Would you have helped me get out of the mayor's house if you didn't know I was one of you?"

Now that it's dark, I can barely see his face. His shadowed hand lifts, and a finger gently traces the white scar on my earlobe.

"Aya, I knew you were like me. That's why I crossed that stream in the first place."

A stick snaps some ways away. It's only a twig on the forest floor, but it's enough to shatter our privacy. I jerk back, and Kiran lets me, though his movements are slower, like he's thawing from a swim in a freezing river.

It's Lorcan, and Daphne with him. They're both riding, and Dell's tethered to Lorcan's saddle. At the very sight of my supposed father, anger boils up inside me.

"Oh good, you're alive," Daphne says to me. "Thanks for the update."

I back another step away from Kiran.

Lorcan dismounts, returning my wary stare.

"I suppose he wants to come, too," I say under my breath.

"He's got an idea," says Kiran.

"I have my own idea," I counter.

"We're going to make jewelry for Clover to sell on Trader's Day," says Daphne. Her words make me stand a little taller.

Kiran's brows raise. "Where'd you get the credits to pay the booth fee?"

I fidget.

He gives me a half smirk. "There's only two reasons the Watchers let a Driver into the city: If we've got a team of fresh rentals, which we don't. Or if we've got enough credits for a booth license to sell goods on a Trader's Day."

He pulls a small leather pouch from the back of the saddle and gives it a little shake. Something jingles inside. Coin. From his days working at the rental barn, no doubt.

"We'll have enough to worry about without sneaking past the Watchers."

I nearly throw my arms around him, but stop just before I get there and awkwardly pat his arm. My face feels like it's on fire when Daphne snorts.

"There's one more thing," says Kiran. "Your father's seen your family."

I freeze. Turn slowly to face Lorcan.

Kiran continues to translate. "He went there to look for you.

He never saw you, but he found your cousin in the Merchant district. He knows where she works."

I am rooted to the spot, unable to move.

"And the twins?" My voice is weak.

Lorcan shrugs, mouth a tight, thin line.

"He never saw them."

"You looked for me?" I ask Lorcan.

After a beat, Kiran answers again. "Aran wouldn't let him into the barn, I guess. He *is* an outcast. Had he gone inside, he might have seen you in the solitary yard."

I nod; it's all I can do. I can't decide if it makes me feel better or worse knowing my father has been to the city.

Lorcan reaches into the inside pocket of his long jacket and retrieves a woven rawhide bracelet, embellished with a glowing copper crystal. I recognize the work. I'd made it, years ago. It surprises me that Lorcan kept it. I guess it didn't sell.

It seems we've had the same idea.

Daphne holds her hands out expectantly, and Lorcan drops the bracelet into them. "Ooh, that's pretty! I've never seen anything like it. What is it?"

I gulp. She's looking expectantly at me.

"It's . . ." I hesitate, but I know I need to answer because now everyone's looking at me.

"It's a kiran stone."

Before anyone else can say another word, I grab the palomino's headstall and head back towards camp. I've got four days until I'm going back into the most dangerous place in the world. It's time to prepare.

PART FOUR

THE GLASS
ARROW

CHAPTER 21

MIST SEEPS THROUGH THE trees well before sunrise, lowering the sky, leaving droplets of dew on each tree limb and pinecone. It chills me to the bone.

Today is Trader's Day. The day of a thousand maybes. Today I might finally be reunited with my family. I might be captured. I might be brought back to the mayor's house in shackles, drugged until I can't move, and made the plaything of Amir and his uncle.

I might not even make it that far.

So I breathe in the pine and the damp leaves. My fingers memorize everything they touch: the patterned bark on the trees, the rough surfaces of nearby boulders, the yellow-speckled grouse eggs we've gathered, and the freezing, clear water. And though it brings an ache to my chest, I say good-bye, because I know how it feels to be ripped away without that chance.

Our plan is simple: We'll go to the gates with our wares—the thirty-three trinkets Daphne and I have been staying up late to make and the two bulging sacks of furs Lorcan and Kiran have gathered from the other Drivers. The gatekeepers will grant us a business pass to set up a booth beside the auction stage—used today just for the livestock—but we won't be going downtown. We'll be going to a pharmacy in the residential district of the Merchant class. Lorcan saw Salma there two months back. Three days ago he went back to try to see her again, but did not. I try not to think too hard about what this might mean.

He came back with something else, though: two posters from the city. One with Daphne's body shot from the Garden—the head-to-toe picture that appeared in the leather book the Governess kept in her office. Kiran told us the caption below said that she's wanted for the Watcher death in the solitary yard and that she'll probably be in the Black Lanes hiding.

I didn't know until then that he could read. I pretended I knew what it said too, but I think he knew I was lying.

The other poster was of me.

It was the photo the Magnate had taken during my capture, with a close-up of my face and my bared teeth, my wild eyes, the sticks and leaves in my hair. I imagined this is what the Governess, Greer, and even the mayor must have thought I looked like again after even such a short time away. "*Property of Mayor Ryker,*" Kiran had said. "*Generous Reward.*"

I know the poster said more, but he crumpled it up and threw it in the fire before he told me. I wasn't too upset; it wouldn't have stopped me from going back to that city anyway.

We've gone over the rest of the plan ten or more times. Kiran's going to find some more Virulent costume makeup like he used to mark me when we escaped, and we'll use the same Skinmonger dress—assuming Salma's not already wearing one—to sneak my cousin out. The twins will go in the sacks in place of the furs, and we'll be gone before anyone knows any different.

I don't dwell on the obvious: that Amir's family is looking for me, that the dead Watcher may mean our stretched necks. I don't let myself think too much about Lorcan, who is still here even though he's had plenty of opportunities to disappear, or how whenever he's around I'm silent as he is, because this connection that hangs between us seems to have taken my voicemaker, too. And I definitely don't let myself think about the danger Kiran is putting himself in to help me. But every time I look at him my hands tremble and I've got to fight the urge to beg him to stay behind.

He already told me not to get sore about it, so I won't.

Daphne, wrapped in a fur mantle, comes to sit beside me in front of the pulsing white coals. Her red hair is growing out; it's actually more yellow, like Kiran's. Two nights ago she made me cut it short, almost to the skull. She said it was because of her picture on the posters, but I think it's because she doesn't want any more reminders of the Garden.

She's quiet now, rubbing the line that's formed between her eyebrows.

"You'll be all right, Daphne," I tell her. "The Trackers will all be in the city for Trader's Day."

Which doesn't exactly bode well for me and Kiran.

She scrunches her nose, drawing attention to the explosion of freckles that seem to be multiplying by the day. I feel guilty for leaving her here with no one but Brax for protection, but there's no need for her to take the risk of going in.

"If I don't come back . . ."

"Shut up Clover," she says. "It's bad luck to say things like that."

I snort. "I would have thought those Magnate scientists would've proved there's no such thing as luck."

Her eyes narrow on me. "Well if you catch me screeching to some mother hen, you'll know I've really lost it."

A smile quirks my lips. Daphne's been growing on me these past few days.

"You'll have the horses ready?"

"I've got one job, I think I can remember it." Her face falls. She begins drawing circles in the dirt with a narrow twig.

"Clover?"

"Yeah?"

"Do you really think I could have stopped the new girl from frying herself?"

Straw Hair. Who ran through the electric fence at the Garden the day she was sold. I cringe, remembering the smoke and the sounds and the smell of it all too clearly.

"Maybe. Probably not."

"I keep thinking I should try to stop you."

I take a deep breath, wishing I could say something to make her feel better, but knowing anything I said now wouldn't be true.

"You can't stop me, Daphne."

"I figured that."

Kiran whistles, but before the three of us can make our way down the mountain towards the Witch Camps, I rest my hand on Daphne's shoulder and say a quick, silent prayer for her protection.

WE STOP IN THE last bit of forest shelter before the field of discarded machines. There Lorcan takes the reins of both horses, and Kiran motions me through the trees.

It's quiet here, so quiet I can hear him breathe. We haven't been alone since he came back to find me. He's tried once or twice, but I've always been able to pull Daphne along, or stay near Lorcan. It's hard to think when it's just the two of us, and I can't be losing my head, not with everything we've been preparing for, and not after what happened with the other Drivers.

Definitely not when I know Kyna is somewhere waiting.

When I realize he's stopped, I stop too. He's staring at me, and the intensity in his gaze makes my heart stutter. His eyes are bright and sad and fearful, and as I stare back I feel everything he does, like an echo. For a flash of a moment I think, *This is exactly why I can't be alone with you,* but then the thought vanishes, and all I can do is focus on keeping my legs under me.

It's hard to believe there was a time I used to look at him and wonder what he was thinking. Now it feels like I've always known.

He reaches for my hand, and I let him take it. There are calluses across his palm and the pads of his fingers and they make my hands feel soft and small. Soon they'll be strong again like his, but I don't worry about that now, because when he touches me like this it makes me think we're going to make it. We're going to be all right.

"You ready for this, Aya?" The way he says my name makes me calm and nervous all at the same time and I force myself to swallow because even though it's stupid, it feels like he's not talking about the city.

"I'm ready."

He watches my mouth as I say the words, and that makes me look at his mouth and think about how I've never kissed anybody—never wanted to—which makes me wonder if I'm weak for wanting to now, and if thoughts like these change a person into the type whose only goal is pleasing her master.

"Nobody's ever going to own me again, Kiran."

He says nothing. His expression doesn't even change. The only sign I have that he's heard me at all is that he gives my hand a small squeeze. I think he must know I need to get this out.

"But," I say, wetting my lips, "but if trust was a thing you could hold in your hand, I would give mine to you. I'd let you have it forever and never ask for it back."

I take my hand out of his before he can say anything. My face is glowing, but I needed to tell him that, just in case this goes bad today. There were lots of things I wish I'd told my family before we were separated.

"Any last advice?" I ask.

He gives his head a quick shake and clears his throat.

"Just remember to be silent. If you think it, swallow it."

I nod and absently adjust my hair. It's tightly bound into a folded knot behind my head, just like the girl Driver I'd thought was a boy.

"And don't do that," he warns. I drop my hand and frown. The longer we stand here, the more aware I am of the bandages smothering my breasts. Daphne's tied them so tightly I can barely breathe. At least I don't look like a girl in these baggy clothes.

Without another word, Kiran pulls me down to the mud at our feet and smears my face with dirt. We cover our clothing, our necks, our hair. He even grabs a fistful of horse dung and smears it across my pants. I wish it made me invisible.

"Talk to you later," he says grimly. I nod. And we continue on.

IN THE WITCH CAMPS I don't even have to pretend I'm skittish. My memories from our last trek down this alley are still fresh and my eyes bounce from one side of the road to the other, searching for any of the defective Watchers we saw before. By the time we cross the wooden bridge—the last barrier between the mountains and the camps—I'm spooking at just about everything.

I wish I had Brax with me. I always feel safer with him.

Lorcan takes the lead, pulling the palomino by a grimy leather headstall. Two enormous sacks of pelts are strapped over the animal's barrel-shaped body. Kiran holds steady the right side, I'm on the left. The smell is enough to make me gag. With such little time to tan the hides, they still reek of rot and the brine we used to cure them. Between that and the way I smell, I can barely breathe.

We pass the tower of rusted cars, an ancient sculpture in the gray light, and I swear I feel eyes—seeing or not—on me.

A line of townsfolk from the outlying villages has formed

outside the city gates. Most are dressed in patched-up city clothes and are carrying baskets or pushing carts. A few have been denied entry and are standing off to the side while a Watcher rifles through their items. Fear tightens in my belly. We can't be searched. If they get too close they'll know something's off. They'll see right through me. They'll know I'm a girl, maybe that I'm a runaway, maybe that I killed one of their own. And then I'll never even have a chance to find my family.

"Keep your head down," whispers Kiran.

I do as he says, only chancing a quick glance forward every few steps.

In the mist it's hard to see clearly, but there are at least two parties before us. The man in front is trying to manage a small herd of goats for the livestock sales. Three people wait behind them, and as we get closer my gut clenches. A middle-aged man leads two girls in clean linen dresses. Stock for the Garden from a nearby town. The girls' heads are hung in shame, and as I draw closer I can hear one of them crying. It's the father. He keeps wiping his nose on the back of his hand and trying to hold it in.

"It'll be all right," he tells them with a hitch in his voice. "You'll have everything I couldn't give you."

I don't understand this; if he doesn't want to give them up he shouldn't. There are other ways to live.

The farmer in front is stopped at the open gate by two Watchers. After a few short words, he's ushered off to the side, and half his goats make a break for it. He goes chasing after them, his long staff waving.

We step closer. The man with the two girls makes it through. And then I'm standing in the gatekeeper's shadow.

"What. Have. You. Got." The Watcher is practically yelling in Lorcan's face as he points at the sacks. My spine straightens before I remember myself and slouch again, bolting my eyes to my dirty boots.

Lorcan's showing the Watcher the pieces I've made. Another Watcher shows up. He walks to Kiran's side of the horse and begins rummaging through the pelts and furs.

He keeps digging, and a drop of sweat makes a slow path between my shoulder blades. If he goes too deep he'll find the knife at the bottom of Lorcan's case.

Before he gets to the bottom, the Watcher abandons Lorcan's case and rounds in front of the animal to where I wait. As he begins the same process on this side, I shuffle back, just like Kiran taught me. I'm never to stand too close to anyone. That way it's hard to notice I'm nearly a head shorter than most of the men.

He searches for what feels like hours. Finally he gives the go ahead to the other Watcher who types something into a messagebox, and returns to the glass station. He comes back with a red form and shoves it towards Lorcan. Kiran's told me this is a one-day business pass.

We're in.

I keep my eyes down as we cross the threshold into Glasscaster, but not just because I'm supposed to. If I look up and see those high stone walls I tried to escape from for all those months, my feet might grow a mind of their own and run out of here.

The stones are hard under these big borrowed boots Lorcan gave me, and the buildings in the business district seem even more crowded than they were the last time I was here. They loom over me like Trackers with nets and make it hard not to hurry.

We join the main street I last travelled by carriage. The Black Lanes are quiet; the Virulent are either sleeping off the previous night, or have already begun their journey downtown, leaving just a few of the plagued leaning up against the trash bins and doors. On the side wall of a brothel I catch a glimpse of a line of posters, like the ones Lorcan brought back, but I don't let myself linger.

I become suddenly aware of three men passing by. They're

laughing drunkenly about something one of them has said. Without thinking, I lift my chin to watch where they're going, but Kiran pushes me roughly back to the horse and I nearly fall. The men look over and jeer again.

When I glance up at Kiran, his copper eyes are blazing. But as he shoves me back to my position, he whispers something in my ear.

"The mayor's looking for you. Remember that. Don't let them see your face."

My stomach drops like it's filled with stones. I can hear Amir's voice echoing in the back of my head: *"Where are you?"* My skin is crawling with the memories of Greer chasing me around the bedroom.

More people join us in the following minutes. Mostly townspeople coming to sell their wares at auction, but some Virulent too. Two hungover Skinmongers wobble by on the right. The closest one, in a skintight blue bodysuit, pukes in the gutter beside my feet. Rainwater and muck splash onto my pants. Then she stumbles into me, lifts my arm, and wipes her mouth with my sleeve.

I jerk away and lower my eyes. She casts me a look of disgust.

"Yick," says her friend. "You got Driver on you."

My jaw hurts because my teeth are grinding together so hard.

We edge into the residential district, and the flashes of my last trip here are coming faster. My last carriage ride to auction. The salmon dress and the satin gloves glued to my hands. My soft, filed-down feet within those impossible heels. *Elegance.* I am hardly elegant now.

More people, and with them, Watchers. I pass one on the right and when our gaze connects my stomach leaps into my throat. But he's not staring at me, he's staring through me. Like I don't exist at all.

"Sell goats, not girls!" comes a shout to my right. I remember the activists from my last auction and feel a jolt of hope that the Red Right endures despite the odds. The Watcher's head whips around and he's lost in the crowd.

They might not endure for long.

Merchants and their families push by us. Pips hold back their wards from coming too close and say things like, "No no, that's dirty," and, "Don't touch." Once I am bumped so hard I crash to my knees. The man never looks back.

At last Lorcan turns down a street lined by small shops. One is filled with wires and small machines. Another is all white and has a picture of a man leading a horse, with an X over it. I think this must mean Drivers aren't welcome there. A small medical clinic, and finally, a pharmacy.

It's a green-glass building with a glowing white plus sign in the front window. Not many people are on this offshoot, and those we pass are going the opposite way, towards the market.

We have arrived, and if Lorcan is right, my family has been no more than blocks away my whole time at the Garden. The very thought is enough to make me furious.

Lorcan does not pause to give me any look, warning or otherwise, and without another word, Kiran and I push inside.

"Quick," I hear Kiran breathe.

I want to ransack the place. To turn over every shelf until I find my family, and then to run for the mountains. But I don't. I stay timid. I tell myself to be still.

Two people are inside. A woman and a young boy, looking down a row of glass bottles filled with different colored liquids and pills. Kiran shuffles beside them, careful not to get too close, and grabs a container of sloshing green syrup. It looks like the medicine Kyna gave him. With a small frown I wonder if he still needs it; I haven't seen him use any since then.

He walks to the front and stands in line. I am surprised again. Kiran didn't tell me he had planned on buying anything. Does he even have credits? This was not part of the plan.

"May I help . . . oh, yes ma'am."

I turn to see that the woman and her child have cut in front of Kiran. Anger flashes over my worry, and if this were any other place I would shove her aside and tell her to wait her turn. I don't know how Kiran stands being treated this way. The walk from the gate to the pharmacy has been enough disrespect to last me a lifetime.

I look past the pair to the Virulent woman behind the open window at the checkout counter. She has long dark hair, pinned back in the city fashion, and large brown eyes. A full chest is crowded into a tight white uniform. The tell-tale sign of her class is slashed across her right cheek.

Salma.

My knees weaken. My blood turns to water. She's been marked. I want to kill the Watcher that did that to her.

She couldn't have turned herself in. Lorcan's wrong. She wouldn't have done this to herself. She's too vain.

But she's still so beautiful, and I don't care why she's here or how she came here anymore, because I've found her. I've finally found her. I could weep from the joy of it.

The woman checks out and leaves the shop. The bell ringing overhead snaps me from my trance, and I run to the counter.

"Salma," I croak.

Her eyes shoot up, first to Kiran, then to me. Even through the dirt and the costume and the months between us, she recognizes me instantly. Her mouth falls open. A shudder runs through her body, and then she does the unthinkable.

She slams the divider window closed.

"Salma!" I shout.

"*Aya,*" I hear Kiran hiss. But he realizes that he can't stop me now. Just as I'm jumping atop the counter, shoving the glass barrier aside, he's racing back to the front and bolting the door.

The glass comes away with a screech, and I stuff my body

through to the desktop on the opposite side. There's a credit machine here, and tall shelving units of more glass bottles. I barely register the crash of something metallic in the front room.

Salma's running to the back corner, making a sharp turn around the last shelf. She's afraid of Kiran; that's the only explanation. I need to stop her before she runs out the back of the building and calls for help.

My too-large Driver boots slip rounding the corner, and I grab the edge of the shelf, knocking a dozen bottles to the tile floor. They shatter, sending shards of emerald and blood-red syrup across my pants. My eyes water as the fresh burst of antiseptic hits the air.

"Salma!"

I reach her just in time to stop her from pushing through the exit door, and shove her hard against the interior wall. I kick the door shut.

"It's okay," I say in a rush. "It's me, you know it's me!"

"Let me go!" The tears are already streaming from her miserable eyes. One hand goes to cover her scar, and the move twists something inside of me. I drop her and she slides down the wall like her muscles have given out.

It's shock, it must be.

"We have to go, Salma," I say. "Where are the twins?"

"Why'd you come?"

"What?" I kneel beside her.

"Why, Aya?"

"Salma, it's okay. I'm here now. Everything will be all right. You don't need to be afraid anymore."

"I'm not going back," she says. She will not look up to my face.

A streak of fury blinds me and the next thing I know my hands are gripping her biceps with bruising force and I'm shaking her so hard her head wobbles on her neck. She has to see reason. She *has* to. We don't have time for this.

"Stop it!" I shout. "I'll fix it, you'll see. We'll be safe. I promise."

Something connects hard to the back of my skull and bright white spots explode in my vision. I release her and fall back onto my haunches. When my hand runs along the back of my head, it returns bloody.

"Leave her alone!" cries a shrill voice. I crumble sideways, still blinking hard, and register a little boy with a cap of straight black hair. A broom handle is held fast in his grip. He's tall for his age. *So* tall. And the boyish fat on his cheeks is all but gone. His black eyes are as sharp as knives.

"T-tam?"

"Leave us alone!" says another voice. There, beside him, is Nina. She's wearing a white apron, as is her brother. Her skinny arms stick out from the sleeves and grasp a metal dustpan like a knife in both hands. Her hair is wound up, much like Salma's. In her ears hang long beaded earrings. The sign of the Unpromised.

Their clothing. The earrings. I know what's happened then. Salma has done it. She's turned my family in.

My throat is so tight I have to cough to speak.

"Tam, Nina, it's me. It's Aya."

I need to be softer, gentler. They're afraid, and gentleness is what they need, but it's so hard to be calm.

Kiran appears. There's a metallic box in his hands. A scanner box; he must have gotten it off the ceiling in the main room. He lays it on the floor and stomps the heel of his boot into it.

The twins are looking between us with frightened stares. The fear in their eyes makes me want to curl up and die.

"We've got to go," I tell them. "I'm taking you home."

They keep staring. It's like they don't recognize me. It's like they've forgotten me, when all I've thought of these past months is them.

"Please." What I'm asking for, I don't know, but when I reach forward and grab Tam's arm, he raises the broom as though he'll hit me again.

"I'm your cousin, Aya," I say, my heart breaking. "I'm going to take care of you. I'm here now, it's going to be all right."

Nina's crying. She's looking to Salma now, who is hiding her face in her hands.

"Salma, tell them. Tell them it's true."

Nothing.

"*Aya,*" presses Kiran.

"No," I shake my head. "We have time. There's time." The grief is grasping at my limbs, pulling me into the floor.

Tam whispers something I can't hear.

"What?" I ask, crawling before him and rising to my knees. But he's so tall now, he's a head above me.

"You left us," he says.

"I didn't leave. They took me. The Trackers got me."

"You left us!" he yells. "Salma told how you left us and went to the city. How you didn't want us anymore."

"We came to the city, too," says Nina. "She said you'd be here, but you weren't."

"I'm here now," I say quickly. "I *never* would have left you. You know that. They took me. That's what happened. Tell them, Salma!"

She looks at me, the tears in her round brown eyes all dried up. In their place is pleading, and it makes my chest ache even more.

"We are just women," she says. "Why must you always try to be more?"

I don't know what to say. It's not until Kiran grabs my shoulder that I can even look away.

"It's true," says Salma to the twins. "Aya was taken."

They stare at her and then back at me. Nina's crying. She goes to Tam, and he puts his arms protectively around her shoulders. When did he start doing that? When did he learn to take care of her? Even now I swell with pride.

"I'm taking them home," I tell Salma. "Come if you want."

She does not get up off the floor.

Very slowly, Tam lowers his broom.

"Come on, Salma," he says expectantly. She doesn't get up.

Nina walks tentatively over to me, and after a long, searching gaze, places her forehead against my stomach. The tears stream from my eyes, and my arms, that have longed to hold her all these days, are finally filled.

I remove her earrings and feel them burn my palm.

"Get up!" Tam orders Salma. She looks away from him with shame.

I grab her arm, preparing to hoist her up. The last chance that I will give her. She shakes me off and turns away. I drop the Unpromised earrings, and they make a nest of beads in her lap.

"Let's go." I turn away, my heart tearing, and we head to the front of the building.

I don't look back. Not once.

CHAPTER 22

KIRAN MOTIONS FOR LORCAN to lead the palomino into an alley between the pharmacy and the doctor's office. There we empty the hides from the leather sacks and hoist the twins into their places. I notch small holes in the sacks so they can breathe, and hope that no one notices how the shape of these packs has changed completely from the full stuffing of before.

The twins don't complain. They're the bravest kids I know.

"Aya," Nina whispers as I place a fur over her.

"Yes?"

"The Driver boy can talk."

I smile. "I know. But it's a secret, okay? We can't tell anyone."

"I won't. I'm good at secrets."

"Quiet now."

She doesn't make another sound. The last I see of her is the reflection of her eyes in the darkness, just before I cover her with a pelt.

I blow out a slow breath through my teeth and prepare for what's to come.

We begin our journey back towards the front gates. Lorcan's sticking to side streets, avoiding the main drag. We step over a body in the alley, its eyes red and swollen from the plague. I'm glad the twins don't see him, but I can't help but wonder what other horrors they have seen since Salma brought them here.

Downtown, the music has begun and the market has opened.

I can hear the screech of the speakers, even half a city away. It pumps a new urgency through me.

When the neighborhoods end, we have to cross back onto Main Street to enter the business district. Walking this way places us directly beside the Garden, and my heart beats harder as the familiar chain fence and its cameras come into view. The rec yard is empty today—the girls must be inside for one of the Governess's presentations—but in my mind I can see them in their black dresses, standing in their groups by the water, calling to the men who walk by on their way to work.

I hear the clatter of livestock on the pavement up ahead and think for a moment that it might be the man with the goats. I'm wrong. It's a team of four horses, already saddled, tethered to a single rider on a prancing black gelding. I glance up as we approach. The man has a thin face with high, ashy cheeks. Greasy gray hair. A turned-up snout.

Ferret Face. Aran. The Driver from the barn where Kiran worked.

I place my hand protectively on the leather sack, feeling Nina adjust beneath. Kiran is on the other side with Tam. Lorcan still leads the palomino.

Aran looks at Lorcan and nods quickly. He glances over to me next, and I can feel his stare burning right through my forehead. He knows who I am; he must. There's no reason for him to look at me this long. The need to run hits my feet, and I begin pushing faster. But Lorcan keeps the same steady pace.

Aran pulls to a halt. A quick glance up reveals that he's looking over the animal's back, directly at Kiran. His face grows tight with confusion. Even over the sounds of the horses stamping impatiently on the cobblestones, I can hear his sharp breath.

We walk on briskly, leaving Aran open-mouthed in the center of the street. I pat Nina reassuringly, but this time she doesn't move. Neither of them have made a sound. They're both doing so well. They know how important it is to stay still.

That or they're unconscious, smothered by the stench and the weight of the pelts.

We cannot reach the gate fast enough.

When we pass the Black Lanes I don't look over to see the posters hanging on the wall of the brothel. I keep my head down and my feet moving.

At last we reach the Watcher station, the most dangerous part of our journey. Now, if the twins—especially an Unpromised Nina—are found, we will be lucky to hang. More likely, we'll end up bleeding in the street at the end of a Watcher wire. I shove these thoughts from my mind. There is nothing we can do now but push forward.

Travelers and traders are still attempting to enter the city. Outside, the man with the goats has finally organized his crew and is attempting to enter. The small white animals are bleating loudly, finally tied together by different ropes.

One of the Watchers registers our presence with a stiff tilt of his head. Without prompting, Lorcan opens his long black coat, revealing that the jewelry pieces are now gone. He hands back the red business pass, which we've used for less than two hours, and the Watcher takes it. There are no questions asked about any weapons, food, or machinery.

The man leads his goats through the gates just as we are approaching.

The second Watcher sees us from the station and heads our direction. I can feel the cool knife I've moved from the sack to my hip and hope that I don't have to use it.

He goes to Kiran's side first, intent to check our goods rather than ask the security questions he thinks we won't understand. His monstrous shoulders tower over the bowed back of the stallion and Kiran's hunched form.

Lifting the leather covering, the Watcher reaches inside, inches away from where I know Tam is laying. My eyes focus on the wire strapped to his chest. Every hair on my body prickles.

Before we came, Lorcan promised me one thing. If something happened to me, he would get the twins out of the city. I feel that promise now, riding on my shoulders like a storm cloud ready to burst.

I will trade my life for Tam and Nina's.

At that moment Kiran falters backwards, and when he does, he trips over a goat. In his attempt to right himself, he stumbles into the owner, who releases the ropes binding the small herd together. The goats pull all different directions, bleating while their owner yells at Kiran.

The goats escape down Main Street.

Kiran is brilliant.

The man chases after the herd. The Watchers appear as though they might follow, but first point us through. On the way by, I see one pick up his messagebox and begin typing what I assume is an alert to his comrades stationed farther down on Main Street about the incoming chaos.

The gray wall looms high above on either side, disappearing into the mist and smog as though it was an illusion to begin with. As though this victory is not real. But it is.

We are free.

THE WITCH CAMPS ARE still empty in the daylight, but I am guarded all the same. I will not make it out just to see our success destroyed by a Watcher mutant. I stare at the rusted machines as if my gaze alone will protect us. No one will stop us now.

Finally we cross the bridge. We enter the tree line, and though I want to shout with joy, I keep steady. I won't relax until we're high upon my mountain, surrounded by our Tracker traps and hidden from the city below.

Hastily, we unhook the bulging leather sacks straddling the

horse's back, and Tam and Nina, smelling rank and slick with sweat, poke their heads out. Despite my relief, it hurts inside to see that Nina's face is wet with fresh tears.

I kiss her cheeks and then round to Tam, who doesn't even look at me as I set him on the ground. He tears his apron off, stomps it into the dirt, and walks away.

A part of me will always hate Salma for this moment.

WE ARRIVE AT THE plateau just before sundown. A brook halves the clearing, and on the opposite bank a half-crazed Daphne is poised, aiming a loaded bow at us. She drops it with a clatter. Before I know it, she's sprinted across the short distance and is hugging me hard.

"Were you going to shoot me?" I ask as the air is squashed from my lungs.

She starts to laugh, but there's a hiccup in there too.

"I don't even know how to use it."

I'll have to remind myself to teach her later. If she's going to live out here with us, she'll need to know how to hunt and defend herself.

I stop myself, shocked that I've come to expect that Daphne's going to live with us. The thought of her moving on to a town like Marhollow bothers me. I think back over the last weeks, but cannot pinpoint the moment I started thinking of her less as a half friend and more as a half sister.

An instant later I'm tackled by Brax, who pins me to the ground with his giant paws. He licks my face and nuzzles his wet nose against my neck. I giggle despite myself and bury my fingers in his coat. Silently, I thank him for giving me hope all these months. For making me remember what's important.

"Ooh!" yells Nina. "Aya's got a wolf, Tam!"

He only shrugs.

"You want to meet him?" I ask. Tam shakes his head and stalks to the edge of the stream alone. I rise to follow, but Kiran stops me.

"Give him some space," he says.

I cast him a narrow look. "You don't know what he needs. He's just a kid."

"Doesn't look like he's been a kid for a while." Kiran removes his dirty shirt to launder, and replaces it with another from his saddlebag. My eyes trail over the bandages on his chest and the bruising that leaks out from beneath them. I look away, embarrassed, and catch sight of a green bottle in his pack he stole from the pharmacy. With a flash of fury I think of Salma.

As much as it pains me, Kiran is right. My little cousin has permanent shadows beneath his eyes. His youth has been stolen by the terrible things he must have seen in the city. I wish I'd been there to protect him.

We sweep the area clean of our tracks and leave at once. The strongest riders take the twins. Nina with Lorcan on the palomino. Tam with Kiran on Dell.

Daphne and I follow on foot. A warm, reckless feeling is expanding inside of me, but I refuse to let it loose. *Not yet,* I tell myself. There will be time to celebrate once we make it to the mountains. Time for the children to heal. But I think I might erupt as the miles between us and the city add up.

After a while Nina trades places with Daphne. She walks beside me, her little warm hand in mine. Every once in a while I catch her looking up at me as if to make sure I'm really here, and when she does, I kiss her head and tell her how brave she is. Behind us, Lorcan leads the palomino while Daphne rests her feet and rides in silence.

As the night darkens, I hear Kiran talking softly to Tam.

"... so Mother Hawk says she'll give a glass arrow to the first beast to make it across Isor, and whoever wins it won't ever be hungry again. The bear takes the lead ..."

"It wasn't a bear."

These are the first words Tam's spoken since the pharmacy. I slow, but am careful not to turn around and ruin this moment. I'm surprised Kiran remembers this story; it was the one I told Daphne while he was passed out with fever. Hearing mention of it now reminds me of the way my ma used to tell us not to worry because she had the glass arrow. I wish I could tell her I've got it now. I'm going to make sure they're safe and healthy. I'll do whatever it takes.

"I'm glad to hear it," says Kiran. "I'm not so keen on bears these days."

I wince quietly.

"It was a fox," says Tam. "And a deer."

"And the fox wins?"

"The deer wins. You talk funny."

"Not nearly as funny as you."

"*Neely*," copies Tam.

I can't help it, I laugh into my sleeve.

"Great," grumbles Kiran.

I want to hear Tam's voice again. I want him to laugh too, but I realize Lorcan, taking up the rear, has pulled up short. At this warning we all grow very still. The darkness seems to thicken, making it impossible to see more than a few paces away.

Brax backtracks, curving silver tail the last piece of his sleek body swallowed by the night. I wish I could see through those ice-blue eyes to what lurks behind us. To hear what he does, instead of the pulse echoing in my ears.

"Clover?" Daphne whispers, frightened. I hush her.

An instant later we see the narrow beams of the searchlights cutting through the trees.

Trackers.

"Run!" I shove Nina towards Kiran and Tam. He reaches down and pulls her in front of him, and with only a quick, concerned glance my way, turns Dell and sets her galloping into the dark.

Brax begins to bark, a loud warning that ends in a snarl. Fear surges through me. I strain my eyes into the black, but see nothing. Then, Lorcan grabs my waist and hoists me up behind Daphne. One slap on the animal's rump and we're off, running full out through the forest.

It's so dark, I can barely make out the trees as they whip by. Daphne ducks low to avoid the branches, and I cling to her body for dear life, the flex and pump of the horse's muscles making it near impossible to keep my seat.

Shouts break through the rush of the wind in my ears, and I squeeze my heels harder into the horse's ribs. The Trackers are close; I can almost feel their breath on my neck.

"Faster!" I urge, not just to Daphne, but to Kiran too, wherever he is. He must get the twins away. My mind turns to Lorcan, left behind with Brax, and I feel like a coward for leaving them, but I have to make sure the twins are safe.

A shot slaps through the trees, too far away to hit us. Another, this time closer. Guns. The telltale echo warns us an instant before the bullet whizzes past my thigh. A loud *crack,* and a bullet lodges into the trunk of a tree on our right, spraying splinters into my side.

Through it all, I hear the howl. Brax is close; he must be following us.

Daphne's as low as she can get on the horse's neck, and I'm pressed flush against her. I don't turn back now. I can't. The wind and the lowest branches catch my hair, ripping pieces away, searing me with fresh terror.

Crack! This one followed by a high-pitched yelp.

The cry sinks through right to my bones, and I can't help it, I don't even think about it.

I look back.

Just as I'm turning my head, the horse swings around a tree in our path. I slide off the side, Daphne's cry in my ear. My fingers grasp for anything to right myself, fumbling over the thick wool saddle pad. Daphne grabs my knee just as the horse jumps over a fallen log. For one beat I'm flying, weightless and free. The darkness surrounds me. My arms spin like swinging ropes.

And then I crash.

I hit the log first. My hip connects hard, and the rotting wood collapses under my weight. I roll to a stop, my shirt twisted around my neck. The stars waver and grow dim.

My heart pounds, drowning out all other sounds.

The breath returns and with it, pain. It screams through my body like I've jumped into a fire.

"Clover! *Aya!*"

Who is that? Her voice is unclear. My mouth tastes like copper and my face is wet.

"Aya! Get up, *get up!*" Daphne's looking down at me from atop the yellow horse. Foam drips from his muzzle as he chews the bit.

Brax. Panic makes me as strong as a Watcher. I leap to my feet, feeling my muscles flex. My eyes must be bleeding, because I see only red. I must go back for my wolf friend. I have to see what's happened to him.

But I can't.

I reach for Daphne's outstretched hand and hoist my foot into the stirrup just as two more shots ring out.

A ferocious beast appears, black like the sky, fast as a hammer striking a nail. Its muscular chest rams into my body, sending me sprawling again. Its front hooves claw the sky. I scream, realizing I'm about to get trampled, and twist out of the way just as the hooves come down beside my head.

Another horse is coming. I feel the ground shaking with its

approach. When I look over my shoulder, I see her. A chestnut mare with white rings around her eyes.

"No!" I shout.

Kiran's come back for me. Alone.

The familiar *twang* of an arrow, and then the Tracker atop the black steed gives a muffled grunt and slides off the saddle, landing on the ground with the thud of dead weight. His horse bolts. From where I am, I can see the arrow rising from the right corner of the man's chest, but when I look up, Kiran's bow is still notched, and Daphne's hands are empty. They're both looking beyond me, and when I follow their line of sight I see another rider.

I jolt up, but stop myself from running when I see the long, dark jacket, stretching to the man's knees, and the dirt-stained shirt peeking out from his collar.

Lorcan. He's riding a Tracker's horse. Before I can think of what this means, another yell comes from the woods. Lorcan turns in the saddle and releases a second arrow. Somewhere in the dark another Tracker falls.

Two, maybe three downed Trackers. All at Lorcan's hand.

My father has saved us. Almost.

There's one more. He'd been holding back, behind the other three. Now I see his light whipping away as he escapes towards Glasscaster. We have no time to wait. We must press on before he returns with more bounty hunters.

Lorcan nods at us then spins his horse around and tears after them.

Kiran dismounts and leaves Dell's reins with Daphne as he approaches the body. He crouches, removing something from the dead man's coat. As I move closer he crumbles it in his hands and rises to face me.

"You all right?" There's something worrisome in his voice; it's low and trembling, and when I'm close enough to look into his eyes I can see the fury there.

"The twins," I say, grabbing his arms. "Where are they?"

"In a tree by the pond up ahead. They were well hidden before I turned back."

Kiran doesn't even attempt to block my path as I stare down at the face of the man who tried to trample me.

It's Aran. His ferret face is frozen in shock. His silver hair is spread over the ground in long greasy points. I snatch what is in Kiran's hand—a crumpled paper—and bite down on my bottom lip when I recognize my own face on the wanted poster.

"Why's he got this?" I ask. "I thought Drivers were supposed to look out for each other. You said they were supposed to look out for each other!"

He snatches the paper back and stuffs it into his pocket.

"I think . . . he thought he was," Kiran says, muttering curses under his breath. "He must have remembered you from the Garden. He saw me with you once, questioned me for days about it. I never told him who you were. When he saw us in the city, he must have thought I broke the rules." His hands are latched behind his neck.

In my mind I can see it: Aran pulling my poster off the wall, taking it to the Trackers.

"He meant to have you killed," I say. "For stealing me."

Kiran's expression is grim. I look down at Aran again, but any remorse I might have felt for him is gone. He nearly got us killed. He might yet.

"We have to hide the bodies," I say. We have only a short time left before more Trackers come after us.

He nods. "I'll do it."

I shake my head. "It'll be faster if I help." I look to Daphne, but she doesn't need me to say the words.

"I'll find them," she says.

"Keep going until you hit the river," says Kiran. "We'll catch up with you."

She goes, taking my hope with her.

IT'S SICKENING, BUT WE succeed in shoving Aran's body beneath an overgrown manzanita bush. The branches grab at his clothes, but eventually we've finished the job. Kiran doesn't say anything, but I wonder if he wants to. My people bury the dead; to leave him like this is the ultimate punishment. If his soul is not sung on it will stay here, wandering, hopeless for another life.

We don't have time to linger. There's one more body in the dark nearby that we have to find, not to mention whoever was riding the horse before Lorcan.

"Have you seen Brax?" I ask, knowing what Kiran's answer will be.

He shakes his head.

My chest is hurting, and as we search through the dark for the other Tracker, I look for any flash of silver.

"We'll split up," says Kiran. "Stay close. We don't find him soon, we're moving on."

I couldn't agree more.

It's impossible to find anything the forest means to keep hidden. The roots of the trees trip me as I venture further into the shadows, but the body is nowhere. I search around every boulder, trying to remember where that yelp came from, just as I'm trying to remember where the Tracker fell.

I tell myself Brax is fine. When I threw the rock at him in the city he scrammed, and that's just what he's doing now. Sulking. I'll probably pay for it later.

Finally, I find the Tracker. He's already halfway under a felled trunk, and his arms are beneath him, so bent they've got to be broken. I wish more than anything Kiran was with me now. I swallow down the burning bile in my throat and refuse to look at the dead Tracker's face as I get low and shove him into the brush. In a hurry, I grab some nearby branches and cover him up. It's good enough for now.

"Kiran!" I call, as loud as I dare.

First there's nothing, then the crunching steps of someone on foot. He's moving slowly, and for an instant I consider that maybe it's not him—Kiran would be in more of a hurry. But then he makes his way into a small clearing, back bowed to support the weight of the heavy load that heaps over his arms.

My stomach twists so hard I almost double over. It's small enough to be Daphne or one of the twins. I rush towards them, stopping short when I catch a flash of silver in the starlight.

"Brax?"

Kiran meets me in the middle of the clearing and lays the wolf's long body on the ground. He's gentle, too gentle, like he's been carrying a sick child.

I fall to my knees, running my hands over Brax's long face, lifting his head. His neck is limp. I shake his legs, but he doesn't pull them back. His silver coat is soiled by slick blood, gleaming black in the moonlight.

"Come on, Brax," I say, quietly. "Come on, boy."

I hear a rustle in the trees above us. The flapping of a bird's wings. I need to concentrate if I'm going to help him, but sounds are too loud and my fear is too sharp.

"Sh-shepherd's purse. It'll stop the bleeding. You have to find it. It l-looks like a dandelion." I use my shirt to stop the blood. "Kiran, please!" I shout when he doesn't move.

He stands. I think he means to go find the flower, and the twisting in my stomach loosens just a little, but he doesn't. He crouches behind me, and his arms slowly wrap around my body to pry me away.

"No!" I bury my fingers in Brax's coat. He's still warm.

I just need a little more time. I can stop the bleeding. I can heal Brax. I saved Kiran from the wire wound, I can do this. And then we'll be gone, all of us, safely hidden in the mountains.

"Let me go."

Kiran's grip is unyielding. One arm around my shoulders. The other around my waist. I writhe against him. He falls back onto his heels, rocking steadily.

"We don't have time, Kiran!"

Brax is still.

I see him as a puppy. Hear his proud little bark. He watches over me in the solitary yard. My head rests on his shoulder while we sleep. He keeps me alive so I have to keep him alive.

"Let's go home," I say between sobs. "Get up, boy. We've got to go. Get *up*!"

I'm going to teach him how to guard our camp. He's going to come with me to hunt grouse and fish. My wolf is never going to eat trash again.

A rumble begins in Kiran's chest. A low hum parts his lips, pressed against my hair just above my ear. His voice cracks, then grows stronger.

Kiran's singing. He's singing Brax's soul on to Mother Hawk. Like I did for Bian and Metea. Like I did for my ma. I don't ask how he knows to do this, I just wish he'd stop. Brax isn't ready. He hasn't even seen how good freedom can be.

"No," I tell Kiran, shaking my head. My face is wet with tears. We don't have time for this, we have to go.

Kiran doesn't stop. His voice lifts. His grip never loosens and he keeps rocking. Front and back. Front and back. The air is so thick I can barely breathe. The night is so dark it masks all my senses. Everything but the pain.

Brax is dead.

The fight dies inside of me, and I sag in Kiran's arms. My lips stay sealed, but a scream echoes inside my ribs.

Kiran stands slowly, pulling me with him. I rest my head back on his shoulder. It takes me a moment to realize he's speaking to someone.

Lorcan. He stands silently beside us. I don't know how long he's been there.

They want me to go. To leave Brax here, half under the brush with the same scum who took his life. And much as I hate it, they're right.

We must move on. We've already been here too long.

I detach from Kiran's chest.

"Did you find the other one?" I ask Lorcan, my voice weak.

Lorcan shakes his head.

"We should split up, go different directions," says Kiran.

"They're looking for me," I say. It's clear now if they come after me, they're going to find the twins.

My gaze lifts to meet Lorcan's. I don't have the strength to feel as grateful for what he's done as I should. All I can do is beg for his help one more time.

"You have to take care of them. You can protect them. All of them. Daphne too." I hesitate. "And when I'm sure the Trackers won't follow, I'll meet you at our mountain."

A strange look passes over Lorcan's face. His brows pinch, and he runs his knuckles absently down his throat.

"I'll bring her home," assures Kiran. My throat swells with emotion.

A few moments later, when Lorcan and the palomino are gone, I turn to Kiran and say, "I have to bury Brax."

He doesn't say a word, he just nods.

CHAPTER 23

WE LAY BRAX'S BODY to rest between two pine trees, where the ground is soft and less riddled by roots. Because of our hurry, the grave is too shallow. There's not even a stone to mark the spot. It is a far cry from the hero's funeral he deserves, but it's all we can do. When we're done, my fingernails are ripped and dirty and my hands are bright red with cold.

"I'm sorry, Brax."

These are the only words I can think to say. As soon as they're uttered, Kiran hoists me up atop Dell, and together we ride hard southwest.

The sun rises what seems like too soon, and with it, new concern for my family. I hope Daphne has found the twins, and that they've arrived at the river, and that Lorcan is there to protect them. I tell myself right now they're safer with someone else, but it feels wrong.

Every emotion within me is worn thin, like the ragged seams of my clothes. My temper is just on the edge of burning. My eyes are filled to the brim with tears. I even giggle a few times, for no reason. Amidst all these edges is a hole, right in the center of my chest. The one Brax used to fill.

Kiran turns against the sun at a yellowing meadow and retraces our tracks the opposite direction. We branch out southeast and then turn back again. We follow trails that lead to nowhere, then backtrack. Should someone follow, they will be led astray over and over.

My stomach grumbles with nerves and hunger throughout the early morning. The dew dampens our faces and chills my skin. I wonder if the twins are cold and if Daphne knows where to find them food. Tam's so grown up now; he'll probably take care of Nina himself.

Kiran dismounts when we return to the meadow in the midmorning. We've been here four times today taking various paths, but when Kiran crouches beside an outcropping of tracks, it's not just Dell's shod imprints he sees, but the semicircle track of a cheap, hired animal, like the fares at the Driver barn.

Trackers have been here since we last were.

The other prints are lost in the harder ground, and though we search, we find no more.

Kiran remounts, his lips drawn in a thin, straight line. Tucked within his belt beneath the shirt, he's carrying two guns that he stole off the dead Virulent. His bow rests across one thigh. I scan the surrounding area for any sign of movement, an arrow notched in Aran's bow. Every falling pinecone and chirping bird draws our eyes.

"I say we follow Lorcan," he whispers as Dell creeps through the woods.

"We can't. If they're watching us, we'll lead them home."

Kiran shakes his head in frustration.

"What do you propose then?"

I don't answer. I don't know.

We don't rest until the sun is high overhead. The stream where we stop is cool and clear, and I kneel and dip my hands and face into the water to scrub away the dried blood and muck. But it doesn't wash away the harsh memories. I don't think anything can do that.

When I rise, Kiran's staring at me, rubbing the line between his brows with his thumb.

I listen, thinking he's doing the same, but hear nothing but the birds.

"It's too quiet." I roll my tense shoulders.

Kiran is still staring.

It occurs to me that I should thank him. I doubt he's waiting for it, but I don't want him to think I've taken all his risks for granted. He might be used to sticking his neck out for other Drivers, but I'm not used to anyone doing it for me. But when I try to express my gratitude, the words get stuck in my throat.

"What is it?" His voice cracks a little. These last hours are wearing him thin.

I hesitate, wanting to get back on Dell, but knowing she needs a little more time to rest. Carrying two bodies half the night is taking its toll on her. She's lathered in sweat, with white salt lines beside her girth.

"Just . . . Lorcan. I keep thinking about what he did last night."

I don't know why I say this, but it makes some of the pressure between us go away.

Kiran gives a curt nod. "Old man took care of things, didn't he?"

"He protected the other Drivers."

Kiran steps closer, and now we're only an arm's length apart. His eyes are glimmering like the river stones, and the way he's looking at me is like he's touching me. Like I can feel his gaze skimming my skin, making me warm.

"I hate to tell you, Aya, but sometimes you have a hard time seeing what's right in front of you." A ghost of a smile plays across his lips.

I take a step back.

"If he wanted to be my father, he would have stayed close instead of always running away."

"Maybe it was too hard to spend every day staring at your ma's scars."

My temper rises. "How dare—"

"Because," he pushes on, "because he knew he'd been the one to do it."

He lifts his hand and very gently trails an X across my right cheek, exactly the way he had the night I'd asked him to help me break the purity rule. I know then that Kiran wouldn't have been able to live with my scars either. I bat his hand away, but not as strongly as I intend and my fingers end up curling around his on my cheek.

He moves closer, and just like when he first crossed the stream into the solitary yard, I'm stuck in place.

I swallow. "He didn't hold the knife."

"But he might as well have. Don't you see how hard it was? He couldn't talk to her. He couldn't laugh with her. He couldn't tell her he cared about her."

"Well, words aren't everything."

And before I can draw breath again, Kiran's kissing me. Or at least his mouth has frozen against mine. He seems nearly as surprised by it as I am and smirks briefly before his lips soften and his copper-flecked eyes drift closed.

Gently, his other hand skims over my hair, coming to rest at the base of my neck. A quake starts deep inside of me and by the time it reaches my jaw, I know he can feel it. Something changes in his face then. A look I haven't seen before, which surprises me because I thought I knew every one of them. His brows lift just slightly, and draw together. His shoulders rise, just a tiny bit. And it's right then that I figure out the truth: Part of my soul may belong to Kiran, but part of his belongs to me, too.

I don't want this moment to ever end.

With Kiran, I am the barest version of myself, not protected by my walls, not hidden behind the Garden's makeup and dresses. I am fierce and pretty and my value is not recorded by some bodybook or measured by stars on an auction block. I'm not so scared, not so alone, and because being here with him feels so right, I know I can't trust it. We're in danger, and when Kiran kisses me it weakens my shield. I can't defend myself from Trackers without that shield. I can't protect the twins. I can't let my guard down. Not now, maybe not ever.

I push him away, but it's hard because the muscles in my arms don't seem to work anymore. He blinks and opens his mouth to speak, but no words come out. Since I found out he can talk, this is the first time I've seen him speechless.

And suddenly, like a furious punch, I remember Kyna. Maybe Driver men are just like other men in the city; they think they can take their pick of whatever girl they want. Well I'm not built that way. I'm loyal, and if someone wants to kiss on me, they better be loyal too.

A crackling in the brush behind me steals our attention. Instantly, our arrows are loaded and our bows are at eye level. Kiran still has the guns, but he doesn't reach for them. I wonder if he even knows how to use one.

Dell lifts her head, ears pinned flat against her neck, and Kiran places a steadying hand on her nose. She grinds the bit anxiously. Her mouth is edged with foam and sweat.

Keeping low, I follow the sound, softly placing each step so I make as little noise as possible. Ten paces away, I hear murmuring. Ten paces more and I see them.

In a small sapling grove are four men with horses. One is crouching on the ground, pressing his fingertips into what I'm sure are Dell's prints.

Three of them, including the man on foot, are Trackers. I can see the flashlights on their hip belts and the nets tied to the backs of their saddles.

The fourth is Mr. Greer.

He's wearing riding breeches and a silk shirt that shimmers even when the wind is calm. Dark hair hangs in crisp points around his eyes. His face is covered by a black scarf, but the pins holding it in place have been dislodged, and a hint of that jagged, raised scar on the top of his cheek sticks out.

"If she's masquerading as a Driver like he said, they'll kill her. Not in the city, mind you, but out here they would. They don't take well to folks interfering with their kind," says one of the mounted Trackers.

I'm frozen, holding my breath. I wish I'd never met Amir Ryker in that candy shop at the auction. I wish he didn't exist. Mr. Greer too, and the mayor, and all these Trackers. If I'm glad for nothing else in my life, it's that we didn't follow Lorcan home right away.

"It would be a waste if they disposed of her." Greer's voice is rougher than before, like sand blowing against metal.

"Right, because then she can't hang," another Tracker laughs. He spits on the ground and wipes his mouth on his sleeve.

"If she's alive, she won't hang," assures Mr. Greer. "We paid a considerable sum for her."

"Waste to give her to a boy, then," says the Tracker on the ground. "Should save her for a man." He rises and puffs out his chest. The others laugh, Mr. Greer along with them.

Greer adjusts his scarf. "She'll pay her dues, not to worry."

The Tracker, now strutting back to his horse, stops short. "I'd think tangling with the mayor's favorite girl would have made an impression. You've still got one pretty cheek, Greer. Don't lose the other one."

Mr. Greer shoots him in the chest, with a gun I didn't even see in his hand.

A cry bursts from my throat as I topple backwards. The three remaining faces turn my way.

There's no hiding now. I get up and I run.

KIRAN DOESN'T WASTE TIME asking questions. The moment he sees me sprinting his way he swings atop Dell and swoops down to grasp my upper arm. She's already running by the time I'm all the way on her back.

I hang on as tightly as I can, arms latched around Kiran's lean waist, feeling the sweat that dampens his shirt on my cheek.

Something crashes in the bushes behind us, big enough to be a horse and rider. Whether or not it's Mr. Greer, I don't know. I don't look back. Not this time.

Kiran aims Dell through the woods and we stay low, avoiding the branches that threaten to scoop us right off her back. To our right is a crowded cropping of squat, green brush, and Dell gallops straight for it. I think she's about to turn, so I brace to slide, but she jumps and lands in a pool of stagnant water.

The water splashes our legs, soaking my boots. Dell makes her way out, her strong neck heaving. When we're free, Kiran whispers something in her ear and we're off again. Flying. He rides like she's a part of him, an extension of his legs. And I bump along the back with the rest of the gear.

We keep going until there isn't a single human sound for miles, and even when we pull up, we're careful to keep our weapons ready.

"Greer," I heave between breaths. "The mayor's brother. Three . . ." I shake my head, ridding the murder from my mind. "No, two . . . more Trackers. I heard them talking. They're not going to stop until they find me."

Now that we're stopped, the words that had been exchanged between Mr. Greer and his men slam into me. I think of Daphne, forced to lay down with a buyer in a private room. Salma's words echo in my head: *"We're just women."*

If I'm caught, it's the end of me.

"They're not going to find us," Kiran says, but there's worry in his voice.

"You have to go," I say. "They'll take me alive. But they'll kill you, Kiran."

I can't believe I'm saying this. I don't want Kiran to leave. I need him and he needs me. But I can't have his death on my conscience. I can't dig another hole in the ground with nothing but a rock in my hand, and lay him inside as we did Brax. I refuse.

Dell's spinning in a tight circle, ready to run again. Kiran calms her with a soothing hum.

"We'll go back towards the city. They won't think we'd do that," he says. It's desperate. We both know it, but Kiran has a point. The closer to the city we go, the farther we lead them away from Lorcan, Daphne, and the twins.

"You head towards the city," I say. "I'll keep going on foot. They're not looking for us to be together anyway. They said a real Driver would probably kill me out here for *masquerading* as one of them."

A grimace tightens his mouth. "They're right."

We both grow quiet, thinking of Aran, his lifeless body stuffed beneath the bushes not far from here.

I try to dismount, but Kiran grabs my arm. I succeed in swinging my leg back over Dell's haunches, but somehow he goes over the horse's neck and hits the ground before me. He's attempting to wrestle me back into the saddle and I'm struggling to get away from him, but the harder I breathe, the more I can smell the leather and sweat and wood smoke on his skin.

"Let go!" I ram my foot down on his in frustration and he grunts in pain.

"Don't be crazy," he says. "There's another way."

I twist out of his arms at the same time as he clamps down, which results in his elbow knocking me hard in the chin. He lets go then, and I topple onto my backside.

"Yeah." I move my jaw from side to side. "I guess *you* could always kill me!"

He turns away, head down, and kicks a rock into a tree with a dull *thunk*.

"You . . . could kill me," I repeat slowly.

He spins back. "What?"

"You can kill me!" I push myself back up, and though now he seems to be purposefully staying back, I close the space between us and grab his biceps. "I know what to do!"

"You're kidding, right?" His chin lowers until he can glare right into my eyes.

I shake my head, trying to work out the details. It's perfect. Well, perfect enough. Either way, it's all I've got left.

"I'm *not* gonna kill you," he says between his teeth.

"Shoot me."

"You're not getting it."

"With an arrow," I roll on. "That way they'll know it was a Driver that did it. A Driver that saw me dressing up and pretending to be your kind."

"Aya, you *are* my kind!"

"Just listen!" My voice smacks off the trees. The volume makes him wince, and his eyes dart around the woods.

Before he can say anything, I continue.

"I'll be no use to them dead. They don't want to bring me back just to hang me, they want to bring me back to *own* me. They'll leave my body out here to rot, just like the others."

"They're not idiots. They'll know if you're faking."

"They might not." I take a deep breath. The prospect of this plan is making me a little lightheaded. "When you were sick, I gave you bloodroot tea. It knocked you out, but not just that, it slowed your heart."

He releases my arms, a worried look on his face.

"What?" I say.

"Kyna told me she thought I was dead. My heart wasn't beating."

My heart twitches at the name. "It was beating. Just very,

very slowly. You would have woken out of it after a while, but the medicine she gave you seemed to speed up the healing."

"I've . . . I've got that medicine," he says. "Kyna gave me too much of hers, so I was going to replace it. She needs it. For her legs."

I remember the green bottle Kiran stole from the pharmacy, wrapped up inside his saddlebag.

"You could give me some," I say.

His hands fist in his hair. "It doesn't matter if I could or I couldn't because your plan won't work. We're going to keep moving. We'll hide you, and this whole thing will blow over."

"It won't. Not until they find me," I say.

He's digging his heel into the ground, not even realizing—or caring—that he's leaving a new mark for the Trackers.

"So you're going to make some kind of tea and then lay on the ground and hope they think you're dead. By what, poison?"

"You're going to shoot me. With an arrow."

"Forget it. Get on the horse. We're going." I can practically hear his jaw grinding.

"Do it," I say. "Or I'm going to do it myself." Before he can stop me, I snatch an arrow from the quiver tethered to the back of his saddle. The point is sharp enough to break skin, but though my voice is fierce, I'm not sure I can actually do it. I don't know if I'm strong enough or brave enough to jam it in far enough.

"The bloodroot numbs the pain anyway," I add, hoping I sound convincing. Hoping he doesn't see right through me.

"Aya, don't be ridiculous. You'll die."

"The bloodroot slows my heart. It'll slow the bleeding. You'll hit me in the shoulder, here." I mark the spot with my hand, hoping Kiran's got good aim. "Far enough away from my heart, right in the muscle, and make sure they're close enough to find me quickly. Then when they leave, you'll come back and wait for me to wake up."

He's considering it. I can see the plan working through his mind.

"Please," I beg. "They won't stop until they find me. And if I keep hiding, they'll keep looking. I'll never be able to see the twins again."

He's shaking his head. But his words don't match the gesture.

"Fine," he says. "Make the tea. I'll start a fire. They'll see the smoke. We'll find some way to injure you. . . ." he hesitates. "And then when you wake up this'll be done."

"Yes," I say. But the fear has already set in. By the end of today I'll either be free or dead.

WE WORK FAST. KIRAN builds a small fire beside a nearby brook—not enough to bring the Trackers this way yet, but enough to heat a tin cup of water from his pack. I take the remaining stalks of dried bloodroot from my solitary-yard plastic bottle and grind them to a powder between two rocks. When the water is steaming, I sift the contents in.

Kiran's taken the arrow and tucked it in his belt. He's agreed to shoot me himself, though he hardly seems thrilled at the opportunity. I don't blame him. I'm not looking forward to it either.

The unspoken truth lies between us. If Kiran's aim is off, the arrow could pierce something vital and kill me on the spot. The Trackers could do any number of things to my body to assure I'm dead. And even if everything goes as planned and they do leave me, I might never wake up again.

"Kiran." I cough. My throat's so tight it's hard to talk. "If it's not too much trouble, maybe you can check in on Daphne and the twins from time to time."

He doesn't look up.

"*You* and Daphne and the twins," he grumbles. "You'll be there with them."

Dell lifts her head, snorting the air. They're getting close. We don't have much time.

"Please say yes," I say.

He rubs a hand down his face. And then he gives a nod, and my heart breaks a little.

I mix the drink with my finger and swallow it in one chug. It scalds my tongue and throat and tastes so bitter I nearly gag.

"There," I say. It's begun. There's no going back now. Kiran grunts and doesn't look up. He hasn't looked at me once since committing to this plan.

He feeds the fire from a pile of dry pine needles, and a plume of white smoke rises into the afternoon sky. I stand, and then blink and grab onto Dell's saddle while the forest spins around me.

"You took enough, right? You won't feel much?" Kiran asks. He's tapping an arrow against his thigh.

"I took twice as much as I gave you," I say. My head feels very heavy. The fire is bright orange and draws my stare. It's so beautiful. I shake my head to clear it.

"Oh. That's good, I guess," Kiran says.

"Too much is *definitely* not good." Some part of me knows I shouldn't keep on, but I can't seem to stop myself now. Kiran doubles before me, and I reach out to try to figure out which one is real.

He grabs my outstretched hand, and soon his arm is around my waist, holding me upright.

"Oops," I say. "We're almost dancing." I bump his hip with mine and smile, but he doesn't seem to think it's funny.

"Why? Why isn't it good?"

"Well, we gave it to my ma when the fever hit. It helped her die."

"Are you joking?" He grips my waist tighter. It makes me giggle.

"I'm not a very good joker," I admit. He knows this. I don't know why I have to tell him.

Dell begins to prance, and Kiran turns away. In the distance, I can already hear the steady cracking of twigs and dead leaves on the forest floor.

The Trackers are coming.

"You'd better do it," I say. "Wait a second. I want to close my eyes."

He's staring at me, pain in his river-stone gaze. He doesn't want to do this anymore, and like something from a different life, I remember how it felt the night I asked him to help me earn a Virulent mark in the solitary yard.

"Gimme the arrow," I say. He'd better hurry up with it, because I might just accidently stick something important if we wait much longer.

"I'll do it," he says.

"Wait!" I say, almost having forgotten what I needed to tell him. He jerks forward, grasping my elbows for support.

"You've got to make sure they made it. The twins. You'll do that right?"

His face falls. "I'll do it. We both will."

"Even if I don't make it. You'll make sure, right?"

"Yes."

"And Kiran?"

"Yes?"

"Don't let them take me." I don't have much time left. I can barely see him through the darkness. But it's only afternoon, it shouldn't be dark yet. . . . Why does Kiran look so sad? I don't like that look at all.

"I won't let them take you," he says.

"You know what to do, right? If they take me?"

I can't go back to the city again. I won't make it out once

they bring me to the mayor's house. I take the arrow he's notched in his bow and aim it towards my heart, showing him what I mean for him to do. The tea is so strong it makes my hands clumsy, and the metal arrow nicks my finger. I wince, and he swears and pulls back the bow.

"I thought you said it wouldn't hurt," he says, more to himself than me.

"Thank you," I say. "For helping me out of the Garden. And for singing Brax's soul. And for telling me about my father. If I die, I'll remember you in my next life and all the lives after. I won't ever forget you."

I'm not scared anymore. Not of anything. Not even of dying. A flush of relief fills me as I realize my ma might not have been afraid either. It makes the cold seeping over my body more bearable.

Kiran's finger brushes my scarred earlobe again, just as it did the night he returned. Time seems to pause. Though I've fought it all my life, maybe someone—Kiran—does own me. Pieces of me. Moments with me. Maybe I own him too, in those same scattered pieces. And maybe it's only the buzzing in my head, but this suddenly doesn't seem terrible at all.

The Trackers are getting closer. The ground has begun to tremble beneath their hoofbeats.

Kiran backs up, one step at a time, until he's fifteen paces away. There are tears running down his face. I widen my stance to hold as steady as I can and pinch my eyes closed.

"Goodbye," I whisper, just in case.

Nothing happens. I blink my eyes open again and there is Kiran, aiming the arrow at my chest, but unable to release the twine.

"It's okay," I tell him. "I'm not scared."

He lowers the bow and in a flash picks up a stone off the ground and heaves it with all his might into a tree behind him. I can hear the air release from his lungs in one hard whoosh.

And then he spins back, lifts the bow, and fires.

I feel the pressure first, like a dull branch prodding my right shoulder. It shoves so hard against me that I'm knocked off my feet and land on my back beside the fire. When I turn my head I see the narrow rod rising from my skin. It's in that moment, between the shock and the fear, that I think of Deer in my ma's old story and wonder if this was the last thing he saw before Mother Hawk took his soul.

The pain comes a moment later, stabbing into my shoulder and sending bolts across my chest. It's worse than the wire, worse than a Watcher beating. I can't move. I'm pinned to the ground.

I can't even remember how I got here.

I hear a crashing through the darkness above, beyond, surrounding me. Hooves striking the ground somewhere close. Someone's here. Is it Kiran? Where is Kiran?

"Found her!" someone yells. The gritty sound echoes in my head.

"He won't be happy," groans another.

I close my eyes and see my ma. Her long, dark hair hanging in tight ringlets to her hips. The mark on her cheek that warps when she smiles.

"Aya." She still sounds the same when she says my name, as though she's never been gone. She sits on the ground beside me, cradles my head in her lap and sings my soul away. Her fingers are warm, skimming across my forehead. And Brax is here too. Licking my face. Snuggling into the crook in my arm. Here there is no blood, no fever, no grief. Here there is only peace.

I've fought well, just like my ma taught me. Just like I was supposed to do. It finally feels all right to let go, and when I do, I can breathe. It feels like the first time in years that I've really breathed. Everything is okay now. Everyone is safe. I am free.

I've got the glass arrow.

It protrudes from my shoulder, wavering the slightest bit, and shining in the firelight. The blood of my life seeps from it, blossoming on my Driver shirt, soaking into the ground.

My sacrifice will allow my family to live.

I am filled with joy.

CHAPTER 24

I COME BACK BIT by bit. One bright dot appears, growing larger, eating up the darkness.

At first, I'm only aware of the pieces—my frozen feet, my aching head, my arms crossed over my chest. There's a pebble stuck under my hip. A rough wool pad under my head. My stomach is empty, and I'm starving.

I'm so tired. I go away for a while, but when I come back there's a noise breaking through the crackling of the flames. A voice I recognize. He has a funny way of talking. Kiran, that's his name. Kiran.

". . . She always wanted to do whatever I did, and our mother stuck her with me, too. 'Don't you leave Kyna,' she'd say. Every single time I left our house. I didn't always mind. Well, maybe I did. But I was just a kid myself, you know."

Kyna. Behind my closed lids I can see her in the buckskin dress with the boards on her legs. Her hair shimmers in the sun. It's golden. Just like Kiran's. They resemble each other, now that I think of it. The same nose. The same lanky build.

Kiran's telling me stories. Like the stories I used to tell him in the city. In the Garden. I remember now. Long nights, when I talked and talked, thinking he didn't know what I was saying. I remember.

"She was four and I was seven when I let her ride for the first time. My father wanted her to wait until she was bigger, but he was working in the city and my mother was cooking, so I took her out back and set her up on this old paint gelding we had. It seemed harmless enough. Kyna loved it. She was laughing." He clears his throat. "Neither of us saw the snake on the ground until it was too late. It spooked the gelding, and she fell. He ran her over trying to get away."

Kiran says nothing for a while. I wish he would talk again. I wish I could do something to make him feel better but my shoulder's begun to throb. I can't remember why it hurts, though I feel like I should.

"I carried her back to camp, to the doctor, but her legs were crushed. During the operation I thought of all the times I'd told her to stop following me and leave me alone, and I promised to take care of her from then on. I still try, though she doesn't need me much these days. I wouldn't have left home, but the city medicine helps her legs. I took that job at the rental barn in Glasscaster so I could get it."

He sighs.

"I wish you'd wake up already, Aya."

My name. Aiyana. Aya. I was supposed to die, but I didn't. I was sold, but I escaped.

A moan whispers from my throat, but it takes too much work and grows quiet.

"Aya?"

A cool hand presses against my neck, searching for my pulse. It must take a long time for those fingers to find what they're looking for because they linger through more than a dozen throbbing beats of my heart.

"If you can hear me, they're gone, Aya. The mayor's brother and his men. You were right. And that's the last time I'm going to ever say you were right about that, because you're not talking me into shooting you ever again."

He moves the hair from my forehead, leaving a tingling sensation wherever his fingertips brush.

"You're safe now. It's been discussed by the elders. You and your family, even Strawberry. We're taking you all in. The outcast—your father, I mean—they're still not sold on him, but the rest of you, you're going to live with us now. If you want, I mean."

He waits a beat.

"I hope that's what you want."

In the quiet, the rest of my memories return, beginning with the past and catching up to the present. Kiran has followed the plan, and now we're all safe. My family is free. Tam. Nina. Lorcan. Even Daphne. They're waiting for me in the mountains. Or maybe they're already at the Driver camp.

We're going to be safe.

I think of Salma's last words to me in the shop—that we are just women. As if that weren't enough. It makes me sad—not angry, not bitter. She always wanted more and in the end settled for nothing.

I see all of it then. Watchers, Pips and their beaters, the medical check. All the fights, all the running, every time I should have given up but didn't. I see a gray wolf and a boy in the solitary yard with gold flecks in his eyes and a man with a scar on his throat who was there for me when it mattered.

I see Daphne and am proud of the friend she's become. I see us age—see our hair grow long and wild and our skin tan in the sun as the last of the treatments from the Garden fade away. We are strong and proud and beautiful and there are not enough stars in the night sky to measure our worth.

I will honor my mother and take care of my family.

Yes, I think. I am just a woman.

I'm awake now. I could open my eyes and tell Kiran I'm back, but something in his tone tells me we have time, so I keep them closed.

I think I'll let him talk a little longer.

ACKNOWLEDGMENTS

I AM HONORED TO be able to thank the following people, because they have been absolutely awesome to work with:

Melissa Frain, who is more or less the best editor/friend/comedian ever. (See what I did there? I used "more or less" right!) How she continues to put up with my rapidly firing anxious e-mails and my brilliantly executed (if I do say so myself) pranks, I'll never know.

My agent, Joanna MacKenzie, who always knows the right thing to say about pretty much anything—revisions, contracts, chocolate, you name it—and Danielle Egan Miller, who is fierce in the best way, and ever encouraging.

Kathleen Doherty, the kick-ass publisher of Tor Teen, who took a chance on me with *Article 5* and has quite literally made many of my dreams come true. Alexis Saarela, my wonderful publicist, who has been kind enough to help me schedule all things bookly around my son; Seth Lerner for all the beautiful covers he has made for my books, including this one; and Christopher Gibbs for lending his incredible talent to create the artwork. And of course, a huge thank-you to Amy Stapp, the best pranking accomplice ever, for all of her help.

I am grateful for wonderful writerly friends, including Katie McGarry, who has pulled me out of more plot holes than you can imagine; and Kendare Blake for her encouragement and thoughtful reads. And for the people who dance with me at Jazzercise, and all the bloggers, readers, teachers, and librarians who have shared their enthusiasm.

Every day I am thankful for my family. For my mom, who is as proud of me now as she was when I was writing stories about my hamster when I was seven; and my dad, a real genuine cowboy, who taught me responsibility by feeding horses and cleaning stalls and who was there to welcome a little chestnut filly, Dell, into the world when I was fourteen. For the support and unending love from the Simmons side, and for open arms and patient hearts of the Fairfields.

And last but not least, I am grateful for my boys. Thank you, Jason, for giving me the best story of all: our story. And thank you, Ren, for filling the pages.